BRIAN STABLEFORD

AFTER
THE
REVELATION

THIS IS A SNUGGLY BOOK

ISBN: 978-1-64525-085-2

The cover shows *The Mark of a Dying Star*, provided by NASA/
JPL-Caltech/ESA.

AFTER THE REVELATION

I

When Denise Corcoran woke up to find that she could no longer tell which way was up, it took her a few moments to realize that the fault was not in her but in the darkness in which she was contained. The darkness no longer had an up or a down. The capsule had, of course, been designed with that occasional circumstance in mind, so the section of the wall to which the sleeping bag was attached, which had been down before she went to sleep—albeit not very down, because she had already lost most of the "weight" simulated by the deceleration of Minerva—was sometimes obliged to be something other than down, and the bag's attachments, like the attachments of the capsule's other facilities, could be relocated in response to convenience.

The screen, however, was always in the same place relative to the sleeping bag, so Denise knew where to reach out for the pod's control panel. Having found it, she should have found the right buttons to press in order to turn on the light and the screen display with equal ease, but uncertainty struck her again with a mocking irony. She had left Earth three years ago, but she had spent almost all of that time in an induced coma, thanks to Minerva's overprotective AIs, and she had not had time to undertake the limited training that was available aboard ship, as well as having missed out on the entire training program that should have been obligatory even before she set foot on the ladder leading to the hatch of the starship—which had then had a very definite down, otherwise known as Earthwards.

"Bloody end of the world," she muttered. "Couldn't even wait one more month. Bloody Captain Kemmering, playing press-gang and hero. And bloody Zeph, for getting me into this." She knew that she was being monumentally unreasonable, and that simply not being able to put her finger on the right button for a few seconds, and not being able to be perfectly certain in her own mind, once she had, that it *was* the right button, ought to have been insufficient to plunge her into a state of existential crisis, but while on Earth she had never been the kind of person who had difficulty finding the right button to press, and she had always taken pride in that, even though it did not set her apart from the majority of humankind.

But on Earth, she had had weight. She had been ponderable. She had always known which way was up. Now, all that had changed.

She found the right buttons. "Let there be light," she murmured, sarcastically. She knew perfectly well that not only was she not God, but that she and Zeph had not made contact with God, no matter what Marie MacLaughlin might think. She was not as crazy as some other people apparently believed.

But there *was* light. And after her eyes had adapted to the dazzle, she switched on the screen. That gave her a sideways, if not an up, and it enabled her to deduce which way was down— Saturnwards, that is—relative to Minerva, now in orbit around the monster world. She had got her bearings, after a fashion.

There had been a time, she remembered, when recently-switched-on screens had displayed a *Hello* or a *Welcome*, because they were programmed to simulate friendliness. The ones aboard Minerva didn't bother; this one just told her that she had numerous messages waiting to be read, including one marked MOST URGENT—presumably an order from the captain— and its implicit tone seemed to her to be a rebuke and a reproach, for having slept too long.

Because her body was still imprisoned in the sleeping bag, she had no difficulty in controlling the reach of her arm to pose her hand over the keyboard, but making her fingers dance was a different matter. She managed to refrain from further futile curses, however, until the message came up.

It was curt and to the point: AM BUSY. TALK TO MIREILLE.

"No hello, and no please," she observed, but self-discipline had taken hold by now, and she knew better than to take offence at the apparent rudeness. Chris Kemmering was not a boorish individual, and if his iron military discipline had slipped a little of late, prompting him at one point almost to assault a member of his crew, it was not his fault, and if he was so busy that he had even omitted the personal pronoun from his message, then he must be *really* busy. Denise knew that she had to obey the order—but not until she had got her bearings a little more securely within the not-quite-upless pod, and not until she had made the heroic demands on her memory that would permit her to employ the hygienic rituals to which the capsule was designed to cater.

In all honesty, the latter really were so simple as to be foolproof, but that did not make them comfortable, especially for a weightless person who had spent the entirety of her conscious life being ponderable.

She knew that she would not be weightless for long. Minerva's future was no longer absolutely certain, but she would not be parked in a long orbit around Saturn for more than a few Earthdays, at the most. In the meantime, however, Denise would have duties, which would require her to float around the ship. As the only member of the crew who had not undergone training, and one of two who had not spent years in deep space on one of the Olympus missions, she would be an odd one out, even odder than Helen Arkheimer, who had not only undergone the full training program at Fairbanks but who had been awake on Minerva for the three years that Denise had been in a protective coma.

I'm going to look like an idiot, she thought, ruefully. But then she added: *Perhaps I am one. Would anyone but an idiot be here?*

And she had to admit that the answer to that might be no. She had had a choice. Captain Kemmering had been very scrupulous about that, and equally scrupulous in apologizing because he had neither the authority nor the time to tell her what she needed to know in order that her consent might be informed.

She could have said no. Perhaps she should and would have said no, if she had taken the time to weigh things up rationally. But she hadn't. She had reacted spontaneously, almost mechanically. Helen Arkheimer had wanted her aboard Minerva because she was Zeph's sister, and that was exactly why she had said yes: because she was Zeph's sister. But what sort of reason was that, if considered rationally and dispassionately?

She hardly knew Zeph. They had never been close, even though they were brother and sister, and when he had made his life-changing decision to join the crew of Olympus Five, he hadn't even had the decency to call her. She had had to learn it from the news. Admittedly, he had never been one for spontaneously making calls; he had not even called her when he found out that the world was about to end, which he must have discovered hours in advance of her—but the fact that it was an aspect of his personality wasn't an excuse, and didn't mean that she wasn't entitled to hold it against him. She didn't owe him anything, so she hadn't been obliged to go along with him when his exotic affairs caught her up like a drunken tornado and whipped her clean out of her old life.

The end of the world would have pretty much done for her old life anyway, but she could have headed for Snowdonia, and could probably have got there before the protective dome was sealed. Captain Kemmering would even have helped her to do it, if that had been her decision. He had a squadron of the US Air Force at his beck and call, and he would have used it, as a matter of duty, to get her out of a situation in which he had played a major role in involving her.

But who was she trying to fool? She had not even thought about saying no. She had been impelled, if not by Destiny or Coincidence-with-a-capital-C, then by something inside herself, some hidden imperative over which she had not had any control, in spite of free will. And that imperative had been correct. She *had* been necessary to Zeph, and to Minerva. She had eavesdropped on Zeph's revelation, which even his own conscious mind might not have been able to seize and capture, and perhaps—only perhaps, but maybe as much as probably—she had been the only person capable of doing so. Perhaps Helen Arkheimer could have done it, given that she actually claimed to understand how her stupid machine worked, and the insane math behind it, and perhaps Mireille Angevot could have done it, because she surely knew Zeph a lot better than his sister ever had or ever could, but perhaps—and maybe as much as probably—not.

Perhaps . . . probably . . . Denise had been necessary to Zeph, to Minerva and to the future of humankind. But was that really something about which she ought to be glad? Might it not have been preferable to have been free to say no?

Don't beat yourself up, Denise, she said to herself. *You've done that far too often for far too long, but that world is over now. Humankind will survive, in the domes and the bunkers, at least for decades, probably for centuries, and perhaps long enough to reterraform the Earth and build a new Eden, but the old world is still dead and buried. It would have been time to move on even if you hadn't volunteered to be a space pioneer tied to your crazy brother's apron strings . . . but the fact that you did was more than a commitment to listen in on his first contact with the Bells. It was a commitment to a new life and a new identity, and it will be far better for the new you if you can discard some of the bad habits with which the old you had cursed herself.*

But it wouldn't be that easy, she knew. Like Rome, new yous could not be built in a day; and like Rome, they only had one short step to take from glory to decline and fall . . . especially when you hadn't gone though basic training and had to work hard even to figure out which buttons to press, and then control your imponderable fingers effectively enough to press them.

She knew that she ought to emerge from the sleeping-bag-cocoon and try to find her metaphorical butterfly wings. She ought to stop lying down and stand up straight—except that there no longer seemed to be a down in which to lie or an up in which to stand, and assuming an upright position would be problematic anyway because to the lack of space.

Instead, she fumbled for the button that would make the capsule translucent, so that she could at least look out on a slightly larger prison cell and see where she would have to take wing.

She did that. There wasn't a lot to see, but enough . . . perhaps more than enough. She couldn't see the pod "below" her own, in which Zeph was probably still sleeping or comatose, similarly stuck to the wall that had once been "down," but she could see the capsules opposite. What had been the lower one was translucent but empty; the former upper one was occupied, not by Helen Arkheimer, its usual tenant, but by Mireille, who was looking right at her.

When their eyes met, Mireille beckoned to her. Presumably, she had orders to talk to Denise, and presumably, she was getting impatient. Her gesture was a trifle awkward, reminding Denise that even though Mireille had been awake for the last three years, and was a veteran of the Olympus program, she couldn't have spent much time being completely devoid of weight.

It took Denise thirty seconds or so to realize that the Frenchwoman's gestures were intended to tell her to switch on her voice-receiver. Feeling stupid, she did that.

"Sorry, Denise," said Mireille. "I need to talk to you."

"I know," said Denise. "Captain's orders. So talk." *No hello,* she thought, *no apology. It must be catching,*

Mireille waved her hand in a gesture of negation. Because she was imponderable, the Newtonian reaction waved her body. Even though there had been no apparent down in which to sit, Mireille had been in a pseudo-sitting position relative to the pod's neatly folded sleeping-bag—old habits. Now she was all over the place.

Maybe I won't be such an odd one out after all, Denise thought. *I bet the captain is infinitely more balletic.* Then, dutifully, she wondered what the gesture of negation meant—apart from *no,* of course.

Logically, it had to mean that Mireille wanted to speak to her in private, without the ship's recorders logging the conversation. That was possible on Minerva, although it hadn't been on Olympus—with farcical consequences, as things had turned out—because Minerva's capsules had been rigged for authentic privacy. But whose belated eavesdropping did Mireille want to keep at bay? The captain's? Earth's? Helen Arkheimer's? Probably the last . . . which implied that all was not harmony in Minerva's improvised crew . . . which was not exactly a surprise.

But in order to speak to Mireille in private, one of them would have to exit her open pod and float over to the other—in theory, the simplest maneuver in the tiny world, but in practice . . .

Mireille was gesturing again. She had anchored herself this time in a huddled crouch that would surely have been uncomfortable if she had not been weightless, so the mime was clearer. In brief, it meant, *your place or mine?* Again, in theory, the simplest politeness in their little social microcosm, but one that might not be as simple as it seemed. For one thing, someone was going to have to exit their capsule, float across the intervening space and clamber into the other capsule—and probably look ridiculous doing it. For another, the two of them would end up in the same enclosed space, cut off from the universe, either extended along the axis of the pod in parallel or hunched in some ungainly contortion . . . and it was not improbable that the dialogue might be a trifle touchy, not to say spiky.

But, circumstances being what they were, Denise knew that she and Mireille would be cell-mates in the same prison for many years to come, possibly for life. It would be greatly to her advantage to get past the phase of their relationship in which dialogues were touchy, bordering on spiky, and in which sharing the same confined space was inherently uncomfortable in more ways than one.

Be brave, Denise, she ordered herself. *You're committed, there's no way back.*

She mimed *Hold on, I'm coming*, as best she could—which, in all honesty, was not very good, because she wasn't securely anchored and the reaction sent her into a spin, but she got the message across, probably because her problematic interlocutor was so glad to receive it.

And, one way or another—or all at once, given that the traditional alternatives had been banished psychologically to multidimensional confusion—she managed to get out of her own capsule and across the brief interval to the other without suffering any excessively awkward collisions or giving the impression of being an innocent lost in chaos. Before Mireille had sealed the capsule and screened it with opacity, she had contrived to arrange her bodily posture in a half-lotus position, only bumping her head twice. Unlike Mireille, Denise had to hunch herself up slightly in order to avoid further contact between the top of her head and the "ceiling" of the pod.

You'd think they'd have designed these pods so you could at least sit up straight, she thought, although the thought reminded her that she was the tallest of the seven women on board, if only by an inch or two, and that it could thus be argued that it was her own fault that she didn't quite fit, and that the occasional bump on the head was simply a more graphic instance of beating herself up.

She anchored herself successfully to one of the walls, at what seemed to her—improvising, with no experience on which to draw—to be a suitable social distance for two people whose communications to date had been a trifle wary.

"Thanks," said Mireille, mirroring her half-lotus with an apparent easy expertise. "Sorry, but I really do need to talk to you. The captain's locked in a slow and awkward three-way with Helen and Earth—you can imagine how tedious that is, given that they're having to relay the signal via Jupiter because the Sun is in the way of the direct beam, but he's under orders to stand by. Alessandro's with them, but I don't envy him having to referee that particular contest. Has to be done, though, and settled once and for all."

Denise had no difficulty guessing the pivot of the controversy.

"Helen wants so-called Mission Control to give the captain a formal order to follow her instructions?" she queried, although she presumed that the question was rhetorical. "But they're not going to do that, are they?"

"Probably not," Mireille agreed. "Although, between you, me and the privacy screen, it wouldn't matter if they did. The captain is the captain and he's no longer in a situation where he's going to take orders meekly from Earth any more than he's going to take them from Helen. This isn't Olympus; Minerva is a microworld in her own right, and even though the captain doesn't like playing tyrant, the responsibility of commanding it is his and his alone. The problem is making Helen understand that. I'd like to be able to say that it isn't our problem, but the simple fact is that it's everyone's problem."

"Because we're all stuck with Helen as a cellmate, serving a life sentence?"

"Not the analogy I would have chosen, but yes, if you like. And there's all the difference in the world, alas, between the happy ship that Olympus nearly was and the happy ship that Minerva, thus far, certainly isn't."

"But I thought that you and the captain got along quite well with Helen while the three of you were awake and the AIs had the rest of us in precautionary hibernation?"

"Sure—because we were all playing the same waiting game by the same rules. It didn't matter that Helen thought of herself as being in command while there was nothing she wanted to command the captain to do. Now . . . well, everything is confusion and choice. *Merde*, not to put too fine a point on it. *Bonsoir liberté, egalité et fraternité* and *à bas la révolution* . . . I'm exaggerating, of course, but things aren't good. You really put the cat among the pigeons, to revert to the English idiom."

Denise would have liked to be able to reply *Me? What have I done?* But she knew perfectly well what she had done. She really had put the cat among the pigeons. In a stammered speech that had only lasted a few minutes, she had torpedoed Minerva's original mission, and in her conscious mind she had no more idea than anyone else whether what she had reported in her somniloquistic state—her whole account of the Bells' message and her revelation of the true nature of life in the universe—had been anything but a dream, a spontaneous concoction of her unconscious mind. She could not even remember clearly having said it, although she had not been oblivious—at least dreaming lucidly if she had been *only* dreaming—and she had listened to the recording often enough to know it by heart.

She did not know, as yet, whether Zeph would be able to confirm the message from memory, when he finally woke up. On past experience, perhaps not. At present, she had nothing to go on but her own psychological certainty—and how reliable was that? Helen believed her, of course, but Helen was, notoriously, as crazy as a sackful of monkey-nuts.

"How has the vote of confidence developed while I've been under?" she asked, meaning the vote as to whether people believed that she really had made contact with an alien intelligence, rather than simply being delusional.

"In the crew, unanimous," Mireille assured her. "The captain says yes, and that's good enough for the rest of them."

"Them?" Denise queried. "Not *us?*"

"I say yes too, but not just because the captain says so. On Earth . . . well, there's a three-way split. I don't have precise statistics, but the believers are in a minority—and to be honest, the fact that your friend the chaplain is spreading the word loudly that you're now God's emissary to humankind, with a divine duty of prophecy, isn't really helping to convince the agnostics. The majority seems to be about equally split between those who think you're sincere but deluded and those who think that you were lying through your teeth."

Denise took legitimate offense at that. "Lying! Why would I have been lying?"

"Conspiracy theories are all the rage back on Earth at present. The members of the so-called Cabal believe—quite justifiably, no matter what one thinks of their politics—that they've saved the human species from extinction, and that anyone who speaks the slightest whisper of disapproval is an ingrate and a traitor, but ingratitude is normal, and the Cabal have been running the world covertly and slyly since the mid-twentieth century, so it's hardly surprising that skeptics want to find one more confidence trick in this affair. Everything Zephaniah brought back from Walter Halleck's Sling was dismissed as delusion or deception by a large sector of the population before and after he went to Jupiter, so your supplementation just seems to them to be an extra chapter in the twisted fantasy saga."

"Fuck!" said Denise. "Or, as you would put it, *merde*."

"Precisely. But that doesn't matter. All that matters *here* is that the crew members are unanimously behind the captain, and the captain is backing you. He's always had faith in Zephaniah, and now he has faith in you—but he needs to know that you have faith in yourself. Helen wants to dictate the future use of her Coincidence machine entirely in accord with her own aims and whims, but the captain won't stand for that. He won't make a move or formulate a plan without Zephaniah's consent—and, by extension, yours. You're his advisers now; he's looking to the two of you to guide him. Are you willing to use Helen's machine again?"

"Of course I am, if it's necessary."

"You might want to pause to think about what would qualify it as necessary," Mireille observed. "The captain has his doubts about its desirability, even though he trusts what you said about the ring intelligences and accepts the fact that further confirmation and elaboration might be vital—for our own information rather than the mere matter of persuading the skeptics. There's a lot at stake."

Denise knew that. On the basis of what she had reported of Zeph's revelation, Minerva was now ready to head for Uranus with an alien hitchhiker, and then plot a course for the stars with the aid of the ring intelligences' advice as to which of the nearest stars to Sol was likely to have an Earth-like world in orbit around it, complete with an oxygenated atmosphere and organic life. If Zeph's revelation turned out to be a fictitious dream, whether it was his, or hers, or a *folie à deux*, that would be the ultimate fools' errand.

Hence, further use of the machine was necessary, in spite of the danger—and danger there was, if the measurements made of

Zeph's brain activity before, during and after the contact could be trusted. In purely materialistic terms, Zeph's "revelation" was just a set of neuronal responses in his brain seemingly triggered by external stimulations of a kind never encountered on earth, and those stimulations had created novel pathways in his neuronal cytoarchitecture. That was not necessarily damaging; something similar, albeit more limited, had happened during the experiments with Walter Halleck's Sling, and Zeph was firmly convinced that any alterations had been benign. According to his subjective judgment, any effect on his conscious self had been beneficial—but how trustworthy was his subjective judgment?

Denise knew, too, that repeating the experiment with Helen's machine, even if it had the same or a better result wouldn't prove anything beyond a shadow of a doubt. If she or Zeph had been deluded the first time, a rerun might simply repeat and elaborate the delusion. Skeptics would, at any rate, be free to argue that, and conspiracy theorists would regard whatever might be reported as simply another phase of the conspiracy.

"Are you saying that the captain might not permit another experiment?" Denise asked her interlocutor uncertainly.

"I don't know, and I strongly suspect that he won't make up his mind until he can consult Zeph, and Gabrielle has passed Zeph fit to respond. That's mainly what he and Helen are arguing abut. She's adamant that the machine has to be used, not just once more but rapidly and repeatedly. In her view, it's the only opportunity we have of establishing communication with truly alien intelligences, with all the potential rewards that implies. To achieve that, she thinks that any risk is acceptable, and she says that if Zeph is reluctant to go ahead—or you—then she's determined to try it herself."

"But she hasn't got Zeph's artificial wiring, or his experience in the Sling, or his seemingly natural talent. He might be the only human being alive capable of making the contact."

"She knows that. She'll doubtless call for other volunteers as well—in her view, we all have to attempt anything and everything to obtain the pay-off, and if it turns out to be a suicide mission for some . . . well, the world has already ended; in her view, it's not just a gamble worth taking but a gamble we can't refuse to take."

"I see," said Denise. "And whose idea was it to leave me out of the hot discussion they're having up in the control room?"

"The captain's, obviously. He's not attempting to deny you a voice, just trying to take things one step at a time. You can be certain that he won't make any decision without consulting you, Zeph and everyone else aboard. Ideally, he'd like a universal consensus—but if he's to stand any chance of getting that, he has to square things with Helen first. Hence the present situation, and the fact that he asked me to fill you in when you woke up. He didn't want to rush you—he's worried about possible after-effects of what you went through."

It was on the tip of Denise's tongue to assure her interlocutor that she was perfectly fine, suffering no after-effects of being wired up peripherally to Helen's machine—but how reliable was her own subjective judgment of that?

"The captain told me that Zeph had some kind of fit while he was in contact with the Bells," she said tentatively. "What was the AIs' interpretation of that?"

"The monitors could only track the event; they couldn't provide any explanation of it. AIs work on precedent, and whatever happened to Zeph, there's no recorded precedent. Whatever happened to Zeph's brain as a result of the contact, it's nothing that has ever been observed before, even in the Halleck Sling. Gabrielle's expertise has to do with the brain's software rather than its wetware, but she understands the documented research well enough; she says that she can't find any evidence in the recordings of any permanent physical damage, and that the momentary epilepsy might have been trivial, but she's not willing to offer any guarantees. The AIs are still keeping him comatose, as a precaution, and the captain hasn't overruled them yet, but they'll allow him to wake up soon of their own accord, posting a token warning about their uncertainty. We'll find out then whether he's still his old self, but for the moment, there's no very strong reason to think that he might not be."

"If he is," Dense opined, "he certainly won't refuse to go into the machine again. There was no shortage of people to advise him not to risk himself in the Sling, but he went ahead anyway."

"Ultimately, though," her interlocutor pointed out, "it isn't his decision."

Mireille didn't labor the point. She didn't need to. The point she had evidently been ordered to make in conversation with her cellmate was that, since the captain had the authority to decide what should be done with Helen's contact machine in the future, when and by whom, he also had the responsibility of making the right choices . . . and unlike Helen Arkheimer, he was not only willing to take advice, but thought of it as his duty to do so. It wasn't simply a matter of asking for volunteers and then giving them *carte blanche*; he was responsible for his crew, and for the mission . . . a mission on which the future of the human species might depend . . . and might have done even if it had been only a publicity stunt mounted by the world's no-longer-covert rulers for Machiavellian reasons.

"It wouldn't necessarily have to be Zeph," Denise said, thinking aloud, "any more than, if it is Zeph, I would have take the secondary role. If we are to secure and strengthen the communication link with the Bells—assuming that to be possible and practicable—then the responsibility can't remain entirely on Zeph's shoulders, and mine."

"True," Mireille agreed.

"And that's why the captain wanted you to talk to me?"

"Partly, as I said. He needs you to understand."

Denise refused to laugh. She contented herself by saying: "I've got a long way to go before I get there, if I ever do. I can't say I'm confident. But I volunteered for the mission, and I'm committed. Whatever seems necessary, I'll do . . . but I need his advice even more than he needs mine . . . and I need yours too, I guess," she added, a trifle reluctantly.

"Mine isn't important . . . but if you need it, it goes without saying that you can have it." Denise wondered whether her informant might be trying a little too hard to be obliging and whether there might be a certain amount of resentment or envy behind her mask . . . or at least a certain wariness.

"Of course it's important," Denise assured Mireille, trying to keep her own residual resentment, envy and wariness from showing, even though the conversation was getting uncomfortably close to potential triggers. "Quite apart from the fact that you're a chemist, and more qualified than I am to offer an opinion as to the likelihood of the ring intelligences being real and to offer an opinion on what the dangers of communication with them might pose to the human brain if they are, you know Zeph far better than I do, having got closer to him than I ever have or could, and Helen was all set to hook you up in parallel with him before I woke up . . . and before he woke up himself. But for a freak of chance, you'd have been the relay instead of me, and you might have done a better job. When the time comes to look for supplementary evidence, you'll be first in the queue for the hot seat . . . either hot seat."

"I suspect you're right about your being a long way from understanding the way things are," Mireille said, a trifle ambiguously, "but you'd probably be wrong to think that I'm any closer than you are . . . to understanding the ring intelligences, or to Zephaniah. As for freaks of chance, you know full well that Helen believes that there's no such thing, and that everything that has happened to us . . . to you and me that is . . . is down to the mysterious workings of the mathematical Great God Coincidence."

Denise did not take the invitation to return to more theoretical conversational terrain, although she knew that it might be wiser to do so. "You're still being falsely modest, Mireille," she accused. "You spent seven years on the Olympus Five mission with Zeph. You had sex with him . . . which, so far as I know, no one else had previously contrived to do, and which, if the leaked tapes are a reliable guide, you did far more frequently than any of your fellow crew members. So yes, you're definitely closer to Zeph than I am, and there's no denying it."

Mireille only seemed startled momentarily, and not resentful that her invitation to deflect the conversation away from touchy subject matter had failed. Denise didn't know whether to attribute that to the fact that the atmospheric chemist was exceptionally well disciplined, or whether she, Denise, had just rushed in where angels would and should have feared to tread.

"Hasn't Zeph explained to you how things worked aboard Olympus?" Mireille asked, and then added, promptly: "No, silly question: of course he hasn't, at least with regard to personal matters. The captain, then? He must have made some attempt to explain, to fill in for the indoctrination you missed?"

"He hasn't really had an opportunity. The only real conversation we've ever had was in the car taking us from Kilburn to the US Air Base off the M40, and there were a lot of things on his mind. The end of the world hadn't been officially announced, but he was already on whatever the highest level of alert is code-named nowadays. He did try to explain, but, to be honest, it was rather garbled. Zeph told me that in order for fourteen people to live in close proximity inside a tin can for five years, there had to be strict social rules but, Zeph being Zeph, his account was purely theoretical. He never mentioned your name."

"But you'd heard it, or you wouldn't have looked at me the way you did when you saw me on the plane. I thought we'd got past that reflexive instant dislike . . . sorry, I shouldn't have mentioned that. And please don't blame Zeph or the captain for not explaining things more clearly; it's complicated, and you hadn't gone through indoctrination. You understand the theory, though? Why the supposed experts in psychology planned the mission the way they did?"

"Yes. The Olympus crew had to constitute a microcosmic society that was stable and amicable, as free from tensions as possible, so its institutions were designed that way. It was a society in which everyone was supposed to be equal, in which even the captaincy was just a specific role within the organism rather than the pinnacle of a hierarchy. It was designed as a society with all property held in common . . . including sexual property. No jealousy and no envy . . . hence no couple-formation . . . everybody free to sleep with everybody else . . . or not to, if they didn't want to . . . except that it was the captain's duty to treat all his potential partners equally, without any hint of favoritism; so, the fact that he slept with all the female crew members wasn't because he was the Don Juan that the yellow media mocked and vilified, but because it was his duty. And it seems, by all accounts . . . his and Zeph's accounts, at least . . . to have worked reasonably well. Are you going to tell me that you sleeping with Zeph was just a matter of duty, because someone had to, and you drew the short straw?"

This time Mireille did not control her surprise, not to say her shock—but it only took a few seconds for her to control her reaction, as befitted a responsible citizen of a microcosmic utopia, or a fearful angel.

"I'm glad that we're behind a privacy screen," she said, "because I really wouldn't have wanted anyone else to hear you say that," she said, reproachfully, "but perhaps the point needs clarifying. Yes, the first time I had sex with Zephaniah it was mainly a matter of duty. As you say, someone had to, and I was one of the people who knew him best, because I was on my way to Jupiter to study the clouds and he was on his way there to study the cloud whales, so we had had a lot of speculations to discuss. But duty went by the board after our first contact, if you'll forgive the phraseology. After that, it was purely for pleasure—hopefully on his part as well as mine. It wasn't exclusive, but that didn't mean that the personal warmth wasn't real. Exclusivity was tacitly prohibited, and we were both committed to the principles, and took them seriously, to the extent that we dutifully went our separate ways once the debriefing in Greenland was over . . . but if the Cabal hadn't brought us back together again with a sudden crash, we would have seen one another again, eventually . . . purely for pleasure. As for knowing one another . . . that's really a different matter. I couldn't say, in all honesty, that I *know* Zeph at all, but I do trust him, and I'd be prepared to risk my life for him. I will, if that's what it takes in the present mission . . . and I'd like to be able to say the same about you, eventually, given that we're serving the same life sentence aboard Minerva."

"You want to sleep with me too?" said Denise, sarcastically, before she could stop herself, and hating herself for yielding to the stupid impulse, which was surely utterly unbefitting a responsible citizen of a microcosmic utopia, or any kind of angel.

"If or when I do," the chemist said, pulling a face, "I'll ask politely . . . but for the sake of honesty, it's not my natural inclination. I've had to be versatile these last three years, but that really was a matter of duty, which remained a matter of duty. You can have no idea how I yearned for Zephaniah to wake up . . . and Victor, Birstan and Alessandro. But none of that is anything for which I have to apologize, to you, to Zeph, to Helen, or to anyone else . . . and I hope you can understand that."

"I'm sorry," Denise said, belatedly. "I hope so too. If I'd had time to think about it, I probably would understand. If I'd had time to adapt to the . . . principles, I think I would . . . but for me, it's only been a matter of days since I was an averagely unhappy Londoner teaching paleontology at Imperial College to students who knew that the whole exercise was pointless, and spending much of my spare time poring over dubious genomic analyses of ancient DNA. I hadn't even adapted to Zeph having come back to Earth, let alone being co-opted into his new life and trying to forge a relationship with him that might begin to make up for past neglect. I fear that I'm a slow learner—evolutionary biology isn't exactly a fast-paced science, and I lived my private life in accord with my professional life until the great upheaval climaxed. I'm sorry that I reacted badly to you when we first met, but it was Zeph that I was annoyed with, for not having called me, not you. I did know that it couldn't be your fault but . . . well, things were moving so fast that I was dazed, not thinking straight. Things haven't exactly improved since, pace-wise."

Following that confession, which ought perhaps to have made her feel better, but didn't, Denise paused to draw breath. Mireille, perhaps showing unusual sensitivity or perhaps simply not knowing what to say, gave her a few seconds to recover before formulating her reply

"Nor are they likely to improve, I fear," was her eventual far-from-reassuring reply. "Our situations aren't so very different—I was co-opted into this at the last minute too, purely because of my association with Zephaniah, regarding which Helen and her backers presumably jumped to much the same conclusions as you did. Maybe I'd have done better to stay in France, where the domes are presumably abundantly stocked with decent wine . . . but how can I regret, rationally, being a part of the last great adventure of humankind? . . . if that's what this turns out to be, rather than a monumental flop." She took a pause herself after that confession, dutifully mirroring Denise's embarrassment.

After the obligatory interval, Denise said: "At least you've done it before—living aboard a long-haul spaceship, that is. You know you can do it."

"It's not the same. Olympus Five had a rigid itinerary and timetable. We all knew that it was just an interval in our lives, from which we'd return to previous familiarity at a defined point in time, if everything went to plan. That helped enormously to make everything bearable, even enjoyable. And the crew had been very carefully selected for compatibility. Zeph was the odd one out, to some degree, more because he was our equivalent of a manual laborer, charged with maneuvering all the surrogates, than because of what he calls his autistic tendencies—but we all had those, to some extent, and we all sympathized with him. We'd all been misfits early in life, categorized as oddballs by our fellows, all veterans of social exclusion. You might have avoided it, thanks to being pretty, with long blonde hair, but . . ."

"I didn't," Denise assured her. "At least until I settled in at Imperial, where being intelligent and obsessed was perfectly normal, within the walls, and being a thinker wasn't regarded as a social disease. Surely it must have been the same at the Sorbonne?"

"Oh, the French education system has always had the tokenistic aim of enabling everyone to become a *philosophe*, and the universities selected out the successes, but the true intellectuals couldn't isolate themselves from the surrounding society the way that the walls of Olympus and a moat of a few million kilometers of hard vacuum did."

"And Zeph really managed to fit into that social microcosm?"

"Yes, he did. His acclimation took time, but so did everyone else's. Some people are far more naturally inclined to that than others, and, implants or no implants, and whatever superficial appearances suggested, Zephaniah is a natural-born *philosophe* . . . just like you. I'm not surprised that he couldn't fit in to what passes on Earth for normal society, but he could and did fit in aboard Olympus once things had settled down, just as the captain fitted in, in spite of his military training and stubborn pragmatism. This time, it's different. Zephaniah and you constitute a unique pair now, tacitly separated from the rest of the crew, and Helen Arkheimer, even though she's had the basic training and the attempted indoctrination, is never going to be *one of us* unless she can discipline herself to accept the principles and behave accordingly. Nor do we have a defined itinerary—not any longer, at any rate—or any realistic prospect of ever returning home, even though we have no idea how long a potential lifespan we might have, with all our sophisticated internal technology and AI-guided medical support."

"Your tone of voice isn't as pessimistic as the words you're employing," Denise observed.

"No, it isn't," Mireille agreed. "I have confidence in the captain and I have confidence in Zephaniah. If anyone can weld the dirty dozen that he's been stuck with into a crew that can function smoothly until we all grow old, it's Chris Kemmering, and if anyone can find us an atom of hope in contact with the Saturnian ring-intelligences, it's surely Zephaniah, at least with your help. And given that I have to spend the rest of my life in a society of twelve people, so far as the flesh is concerned, I know that while the twelve include the captain, Zephaniah, Alessandro, Mellita and the others with whom I've served before, it will have its rewards and comforts. Things could be a lot worse, don't you think?"

"Probably—I'll let you know when Zeph wakes up . . . if he does."

"He will. The AIs say so. I suspect that the captain only refused to overrule them when Helen demanded that he do it in order to spare Zephaniah the argument that's raging nosewards and postpone the pressure that Helen will doubtless put on him when he does wake up to go back into her rigged capsule right away . . . you might have to steel yourself for that, when the medical AIs do bring him round and classify him fit for duty, or even beforehand, if and when she stops ranting into an absurdly slow com link demanding her instant promotion to admiral of the fleet."

"If *and* when?" Denise queried. "Not if *or* when."

"She will. I've got to know her reasonably well during the last three years—probably as well as anyone can, herself certainly included. She'll run out of steam and capitulate. She's a mathematician: once she's convinced that Chris really is the *de facto* captain and that nothing can possibly change that, she'll accept the situation and adapt. She'll sulk for a while, but she'll get over it. Logic won't let her do otherwise, and she prides herself on her respect for logic."

"Don't we all?" muttered Denise, wishing that she had a little more of that kind of pride.

There was a sudden buzz from the direction of the screen, which was situated behind Mireille in their present position.

"That's the captain," said Mireille. "He's the only one with a license to break through the privacy barrier."

She pressed a button but the screen did not light up. "Go ahead, Captain," said Mireille.

"Is Denise with you?" the captain asked, curtly.

"Yes," said Mireille.

"Well, switch on the video link, damn it, so we can all see one another."

Mireille did as she was asked, but Denise still couldn't see much of the captain, because the wiry but solid atmospheric chemist was in the way.

The caller evidently decided to overlook the inconvenience. "I'm still tied up," Captain Kemmering declared. "The time delay between Q and A is driving me mad, but I need to stand by. It's best for everyone if we can maintain the illusion that we're all in the same fleet even though we're not all in the same boat. Has Mireille brought you up to date, Denise?"

"Yes, sir," Denise confirmed. "I think I have a reasonable idea of where we're up to and what I'm in for."

"Good, because Helen will be arriving in your cabin at any moment, and she's not in a good mood. Handle her with kid gloves, please. With luck, we'll all have to live together until we grow old, and she needs to be persuaded, even more than those oafs on Earth, that we're a team, with identical interests at heart, and that we have to pull together. You might have to protect Zephaniah, because he tends to be a little too tractable for his own good, but as his sister, you presumably have form in that regard going way back."

"I'll do my best," Denise promised, sincerely, thinking meanwhile that her form figures in that regard were not as strong as Chris Kemmering would like to assume. She was, after all, only Zeph's younger sister, and such protection as she had been able to provide while they were children would have been very thin even if she had been more able and willing to provide it.

"Good," was all the reply she got before someone started hammering on the door of the cabin—insofar as effective hammering was possible for a weightless hammerer with a bare fist, however angry they might be.

Mireille switched off the screen before opening the door and removing the opacity screen over the capsule. "Good luck," she murmured to Denise, probably wishing as she said it that the form figures for that particular species of Coincidence were a little more encouraging.

II

"Can you come to the machine cabin, Denise?" said Helen Arkheimer, "I need to talk to you in private." The glance she shot at Mireille was not exactly hostile, but did not even strive to be apologetic, let alone affectionate.

"I dare say," Denise replied, but felt obliged not to seem to be meekly capitulating and was quick to add: "We can use my pod, if you like. I think I've mastered the control panel well enough to ensure privacy."

The great mathematician hesitated over the problem in diplomacy—by no means her strong suit—but she finally agreed to the proposal.

Denise managed to make it across the gap without seeming too maladroit, at least to herself, and waited for Helen to assume a half-lotus and anchor herself before choosing a position of her own, a little further away than the social distance she had thought appropriate to her confrontation with Mireille, with her back to the screen. Denise mirrored the pose without undue effort—she only bumped her head once, and not too painfully—although she couldn't help feeling that Helen, being shorter and even wirier than Mireille, must seem far less ungainly.

Perhaps surprisingly, the mathematician, succeeding better than might have been expected in keeping her frustration under control, felt a need to observe polite formalities. "How are you feeling, my dear?" she asked, solicitously. Denise had already observed that three years in close company with the captain and Mireille had not cured Helen's annoyingly condescending habit of addressing people as "my dear," with a tacit suggestion that they were not dear to her at all. As a strategy intended to make herself seem friendly and likeable, it was unfortunately counter-productive, but Helen appeared to have no Plan B.

"I'm fine," Denise lied, politely.

"Good. I can assure you that Zeph is fine too. I've been monitoring him, with a more intelligent eye than the medical AI possesses, and I've analyzed the EEG traces of his so-called fit very carefully. His life was never in any danger, and although the captain's over-reaction might qualify as natural, it was never-theless unnecessary. The machine is perfectly safe to use, and I'd strap myself into it without hesitation if there were anyone else I could trust to operate the controls. I *will* go into it myself, just as soon as I've educated someone else adequately . . . someone other than the captain."

Denise had no idea how to respond to the deliberate insult to Chris Kemmering, and could not tell whether Helen had only uttered it to test her response, so she ignored it. Instead she said: "Have you made a start on analyzing my brain scans as well as Zeph's?"

"Yes, of course," the mathematician replied. "The neurocien-tists at Fairbanks are stubbornly unconvinced that Zeph's brain was reacting to external input, and although they can't deny the synchronicity between your cerebral reactivity and his, they refuse to jump to the necessary conclusions—but they're idiots, mathematically and conceptually speaking, who wouldn't recog-nize the truth if it cut their throats with a razor. There's not a shadow of doubt in my mind that the contact was real, and that what you reported was a faithful echo of what was going on in Zephaniah's cerebrum, behind the censorship of his conscious filter. The captain refused to order the AIs to wake him up, even though the AIs acquiesced in deeming it safe to do so, but I hope that when he does wake up, he'll report a measure of leakage into consciousness. Eventually, I'm sure, repeated contact will become fully conscious, just as Zephaniah was gradually able to obtain a conscious rapport with the so-called Dancing Rats. I notice that you have hundreds of unseen messages awaiting your attention—please don't worry about those that refuse to take what you experienced seriously. There are people on Earth with a vested psychological interest is refusing to believe what you and I know to be true, and trying to write the whole thing off as a Machiavellian publicity stunt, just as their great-grandparents refused to believe that the first moon landing had actually taken place. There is no limit to potential human willful blindness on Earth, but we're in an infinitely better position to make accurate judgments."

Are we? Denise wondered. Aloud, she said: "Zeph and I need time to recover and talk things over between ourselves. Even if the medical AIs pass us physically fit for duty, mentally, we need time to think it through, to consider what happened carefully . . . very carefully."

"Of course we do, my dear," Helen replied, even though Denise hadn't actually included her in the *we* of her own summation. "I know perfectly well that the scans only tell part of the story. What happened in Zephaniah's brain was unprecedented, and the neural pathways that opened up in response are evidently novel, but there's no evidence that they pose any physical danger."

"No neurological evidence, you mean."

"Of course. What other evidence is there?"

"The evidence of evolutionary biology," Denise said.

Helen's eyes narrowed slightly. "I know that's your specialty, Denise," she said, attempting unsuccessfully to maintain a honeyed tone, "but I can't see its relevance to the present case."

"I can," Denise told her bluntly. "You imagine that what happened to Zeph was the stimulation of a sense that is normally mute in humans: a Coincidence sense. Is that correct?"

"Put crudely, yes . . . except that I wouldn't use the term *mute*. It's not the sense that's mute, in my opinion, merely that ordinary human consciousness is incapable of apprehending it. I suspect that it's our conscious minds that are deaf to it, although our unconscious minds certainly react to it, enabling a certain filtration into emotion and dreams . . . a filtration that you were able to pick up, with the aid of the neural connections established by

31

the machine, even though Zephaniah's consciousness censored it . . . partially, at least. My hope is that, with the aid of the machine, Zephaniah will soon be able to bring the communication to the level of conscious apprehension, even if he didn't manage it during the experimental run. I'm sorry you didn't understand that; if I'd been able to brief you more fully . . ."

"I do understand it," Denise interrupted, although she was aware of the exaggeration of the claim. "I understand it well enough to ask a question that you apparently haven't—which is where evolutionary biology comes in."

Helen tried to make a dismissive gesture with her hand, but exaggerated it too much, because of her weightlessness, and it became rather grotesque.

"You mean the question of why natural selection in humans has favored the censorship in question. Look at history, my dear. Natural selection is a crude instrument of evolution, motivated by successful reproduction. My reading of history suggests that a few visionaries capable of consciously accessing information via the Coincidence sense have certainly existed, but that their visionary aptitudes haven't exactly helped them to produce off-spring . . . quite the reverse, in all probability. But reproductive selection is context-dependent. We're no longer living in a brutal society; we're capable now of taking over the task and the responsibility of eugenic selection ourselves. If we had a few centuries to spare we could probably produce and refine expert visionaries by means of careful selective breeding. Unfortunately, we don't, so we need a short cut. Walter Halleck's Sling wasn't intended as an abridgment, but it seems to have had that side effect, or at least enabled a link with the so-called Dancing Rats that permitted them to effect a short cut. My machine is better—and the ring intelligences appear to be better equipped than the Dancing Rats to make use of it. Believe me, my dear, I haven't left any questions unasked . . . or unanswered."

"So you're assuming that in the Dancing Rats, and more so in the Earthly generations to come after them—and even more so in entities akin to the Bells—the consequences of employing and developing Coincidence sensibility have favored reproduction, and thus have been positively selected rather than negatively."

"Yes, indeed. Doesn't Zephaniah's experience in the Sling, and his brief experience in my machine, confirm that magnificently?"

"Perhaps. But it opens up the possibility—the strong possibility—that Zephaniah's merely human brain is ill-adapted by physical evolution for the kind of communication you're trying to force him to receive. It reacted last time with a minor epileptic fit; next time, the fit might not be so minor."

"The reaction was momentary," Helen countered. "Zephaniah's brain coped and suppressed it. Perhaps some brains wouldn't, but his clearly can. He's an exceptional person, Denise, and we have to make the most of his exceptional qualities."

"And you're the person who gets to decide how that's done, and when?"

Helen was utterly unfazed by the challenge. "Of course," she said. "After all, I have relevant experience to draw on. I have an extra sense too—a mathematical sense. The same argument applies: throughout history, mathematical genius has cropped up, rarely but insistently, in human brains, but it hasn't led to reproductive success. So, most human brains not only can't do advanced math but protect themselves against it with willful blindness and antipathy, and most of the willfully blind treat the mathematically gifted as lunatics, in spite of the fact that mathematics is the only provable truth, the only genuine logic. Evolutionary biology, my dear, is idiotic, just as artificial intelligences are idiotic. Zephaniah and I are members of an advanced species—*Homo superior*, if you like pretentious Latin, or *übermensch*, if you prefer Nietzschean philosophy. On Earth, evidently, natural selection will win out and ill-named *Homo sapiens* will eventually become extinct, leaving the descendants of rats to carry the torch of intellectual progress further, but you, Zephaniah and I are no longer on Earth, and we have a chance to open a new evolutionary tributary in the great river of life. I think—I *know*—that our brains can take aboard the necessary adaptations, because Zephaniah and I already have . . . and even if there's a mortal risk, it's our responsibility to try."

Merde, Denise thought. *She really is crazy.* But she felt guilty immediately after having thought that, because she knew that it was exactly what Helen would expect of a mere *Homo sapiens*, even a certified *philosophe*. And she had heard Zeph lecture her more than once on one of the very few topics about which he was willing and able to talk loquaciously to his fellow human beings, regarding his conviction that there were alternative sanities, some of which were far superior to the vulgar "sanity" misnamed "common sense." She believed that herself—but she also believed that some people thought to be mad really were simply mad.

In order to gain time rather than to build an argumentative wall, she said: "We're not exactly in a position to start a new evolutionary tributary of humankind," she said, "being seven women and five men locked in a tin can for at least a generation."

Helen sighed. "You missed the briefings, my dear," she said. "The cargo hold contains enough frozen sperm and ova to populate a planet, if the opportunity to do so ever becomes available, and the technical capacity to build artificial wombs by the score if the raw materials become available. Perhaps it's a million-to-one shot, but mathematically speaking, that's better than zero. There's also provision in the mission plan for one or more of the fortunate seven to give birth aboard, if the conditions require or favor it. Minerva is a powerful and resilient machine, capable of functioning as what the jargon of science fiction used to call a generation starship. Read the protocols, when you have time."

Denise resisted the reflexive temptation to think *Merde* again, in favor of getting back to what seemed to her to be the point. "But the bottom line," she said, "is that the changes that your machine makes to the human brain, with the aid of alien input, are utterly unpredictable."

"The machine doesn't make any changes," Helen objected. "It merely facilitates the brain's ability to change itself: a perfectly natural ability, absolutely routine in youth, which is never completely lost, even when the neural pathways become ingrained by habit. Contrary to popular parlance, ways of thinking are not set in stone, and old dogs can learn new tricks."

"Even so," Denise insisted, "the effect of such changes is unpredictable, and always likely to be harmful."

"There are risks involved," Helen admitted, "but they're risks worth taking."

"Are they? It seems to me that the likelihood of induced psychosomatic transfiguration equipping us with superpowers, the way that mysterious radiations used to do in ancient comic books, is far inferior to the likelihood that they might fry our neurons instead and turn us into zombies . . . or corpses. Any serious student of the mathematics of probability would surely agree with me."

"Very succinctly put," said Helen, sarcastically, "but totally lacking in genuine mathematical and moral sophistication. Think about it carefully, my dear, with a proper appreciation of what evolutionary biology has contrived to do for the human brain thus far, and I have every confidence that an intelligent woman like you will see that I'm right, just as I'm absolutely certain that Zephaniah won't doubt it for a moment."

"That remains to be seen," said Denise, weakly—and silently cursing her weakness, while admitting that the mathematician was probably right about Zeph's lack of doubt. "He'll have to wake up first."

"Obviously—and he'll have to be fully debriefed . . . but an argument seems to have developed, quite unnecessarily, as to who ought to conduct that debriefing, and who ought to take the lead in the subsequent discussion. Obviously, I'm the only one qualified to make accurate scientific judgments in this matter, and, with all due respect to the captain's presumed authority, it really would be better if individuals without the necessary expertise to form an informed opinion were excluded from a discussion to which they can make no helpful contribution." She didn't even bother to add *don't you agree?*—which would surely have been taking the implied insult a step too far.

Not unnaturally, Denise didn't agree. "You can hardly exclude the captain from leading the discussion," she said, mildly. "It's his responsibility to command the mission and to determine its itinerary. He's the one who has to decide whether or not to make a port of call in the rings of Uranus, and what our heading ought to be when we eventually exit the solar system. He might not be an expert in the scientific aspects of the contact that Zeph made, and he probably doesn't understand Coincidence theory and cerebral neuroarchitecture any better than I do, but he's still the one who has to make the crucial decisions."

"So he seems to believe, absurd though that is," the mathematician observed. "His obtuse military mind seems to be incapable of understanding that the machine is mine, the mission is mine and Minerva is mine, and that he's just a figurehead . . . and his supposed superiors back on Earth are insisting on maintaining him in his delusion of authority, even though they're the ones who gave me the task of constructing the machine and gave me the ship to put it in. But you and I aren't part of the little hero-worshiping society left over from Olympus—you're an outsider, like me, potentially capable of objective assessment. You can see the real logic of the situation, which is that you and I are the only ones capable of making sense of what you and your brother experienced and determining how the investigation ought to be carried forward. We three are the ones with the real responsibility—the only ones. We can't allow ourselves to get into the situation in which Walter Halleck currently finds himself back on Earth, prohibited from using his Sling because a gang of suriphobic fools don't approve of what he found by means of its operation."

It took Denise a moment or two to recall that suriphobia was the currently popular pseudotechnical term for fear of rats, although it was pedantically mistaken, the Latin prefix referring to mice rather than rats. As a biologist, she naturally disapproved of that insult too, but it wasn't worth querying, given the far more dubious implication that anyone who disagreed with Helen's assessment of any and all situations was a "fool" or an "idiot."

In all fairness, Denise could see that Helen's argument that she was the only person with the expertise to interpret the electroencephalographic recordings made by her machine might have a certain justice to it, but she could also see the numerous objections that could be raised to her far-from-mathematical summation of the general situation—so numerous that it wasn't easy to choose which one to take up first. Once again, she was drawn to the personal rather than the theoretical, although she wasn't at all sure that it was the right way to go, in the circumstances.

"I might be an outsider in the crew," she pointed out, "but Zeph certainly isn't—he was aboard Olympus Five, and he has a great respect for the captain. So have I, in fact . . . and he isn't your enemy. However the attempt to communicate with the ring intelligences eventually works out, we're all going to have to work together. Conflict is surely unnecessary, and could be disastrous. From that viewpoint, everybody aboard Minerva needs to be involved in the discussion, however limited their understanding of particular aspects of the science and mathematics might be."

"Oh, Denise," countered the mathematician, putting on an unconvincing show of weary sympathy, "you can't really believe that. It's all very well for the captain and Mireille to pay lip service to the ridiculous principles of Olympus Five's microsociety, but you and I and Zephaniah know full well that there was no real equality aboard Olympus, no matter how dutifully its crew members were willing to pretend, and there's even less aboard Minerva. For the moment, at least, Zephaniah and I are each unique, and you might be too, although it's a matter of extreme urgency to test that hypothesis. Eventually, others might be able to make contact with the ring intelligences, and make it consciously, but only if we can figure out exactly what needs to happen in their brains and cultivate the ability. One or two of the crew members might be able to make a contribution to that, eventually if not immediately, but the investigation has to begin with the three people who made the first contact, and it has to be conducted with the maximum possible expertise and the greatest urgency."

"And within your hypothetical trinity of contactees," Denise suggested. "Zeph is only a hapless Christ and I'm just the paraclete, whereas you're the Creator, the Mother Goddess?"

"You really shouldn't pander to stupid religious fantasy, my dear; its language distorts things terribly. Next you'll be suggesting that the captain has to be regarded as Satan, which would surely test the analogy to destruction in your view. But I *am* the only person aboard Minerva who understands Coincidence Theory, and—with all due respect to Gabrielle, who doubtless has the delusion that she knows something about neuroscience—the only one with sufficient mathematical acumen not only to decode brain scans accurately but to assess their implications fully. Who do you think it was that decoded the transmissions sent from the future by the Dancing Rats?"

"Walter Halleck," suggested Denise, letting the insult to Gabrielle, Minerva's official psychologist, pass unchallenged.

"Don't be naïve, my dear. Walter Halleck is a mathematician of genius, and without his theoretical shoulders to stand on, neither I nor the Chinese team could have seen as far as we did, but even the Chinese genius was able to see further than Walter could, and I can see further than either of them. There's no equality in that kind of analysis and intuition. I'll readily admit that Zephaniah has a different kind of intuition, in which he is certainly as unique in his genre as I am in mine, but that means that the two of us complement one another and need one another, just as you apparently complement him, in your own way, in order to complete a triad . . . or a trinity, if that's the term you prefer. United, we can stand, divided, we'll surely fall."

"Very poetic," Denise commented, dryly. "But I'm not sure as yet, exactly where and how I fit in to a duality with Zephaniah, let alone an unholy trinity with you."

"That," said the mathematician, "is precisely what we need to determine. Evidently, there's a particular Coincidence between your brain and your brother's, probably partly determined by genetics, but surely not limited to that. We need to test its nature, quality and potential range experimentally. I had Mireille added to the crew because she seemed by far the likeliest secondary candidate to form an *ad hoc* duality with Zephaniah, but what you told me in the jeep back in Alaska, before that unfortunate accident, suggests that even the captain might not be incapable of a certain Coincidental resonance with your brother. He and Zephaniah got to know one another quite well aboard Olympus—not as intimately as Mireille, obviously, but I doubt that sexual intercourse is a genuinely defining factor, any more than genetics is. Having analyzed the tapes of their encounters aboard Olympus, I can't detect any crucial significance, although comparing them with tapes of my encounters with Mireille and the captain certainly indicates a qualitative difference, which will require further investigation to be properly evaluated . . ."

"You've been spying on Zeph's . . . encounters with Mireille aboard Olympus?" queried Denise, momentarily aghast.

"Of course I have. The tapes are ludicrously inadequate, of course . . . very little to be seen, and almost as little to be heard, and no electroencephalographic data at all . . . but one has to make the best of the data one has."

"It didn't occur to you that it was an invasion of privacy?"

"Of course it did—but I did it for a good scientific reason. The millions of other people who have watched and listened to the bootlegged tapes purely for casual prurient interest have no such excuse. Haven't you looked at them yourself, simply for the sake of curiosity?—the ones featuring the captain, if not the ones involving your brother?"

"No," said Denise, heartily glad that it wasn't a lie. She had, in fact, avoided looking at the tapes of the captain's performance of his duties, and Zeph's adventures; if she had glanced at other bootlegged tapes it was purely out of academic interest.

"Well, you might be in a minority," Helen said, without making any skepticism she might have felt manifest, "although I commend your wisdom—any pornographic interest they might have is entirely in the imagination of the beholder. You're not interested, then, in any conclusions I might have reached regarding the uniqueness of your brother's brain, because you want to respect his cerebral privacy?"

Anyone else could only have said that with flagrant sarcasm, but from Helen Arkheimer, Denise couldn't be entirely sure that it wasn't a serious question—to which she didn't know the answer. She was uncomfortably aware, though, that only a few minutes before, she had been prying into Zeph's relationship with Mireille herself, by provoking confidences from the latter, and although she wasn't sure how to evaluate the information she'd gleaned, there was no doubt that she had found it interesting and intriguing.

Backed into a metaphorical corner, she said: "Zeph's sex life is none of my business, and certainly none of yours."

"Oh, but it is," Helen countered. "It has always been in your interest and well as mine to know whether his apparent ability to empathize with alien minds is real or illusory, and given that we both know, now, that it *is* real, it's in your interest as well as mine to discover as much as we can about how it works and what its limitations are. The objective features of his exchanges of information with the Dancing Rats have been immensely valuable and interesting, but it would be a great mistake to overlook its subjective elements. The same is true of his interactions with other humans. Vulgar minds have suggested for years that his ability to empathize with the Dancing Rats was a complement to, or even an aspect of, his apparent inability to interact efficiently with human beings in what passed on Earth for everyday social circumstances, but that was always glib and sloppy thinking. Now that we know that he was able to learn to interact efficiently with the other crew members of Olympus Five, without overmuch effort, and that he was able to form close relationships, of different kinds, with Captain Kemmering and Mireille, and thus become determined to forge the close relationship with you that he had been unable to form before, the substance of those relationships becomes intensely interesting, scientifically, including, and perhaps especially, the sexual component of his relationship with Mireille. I intend to investigate it as fully as I can . . . although I anticipate that direct interrogation will be difficult, precisely because their immediate, reflexive reaction will be the one you just voiced."

"I'd go so far as to suggest that it might be counterproductive," Denise observed, mildly, "generating more hostility than useful information."

"I suspect that you're correct," Helen admitted. "Experience certainly suggests so—but we're all scientists, are we not? All *philosophes*, as Mireille puts it. It ought to be possible for us to reach an understanding . . . an empathy, if you wish. We all have the same objectives, and it would surely be foolish of us to allow stupid taboos formed by our ignorant ancestors on Earth to inhibit our investigation. I simply can't agree that that makes me, to use the favorite phrase that dogged my footsteps on Earth, *as crazy as a sack of monkey-nuts*. Personally, I'm certain that I'm absolutely sane . . . and with all due respect to Zephaniah's theory of alternative sanities, I cling to the conviction that my sanity is the only true one . . . and please don't tell me that you'll have to agree to differ, because mathematicians can *never* agree to differ with regard to their conclusions, and without two parties there can be no agreement."

It took Denise a few seconds to realize that Helen had not plucked the monkey-nut analogy out of her private thoughts, or even consulted the stored tape of her not-entirely-private conversation with her fellow crew-members not long after their general emergence from hibernation, in which she had casually echoed the second-hand judgment. Again, it seemed best to let it pass without comment.

"I'll refrain from employing that particular cliché," she conceded, aloud—meaning the *agree to differ* cliché—"but although it takes two to agree, it only takes one to differ, and I differ. So, I suspect, does everyone else in this world and on Earth . . . but I don't suppose you're in the least intimidated by being in a minority of one?"

"On that matter, no. Since you appear to care, though, might I remind you that in the other matter that ought to be our immediate and urgent interest, there's no rational reason why any of us should differ. We all want the same thing: to understand, as much as may be humanly possible, the nature and contents of the universe in which we find ourselves. In that regard, my dear, you and I are presently in a privileged position, which we share with a limited number of others, and in which your brother, and perhaps Mireille, and perhaps even the captain, can lend us invaluable assistance, if only they can be persuaded to do so. Zephaniah, I'm convinced, will lend me his wholehearted support. Yours will evidently have to be earned by persuasion, which is what I'm endeavoring to do."

"I see," said Denise, feeling a little like the proverbial blind man who said *I see* when he couldn't see at all. "As I said, I'll have to think it over . . . and talk it over, with Zeph. It might take time."

"Obviously. I'm taking it for granted, of course, that you're willing to join Zephaniah in a second experiment with the machine, and also that you have no objection to other people substituting for you in future runs . . . but it's necessary that you and the others involved go into those runs with informed and enquiring minds, ready to record data if or when it evades the reflexive censorship of consciousness. It won't be easy to overcome those inherited taboos, but Zephaniah has already proved on Earth that he's capable of doing it, with assistance and practice. You might think it indelicate of me to follow the train of thought, but I believe that his experience with Mireille, in which he broke through a number of previously strong personal taboos in order to attain a satisfactory relationship, suggests strongly that he is still expanding his personal capabilities in multiple directions. It adds to my confidence that he might be able to obtain the same success with the ring intelligences as he did with the sentient rodents and insects in Earth's far future."

Denise couldn't resist that bait. "You're convinced that, because he learned to love Mireille, just as he learned to like the Dancing Rats, he can also learn to like the Bells?"

"*Bells* is a silly term, the use of which only serves to confuse matters . . . but I could say the same for *love*. In crude terms, though, yes, I think there's every possibility that, with practice and a little wise guidance, Zephaniah will be able to make a conscious contact with the ring intelligences that is not only fruitful but pleasurable, for him and for them. For the time being, that is the working hypothesis on which I'm making my plans."

Inevitably, Denise remembered what Mireille had said about her relationship with Zeph having become, albeit not without preliminary hesitation, "pure pleasure." She also remembered that Mireille had said that she didn't really *know* Zeph at all. All she said to Helen Arkheimer, however, was: "Pleasure and understanding are very different things."

"Of course they are," the mathematician agreed. "The synthetic relationship between them is very complicated . . . but certainly not non-existent, in terms of Coincidence. If Zephaniah can be enabled to obtain pleasure from contact with the ring intelligences, and if that feeling can become mutual, I suspect that the data they exchange will be more prolific, and more productive. Initially, at least, that information might have to be filtered through you . . . or someone else . . . and for that reason, it will doubtless be useful if you could . . . share his feelings."

"Very delicately put," said Denise, wryly. "I'll do my best to like the Bells . . . but I can't guarantee that they'll like me in return. Experience suggests that I'm not a very likeable person."

"It's very interesting that you should say that, my dear," Helen Arkheimer informed her, obviously taking the remark literally rather than crediting it with the sarcastic flippancy that Denise had intended, "and if you're being sincere, I could certainly say that I know how you feel. But for what it might be worth, I can assure you that Captain Kemmering likes you a great deal more than he likes me, and the same is almost certainly true of Mireille. I've had plenty of opportunity to make the relevant observations. The ring intelligences might have very different tastes, of course, but I'm prepared to be optimistic until I find evidence to the contrary. If my reading of his personal history is correct, there was a time when almost everyone who met him, probably including you, thought that Zephaniah wasn't a likeable person, but that wasn't the case abroad Olympus Five, just as it wasn't the case with the future generations of Earthly evolution. In the unlikely event that what you just said wasn't simply hypocritical false modesty, please don't sell yourself short."

Anyone else, Denise thought, would probably have assured her that *she* liked her, but Helen Arkheimer was a mathematician, only given to hypocritical politeness when it fitted her calculations. Aloud, Denise said: "The last three years must have been difficult for you, stuck in intimate proximity with two people you don't like."

"Not really," said Helen. "They both felt that it was their duty to pretend, and even to try, to like me, even to the extent of having sexual intercourse with me occasionally, for which I was duly grateful. I like them well enough, I suppose, to the extent that I've ever liked anybody—but you can't imagine how I yearned for the others to wake up . . . especially Zephaniah."

"You probably weren't the only one," Denise observed, confidently.

"Indeed not . . . but I really ought to have tried harder to like the people I was with, given the circumstances. The sexual intercourse should have helped in that, but the captain is too disciplined for my taste and Mireille . . . well, she's an atmospheric chemist. People's professions, alas, often reflect their personalities."

"I'm an evolutionary biologist, alas," Denise remarked, "and you're a mathematician."

"You say that as if to imply that those are bad things, my dear, but you know as well as I do that they're not. Can't we try to be a little more honest with one another? Difficult though it might seem, and as experience suggests that it is, I really would like you to like me . . . or at least to understand me . . . to the extent that it might be possible."

Denise thought: *Perhaps you ought to try a little harder to be likeable, then*, but she didn't say it. She suspected that the other woman actually was trying as hard as she could to obtain that effect, in her own peculiar way . . . whereas she was not making any such effort herself. "We're going to be sharing the same prison for a very long time," she observed, reflexively, addressing herself rather than her interlocutor, "so it probably would be a good idea."

"We aren't in prison, my dear," said the mathematician, "and I'm not just referring to the ability of the VR-hoods to take us to an infinite number of virtual environments. To mangle the words of the poet whose name I never bothered to memorize, metal walls do not a prison make, nor stony expressions a cage. You and I are as free as any human beings have ever been, and perhaps freer. The people on Earth are all in cages of their own making, and were long before the retreat to the domes gave them a material symbolization of their existential situation, but the elite of humankind—the real elite, not the stupid political Cabal—have always been free in their minds and in their hearts."

"Lovelace," said Denise, reflexively.

"Pardon?" said the mathematician, perhaps having heard it as *loveless*.

"The poet whose name you can't remember was Richard Lovelace."

"Oh. Thank you. I'll remember it in future; it's important for mathematicians not to seen uncultured. You followed the wordplay, though? And since you know the poet's name you presumably know the actual text of the poem?"

That was a challenge. "Only the last few lines," Denise admitted, regretfully. "Stone walls do not a prison make, nor iron bars a cage. Minds innocent and quiet take that for a hermitage. If I have freedom in my love, and in my soul am free, Angels alone that soar above enjoy such liberty." She had memorized the poem as a child, perhaps in thoughtless imitation of Zephaniah's memorization of *Kubla Khan* for therapeutic reasons. Unlike Zeph, however, she had not been able to retain all of the Lovelace in her memory permanently—although, oddly enough, she thought she might still be capable reciting *Kubla Khan*, with or without Zeph's playful amendments.

"Very good," said Helen, with apparent sincerity, "and very apt. Do you?"

"Do I what?"

"Have freedom in your love and in your soul."

That was a challenge too, but Denise knew that the mathematician wasn't merely playing games. The question was serious—and pertinent.

"No," she admitted. "I don't . . . yet"

"Nor do I, yet, my dear," Helen conceded. "Nor, I suspect, has anyone else achieved it yet, including the aptly named Lovelace. But I suspect that Zephaniah is capable of a temporary liberation, with the proper assistance. We must try to make what contribution we can to that assistance, I with my math and my machine, you with . . . whatever you can muster."

That, at least, was not a petty challenge, and it demonstrated that the other's relentless pedantry was no mere bluster.

"I'll do my best," Denise promised, "but even regarding sisterly love, I fear that I've never shown much natural aptitude. I'm a conspicuously ordinary person, affection-wise." *But not such a cripple as you*, she scrupulously refrained from adding.

Helen sighed. "Please set the false modesty aside, Denise, and admit that you're one of us . . . one of the elite, that is. We've already proved experimentally that you are *not* ordinary. The three of us need one another, but together with Zephaniah, you and I can make history."

"If the number of queued-up messages indicated by the screen behind me is anything to go by," Denise said, "we already have."

"It isn't," Helen retorted, flatly, "and we haven't. Those messages are just idle gossip, not history. We've pried open the door of historical possibility, but we have yet to go through it. Vague preliminary revelations might provide acceptable endings for Bibles and other fairy stories, but in history-making terms, it's what happens afterwards that matters. History isn't what the yellow media report, as you must know, but what happens deeper in the collective unconscious of the race—and whatever anyone else thinks, we're the ones who are making it . . . you and I and Zephaniah, that is, with only spear-carrying roles for the other crew members at present, although we must hope that they will be able to play their parts more fully in future. The captain thinks that he ought to control the pace of the plot and the finicky detail, but at heart he's a critic, not a creator, and he needs to be kept in his place. You and I can do that if we work together, Denise . . . and we need to do it. We're the ones who need to orchestrate the story, and when you've had time think about it, you'll see that I'm right. You're an evolutionary biologist, after all, not a soldier or a weather girl."

Wow! Denise thought. *Lyrical abuse as well as crude poetic flattery, from a mathematician—such ingenuity. But people who think they understand Coincidence math, as well as those who can't begin to do so, concede that it's horrendously convoluted—and she* is *a certified genius, even if she's as alternatively sane as a sack of monkey-nuts.*

"I will think about it," she promised, just as the screen buzzer sounded.

The captain, who had the privilege of overriding almost all of the prohibitions built into the ship's programming, was using his prerogative to transit a message in print, which read: FINALLY FREE. COME TO THE CONTROL ROOM IMMEDIATELY, DENISE.

No *hello*, no *please*, not even an *as soon as possible*. For a captain who preferred manipulating with a velvet glove and claimed to detest tyranny, Chris Kemmering was certainly not shy about deploying the iron fist when the mood took him.

III

Captain Kemmering was alone in the so-called control room when Denise finally contrived to float through the access hatch, preserving her cranium from harm and only inflicting mild pain on her sensitive elbows as she did so. Alessandro—a theoretical physicist who probably thought that he understood the basics of Coincidence theory, although Helen Arkheimer and Walter Halleck would presumably dispute the claim—had already withdrawn, perhaps exercising tact rather than having been ordered to do so. Denise anchored herself in response to the captain's invitation, making sure that the tethers were firm, and then assumed a very tidy half-lotus, although there was plenty of room to extend her legs had she wanted to do so; she wanted to put on a show of the utmost stability.

"I'm sorry about the delay," the captain said. "I wanted to be there as soon as you woke up, but I'd received a specific order from Mission Control to remain at my post, and it didn't seem to be the right moment to let Fairbanks know that their orders have lost all meaning, since they seem to be still under the arrogant illusion that they really are controlling the mission. We need the information they're relaying to us, and I don't want to offend them. You can't imagine how frustrating it was, though, having to twiddle my thumbs during the long gaps in conversational exchanges that were, in the ultimate analysis, meaningless."

"Do the people at Fairbanks believe that the contact we made was real?" Denise asked.

"Provisionally, yes they do, perhaps more because they want to than because they find the evidence completely convincing.

For both reasons, though, they want more evidence, and soon. Their masters in the Cabal are busy formulating the message they want to receive, shaped by their perceived political needs, but the people in Mission Control have a far greater commitment to the truth. If and when we send them a message of which the masterminds of the Cabal don't approve . . . relations could become strained. They can't play censor, with the European and Asian stations equally capable of picking up our transmissions, and no imaginable encryption being able to protect them. For the same reason, they can't give me a direct order to lie . . . but that particular diplomatic tangle is my problem, not yours. How are you feeling?"

"In myself, fine. In respect of Helen Arkheimer and her convoluted aspirations of grandeur, somewhat confused. My head's still spinning. I can't quite see why she's in such a mutinous frame of mind, though, given that you and she have exactly the same objectives . . . don't you?"

"For the moment, yes . . . but she's thinking ahead. She has no idea what Zephaniah might experience if he agrees to make use of her machine again, but she's afraid that she and I might soon come into conflict as to how best to proceed, or how rapidly. If she could only wait patiently to see how things pan out . . . but she's not a patient person. If her thinking didn't happen in perpetual overdrive, she presumably wouldn't be a mathematical genius, but the side effects are . . . how shall I put it . . . ?"

"Counter-productive?" Denise suggested.

"Not always," said the captain, with scrupulous fairness, "but sometimes, yes. I wouldn't say that she's her own worst enemy, but in social matters she's not her best friend either. You're not used to her yet, but you'll learn to make the necessary allowances. I was succeeding quite well in that, as was Mireille, while things were quiet, but since they've become several orders of magnitude more complicated, in a matter of Earthdays, I fear that I'm not coping as well as I should, and must."

Denise was not confident that she could do half as well as the captain, but she did not voice the fear. "You said *if* Zeph agrees?"

she remarked instead. "Helen is taking it for granted that he will, and so am I. Do you have any reason to think that Zeph might refuse?"

"No, but I'm still prepared to consider the possibility that it might be expecting too much to allow him to continue. Until Zephaniah has been debriefed regarding the conscious component of his experience, if there was one, we can't make a good estimate of that. Walter Halleck was always able to bully him into taking further shots with the Sling, but things change. He might be more vulnerable now than he was before the seventh generation contact, let alone the contact with the ring intelligences. Helen might think that she has a God-given right to plan and control future experiments, but in fact, the only person who has that right in Zephaniah . . . and the only advice he'll take in the first instance won't be Helen's . . . it'll be yours."

Will it? Denise thought. *He's never shown any sign of preferring my advice to that of others, or of any inclination to take it.*

The captain's attention was deflected for a moment, in order to cast a glance at the screen display of an incoming transmission, but it only took a few seconds for him to scan it and for his fingers to perform a routine dance on his keyboard. Denise had observed his expertise in that kind of multitasking before, and she knew that she still had his almost-full attention.

"Helen seems to have the same opinion," she said, in slightly belated response to his last comment. "She's just been giving me an urgent indoctrination regarding the necessity of my supporting her right to command the investigation. She refused to endorse a fanciful symbolism constructing a holy trinity in which Zeph is the sacrificial Christ and me the paraclete, but she was suspiciously quick to deny that you might figure in the pattern as Satan. Her thinking doesn't seem to be as stubbornly literal as one might expect of a mathematician."

"What you and I think of as mathematical reasoning comes unstuck in confrontation with Coincidence theory," the captain observed, with a slight sigh. "We're not capable of following her into that logical wilderness . . . but we can't afford simply to dismiss it as insane, as most people on Earth seem willing and eager to do. As Zeph was fond of saying on Olympus, there are alternative sanities, which can't simply be dismissed by those who don't have the right mental configuration to sympathize with them."

Yet again, Denise refused the theoretical in favor of the personal. "You like Zeph, don't you?" she asked, interestedly. "Not just as a matter of duty, the way the principles in operation aboard Olympus Five required you to do, but because you really did learn to like him?"

"Of course," said the captain, evidently puzzled by the question. "Isn't that obvious?"

"Yes. Do you think that Mireille loves him . . . and not just as a matter of duty?"

"Ah!" said the other, as if that sequel explained the puzzling aspect of the earlier question. "That I don't know. Has Mireille said something?"

"Very little . . . but enough to enable me to deduce that the mythology of romantic love was something of a taboo subject aboard Olympus, and that he and she have been scrupulous in refusing to think in those obsolete traditional terms. But that self-censorship, however useful it might have been in the context of relationships between the crew members of Olympus during a seven-year mission, might be an obstruction in trying to determine exactly what kind of a bond Zeph was able to form with Mireille. It's presumably irrelevant to the bond that he seems to be in the process of forming, a trifle belatedly, with me, as well as the bond he was able to form even before he was co-opted by Olympus, with the Dancing Rats, but the comparison might help to provide insight into the whole picture."

Oh shit, she thought, *it's infectious. I'm talking like Helen . . . perhaps counter-productively.*

"Did Helen say all that?" the captain enquired curiously, evidently having noticed the atypical style of expression.

"No, but she's obviously been thinking along the same lines," Denise replied, trying hard to sound more like her self . . . her old self, at least, "and I suspect that it worries her, because she thinks that her brand of sanity might not be equipped for understanding that component of Zeph's relationships. And at the risk of selling myself short, to use her phrase, I'm not at all sure that I'm equipped for it either. Are you?"

The captain laughed. "If I understand that question correctly, you're asking me whether I think I'm genuinely capable of love rather than putting on a dutiful act shaped by the formal principles of Olympian society. There was a time when I would instantly have replied yes . . . but I've learned to think in more convoluted ways, polluted by Coincidence theory even though I can't begin to understand it the way Helen claims to do. But I'll stick my neck out, and still say yes, in spite of the complications inherent in the notion. So is Mireille, if my judgment can be trusted, although she's understandably inhibited in thinking about it, let alone talking about it. I'm certainly prepared to say that she loves Zephaniah, even though she won't say so herself. Helen probably isn't capable of love, in the way that you and I presumably understand the term, but I might be wrong about that. I don't know you well enough to form a confident judgment yet, but if I had to bet, I'd put my money on yes."

Would I? Denise thought, but abandoned the train of thought, because the captain hadn't finished speaking.

"Whether that can possibly help to explain the bonds that Zephaniah now seems to be capable of forming with other humans and alien intelligences," he continued, "I don't know, but I certainly hope so."

"Why?" Denise countered, automatically, still postponing the matter of thinking through the various implications of what the captain had just said.

The captain evidently had not been expecting that challenge, so he took a moment, dutifully, to think about it.

"Because of what happened in his communications with the Dancing Rats and their descendants, and the insectile species that replaced them," he replied, judiciously. "It seemed insane to many people that he could say that he liked those alien species and that they liked him. The prevalent opinion in Fairbanks, so far as I could judge, was that if the Rats were pretending to like him, it was because they had an intrinsic interest in feeding him the information they wanted humans to have, because it would favor their own evolution . . . but that's just anthropocentric paranoia. Personally, I prefer a secular variant of your friend Marie's interpretation . . . that Creation is essentially benign, and essentially affable, because that's a necessary condition of the past and future evolution of intelligence. Either way, we need an explanation, in order to plan our strategy in forming our future attempts to bond with alien intelligence intelligently . . . and perhaps even to carry forward our strategies of form bonds with one another with due intelligence."

"Do you really believe that Creation is essentially benign?" Denise queried—not because she doubted the captain's honesty, but because what he had said flew in the face of conventional secular wisdom that the universe was essentially indifferent.

"Belief might be too strong a term," he confirmed, "but I'm certainly prepared to hope so and to accept the possibility. Unlike Helen, though, I'm able to agree to differ with people who think that it can't be so. She thinks that I'm just a clodhopper, intellectually speaking, but I'd like to think that she's wrong, and that my opinion has some weight even though my body, for the moment, doesn't. And I think that the questions you just asked me are good ones, and that Zeph's . . . what we have to call empathy, for want of a better word . . . is crucial to his ability to made contact with other intelligences, both human and alien."

"When we were young, he was educated to think that what he had was a lack of empathy, and hence an *in*ability, something unfortunately built into the configuration of his brain. Attempts were made to cure him of it. I was never wholly convinced, though. I always had the impression that his behavior was partly pretence, or at least exaggeration. I was probably being unfair to him."

"I suspect so," the captain agreed, "but it was certainly far more complicated than a matter of an ability or inability to relate to others. He was, or at least became, a different person aboard Olympus, partly as a result of the experience he'd had in the Sling, with the rodent and insect intelligences, but partly because he simply had more in common, intellectually and emotionally, with the other members of the crew, than with most of the people with whom he'd had to associate in the past . . . and partly, too, because he and Mireille were able to form a particularly intimate bond. I know that he was very grateful for that, but I suspect that widening the scope of his personal relationships did exactly what he had always been consciously and unconsciously afraid of—it made him more vulnerable emotionally. On Olympus, he was shielded from excessively awkward emotional difficulties by the principles . . . but I was worried that the shield might turn to tissue paper as soon as he was out of rehab, and that repairing it might be impossible."

"So you're afraid for him?" Denise said bluntly. "Not just because the alien input into his brain via Helen's machine might cause physical damage, but because he might get hurt emotionally."

"The apparent alternatives might not be distinct. Yes, I'm afraid for him, and not just because it's my duty as his captain. Aren't you?"

"Yes . . . but I'm having difficulty explaining to myself exactly why, beyond the mere physical risk."

"Join the club. I suspect that Zeph is probably right to believe that his brain is not only preconfigured to receive information from alien intelligences—and thus, indirectly, from all the other intelligences with which some alien intelligences are in communication—but that his personality is configured to be able to like them, or even to love them. Unfortunately, circumstances being what they are, I haven't had a chance to discuss it with Gabrielle, and she hasn't had a chance to evaluate Zephaniah, so my assessment is simply my own, based on what Helen would call crude guesswork. Obviously, though, Zephaniah's recent cultivation of his ability has been far from easy; I presume that, as his brain developed in youth, it spontaneously built barriers designed to exclude the special kind of empathy that he seems to have, and other kinds of empathy were bundled with that exclusion."

"It certainly seems so," Denise confirmed, exercising hindsight in reevaluating her memories.

"But those neurological dams began to crack as soon he was put into Halleck's Sling," the captain said, continuing his own train of thought, "and they continued crumbling until he volunteered to serve aboard Olympus Five . . . and during the seven-year mission they were probably reduced to metaphorical dust. His vulnerability wasn't seriously tested aboard Olympus, or even during the brief interval he spent back on Earth, and he spent his first three years on Minerva in a coma—but when Helen plugged his contacts into her machine . . . well, you were there, and you saw what happened. The medical monitors say that his life wasn't in danger, and Helen swears it, but they're not qualified to assess the physical trauma that his brain might have suffered, let alone any danger that his mental software might have been in. No one, on Minerva or Earth, is competent to analyze the electroencephalographic traces that have been recorded while he's been comatose—there's nothing on record with which to compare them."

"When he woke up before," Denise reminded him, "he didn't remember anything, and he didn't seem to have suffered any ill effects."

"No . . . but I've been regretting ever since that I let Helen hook him into her machine so rapidly. I should have asked Gabrielle to make a full examination, and kept Helen at bay until it was complete, to Gabrielle's satisfaction and mine. She's flying almost as blind as I am, but she's the nearest thing to an expert we have, even though Helen dismisses her as an irrelevance. She wasn't on Olympus Five, so I don't know her that well personally, but her record on Four certainly entitles her to respect."

"I'm not sure that Zeph would have liked submitting to Gabrielle's assessment any more than Helen would, and even though he seems to like you, as a person, better than he's ever liked anyone else, with the exception of Mireille, I'm not sure that he'd consider you qualified to make decisions on his behalf."

"I'm sure that he wouldn't—but if I had told him that I needed a full psych assessment, and needed to take responsibility for decisions regarding his welfare in order to fulfill my duty as captain, he would have agreed. In retrospect, that's what I should have done. I made a mistake . . . I wasn't thinking fast enough."

"Nor was I," Denise observed, quietly, and a trifle ominously. "He assured me that he was fine, and I believed him. But when we were kids together, on the rare occasions that I actually bothered to ask him whether he was all right, he always said that he was fine . . . and I always took his word for it, even when I knew full well that he wasn't all right. I wasn't a very good sister . . . but Mum was always there in those days to make up for my failings. Now . . ."

It was the first time that she had been forced to bring to mind what had happened to her mother, and the fact that, unlike Zeph, she hadn't had a chance to talk to her before the old lady and Earth's atmosphere had both run mortally short of oxygen. She cursed herself for the absurdity of the determination she felt not to weep in front of Chris Kemmering.

Perhaps he observed that, and, as the good captain that he was reputed to be, tried to contrive a diplomatic deflection . . . or perhaps he was still caught up in his own train of thought. Either way, he continued: "But I won't make the same mistake again, if I can help it. This time, when Zephaniah wakes up, I want him to be properly assessed before I allow him to hook up to any kind of machine again, and I want you, as well as Gabrielle, to assess him as carefully and as closely as you can. Whatever Helen thinks, and whether or not she can bully Zephaniah into supporting her, I want to take things one step at a time. I do understand Helen's sense of urgency, and I also understand her argument that, as we have no choice but to repeat the experiment eventually, it might be best to get on with it right away . . . but I've always had some sympathy for the view that hesitation isn't a bad thing, if it prevents fools from rushing in where wise angels would fear to tread."

"Fair enough," Denise conceded. "But I'm really not sure what my assessment will be worth. I don't know anything at all about neurology and electroencephalography, and hardly anything about Zeph's peculiar mind. If we really do have some mysterious Coincidental connection, it has no conscious component."

"I know that," the captain said, "but I'm prepared to trust your intuition, since it's all that we have."

"If you knew my personal history," Denise observed wryly, "I'm pretty sure that you wouldn't think of my intuition as something trustworthy. I don't."

"I know more about your personal history than you might think," the captain countered, "but I don't think that's relevant. And I could say the same about the trustworthiness of my intuition . . . but it hasn't always been at fault, and I liked you from the first moment that I saw you."

"I thought you were just flirting with me at the Embassy because it was your duty, or simple habit."

"It wasn't my duty, at the time, and although I can't deny the habit, I'm prepared to think that the fugitive empathy was real. How about you?"

Good question, Denise thought. *I automatically put up a defensive barrier the moment I felt the first twinge of sexual attraction, but isn't that just a symptom of my own social disability?*

"I don't even know whether the *fugitive empathy* I now feel with Zeph is real," she countered, aloud, "but I'll give it a try, for lack of any rational alternative."

"Good. Obviously, I'll convene a full crew assembly before taking any further action, unless I'm forced to react to changed circumstances. The final decision as to what our next step will be has to be mine, but everyone's life is on the line, and everyone is entitled to voice an opinion. If we can't achieve unanimity, that will be a minor catastrophe in itself, but we have to try. Don't you agree?"

"I don't know," Denise replied, although she was fully conscious that it was not the most diplomatic reply she could have chosen.

"Why don't you agree?" asked the captain, bluntly.

"Because I haven't heard yet what Zeph has to say, and when I have . . . well, I know it's contrary to the principles on which you and the rest of the crew—with the exception of Helen—have all adopted, but I haven't signed up to them, and with all due respect to your crew psychologist and my suspicions regarding my own incapacity, I want to make my own assessment of my brother's state of mind, and make my own decision as to what's best for him . . . and for me. Whether the crew—or you—agree with me or not isn't a matter of great importance in my mind. If that makes me a bad utopian, so be it."

If Chris Kemmering was disappointed by that response, he didn't show it. Discipline prevailed. "That's perfectly under-standable," he said, "but might I remind you that Zephaniah *has* signed up to the social conventions applicable to Minerva, and has seemed in the past to be fully committed to them. Unlike Helen, he's surely the kind of person who will honor them scru-pulously . . . and who would want you to honor them too."

Sly bastard, Denise thought, reflexively, but immediately reproached herself for blatant inaccuracy. The captain was not being sly, nor was he being anything less than a perfect gentle-man. And in any case, she had no rational grounds for objecting to the captain's declaration. Being Zeph's sister did not constitute reasonable grounds for claiming that she and she alone ought to have the prerogative of deciding what was good for him, or even for herself.

"This discussion is a trifle premature," she suggested. "Until Zeph wakes up—until you consent to letting him wake up—we have no idea what Zeph is likely to remember, or to say."

"I don't think it's at all premature from my viewpoint," the captain replied, in a honeyed tone intended to soften the flat con-tradiction. "I need to consider all the possibilities in advance—if only because, as you just pointed out, I'm the one who has been delaying the moment when Zeph can tell us himself what he ex-perienced and what he thinks our next step ought to be."

"Of course," Denise conceded. A sudden thought occurred to her then, and she asked: "Is this conversation private?"

"We're the only ones here," the captain pointed out. "But if you mean, is it *secret*, the answer is no. Anyone will be able to access the automatic recording, if they wish. The conversation you had with Mireille was anomalous, in being fully screened—that was as much for your benefit as to separate our account of the situation from Helen's. Helen had her own reasons for wanting the account she gave you to be confidential. As you say, you haven't formally accepted the rules of conduct to which the rest of us are accustomed, and are unfamiliar with our etiquette, but we're all hoping and expecting that you'll be able to adapt. Helen hasn't, thus far, but given time, we hope and believe that she will."

"I see," said Denise, reflexively. "I fear that I might test your patience a little . . . I'm a slow learner . . . an intellectual clodhopper, as Helen would put it."

"Even the fastest thinker in the solar system sometimes gets cramp," the captain assured her, scrupulously mentioning no names. "Thinking is a complicated business, and it sometimes takes its own time, especially when we try too hard to get ahead of ourselves. You're a highly intelligent person and—perhaps more importantly—a thoroughly benign one. Fundamentally, you're *one of us*; we have every confidence that you'll fit in."

Denise observed the irony of the fact that when Helen Arkheimer had assured her that she was *one of us* she had had a very different *us* in mind; an example of the perversity of coincidence, if not Coincidence.

"But it makes no difference," Denise said, thinking aloud rather than responding to her interlocutor. "Zeph will doubtless put on a show of playing by your rules, but while I've known him he's always been stubborn, and he's always been selfish. Once he makes up his mind to think or do something, he's as bad as Helen. He won't back down. Believe me, if I do know him, that's one thing I know for sure."

"I believe you," the captain said, "but if I know him, on the basis of our relationship on Olympus, he's capable of taking advice—perhaps not from Gabrielle, and perhaps not even from me, if he doesn't like the advice . . . but I do believe that he'll listen to you."

That, Denise knew, was exactly what Helen thought, and that was why the mathematician and the captain were both striving, in their different ways, to recruit her to their causes.

"But this conflict, if it is one, is absurd," she opined, carefully. "We all want exactly the same thing—to make productive further contact with the Bells and to discover what they know about the universe and the minds within it."

"The problem," the captain reminded her, "is how best to go about that, given that the only potential conduit of information we have, at present, is Zephaniah. For Helen, that's purely a matter of mathematical calculation of risks and potential rewards, but you, Zephaniah and I can't think that way. We can't decide whether the risks are worth taking simply in accordance with a calculation of hypothetical probabilities."

"Zeph might," Denise said, pensively. "He's the stuff of which heroes are made, alas."

"Which is exactly why you might need to make a more sensible decision for him."

"A cowardly decision, based of fear and anxiety?"

"A sensible decision, based on human fellow-feeling, on love. But I'm not giving you an order . . . I'm just trying to make sure that your conduct is as fully informed as possible as to where I stand. Circumstances being what they are, there's bound to be a . . . let's call it a lively discussion rather than a fight . . . when Zephaniah wakes up, whatever he remembers, or whatever judgment he makes regarding your little sermon, if he doesn't remember anything at all. You'll be a crucial player in that argument, and it's important that you figure out for yourself where to take your stand . . . just as Helen and I have figured out our own starting positions.

Denise cursed the slowness of her own thinking, the depth of her own uncertainty, and the unfairness of the position in which Fate or Coincidence had placed her.

"But whatever judgment you or I might form," she said, "it won't make any difference if Zeph decides otherwise. And whatever he decides, you won't actually forbid him, will you, even if you come to consider that it's your duty as captain to oppose him?"

"That remains to be seen," Captain Kemmering said, sternly. "But you're absolutely right in saying that we all want the same thing, and please don't think, because I'm anxious and fearful, that I'm not hopeful that we can and will achieve it. I believe in Zephaniah, in his ability and in the necessity of trying to make the most of it. I hope and believe that he can continue his own personal evolution—that he really can continue to forge a viable connection with the ring intelligences and hence with the universal community of minds, whose Coincidental links go all the way back, in embryo, to a brief interval after the hypothetical Big Bang . . . the evolving cosmic mind, if you like; but I can't believe that that will be easy, or comfortable, and I'm afraid that it might endanger his sanity and his life, especially if it's rushed. That's why I want to tread very carefully in licensing and pacing the further use of Helen's machine . . . but she dismisses most of my train of thought as nonsense or cowardice. It doesn't fit with her reckless frame of mind."

Denise couldn't bring herself to say *I see*, or to make any other tokenistic gesture of endorsement. Instead, she said: "You've given this matter a great deal of thought, then—even before my so-called revelation?"

"Obviously—long before. Hasn't Zephaniah told you about our long theoretical discussions aboard Olympus? You friend Marie seems to know a good deal about them."

"No, he hasn't—his mind was on other things. Marie's wasn't. You've been exchanging social chitchat with her too, then? Even at a distance of several light-hours, she's been pestering you the way she pestered Zeph during our brief interval on Earth?"

"Indelicately put, but yes. Don't think you'll get away—I presume that you haven't had time to read your messages yet, but you'll see what I mean soon enough. She's firmly convinced that there is but one God, that Zephaniah is now his prophet, and that she has been selected by Coincidence to be the prophet's mouthpiece on Earth. But even if her viewpoint is skewed by faith, she's one of the few people who currently feel the need to consider such questions very carefully and very seriously. Coincidentally or not, you and I can hardly avoid that responsibility. I believe we can do it—the evidence of your testament says so. And however uncertain you might be about Zephaniah's relationships with other people, you must know how you feel about him."

"If only," said Denise. "That secret, I suspect, is buried in my unconscious, behind barriers that have barely begun to crack, let alone crumble."

"You're here," the captain pointed out. "You might not know why, consciously, but you know the heading that your unconscious compass has set. Zephaniah loves you and you love him; you couldn't avoid that even if you wanted to . . . which you don't."

"What about Zeph and Mireille?"

"Same situation, although they'd inevitably feel compelled to be wary in their choice of words."

"Purely for pleasure," Denise recalled, aloud.

"That would certainly be Mireille's way of putting it . . . but she knows full well that there's nothing simple about pleasure, let alone pure. Zephaniah will probably put it differently, if you can pry an explanation out of him . . . and I strongly suggest that you do so. There is a school of thought that thinking too much about those kinds of *rapports* injures or spoils them, but even if it's true for some people, I don't believe that it can apply to you or Zephaniah."

"Because we're *philosophes*."

"Precisely. You not only *can* understand, you *need* to understand."

"Even if it kills us or drives us mad?"

"Understanding won't do that—but using the machine might, I fear. I was present during Zeph's last experiment with the Sling, just as you were, as well as the test run of Helen's machine. Walter

Halleck played down the danger that Zephaniah had been in, just as Helen did, but they weren't standing where you and I were standing. We know how close he came to having his mental capacity blasted. Zephaniah probably suspects, but he didn't have our distanced viewpoint either, and as you say, he's a dyed-in-the-wool hero . . . or victim. You and I are the ones who have the responsibility of protecting him, so far as he can be protected."

"From Helen?"

"From himself. You're his sister and I'm his friend. Nobody else has our standpoint, and our responsibility . . . not even Mireille. She's his lover, although she won't use that vocabulary, at least unless and until he does, but we've known since time immemorial that that kind of love is blind."

"And our kinds aren't?"

"We must hope so, mustn't we? Else what are friends and siblings for?"

"Helen thinks that she's the only one capable of making a rational decision."

"She's probably the only one capable of making a *dispassionate* decision—but I suspect that the last thing we need is a dispassionate decision."

"*We* being you, Zeph and I?"

"No, Denise, *we* being the human species and the ring intelligences. You, Zephaniah and I just happen to be situated at the crucial conjunction."

"Coincidentally? With a large C?"

"Perhaps. Better that than coincidence with a small c . . . but even Coincidence with a capital C isn't a species of Providence. We're the ones who have to determine how this plays out, with no aid but our own feeble and direly perverse brains, which work in mysterious ways. We have no God or Destiny to help us."

"I'm not sure that the odds are in our favor," said Denise, trying to sound heroically flippant.

"I'm quite sure that they're not," the captain replied, dryly, "but it's not as if we can refuse to throw the dice, is it? In theory, we could mothball the machine, put Helen under lock and key and set a course for Proxima b or back to Earth . . . but you understand why, as the captain, I can't do that. I have to risk further attempts at communication, even though they might involve a risk to Zephaniah's life, or at least his ability to think. All we can do is make what efforts we can to minimize that risk. In theory, of course, you could advise me to do the other thing, but we both know that, in practice, you can't."

Denise didn't bother to deny it. "I haven't been fully debriefed yet regarding the first contact," she reminded the captain.

"No," he agreed. "Nor can you be, until Zephaniah wakes up. I can let that happen any time, but I've been waiting for you to give me the green light."

"You don't need my permission."

"Technically, no—but personally, I do."

"Well, if you're really giving me the choice," Denise said, thinking furiously, and far too rapidly for her own comfort. "I have a condition to impose on that permission."

"I thought you might," the captain countered. "Let me guess: you want to be alone with him when he wakes up—to talk to him before everyone else starts pestering him, behind the kind of secrecy screen that I instructed Mireille to impose when she talked to you on my behalf?"

Denise knew that she ought not to be surprised by that, nor by the fact that the captain was evidently trying to maneuver her like a piece in his own diplomatic game. She was prepared to believe that he was honest in saying that he wanted her to make up her own mind about the square on which she wanted to stand—but that was because he was firmly convinced that she would reach the same conclusion as him.

"Yes," she said, answering his question bluntly. "It's necessary—certainly for me, and I suspect for him too. He and I need to get our story straight before we try telling it to anyone else . . . and I don't mean that in the vulgar sense of concocting a collaborative lie about our shared experience."

"I didn't imagine for a second that you did. Yes, you can have your *tête-à-tête*—as long as you need. I think it's a good idea."

"Helen won't . . . and she won't like it."

"I'll have to try to explain to her why it's necessary . . . and if she still doesn't like it, she'll just have to lump it."

"Because you're the captain?"

"Absolutely."

"And you take your duties very seriously."

"Of course."

"And it's a pleasure for you to do your duty in a disciplined fashion?"

"Not always, but in general yes. Call me a megalomaniac, if you like. Helen does . . . but she really doesn't understand. It's not her fault—she just has difficulty accommodating things that don't fit in easily with her way of thinking. She really does mean well, and she's probably not as inflexible as she thinks. At present, she doesn't like me, but she'll come around eventually. I'm very likeable, as captains go. She's already trying hard to like you, and even if you have to disappoint her slightly in the short term, she'll eventually come around."

"And if I disappoint you in the short term, will you come around?"

"There'll be no need—not because you can't disappoint me, because you certainly could, but because I can discipline and digest disappointment. I doubt that anything could stop me liking you."

"You don't know me yet; don't count your likes before they're hatched. How long can I have?—alone with Zeph, I mean, not to make an impact on your affection."

"As long as you need. I won't override your privacy seal unless there's a full-scale emergency. Is there anything you need before you start?"

"Yes, some food and a little floating time, in order to become a little more comfortable with my weightlessness. An hour should be adequate—if I take any longer the pestering will intensify."

"Undoubtedly," the captain conceded. "An hour it is, then, and then as long as you need to talk in private, and in secret—but afterwards, I'll need to do my own debriefing, and not in private or in secret. That might easily become chaotic—which is one of the reasons why I think it's a good idea for you to go first, in order to help Zeph get his story straight, as you put it. An hour probably won't be enough for that, whether he remembers the communication or not, but it will help. I don't need to beg you to handle him gently, obviously, and you're probably as well prepared now as you can be, given the urgency with which we're working, but if there's anything else you need, say so."

Having no idea what the captain had in mind, Denise simply parried the invitation, countering with: "Is there anything else you think I need to know?"

"Not urgently," the captain said, "but other opinions will certainly differ. It might be wise not to start scrolling through your messages immediately—or, if you do, use a very fine filter— and to avoid getting sucked into earnest conversation, even with Alessandro or Victor. You'll undoubtedly find it useful to talk very seriously to Gabrielle, and also Savina, when you have time, but leave all that until later. You'll have plenty of time to catch up with everyone once we've decided where we go next—wherever it might be, it'll take a long time to get there. Give my regards and my apologies to Zephaniah when you see him, and tell him that I need to see him *very* urgently, as soon as you've had your private discussion."

"I will," Denise promised.

IV

The first thing that Zephaniah Corcoran said, when he woke up, blinking furiously against the light, was: "What the hell are you doing in my bed?"

"It's not a bed, Zeph," Denise said, quietly, quelling the flood of relief that almost overwhelmed her when she saw that her brother was not only awake but *compos mentis*, at least to the extent of being rude and aggressive, "and I'm not in your sleeping bag, I'm just tethered alongside it, in a position that could be described as lying down, if up and down hadn't lost their significance temporarily."

"Denise?" he queried. "Get out of my pod, damn it. It isn't big enough for two."

"There's plenty of room, Zeph; the capsule was carefully designed to accommodate two people, if necessary or desirable."

He started to protest, perhaps to say that she was his sister, and didn't qualify as necessary or desirable, in the circumstances, but he seemed swiftly to remember that he didn't know what the circumstances were.

"Has something happened?" he demanded, presumably meaning some kind of catastrophe. He didn't pause to hear the answer before saying: "How long have I been out?" thus demonstrating a certain confusion of ideas, although the fact that he was capable of reacting to that confusion in what seemed to be a perfectly sane and normal fashion was reassuring.

"You've been comatose for a few Earthdays," Denise told him, stacking her answers in reverse order. "Purely a precaution—the medical AI has passed you physically fit, to the extent that it can.

We're in orbit around Saturn, in free fall, hence the weightlessness. Stay in your sleeping bag for the time being, and don't make any reckless movements. You're obviously lucid, so what's the last thing you remember?"

That required an evident effort on Zeph's part, and provoked a frown of uncertainty. Eventually, he said: "I'm not sure. I don't feel confused . . . in fact, I feel fine . . . but I have a curious feeling that perhaps I ought to feel confused . . . even worried, given that I can't quite remember, for the moment, where I was up to when I lost consciousness. We're in orbit around Saturn, you say?"

"That's right," Denise confirmed.

"In the plane of the rings?"

"Yes, not far away from the C-ring."

"That's not a good idea. We need to move outwards."

"Why isn't it a good idea, Zeph?"

There was a pause before he said: "I can't answer that—but I know it's not a good idea. Don't pester me—I've just woken up and I need to pull myself together. Give me a minute."

"Of course," Denise acquiesced, but couldn't help repeating: "What's the last thing you remember?"

"I don't know," he replied, automatically. "Give me time, damn it . . . I'll get there." After a pause he continued: "Let's see . . . I remember the blast-off, obviously . . . and being scared when you didn't come out of your coma. Just a precaution, the captain said, just like you, but . . . anyway, that was way back. After that, though, things are difficult to put in order, or even to recall. I was ill, wasn't I? And then I woke up. You were awake by then . . . and Doctor Arkheimer. I remember that. Then I had to go into her Sling . . . well, it's more like a pod, obviously, but I was hooked up, and I felt as if I were in the Sling. I wasn't hooked up in order to operate a surrogate . . . I remember reaching, as if I were in the Sling, trying to focus on a lens, searching for ghosts . . . that's probably the answer to your question. That's probably the last thing I *remember* . . . but I have a weird feeling that it isn't the right question. What I remember isn't the important thing . . . if that makes any sense."

"Don't worry about that, Zeph. Just try to remember."

"I just told you," he snapped. "That isn't the right question. Stop pestering me and let me think."

"I'm not pestering you, Zeph," Demise assured him, soothingly. "I'm trying to help."

You shouldn't be here," he said, waspishly. "I need to speak to the captain. He needs to move Minerva."

"Why? Are we in danger?"

"Yes. They can't help it. They'll do their best, but if we're close to the rings we need to move Minerva . . . outwards. I need to tell the captain."

"Who is *they*, Zeph?"

"The Bells, of course. You *know* that. I know you know."

There was a world of implication in those three sentences, and Denise knew that it was going to take a while to process those implications.

"The captain wants to talk to you, too—but he thought that it would be a good idea if I saw your first, so that we could compare notes on what happened. I wanted to do that because I was worried about you, Zeph . . . we all were, but I'm your sister. I needed to make sure . . ."

He cut her off abruptly. There was a time when he had done that often, even routinely, but he had shown no sign of that behavior pattern since returning to Earth from the Olympus mission. He had learned different behavior patterns on Olympus Five, but he was still the same Zeph, fundamentally. She didn't have time to think about that, though, because of what he had interrupted her in order to say.

"That's right," he said, abruptly. "Someone was in my head, and it was you, Denise, wasn't it?"

"Yes, it was," she said. "That's how I know about the Bells, remember?"

"Stop saying that," he retorted. "It's *not* remembering . . . but I'm sorry. You were in my head, and I tried to make you get out . . . didn't I? Not for the first time . . . but it was different. You were trying to calm me down, the way you always used to do in the days when I couldn't control the meltdowns and reciting Cobbler Ken didn't work . . . when I was a kid, and things got on top of me, and even though you were even younger . . . but this time, you actually got inside my head . . . through the contacts, like . . . no, not like a ghost. I don't know what it *was* like, although . . . but no, that doesn't matter. You were in my head in order to feel . . . to listen . . . in order to *be me*, because I couldn't, quite, for the moment . . . this makes no sense, damn it . . . but you were definitely there, although you had no right to be, just as you're here . . . except that it's really okay for you to be here, and it was okay for you to be there, because I'd agreed . . . I actually let you in . . . and I was right, wasn't I . . . ?"

He paused, evidently struggling to recall—except that he seemed perversely insistent that it wasn't a matter of remembrance. Did that mean that it might, in fact, have been a delusion and not an alien contact at all, Denise wondered . . . that everything she had reported orally might, in fact, have been nothing more than a dream?

No. It had been real. She *knew* that. She was the one who had given the ring intelligences the improvised name of Bells while she was struggling to understand what was happening to her, but neither she nor Zeph had invented them. They were real—bizarre but real. She really did *know* that. She didn't know how she knew it, but she knew it.

Zeph had already resumed his account, gradually becoming more fluent in his loquacity—his unaccustomed loquacity, given that he wasn't following one of the temporary obsessions that had gripped him in his youth: "I was furious, for a moment or two . . . but then I realized that what you were trying to hear, and managing to feel, were . . . images, if that word applies . . . images that weren't mine, even though they were *there*, in *my* head. I didn't know what they were . . . not like dreams, not like hallucinations . . . something that had no right to be there, obviously, but they were real . . . I thought for a while that I must be crazy, that I was losing my mind, but I knew that I wasn't. I *knew* that . . . well, I didn't know exactly *what* I knew, but I knew that I knew it, however crazy that sounds, now that I'm awake. I *am* awake, because what always happens when you wake up from a dream is happening now . . . has already happened. I can only remember fragments . . . which run away as soon as I try to focus on them and organize them, the way dreams always do . . . except that they leave traces, even though they can't be brought to consciousness. Remembering isn't the point . . . it isn't the right question. But you shouldn't have been there, Nise, even if I did invite you in, like a vampire. That shouldn't have been possible . . . I'm sorry, but . . ."

He trailed off then, as if he had lost the thread that he had been following, once again. He was still frowning, still groping, but he had lost the thread—momentarily, Denise hoped. She resisted the urge to put her arms around him, to stroke him, because she couldn't be sure that he wouldn't react to that with his old phobia, even though he had been so much more comfortable back on Earth . . . probably thanks to Mireille, whose soothing touch had surely never made him flinch . . . or, at least, not for long . . .

"You don't have to be sorry, Zeph," Denise assured him, trying to restore a measure of serenity by means of her voice alone. "You haven't done anything wrong."

It seemed to work, after a fashion—but it didn't enable him to pick up the thread of dubious remembrance right away.

"I *do* have to be sorry," he insisted. "I shouldn't have told you to get out of the pod just now. I shouldn't have tried to drive you out of my head, back then. That was stupid . . . knee-jerk stupidity. I should have thought . . . but what are you doing here, Nise? Surely you shouldn't be sealed in a pod with me . . . unless something has gone disastrously wrong. Where's the captain? I need to tell the captain to get away from the ring. We shouldn't stay. It's not safe. Where's the captain? Why isn't he here?"

Denise took a deep breath, unsure as to whether to cut the interview short and summon the captain—but she wanted a better explanation herself before she turned the problem over to anyone else. She was his sister, after all. "The captain isn't here, Zeph," she said, mildly. "We really couldn't fit three of us in—we'd be packed like sardines. The captain is in the control room, trying to cope with a flood of time-delayed communications from Earth, but we need to straighten out your ideas before you see him, so that you can make your report coherently. For the moment, you need to calm down. Once you've told me what there is to tell, you'll be much better able to tell the captain in a reasonable and orderly fashion."

He condescended to give that a moment's thought, and then said: "You're right, as usual. I need to get things straight, because I can't afford to get tongue-tied. But I really do need to talk to the captain urgently. He has to move the ship."

"He will, if you can explain to him why it's necessary—but in order to do that, you need to get the explanation straight."

Zeph's frown deepened. "You're right . . . except that . . . I'm not sure it *is* straight. He ordered you to talk to me first?"

"That's right," Denise confirmed, although it was not strictly accurate, and her conscience compelled her to issue a correction. "I asked him to let me talk to you first, and he gave me permission. I need to bring you up to date, since your memory is a little confused. You made contact with the ring intelligences, Zeph . . . or, perhaps to put it more accurately, they made contact with you."

"I *know* that," he told her.

Denise ignored the rudeness of his tone. "The ring intelligences tried to let you know certain things, Zeph," she said, thinking that it might not be a bad idea to get her own ideas straight. "I really was in your head, eavesdropping. I didn't pick up all of it, and couldn't make much sense of what I did catch, or remember very much immediately afterwards . . . but I talked in my sleep, and what I did manage to catch was important . . . so it would be really helpful if you could remember something . . . anything . . . before we try again . . . if we try again . . ."

"You're rambling," he said, sternly. "Pull yourself together, girl."

"I'll try," she promised. "As I said, I can't really remember the detail, if there actually was any detail, but I talked in my sleep, and I was conscious of doing that, and what I said, if it was true, was important. It would be very helpful if you could remember something that would confirm, if only for my benefit, that it wasn't just a dream. At this moment, Zeph, you're probably the most famous man in the solar system, but not entirely in a good way. The people who thought you were crazy before still think you're crazy, and they think that I'm either crazy, or a liar, or an actor in some crazy publicity stunt cooked up by the Cabal . . . but there are hundreds of thousands of people who do believe us. Some of those have got hold of the wrong end of the stick, like Marie MacLaughlin, but one way or another, everybody on Earth is talking about us, and everybody in the solar system is . . . expectant. So if you can remember anything . . . anything at all . . . about what you thought, or felt, or dreamed while I seemed to be in your head, however slight . . . we need to know, Zeph. You and I, at least, really do need to know. Sorry to be so urgent but . . . well, it *is* urgent."

"I see," he said, although he clearly couldn't, in the sense that he meant the phrase. His eyes could see; they were moving back and forth, looking at the opaque surface of the pod, trying to look through it, trying to look . . . somewhere else . . . but his mind's eye was still having difficulty peering through the existential murk

"It wasn't a dream," he said, after a long pause. "It wasn't like the last Slingshot, when there were actual images in my mind's eye . . . things I *could* see. I don't believe that I could *see* anything at all . . . but I could sense something. I could sense the rings."

"That's good, Zeph," Denise told him, while her heart leapt in hopeful anticipation. "What could you sense?"

"They're big."

"Yes, Zeph, I know they're big. What else?"

"No, Nise, you don't know. You don't know what big *is*. You're thinking about photographs, taken from an angle that show the rings as a kind of halo or nimbus around the planet—but that's an illusion, because the real rings aren't solid, except for a tiny fraction of their physical being . . . a sort of anchorage in baryonic matter. I'll have to discuss that with Savina, when I get the chance, and with Mireille, although they aren't atmospheric, like the cloud-whales. What you can see in your imagination is just blurs of light, reflected from tiny particles, like a cloud of sorts, but not like the clouds of Jupiter. The rings aren't really like that at all; that's a construction of our crude senses. The halo . . . the planetary nimbus . . . is just an optical illusion. The rings aren't just big in the crude way that a cloud is big, or a planet. What you think of as the material part . . . the kind of matter that you and planets are made of . . . is only a fraction of their being, but that's the only part that eyes like yours can see, and even then it's mostly an optical illusion. What you can see isn't even a ghost, and they're not ghostly themselves, but there are . . . vibrations. They include the vibrations of subatomic particles . . . the raw materials of baryonic matter . . . but that's not the whole of it. Electromagnetic vibrations, including the light visible to our eyes, are part of it too, but there's much more. In a way, they're more analogous to sonic vibrations, but in the fabric of space-time rather than in air. The baryonic matter and the energy associated with it is just one part of the weave, one aspect of the pattern. How can I put it . . . ? They're not like rosary beads, for sure, nor fancy carpets . . . more like . . . a carillon of bells . . ."

"Bells?" Denise interrupted, unable to help herself. "Where did you first get that word, Zeph . . . that idea?"

"From the dictionary, of course," he said, dismissively. She tried to take offense at being denied the credit she felt she was her due, but it was not a time for that kind of selfishness.

"Try to concentrate, Denise," he said, unfairly, "this is *important*. It's difficult, I know, but it's . . . more than important. Much more. This is *big*, Nise. It isn't something I heard, or remembered . . . it's something I *know* . . . something that I didn't know before, something important. The sounding of the carillon, or the equivalent of *sounding*, since it isn't an actual *noise*, means something. Changes of some sort are being rung . . . a huge number of changes . . . but not infinite . . . *big*, but not infinite. Most of them aren't even deliberate, let alone intelligent, but there's intelligence in there . . . intelligent entities, intelligent thought. And

there are resonances . . . distant resonances. There's meaning . .
. and emotion. The carillons can signify things . . . lots of things
. . . but even without learning their language, I can understand
that they can signify *joy*. They're always joyful, Nise . . . but right
now they're *glad*.

"They enjoy harmony . . . they don't like disharmony, because
it offends them . . . perhaps it even hurts them . . . so there's far
more harmony in the changes, even the unintelligent changes,
than disharmony, but it's not all harmony, because that's impossible . . . There's work to be done to produce and sustain complex
and sophisticated harmony, and to find new combinations . . .
and that's not easy. There's art in it, and science, and evolution.
It's slow, I think, very slow and ponderous . . . not by our fleeting
standards, but by theirs. But for the moment, at least, they're
glad . . . if they were rats, they'd dance, but they can't. Movement
is difficult for them, even for their baryonic components . . .
not impossible, within limits, but difficult . . . For the moment,
though, they're ringing joyful changes. They're glad that we're
here . . . but that doesn't mean that we're not in danger. I have to
make the captain understand that . . . or a least to take my word
for it, if he can't."

Denise took note of the fact that, in spite of all his hesitations
and narrative swerves, Zeph did not seem to be in an alternative
state of consciousness. He did not seem to be entranced, as if
he were talking in his sleep. His facial expression reflected puzzlement and effort, but he was wide awake now, and his tone,
although pensive, was almost conversational.

When he paused again, Denise was initially afraid to interrupt, but when the pause began to drag on, she prompted: "Go
on, Zeph. Why are they glad? What do they want from us?"

"They're glad because they're surprised. We're not dishar-
monious. That surprises them, and the surprise is inherently
pleasant . . . at least, they hope so. They don't rush to judgment.
We move so fast that they could barely sense us, at first, but
they're concentrating hard. They're being very careful . . . so
very careful . . . because they're frightened that they might hurt

us. They don't mean to be dangerous, but they are, just by *being*, just by ringing the changes. They really don't want to hurt us, but they're afraid that they might, accidentally. They want us to go somewhere else, for our own safety."

"Where?" Denise prompted, although she already knew the answer.

"Outwards, further from Saturn . . . and ultimately, further from the sun, if they can achieve a stable and safe physical relationship with the shell of Minerva. They believe that they can . . . and they desperately want to try . . . but they're afraid it might be dangerous . . . to us, at least, and perhaps even for them . . . but they feel a necessity to try. They want us to go . . . but they want something, or someone, to go with us."

"To Uranus?"

"If we're willing. It isn't completely safe . . . they don't know exactly how dangerous it might be, yet, but they know it isn't safe . . . yet. But they also think that they can make it safe, and that it would be harmonious to do so. They'd be glad if we did take one or more of them to Uranus . . . very glad . . . but they admit it would be a risk, because they're fundamentally honest, and benign. They're afraid for us . . . and they'd like us to go further out, at least for the moment . . . and soon."

"And in exchange for our going to Uranus," Denise said, remembering the substance of her first report on the contact, "they'll tell us something about the distant vibrations they can sense, about the distribution of different kinds of life among the nearest star systems?"

Zeph had to think about that one; his brow was still furrowed in concentration.

"I don't know," he said, eventually, "I don't think they have the concept of barter, absurd as that may seem. They're many, not one, but they don't seem to *trade* . . . they're more akin to the different instruments in an orchestra trying to play a symphony than independent merchants trading things. The spectrum of their needs and desires isn't like ours. So far as I can tell, it would give them pleasure if we went to Uranus, because it would be harmonious, but as I said, they're conscious of a risk and that makes them anxious. They aren't begging, and they aren't offering any kind of bargain. But they want to like us—because that would be harmonious—and they do like us, unconditionally. They see us as part of the *work*, part of the symphony, part of the evolution . . . a tiny part, but a part—and even though they're so very big, and we're so very tiny, that part can't be insignificant, because pleasure . . . joy . . . has no dimension. It just *is*. It's . . . mercurial, evanescent and fragile . . . but it *is* . . . Joy exists, Denise, and it's important, to them, and to us, even though we twist it slightly in our consciousness. Even there, it's real, and important. You know that. *We* know that. Everybody knows that . . ."

"*How* do you know all this, Zeph?" asked Denise, cautiously.

"I don't know. I just do. I didn't know before, but I do now, without being told, or having seen. I'm just *vibrating in resonance* . . . somehow, I can do that, although it isn't easy and certainly isn't easy to bring it to consciousness, on either side. Changes have been rung, in me . . . and not only in me. Somehow, I could always sense Coincidences more fully than other creatures of my kind, but now I can sense them *much* more fully . . . I can hear the inaudible music of the spheres and I'm no longer tone deaf . . . but it's dangerous, for me, and creatures like me, and even for entities like them, if they aren't very, very careful. That why they want us to go, and soon . . . but not inwards and not forever, because we are . . . or can be, at least . . . part of the universal concert. We have a part to play, and it's worth the risk. In the long run, it's *always* worth the risk. There's no progress without death and destruction, but there *is* progress, and ultimately, progress and harmony have to prevail over disharmony and death . . . at least, they hope so, and so should we . . .

"I'm not *remembering* this, Nise; it isn't as if I were reaching into my memory, striving to remember something once experienced but half-forgotten. That's not where it's coming from. It just . . . well, *materializes* would be entirely the wrong word, but somehow it comes into being, in mind and thought. It feels like *creation ex nihilo*, but it isn't, obviously. Somehow, the potential is there in the human brain, but it has to be shaped, by skill, by artistry. It's not easy . . . far from it . . . but it *is* possible. And, alas, dangerous. It's Coincidental . . . with a capital C . . . but not all coincidences are harmonious . . . and discord is never far away. *Clinamen*—spontaneous discord, that is—is real too. The universe couldn't exist without it, because it's an essential condition of change, or reorganization, and hence of progress. Life can't exist without it, and life *is* progress, because it has to be more than mere endless repetition, more than mere monotony. There has to be noise in order for there to be music, but music is always in danger of dissolution into cacophony. Harmony is difficult . . . but it's worth every risk, because without it . . . there's next to nothing. No substance, no *joy*.

"There are terrible risks, Nise, for beings as tiny and as incompetent as us . . . even the plant intelligences of the fifth and sixth Earthly generations and planetary rings aren't immune to the hazards and the stresses of big slow planets as well as the flickers of little quick ones . . . but there *is* a harmony and there *is* joy . . . not just here and further out, but *everywhere* . . . however difficult, everywhere there is . . . affection and beauty and joy. It's evanescent, fragile, unstable . . . but it does exist . . . and it's workable, even for creatures as tiny and as rapid as us. And if we want to, if we're so minded, we—you and I and Minerva, that is—can add to it. We can go outwards, first within the system, and then without . . . to where there are other suns, other carillons, other big and small planets. It wouldn't be easy, but if we were minded to try . . . they'd like us all the more for it, and we'd like ourselves for it, or ought to . . ."

Zeph stopped. There was no evident change of psychological state, so far as Denise could judge. He had not been in a somniloquistic trance; he had just been talking, in a level tone of voice. He had seemed perfectly lucid all the time, in spite of all his hesitations, his necessary groping for words of expression.

"You *know* all that?" Denise said.

"Yes, I do. It's not just hearsay. I *know* it."

"How much more do you *know*?"

78

"I don't know, if that's not a paradox. That's all that comes to mind, for now. Perhaps that's all there is. Perhaps more will come to mind, when the right stimulus comes along . . . but my dutiful conscious paranoia wants to remind me that a little knowledge is a dangerous thing, and below the level of consciousness, a monster unease is lurking. I suspect that I got more than they did out of our brief contact, but that was their intention. They'd like to know more . . . they'll need to know more, if we're to head outwards, but if I try to give them more . . . it might be dangerous. They're probably too big to be mortally imperiled, but I'm certainly not. *We*'re not . . . and by *we* I mean everyone aboard Minerva, to varying degrees. But we already knew that we're tiny, and vulnerable, and endangered.."

"Did we?"

"Yes. Perhaps not consciously, but we knew it. Even the AIs detected it. That's why they put most of us—and all of the Cronos crew—into hibernation. They might do it again if something in the Rings becomes too clumsy, or too curious. Next time, there's a possibility that we won't wake up. As for me, or anyone else, going back into Helen's machine . . . well. there's an element of Russian roulette about it, and we don't know the proportion of live bullets and empty chambers . . . but we'll have to try, won't we . . . and soon?"

"*Merde*," said Denise, reflectively.

"Can I report to the captain now?" Zeph asked, after another pause. "I need to tell him to move us out of our present orbit."

Technically, Denise knew, he didn't need her permission. All he had to do was flick a couple of switches and float out of the pod. Personally, though, perhaps he did need her permission. Even though she was only his little sister, for some private psychological reason, he had needed her presence aboard Minerva, and he needed her permission now.

"Why am I here, Zeph?" she asked him, perhaps out of sheer perversity, or the pleasure of exercising a power she hadn't known she had.

"I don't know," he said, brutally. "Why are you here?"

"Are you saying that you didn't invite me? That you didn't want me here?"

"Oh, I want you here . . . but I didn't invite you. You made your own decision—but I'm glad you made it the way you did, and if we're being honest, I never doubted that you would."

"Oh," said Denise. "Well, if we're being *honest*, did you invite Mireille? And are you glad she's here?"

"No, I didn't invite her, but yes, I am glad she's here. I think you know why."

"Because you're in love with her?"

"We don't use those terms. That Earther mythology has no place aboard a long-haul spaceship."

"Why, then?"

"For pleasure, of course . . . no, not for vulgar pleasure. For joy. For harmony, insofar as our feeble brains are capable of feeling joy and appreciating harmony. And we all are, no matter how suspicious our conscious selves are of the unconscious fraction of our minds. Even if we were *only human* . . . but we're not . . . we're better than that . . . all of us, even though most of us, back on Earth, wouldn't admit it."

"I see," she said, and actually thought that she was beginning to catch a glimpse of an understanding. "And what about me? Why me, assuming that it's not for pleasure or for joy . . . or even for harmony."

"Oh, but it is. Sexual intercourse is . . . well, not irrelevant, but certainly not necessary or sufficient. I've told you before, Nise, that you don't understand the way things were aboard Olympus Five. I didn't really understand it myself, at the time, but in retrospect, I'm beginning to see the sense of it, as well as joy and the harmony."

"And do you also understand how things are aboard Minerva— with Helen Arkheimer?"

"Not yet . . . but I hope that I might make progress, when I've had a chance to talk to the captain."

"Not unnaturally, he seems to be hopeful that he might understand things a little better when he's debriefed you. Having

80

heard what you have to tell him, though, I'm not so sure that he will. The one thing I *am* sure of, though, is that Helen will want to stick you inside her machine again before you can even stick the nozzle of a food tube in your mouth. My advice, for what it's worth, is that you and the captain tell her to wait until you're good and ready, and then take things *very* slowly."

"Thanks," Zeph said, without a hint of sarcasm. "I know you mean well, and I'm truly sorry that I can't take the advice."

"Why not?"

"Because I need to move quickly, even by human standards. I need to talk to the captain, and then I need to talk to the Bells, if I can."

"But you didn't need me to tell you that that would be danger-ous," she observed, keeping her tone scrupulously level, as befit an apprentice utopian. "In fact, you don't really need me at all."

"I'll always need you, Nise. For thirty years, I thought I didn't. Sometimes, I even thought that you were a bit of a pest, but that was utterly stupid of me. I didn't realize how much I needed you—loved you, if you prefer—until I was tens of millions of klicks away from you. Then I found a disharmony in my life, which had always been there but which I'd somehow contrived never to notice or appreciate, and about which I felt that I had to do something. I didn't know what, as you presumably noticed, but I made an effort . . . and I must have done something right, because here you are, just a little too close for comfort for the moment, being a precious pest yet again. Without you there'd be . . . I don't know. Not a void and not exactly a cacophony, but something bad . . . something I could feel . . . in my bones, as the saying has it. Again, I'm truly glad you're here . . . but I really do need to see the captain, urgently, and I have a gut feeing that he really needs to see me. Otherwise we might be going round in dangerous circles for a long time . . . far too long."

"Sometimes," she told him, but not coldly, "I miss the old Zeph . . . the unholy innocent. Talking to the new one is . . . a trifle awkward."

"I know how you feel."

"You feel awkward talking to me?" She didn't believe it, even though there had been a time, even recently, when it had been patently obvious.

"Oh no—talking to you is surprisingly easy now, even in a claustrophobia-inducing imitation sarcophagus. I meant talking to myself. Once upon a time, I used to have a fairly accurate idea of what I was going to say, and I had a series of contrived scripts to draw on . . . now, I'm full of surprises. But I'm not really mad . . . or bad . . . perhaps just a trifle dangerous."

"Zephaniah Corcoran comparing himself to Byron—now I've heard everything."

"I suspect," he said, "that that might be a long way from the truth."

"Good," she said, pressing one button to make the capsule transparent, and leaving her weightless finger hovering hesitantly, and awkwardly, over the one that would open it up—in spite of the fact that the transparency had revealed Captain Kemmering and Helen Alzheimer, floating impatiently in the cabin—and Denise took leave to wonder, aloud, whether Zeph was wearing any clothing inside the sleeping bag from which, obediently, he hadn't yet emerged.

He didn't answer, but he reached out, pushed her hand gently out of the way, and pressed the button that opened the capsule himself. All he said to the expectant pair, in a perfectly composed tone, was: "Please wait for me in the control room, Captain—and you too, Doctor Arkheimer. I'll be there in two minutes. I have a lot to tell you. I assume that you have a course for Uranus already set? We'll have to leave quite soon, preferably right away." He was in pseudo-utopian mode now, a practiced Olympian.

The captain, even though he was the captain, with the sole privilege of command, didn't challenge Zeph's assertion of necessity, and Helen Arkheimer, her lightning-fast mind perhaps able to take in a whole host of implications from Zephaniah's brief statement that the captain had barely glimpsed as yet, looked positively radiant—as glad as glad could be, for someone who was far from expert in sensing and communicating joy.

"Wait here, will you. Nise," Zeph said to her. "Let me handle this. I'll send for you if I need you, but otherwise . . ."

"It's all right," Denise assured him, although she couldn't help feeling hurt by the sudden stern exclusion. "I'll be here when you need me, as always."

V

Denise accepted the order that Zeph had given her, even though she wasn't at all sure that he wouldn't need her moral support in his confrontation with the captain. She knew that she ought to make a start on the multitudinous messages that had stacked up in her virtual in tray, or at least to make an effort to catch up with the news from Earth, but she wasn't in the right frame of mind. For a while, she listened in from her pod on the report that Zeph was making to the captain, which wasn't protected by a privacy screen, but she had heard it all already, albeit in more disjointed fashion, and the questions with which the captain and Helen were continually interrupting their informant were annoying.

Eventually, she decided that she felt hungry, and thought that assuaging the hunger might be a pleasant distraction. It would have been easy enough to eat in the pod, where Zeph had told her to stay, but she decided that she didn't have to take that part of the order too literally, and that more space and freedom of movement would also answer a temporary psychological need, so she decided to go "down," or to what would previously have been down, to the common space, in search of a tube of food and a bulb of water.

There were three people already there, clustered around a screen, which was still displaying the three-way conversation between Zeph, the captain and the mathematician, but they were apparently satisfied that they had heard the gist of the report, because they were no longer paying close attention, and had engaged in an intense conversation of their own—a conversation that fell silent as soon as Denise appeared, although the attention of the three women did not revert to the screen.

Denise recognized Mireille, but she had to delve into her memory to identify the other two, whom she had only seen briefly and to whom she had barely been introduced. She knew that the Afro-American Paula was not among them, but she had to think for a moment and weigh up the alternative possibilities before concluding that the other members of the variously paler trio were the xenobiologist Savina and the psychologist Gabrielle.

Unsurprisingly, it was Mireille who spoke first when she joined them.

"I can only assume that you aren't with the captain and Helen in the control room because you've already heard what Zephaniah has to say?"

"That's right," Denise said. "I wanted to be there when he woke up because I didn't know what state he'd be in, and I was afraid that he might be in need of moral support that only I could give him, but I'm superfluous now. He's fine, and making as much sense as can be expected . . . which, admittedly, isn't setting the bar very high."

The ghost of a frown passed over Mireille's expression, as if she found a hint of insult in that judgment. All she said, however, was: "He seems to be perfectly all right, from what I can see through the screen."

"That's right," Denise said. "He collected himself very well . . . he didn't need me at all, as it turned out . . . but I needed to put my own mind at rest. I hope you can forgive me for that."

"It's perfectly understandable," Mireille conceded, "including the use of the secrecy screen."

"I'm sorry about the secrecy too," Denise said, "but until I'd heard what Zeph had to say, I didn't know whether it might be politic. When he's completed his report to the captain and Doctor Arkheimer, the captain will presumably convene a crew assembly. There won't be any secrets aboard by then, and hopefully no conflict."

No one challenged the blatant exaggeration. "So Helen's running battle with the captain has all been a waste of time and energy?" Savina suggested—but swiftly moved on to the matter than interested her most, as a xenobiologist. "And your Bells—the improbable ring intelligences—are definitely real?"

"Definitely," Denise confirmed.

"And friendly, it seems?"

"Yes. Dangerous, apparently, but definitely friendly."

"And they really do want us to take them to the rings of Uranus?" Gabrielle put in. That had been in Denise's synoptic report of the revelation of Zephaniah, so the possibility must already have been pondered and discussed extensively by the crew.

"Apparently. As you've just heard, they've suggested to Zeph that we might want to travel outwards anyway, for our own safety, but they'd be grateful if we'd head for Uranus, even though there are risks involved."

"And in return they'll tell us which stars within a few light years have planets that support oxygenated atmospheres and viable ecospheres?" Again, it was Gabrielle who was asking for confirmation.

"Zeph doesn't seem to think that they'll keep anything they know secret," Denise said. "He can probably obtain that information for free, especially if he's willing and able to go back into Helen's machine and form a new communication link."

"Which he seems eager to do," Mireille put in. "As eager as Helen, in fact—and the two of them are ganging up on the captain in order to overrule his brake."

"Will we be able to relay that information back to Earth in the imminent future?" asked Savina, presumably as a diplomatic alternative to asking point-blank how soon Zeph would be ready to take that risk.

"We'll be able to relay anything the Bells can tell us long before we reach Uranus," Denise assured them, a trifle evasively. "If the dome-dwellers at Fairbanks have the technical capability to build and launch another starship, there's a chance that its crew will have a good chart and a choice of potential destinations before they blast off."

"If the ring intelligences are telling the truth," Gabrielle said, in a neutral tone.

"Aren't we supposed to have left that kind of reflexive paranoia behind on Earth," Denise queried, "where our inheritor species will apparently abandon it?"

"Perhaps," said Savina. "As one of the only two Earthers aboard, have *you* left it behind?" Her tone was enquiring rather than hostile, but Denise supposed that it was probably just an act. Denise got the feeling that there had been a certain tension in the group before she had joined it and that her presence was merely deflecting it rather than soothing it. She wasn't at all sure that she wanted to be lumped in with Helen as an "Earther" by contrast with the rest of the crew, but she couldn't in all honesty lay claim to being a spacer yet.

"I've tried," Denise told her, in answer to the question, "but I haven't entirely succeeded, I fear. Zeph seems absolutely convinced that the local aliens are completely trustworthy, and that the generalization can be extrapolated to most of the universe . . ."

"But you don't believe him?" suggested Savina.

"Yes, she does," Gabrielle put in, swiftly. "It's not the aliens that are provoking a certain suspicion in Denise, I fear—it's us . . . and we're the ones at fault for that. Please be assured that there really is no need, Denise. I wasn't on Olympus Five myself, but Mireille and Savina were, and they trust Zephaniah too, which is good enough for the rest of us."

"Never mind the soft soap, Gaby," said Savina. "Why are the ring intelligences dangerous, Denise, if they're friendly and full of universal joy? Which of the models of possible pseudo-life we've constructed hypothetically applies to them?"

"I don't know," Denise replied. "I haven't had a chance yet to look at any of the work you've done since the possibility was raised that there might be minds in the rings, but I'm an Earther, as you say. The further reaches of xenobiology are beyond my expertise, and Zeph's too. With your help, though, he might be able to indicate the likelier possibilities. You've just heard him say that the component of their nature made up of ordinary matter is relatively minor, so hypotheses regarding the exotic states of baryonic matter that can only exist at ultra-low temperatures are probably not central to an understanding of their organization, even if they're essential. As for hypotheses about the nature and the transactions of dark matter . . . it's not my field. Alessandro is presumably the best person to guess and refine what Zeph might mean in talking about vibrations in the fabric of space, and why he used the word *big* so much, but you'll have to put all your heads together to put the conceptual jigsaw together."

"But the crucial implication," Gabrielle contributed, "is that however they're conceived, our present orbit is inside the body of one or more of the ring entities, and that there might be some reaction to our intimate presence that the Bells can't consciously control."

"That's right," Denise agreed. "The impression I got during the first communication was that one or more Bells actually wanted to hitch a lift to Uranus, in which case their presence on the outside of the ship, like our presence in our current orbit, might perhaps entail an initial danger to those of us inside, but that they were hopeful that the danger might be eliminated, given time. That thinking might well be too crude and heavily polluted by my own ignorant hypothesizing, but for what it's worth, that's the way it seems to me."

"If I'm interpreting what he's saying to the captain correctly, you haven't managed to persuade Zephaniah to take things slowly, have you?" Mireille asked, evidently less interested than her companions in the physical nature of the Bells. "He seems to share Helen's determination to stick him back in her machine at the earliest possible opportunity."

"That seems to be the case," Denise agreed, "but it was an immediate, almost automatic response to the ideas in his mind when he woke up; the captain might be able to persuade him to slow down—Zeph has a lot of respect for the captain, and he's not immune to reasoned argument."

"He seems to remember a great deal of his first communication with the Bells," Savina observed, "even though he's oddly insistent in saying that it isn't a matter of remembering."

"He certainly seems to have taken aboard a good deal of information, one way or another," Denise replied, judiciously. "More than me, at any rate. That's good, I think—if he hadn't been able to remember anything at all, or hadn't been able to make as much sense of what the Bells contrived to put into his head, he'd probably be even more determined to learn more as soon as possible."

"But you agree with the captain that he ought to take things slowly?" Mireille prompted.

"I think he might have enough to work through, for a while, without hooking up to the machine again. In fact . . ." She stopped, realizing that she really didn't have anything to go on that could possibly qualify as a fact.

"Go on," Mireille prompted. "*What* do you think?"

"I got the impression . . . perhaps it's just me, and he certainly doesn't seem to share it . . . that he might not need to go back in the machine at all. It seems to me, although Helen would doubtless say that I have no rational grounds for the feeling, that now the link has been forged, the Bells might able to decant further information into his head even without the aid of the machine. Zeph is, as you say, oddly insistent that he isn't *remembering* what he knows . . . or thinks he knows. Perhaps, as long as he's inside the ring, the Bells can operate directly on his brain . . . perhaps they can operate on all our brains, at least accidentally . . . and on the ship's electronic systems . . . even at long distances . . . and that's why the AIs put some of us into defensive hibernation. Zeph says that they're being very careful, and presumably they're better able now to exercise that care because of what they learned from him during the contact, but . . . "

"Oh, *merde!*" murmured Mireille, clearly talking to herself, having apparently stopped listening to what Denise was saying, even though she had issued the initial prompt and it seemed to Denise that the point she had been making was very important.

"What's the matter?" Gabrielle was quick to ask.

"Nothing," said Mireille. "I just . . . glimpsed a possibility because of what Denise was saying. It's a personal matter, of no relevance to anyone else."

"I fear, Miri, that everything might now be relevant to everyone," the psychologist said. "You mean that it pertains especially to you because you've had sex with Zephaniah and Sav and I haven't—we know as well as you do why Arkheimer had you drafted to the crew."

"It's a private matter," said Mireille, stubbornly. "We can sleep with anyone we like, and we're supposed to do so, in order to avoid the alleged risk of *folie à deux*, but what we do and what we feel are still personal and private, and nobody's business but our own."

"Normally," said Gabrielle, "I'd agree with you—but if you've just discovered something in your relationship with Zephaniah that might cast a light on his peculiar ability to empathize with aliens, it might be something that we all have an interest in knowing."

"Well, it isn't," Mireille retorted. "It's something to do with me, not with him."

"So there's no point in my making Zephaniah a belated proposition?" Savina put in, with a wry smile perhaps intended to make a joke of the issue. "The possibility crossed my mind several times, but . . . you know how things were."

"I don't," Denise put in, mildly.

"No, you don't," said Mireille, more than a trifle aggressively, "but now isn't the time for a seminar on the ins and outs of intimate relations aboard Olympus."

"Easy, Miri," said Gabrielle softly. Denise got the impression that if the four of them hadn't been weightless and tethered, the psychologist might have tried to give Mireille a hug, or at least touch her arm reassuringly. To Denise, she said: "It's simple enough to design social institutions to minimize jealousies and resentments, and it works, with the aid of general good will and commitment—in the words of the cynical old adage, love won't work, but courtesy might—but suppressing spontaneous feelings doesn't annihilate them."

"And it wasn't exactly a secret aboard Olympus that no matter how insistently you and Zeph played by the rules, Miri, you had something particular between you," Savina added. "Even Helen Arkheimer knows that, it seems. You're here, and so far as I know, neither of Zephaniah's other partners is."

"So far as you know!" remarked Mireille, waspishly. "You know the number, so you must know the names. Don't pretend that you haven't looked at the leaked tapes. Everybody in the world has—except Denise, apparently, who's so uptight she hasn't even screwed the captain yet."

"Low blow, Miri," said Gabrielle, quietly. "We're all crew now. Denise might not have signed the contract yet, but she's entitled to its protection . . . and this isn't like you. I don't know what the thought was that suddenly occurred to you and gave you a different slant on your relationship with Zephaniah, but it shouldn't have thrown you off balance. We've all been on edge for days, understandably, but . . ."

"Oh, shut up," snapped Mireille. "*You've* be on edge for days—I've been on edge for three fucking *years*. You have *no* idea . . . but you're right, of course. I'm sorry, Denise . . . and you, Savina. I shouldn't let things get to me. Conduct unbecoming a spacer . . . all the more so if the mission is going to extend for thirty years and more, under some kind of mysterious external threat. None of us wants to be the first to crack up, do we? Excuse me."

Having unfastened her tether, she floated away from the group, heading toward the hatchway to the cabins.

Denise looked at the other two, in quest of an indication as to whether someone ought to go after Mireille and whether, if someone should, it ought to be her.

"Let her rest," was Gabrielle's advice. "As she says, she's had things harder than the rest of us. She had to settle into a routine with Chris and Helen, then that was suddenly disrupted, and watching that first experiment with the machine must have been hard, when Zephaniah seemed to be in trouble . . . and then the captain delegated her to bring you up to date, Denise. The news that you and Zephaniah have given us is mostly good and reassuring, but the fact that it was you who gave it to us . . . didn't help, from Mireille's viewpoint. It must have been awkward for her, meeting you on Earth and not knowing how your proximity might affect a relationship with Zeph that already seemed problematic, and she hasn't had a chance to be alone with him since the ship blasted off. It will work itself out, in time."

"I didn't help, I'm afraid," Savina interjected. "A bad time for tactlessness. I'm sorry."

"I don't understand," Denise said, attempting reflexively to mime incomprehension and falling prey to the inevitable Newtonian reaction.

"Nor does Mireille," Savina said, with a sigh. "We once did something stupid, in the early days of the Olympus mission. I thought it was dead and forgotten, but in the new circumstances, it might have come back to haunt her."

"We still don't understand, Savina," said Gabrielle, mildly.

"It was nothing, really . . . just stupid, as I said. She and I decided in conversation that Zephaniah needed to be . . . initiated into spacer mores, and that as we were the two people who worked with him most closely, because of the proximity of our specialties, it was up to one of us to make the breakthrough. So we . . . drew lots . . . tossed a coin . . . however you want to put it. And Miri . . . well, we both described it, in jest, as losing, but it wasn't; we could just as easily have represented it as winning, and it certainly seemed to turn out to be winning, from Mireille's viewpoint. She should have forgotten all about it but . . . well, one way or another, for psychological reasons that you can probably explain better than I can, I never did get round to having sex with Zeph, and Mireille was always aware of that non-event. Neither of us ever mentioned it again, of course . . . but deep down, something evidently rankles. We're not supposed to be possessive, but . . . sometimes, signing a pledge only scratches the itch, if you'll forgive the ludicrously mixed metaphor."

Denise didn't see any need to tell her interlocutors that Mireille had already given her half the story that Savina had just related, and was probably a trifle embarrassed about the part that she had left out, although she surely hadn't expected that Savina would fill it in. Nor did she see any need to repeat Mireille's dismissive semi-confession that her relationship with Zeph had been "purely for pleasure." Instead, she simply said: "Thank you. I fear I'm partly to blame for the tension between us. When Mireille and I were first introduced, I wasn't very friendly. I've explained to her that I was annoyed with Zeph, not with her, but I don't suppose she was able to believe me. She thinks that I don't like her . . . or that I don't approve of her relationship with Zeph . . . but that honestly isn't the case."

"We could say the same," Gabrielle said, with a sigh, "but she's suspicious of our attitude too, albeit not for the same reason. Now she'll be fretting because she let it out, but as I say, it will work itself out, given time, when she and Zeph have had a chance to get together and figure out what their relationship amounts to and where it will go in future."

"And when you've had a chance to screw the captain and figure out how your relationships are going to go in future," Savina added, even though, as she had observed herself, it really wasn't a good time for tactlessness.

"Inappropriate, Savina," said Gabrielle. "We're all on edge—some more than others, but that just means we need to try harder to pull back. Getting back to less trivial matters, do you really think, Denise, that Zephaniah is now permanently linked to the ring intelligences . . . that they might be able to put information into his head without the intermediary of the machine?"

"I don't know," said Denise. "Maybe it's just my paranoia making that suggestion."

"Because, if it's true for Zephaniah, it might be true for you too?"

"Perhaps," Denise admitted.

"Helen's not going to like it if Zephaniah comes to think that he doesn't need her machine any more," Savina observed. "It would undermine her *raison d'être*, as Mireille would probably put it."

"It won't dampen her experimental enthusiasm in the slightest," Gabrielle opined. She glanced at the screen, and added: "I don't think that possibility has been introduced into the argument yet, but it's still . . . well, not raging, as it seems to be very serious and far from angry . . . but the captain doesn't seem inclined to call time yet. He's already agreed in principle to move the ship, but he hasn't transmitted any instruction to Birstan."

"He might as well," said Savina. "He isn't going to get any opposition from the assembly when he convenes it . . . there might be questions raised about ferrying invisible alien monsters and going to Uranus, but nobody will object to leaving orbit, all the more so as the thrust will give us some weight."

"It's not as simple as that," Gabrielle observed. "Chris will have to consult with Captain Fulsom. If we're in danger, so is Cronos, and Fulsom seems to have decided that even though things have changed drastically back on Earth, he ought to stick to his predetermined mission plan."

"Not a problem," said Savina, dismissively. "I helped draw up that plan, and he'll be heading away from the rings himself as soon as he's satisfied that his crew have recovered from their long doze and that his systems are in good order. He's scheduled to head for Rhea and Titan first, and then call in at a couple of the minor satellites before returning to go into close orbit just outside the atmosphere, in order to send in his surrogates and probes. He'd have to go through the rings then if he stayed in the plane of the major satellites, but he can easily loop round and then take up a polar orbit."

"I'm not sure that will be distant enough," Denise observed. "Zeph was very insistent that the rings are big, and Minerva's AIs apparently reacted to their distant probing while we were still in the vicinity of Earth."

"Fulsom will take the risk," Savina insisted. "He's even more military than Kemmering, if that's possible. He has his orders and he'll stick to them, in the absence of *force majeure*."

"But if new orders arrive from Earth, he'll stick to those instead," Gabrielle insisted, "and we have no idea as yet how Fairbanks will react to Zephaniah's enhanced report. The government of the dome has problems of its own, and if I'm reading the reports right, the chances of consensus are slim. You've just seen evidence that even our consensus is capable of developing cracks, if we're not careful."

"Trivia," opined Savina. "With regard to the mission, we're all rock solid . . . even Helen. She's a pain in the ass, but on important matters, she's fully on board."

"Trivial cracks can grow," Gabrielle observed. "We have to be careful. And it's a long way to Uranus, with or without an alien hitchhiker, however unmonstrous."

"I really should be up there," Denise said, anxiously eyeing the screen that was relaying the discussion between Zeph, Helen and the captain, momentarily forgetting that the control room was no longer "up," but merely "forwards" relative to the business end of Minerva—her cargo holds and thrusters.

"If the captain wants you, he'll summon you," Gabrielle said, "but he knows that three's a triad and four's a crowd, in terms of reasoned debate. Don't be offended that he seems to be taking your position for granted—he might well convene the assembly before talking to you again, given that Zephaniah hasn't said anything, or omitted anything, that might generate a serious difference of opinion, but he applies his customary discipline to his consolations and he'll take the opportunity to smooth things over with you as soon as he has time. If you're fretful, check your messages . . . don't worry about the long-distance abuse; your message recorder will have relegated the trolls to the end of the queue, and given top priority to personal acquaintances. If you don't want to do that, let your VR hood take you back to virtual Old Earth and wallow in nostalgia for a while—it's better that than dwelling on the latest prognostications regarding the chaotic fog that is now Earth's atmosphere."

"Is that a prescription?" Denise asked.

"No, just a friendly suggestion," the psychologist assured her. "The VR store has an enormous library of tapes of Earthly environments, and when you're on a deep space mission, they provide a uniquely useful source of pleasant relaxation—I suspect that the effect will be further enhanced now that it seems like traveling in time as well as space, although I have to admit that Mireille doesn't seem to have got as much benefit from visits to virtual Paris and Bretagne during the last three years as I could have hoped."

"Inherent limitations of VR," Savina put in. "You can look at the food and wine, but you can't taste it or get drunk, And as for VR sex . . . maybe it's just a chronic lack of imagination on my part, but it really doesn't do anything for me."

"You shouldn't let your awareness of the limitations spoil your appreciation of the benefits," Gabrielle told her. "It's an invaluable resource, and it answers a real deep-seated need." Addressing Denise, she added: "If you need guidance in the use of the equipment and the library, consult Paula, but you can probably find your own way through the labyrinth without a thread. A short excursion will fill in time while you're standing by, waiting for the assembly, or the captain's call . . . it would probably be more relaxing than gossiping with Savina and me . . . although I'm certainly not trying to make you feel unwelcome."

Clearly, it *was* a prescription, against which Denise reacted almost reflexively. "Or I could just start reading my mail," she said.

"That could work just as well," Gabrielle agreed, affably.

"Not for me," Savina commented. "But then, I don't have a thousand messages in store from ex-colleagues, old neighbors and religious cranks. Anyway, I'm going to confer with Victor. If you want my friendly advice, Denise, which you probably don't, don't bother with VR or the mail that your receiver thinks you ought to read first. Get stuck into some serious xenobiological research, and try to figure out what your so-called Bells really are. That might actually be useful—more so, at any rate, than any kind of escapism."

"Not helpful, Savina," Gabrielle admonished, with scrupulous professional mildness—and as Savina floated away, the psychologist turned back to Denise and said: "If I can help . . ."

"Not just now, please," Denise said. "The captain has suggested that I speak with you—which presumably means that he wants an expert report on the awful condition of my barbaric personality . . . but not now, if you don't mind. You're absolutely right: what I need is to make a start on my mountain of messages, or treat myself to a few visions of Old Earth. Thanks anyway."

"You're welcome," said the psychologist, with apparent sincerity. "And for the sake of honesty, yes, the captain has asked me to make a formal assessment of your psychological fitness, because there wasn't time for anyone to do one at Fairbanks before we took off, but please don't take it amiss—it's just standard procedure."

"I won't take it amiss," Denise promised, "but I can't guarantee to like it. I already know that I'm a mess, and I can't exactly relish the thought of the mess in question becoming the subject of a formal report. Imperial College wasn't a utopia of the kind that Minerva is supposed to be, but it was the ideal environment for hiding one's personal deficiencies, and there's a lot to be said for that, if you have as many as I have."

"Well, you're a utopian now," the psychologist told her, "and there's a lot to be said for that too, believe me."

Denise wasn't sure that she could believe her yet, but she knew that she had to try, if only for Zeph's sake.

VI

Denise floated back to her cabin, and was only slightly disappointed to find that it wasn't empty. The capsule opposite the one that Zeph had recently abandoned was occupied by Mireille. It was open, but the Frenchwoman was extended within the shell in what would have been a prone position had Minerva possessed its usual down, staring at the screen, which was displaying statistics that Denise assumed to be a weather report from Earth.

Instead of floating up to her own pod, Denise hovered hesitantly in midair, thinking that she ought to say something, but not quite sure what. Eventually, she settled on: "Sorry, I just . . ."

"No, I'm sorry," said Mireille, apparently eager to interrupt but having been unwilling to open a conversation that was bound to be embarrassing. "As I've said before, we're shipmates now and maybe for all eternity, so we need to get used to the fact that this is shared space. We have to learn to be comfortable in one another's company—and with Zephaniah's and Helen's too."

"Easier said than done," Denise said, with a sigh, "even with Zeph and in spite of being his sister."

"Ditto," said Mireille, "in spite of being . . . his lover. But it has to be done regardless."

Denise gripped the bottom edge of her capsule in order to steady herself. She was quite a long way from her interlocutor, but the distance seemed appropriate to the nature of the conversation, and there was no way that she was going to clamber into Mireille's pod. The Frenchwoman switched her screen over to the feed from the control room.

"They're going to be at it for some time yet," she said. "It's ground that Chris and Helen have trodden a hundred times before, but the field has been thoroughly plowed up by Zephaniah's new input, and now they're going over it with a metaphorical harrow. Chris is determined not to rush to judgment—he's fanatical about taking things one step at a time, as you'll doubtless have many chances to observe, but you'll forgive him because he's so handsome and has such a nice smile. I'm glad to be out of it, for once, but you might get called in if he thinks your input would be useful. If the ring intelligences really are feeding new information into Zephaniah's brain while the argument is in progress, though, the conference could last for hours."

"There isn't any solid evidence to license the supposition that the ring intelligences have established a permanent link with Zeph's mind," Denise observed, blandly. "Even if they have, I suspect that they work on a much slower timescale than we do, and I doubt that they can keep up with the pace of our arguments. And on a more personal note, even if it is the case, there's no reason to think that it will affect his relationship with either of us." She tried to make the assertion sound confident, but she suspected that her doubts were transparent.

"If an alien intelligence has acquired a firm telempathic foothold in Zeph's brain," Mireille opined, putting on a much better show of confidence, albeit with a definite ominous quality in her tone, "it will affect his relationships with everyone and everything."

Denise wondered whether she ought to challenge the intellectual coherency of the notion of a "telempathic foothold," but decided against it. "We're getting ahead of ourselves," she said instead. "It's not a good idea to get lost in idle speculations devoid of evidential support." She was uncomfortably aware that she must sound like a pompous idiot; that was one of the Earther habits that she ought to be trying hard to shed, now that she was a utopian and not a stuffy academic with a tacit license for pointless pedantry.

"They're not devoid of evidential support," Mireille told her. "I don't know how he seemed to you when you were cozily sealed up in his capsule with him, but what I've seen of him on screen while he's been making his report to the captain suggests strongly that he's already changed, and is still changing."

"And you think that might affect your . . . pleasure?" Denise asked, thinking that any answer she obtained would reveal more about Mireille than Zeph.

"Yes," said the Frenchwoman, "but that's not what ought to concern you, and it's far from the whole of existence for me. Since you're fixated on that aspect of the matter, though, do you know why Captain Kemmering is such a handsome man?"

Denise blinked at the unexpected question, the relevance of which she could not see.

"Just fortunate, I suppose," she said, warily. "I know he's had somatic engineering to adapt him for space travel, and that all somatic engineering includes an element of cosmetic manipulation, but it can't make silk purses out of sow's ears. He must have been exceptionally well-endowed by nature."

"Nature probably had less to do with it than you might think," Mireille told her, "but what I actually meant was: why do you think that the architects of the Olympus-Five mission chose an exceptionally handsome man as captain of the ship?"

Put like that, Denise had no difficulty guessing the answer for which the Frenchwoman was fishing. "You mean that he fit their notion of how a captain ought to look?" she said. "That it assists his authority . . . and his duty of distributing his favors within the utopian microcosm?"

"Yes. Which of the women in the crew do you think is the most beautiful?"

"I don't know—but in an era of commonplace somatic engineering, ugliness had pretty much been abolished in the fully developed countries back on Earth even before the Crash, and exceptional beauty is notoriously rare among career scientists, so it's not surprising that we're all on a sufficiently level playing field for such judgments to be simply a matter of idiosyncratic taste."

"Modest and polite—and true enough, although I suspect that anyone else to whom the question was put would have named you, with a hint of suppressed jealousy, and not just because the rest of us are rather short by current Earth standards, and a trifle masculine in our engineered musculature. You can see the reasoning behind what you call the *level playing field*, can't you?"

"I can see why the selection of a crew for maximum compatibility might include a judgment of that sort," Denise said, judiciously, still uncertain as to where Mireille was going with the argument, "given that the social design was intended to minimize envy and jealousy . . . but it couldn't have the effect of making people interchangeable, could it? They'd still have different personalities."

"All cats are gray in the dark," Mireille quoted. "But no, the selection system couldn't make sexual partners interchangeable, even in the dark. We might all be similarly attractive lookswise—apart from the captain's calculated privilege—but people feel different, and they have different behavioral styles . . . but let's also remember that we're all children of the end of the twenty-first century. Everyone learns sexual technique from screen displays and VR tapes, in spite of the lack of touch in VR, and everyone learns from similar gospels. You must have noticed, however few or many lovers you've had, a certain educated uniformity . . . a standardization of method that, along with the standardization of faces contrived by methodical somatic modification, really does make a great many lovers essentially interchangeable, ideal fodder for the kind of egalitarian society that we're supposed to be."

Denise finally realized what Mireille was getting at. "But not all of them," she said. "Some remain stubbornly exceptional . . . including the captain." She chose that example deliberately, knowing that it was not the one her interlocutor must have in mind.

"No," said Mireille, "not like the captain. In terms of looks, he's custom-designed, literally, to be exceptionally attractive to women, but when the lights are off, he's much the same as the rest—a little more skilled, and a great deal more experienced, but in essence, he's a perfect example of turning standardized theory into practice. He's artificial—a masterpiece, in his way, but a creature, not a creator. Alessandro is a fainter carbon copy. I can't speak for Victor or Birstan, but I'd be willing to bet that they're no different. I'm not the right person to judge the women, although Helen isn't the only one I've fooled around with . . . but again, I strongly suspect they're standardized in much the same way as the men, me included . . . and even you."

Denise had no wish to discuss her own case, and she suppressed her reflexive denial. "But Zeph is different?" she queried.

"Yes, he is. Not to everyone's taste, I imagine, even if you can make a start on getting close to him, and he's certainly not easy to get to know . . . but yes, he's quite different."

"So what?" said Denise. "I can't see any wider implications."

"Nor could I, until a few minutes ago. I thought he was just a precious secret, that I wanted to keep to myself, as far as possible—principles or no principles—but then you opened up a possibility that I hadn't considered before, and suddenly, the situation looked different . . . initially just from my own selfish, corrupt, perhaps perverse viewpoint . . . but then I saw the wider implications. And if I'm right, you might soon be able to see and feel them yourself. Perhaps we all will."

"I'm not following you."

"Not all the way—but you understand what I mean about the interchangeability of the men, don't you? Back on Earth, I'd be willing to bet that you were a desultory serial monogamist, who had about as much time for the antiquated romantic mythology of eternal soul-mates as the designers of the Olympus microcosm."

Again, Denise did not bother with a futile and dishonest denial. "But you've found true love?" she asked, incredulously. "With *Zeph*?"

"No. Those concepts don't apply to him any more than they do to you—probably less so. He and I weren't and aren't *in love*"—she pronounced the phrase contemptuously, as if she were spitting metaphorical acid—"but we had something different from conventionally rehearsed rutting . . . something that was valuable, at least to me."

"Congratulations," said Denise. "But I still don't see . . ."

Mireille cut her off, abruptly, in a hurry to speak now that she had decided to do so. "Zephaniah can empathize with aliens," she said. "He doesn't know how, or exactly what that empathy consists of, and it was very hard for him to get past the conviction that it was just an illusion, that he was simply crazy—but the Slingshots and the Dancing Rats proved to him eventually that it wasn't, and by the time I met him, he'd accepted that it was real, that the difference between him and the vast majority of other people wasn't the simple craziness or mental crippling that other people thought. He didn't know what it was, but he knew what it wasn't. And when his resistance broke down, he allowed me to be an honorary alien . . . he empathized with me. He couldn't do it with the cloud-whales, which turned out not to have a consciousness more highly developed than that of a dog, if that . . . but he was able to do it with me. I expect he tried to do it with the other women he screwed on Olympus-Five, but he couldn't connect, probably because their hearts weren't in it. He connected with me, though . . . and if what he said in the account he's just given you and is currently repeating to the captain can be trusted, he connected with the ring intelligences too . . . and he probably remains connected.

"His connections with the Dancing Rats and the ring intelligences, though, aren't just with them; they extend further, to other entities Coincidentally connected with them, and, however vaguely or faintly, to the mentality of the entire universe. And he had a connection of that sort even before he joined Olympus Five, and even before he first hooked up to Halleck's Sling; he's always had it lurking in his subconscious, and it's always affected his consciousness of his social environment, even though he couldn't begin to understand it until now. But what he experienced when he and I . . . got together . . . what he was *enjoying* when he and I . . . well, it occurred to me that perhaps it wasn't really *me* at all . . . or not *just* me, at any rate . . .

"When that thought first struck me, it seemed horrible . . . it was a category-shift that I didn't like at all. *Merde*, I thought— aloud, because I was careless—but I overreacted. It doesn't diminish me, or reduce my experience to irrelevance . . . and as you say, in your conscientiously optimistic fashion, maybe the changes that are being rung in him won't affect our relationship for the worse . . . certainly no worse than coming down to Earth again, which made it awkward, distant and problematic in all kinds of ways . . . but that remains to be seen and felt, and it's difficult, for the moment, for me to figure out when we might be able to get a moment to ourselves in order to investigate. But if your conjecture is right, and the link that Helen's machine established to Zephaniah is still open, permanently so, becoming progressively more accessible to consciousness, and potentially contagious, then everything has already changed, for me, for you, and for all our shipmates on Minerva, if not for others. By the time we reach Uranus, we might all be honorary aliens."

"What do you mean, *potentially contagious*?" Denise asked, although her memory had already told her, referring back to the moment when she, Mireille, Zeph and the captain had been holding hands aboard the plane transporting them to Alaska.

Mireille did not bother to quote the specific reference. "He's telempathic," she said, simply. "Not easily, but you know full well that he's capable of establishing links of his own without the aid of any machine: weak and evanescent links, perhaps, but real. He's got better with practice, especially with me and even more especially with you . . . and he already knows that continued proximity with the ring intelligences is dangerous, because it can not only mess with his mind, but with yours, with mine . . . and even with the electronics of Minerva's many AIs. And they will mess with us, if they're not *very* careful."

"That's an awful lot of conjecture to build on a few gnomic phrases in a muddled discourse that many people judge to be mere illusion," Denise pointed out, scrupulously.

"Yes it is," the Frenchwoman admitted, "but I have experience that you and they don't. Even you *know* that what he said is true, even though you don't know where that knowledge comes from, or how reliable the conviction is . . . and you've argued yourself that I might be more closely linked to Zephaniah than you are, albeit in a different way . . . so you have to admit that what I'm saying is more than just idle fantasizing and conjecture."

"Yes, I do," Denise admitted. "But I'm still finding it difficult to imagine that there could be anything so superbly out of-this-world about Zeph's sexual technique that it justifies the kind of hyperbole that you're hurling around."

"Wrong end of the stick, Denise. It isn't his sexual technique that's important, but his lack of it. He had never made any attempt to master the kind of conventional sexual athletics that the captain, Alessandro and most ultra-civilized men of the twenty-second century take for granted. For him, sexual intercourse isn't a matter of skill, or dutiful artifice . . . it's just about *joy*, once he feels that he has permission simply to enjoy it. Whatever he's intuited, he's done it through an embryonic Coincidence sensibility. He's shared the joy of the Dancing Rats and the invert generations, and he's learned from that. The religious fantasists on Earth who believe that he's made contact with God and experienced God's grace and divine love directly might be using an inapt vocabulary, but they're not entirely wrong: they're referring to something real.

"What he's connected with, via his primitive but evolving Coincidence sensibility, is the grace of cosmic multiple mentality, and something more elementary, more fundamental, and *purer* than what most humans mistake for love. And he let me share that joy, simply by enjoying *me*, innocently and naïvely, in a way that Captain Kemmering, Alessandro and more than a dozen others in the course of over twenty years of erotic experience, never did . . . except, I suppose, that it wasn't really me that he was enjoying so much as some kind of generalized universal joy for which I was just a conduit while we were having sex. Unlike him, I probably could have been anyone . . . even . . ." She did not pronounce the name that she presumably had in mind.

"I doubt that," Denise said. "In your own way, you're just as unique as he is."

"Bullshit. In any case, I'm not saying that he's unique—far from it, in fact—but he's had more opportunity to develop his innate sensibility than any other human being ever has. He's traveled farther, with better technological aids, and he's seen *much* further; such uniqueness as he has is the result of education and effort, not some fundamental anomaly. He's a self-made *surhomme*, Denise . . . a true Nietzschean *übermensch* . . . and if the stupid world hadn't ended three Earthyears ago, he might have been the first of many . . . but we already know, thanks to him, that the torch will have to be handed on to the überrats and the überants, who will make a better job of it than we could, being better pre-equipped by natural selection to cultivate and enhance joy and harmony. And we Minervans might have time yet to make as much of ourselves as we can, if we have the will and the ambition . . . as well as the machinery and helpful allies."

Denise suddenly remembered that they were talking in an open space, with no privacy screen. The conversation was being recorded. It would be accessible to the other members of the crew, if any of them cared to look . . . and it could be beamed to Earth, if anyone cared to take the trouble. Even if Mireille regretted having let it all out—as she very well might when she got over her burst of confidentiality—it was in the public domain now, an apocryphal addendum to the new gospel according to Zephaniah. How delighted Marie MacLaughlin would be, if she ever got to hear it, once she had reconfigured the vocabulary to fit her own preconceptions!

But Denise wasn't delighted, and not simply because Mireille's flight of fancy set a new record for long-distance conclusion-jumping. Even if it were true, and not simply a tissue of self-deluding conjecture, she couldn't rejoice in it. The fault for that was presumably in herself, not in the stars, but the fact remained. She couldn't believe it and couldn't even enjoy the possibility.

"I came in to look at my messages," she said to the Frenchwoman, brutally.

Mireille didn't seem offended, or even surprised. "I'm sorry for interrupting you," she said. "I keep forgetting that you have a quasi-phobic reaction to talking about sex. I shouldn't have gone off like that, but I thought . . . that you were entitled to an explanation."

Denise was inevitably tempted to deny that she had a "quasi-phobic" reaction to talking about sex, but she knew that it was the kind of denial that could never ring true, and only made the denier seem ridiculous. Instead, she said: "I'm sorry . . . but I do have a *lot* of messages waiting."

"I know," said Mireille. "Don't worry—no one has read them, unless the captain felt obliged to take a peek, but the count is public knowledge . . . and one of them is an absolute *monster* . . . you might want to leave that one for another time, in spite of its high priority ranking."

Feeling that it was advice that she didn't need, and that it constituted an invasion to privacy in itself, Denise scowled. She sealed herself into her pod, although she didn't go so far it to render it opaque or to invoke the secrecy function. She summoned the list to which Mireille had referred on to her screen.

The receiver used a primitive sorting program that gave top priority to private messages from personal acquaintances, and the names near the top of the list were mostly former colleagues at Imperial, but the highest priority of all had been given to a message from Marie MacLaughlin, which was, as Mireille had observed, a real monster, with a bytesize more appropriate to a feature film than a mere letter. As suggested, Denise looked for something smaller and less challenging, and spotted the name *Emily Saverne*, which surprised her in more ways than one. Emily Saverne had been a neighbor of her mother's on the Thames estuary; Denise hardly knew her, but she had a vague memory of Zeph having mentioned her and her young son being picked up by an army truck when the Code Triple Red and martial law were declared by the British government, and noting sorrowfully that wherever it was taking her could not possibly be reckoned a viable safe haven from the kind of disaster that the fracturing of the Earth's crust had abruptly precipitated. Logically, Emily Saverne ought not to be alive.

Curiously, she opened the communication.

Dear Denise, it began, using a formula that had become obsolete decades before she or Emily Saverne had been born, *I expect you will be as surprised at receiving this letter as I am to be sending it all the way to Saturn. I don't even know whether you remember me, but I was a neighbor of your mother and although you had left home before we became good friends, she talked about you and your brother a great deal. My son, Luke, took a great interest in your brother when he joined the crew of Olympus Five, and once spoke to him briefly on Marine Parade while he was visiting your mother after his return to Earth. I dragged him away, I fear, because I didn't want him to pester Zephaniah, and he's never quite forgiven me, especially since you and Zephaniah became world famous. The fact that he once spoke to Zephaniah, if only for two minutes about nothing of importance, is now his own claim to fame of a sort, and that matters a lot to an eleven-year-old, as you can probably imagine.*

We're in Yorkshire now, under the dome, and very lucky to be here, I assume. Jeff, my husband, was in the Army Reserve, like practically every other able-bodied man in the country, and he was conscripted on Disaster Day, even before the news broke, and had to report for duty in Basildon. An army lorry collected all the women with young children when the sky went dark, and took us to some kind of bunker near Stansted. There were hundreds of us packed in there. We couldn't go outside because of poisons in the air, but the army had a huge stock of sealed trucks designed to keep moving even when things got very bad.

We were told that we'd be safe for a while, and that we'd be moved out in small groups to somewhere even safer as and when it became possible. It was supposed to be secret but we all knew that there was a plan, that lists had been drawn up by the government to determine who could get into the big domes that had been built in England, Scotland and Wales. The army tried to move the people at the top of the list on or shortly after Disaster Day, but some of them didn't make it, because the copters crashed or the sealed trucks didn't get through, so more people got moved up the priority list gradually. Jeff was out on the road all the time, but we had screen-time, and he told me that it was all very well organized, because AIs kept track by the hour of any deaths and licensed further transfers.

The priority list was top secret, of course, so no one had any idea where they might figure on it, but we had points, apparently, because of our ages, our health, Jeff's service in the army and because Luke was reckoned to be very clever. After a month in the holding bunker, Luke and I were taken out and driven to Yorkshire. I couldn't see a thing on the way, of course, so it was scary, and there were plenty of pictures on the news of deserted towns and roads, and terrible weather, although they were careful not to show dead bodies. We arrived safely, though, and we were very lucky, because not many people got in after us. Jeff was still driving scavenger trucks for six months afterwards, and it was dangerous work, but he survived.

Life here is actually pretty good, although the rationing is a bit tedious. Luke loves it, although the discipline at the school seems very strict to me. He doesn't mind the homework—he says that we have a world to repair, and that everybody needs to do their bit, even at eleven. I'm not sure that I'm doing my fair share, but Jeff says that the menial jobs are actually the most important of all, because what the world is really short of now is hands, not minds. AIs can do the brain work, he says, but only people like us can do the fetching and carrying. He still goes outside the dome a lot, wearing a spacesuit, and he tells us that it's really not so bad, in spite of what the news reports say about plant die-back and low oxygen levels. The sun has begun to shine again, he says, and where there's light there's life—not much, for the moment, but enough to allow us to come back, given time. Everybody keeps saying that the world has ended, but for us, personally, it's still going on, and hasn't changed as much as you might think.

Jeff reckons that Luke might live long enough to see the day when it's possible to move around outside without spacesuits, when the soil has been reseeded with plants: the New Eden, everybody calls it, and although practically everybody thinks it's a myth, we all try to believe in it, or at least pretend to. Everybody knows, thanks to your brother, that the rats will inherit the Earth in the end, but lots of people pretend not to believe it and those who do say that it really doesn't matter to us because our descendants still have tens or thousands, and perhaps hundreds of thousand of years in hand . . . longer than civilization has existed so far.

There are some people who think that the message you sent back about Saturn and the Bells is fake or fantasy, but Luke won't hear of it. It's true, he says, and it means that you can go to the stars and come back with knowledge that will help us to repair the world and shape the New Eden. Jeff says that Luke and his generation are the hope of the human race, but Luke says that they'll be a much brighter hope if you can make it to another star and come back. He's studying Coincidence theory at school, and he says that it's not as hard as some people make it out to be, and that contact with the Bells might be a great leap forward, especially if you can help them establish closer contact—closer harmony, he calls it—with others of their own kind further out in the solar system.

It may be just gossip and there's nothing about it on the official news—everybody knows that the official news is strictly censored—but Zephaniah's old employer, Walter Halleck, is said to be designing new machines, not for building bridges in time, but for detecting people with brains similar to Zephaniah—Coincidence psychics is the popular term. The first step, Luke says, is to find a way of enabling them to make psychic contact with one another, although it won't let them read or listen in on one another's thoughts, and after that to make contact with aliens. He's madly ambitious to join the program, when he's old enough, although it doesn't even exist yet, officially. Even Jeff says that it will exist, because our government is determined not to let the Americans or the Chinese steal a march on us . . . or even the Scots, now that they've got their independence back.

Anyway, that's my news. You get all the big news, obviously, but I thought you might like a worm's eye view. Luke has written to your brother, but he must have millions of messages, and might not even get around to reading it, let alone replying, and I thought I might have better luck. I didn't see your mother after Disaster Day, but I presume that she died, and I'm truly sorry for your loss—she was *always a good neighbor to me, and very friendly. She thought the world of Zephaniah and you, even though she always said that you were difficult when you were children. She always said that she knew how I felt about Luke, and if she did, and knew how much I think of him in spite of him sometimes being difficult, then she must really have loved the two of you. Please remember Luke to Zephaniah, even if he doesn't remember talking to him on Marine Parade, and we all hope that you make it safely to the stars, and back.*

The missive was signed in similarly old-fashioned style: *All best wishes, Emily Saverne.*

Denise found that there were tears rolling down her cheeks, although she wasn't at all sure why, as the message was all good news—as good as could possibly be expected coming from a world that had supposedly ended, from someone who could very easily have been counted among the casualty figures, if her young son had not been promoted to the rank of national asset by some super-efficient but utterly dispassionate AI to which all the hard political life-or-death decisions had been delegated.

"Good luck to him," she whispered, "and if he took a place vacated by some self-satisfied somatically engineered civil servant with delusions of necessity whose copter choked in a dust-cloud and came down with a bang somewhere north of Watford, three cheers for chance or Coincidence."

She almost began to type a reply, but her connection was over-ridden by a message from the captain—not a personal message, but a summons to the expected crew assembly. Her first reaction was frank annoyance that she hadn't been invited to a private audience before the general rallying cry—annoyance directed more at Zeph than at Chris Kemmering and Helen Arkheimer, because she thought that he owed her a special consultation even if the crucial decision had already been made and a new timetable drawn up for the continuation of Minerva's mission to Uranus. Clearly, though, her endorsement of what Zephaniah now "knew" was no longer considered necessary. Her brief reign as the mouthpiece of the Gospel according to Zephaniah was over; the prophet was now on the soap-box himself, and the game had changed.

As she swung herself out of the pod she nearly collided with Mireille, who was similarly responding to the order, and was wearing what was presumably a similar scowl. She too was feeling left out in the cold, because Zeph had not made an effort to speak to her in advance of the public meeting.

"The die is cast, it seems," the Frenchwoman said to Denise, a trifle bitterly. "There isn't even going to be a vote, and the captain isn't going to put on a pretence of waiting for a reaction from Fairbanks to the discussion that the holy trinity has just held."

It's only a matter of hours since I was a member of the pivotal trinity, Denise thought. *No longer the paraclete, not even an archangel. How are the mighty fallen.*

All she said to Mireille, though, was: "Uranus, here we come. At least I'll have plenty of time to listen to Marie's vast sermon, which looks to be longer than the whole Bible, let alone the mere Apocalypse. And she'll still have a role to attribute to me, even if that ingrate Zeph is squeezing me out."

"Boo hoo," said Mireille, unsympathetically—and then added: "Have you been crying?"

Denise wiped away a residual tear. "Nervous reaction," she said. "Meaningless."

"I hope you're right."

Denise was startled by that. "Why?" she said

"Because if it were a telempathetic reaction," the Frenchwoman said, "it would mean that you were picking up sorrow from somewhere else . . . and if the Bells are weeping, or whatever is equivalent to weeping in their bizarre existence, it probably wouldn't be good news for us."

VII

The crew assembly was not quite what Denise had expected. Having a model in her imagination based on public meetings at Imperial College and other locations in London, she had expected more formality—although the fact that everyone began the meeting weightless and gradually gained weight while it was in progress, finding the floor and progressively cultivating more adhesion to it, did facilitate a more orderly and more ponderous physical arrangement of bodies.

There was no ceremonious introduction; the captain simply spoke to the other eleven people present.

"I assume that most of you listened in to the report that Zephaniah just made, and the questions subsequently addressed to him by Helen and myself, and that anyone who didn't will familiarize themselves with it and study the recording carefully within the next twenty-four hours. There will be plenty of time thereafter to discuss the reliability of Zephaniah's assertions, but if there is even a possibility that they are true, it is clearly necessary, as a precaution, to remove Minerva from its present orbit, further away from the planet. Cronos has already left the ring orbit, in accordance with its mission plan, but we will not be accompanying her in the direction of Rhea's anticipated position. Instead, we will head away from the sun, on a curve that, should we elect not to modify it, will eventually take us to rendezvous with Uranus.

"Helen and Zephaniah feel, and I agree with them, that it remains urgent to make every effort to collect further evidence that might corroborate and elaborate the account of the hypothetical ring intelligences that Zephaniah has given us, initially relayed via Denise but now elaborated by his own testimony. My own feeling is, however, that further testimony from Zephaniah at this time would not constitute an ideal corroboration, although it will doubtless be invaluable in future, for the sake of further elaboration. For the moment, therefore, I have given Helen permission to call for volunteers to place themselves in her machine, singly or in pairs, with the proviso that she allows them to set their own timetable.

"It might well be the case that the initial results will be poor, given that no other crew members are fitted with the artificial neural contacts that Zephaniah has been employing throughout his working life, and the fact that even volunteers who did have such contacts were unable to duplicate the success with Walter Halleck's Sling that Zephaniah achieved. He clearly has natural advantages, presumably including a mode of quasi-sensory perception distinct from the five familiar senses, but he believes that such a sense might be latent, and capable of development, in many living creatures, including all humans, and the hypothesis that Helen's machine might enable its stimulation and development requires extensive and disciplined testing. There are hazards involved in any external stimulation of the brain, so the experiments would not be risk-free, but Helen believes, as I do, that at least some of you will not merely be willing but eager to take those risks.

"As you already know from the communication relayed by Denise, assuming the substance of that communication to be accurate, the ring intelligences would like our permission to attach a certain amount of extra mass to the external surface of Minerva in order that it might be transported to the vicinity of Uranus— something they cannot achieve by themselves using their own resources. Given that we are already within their bodies, one or more of them could simply attach themselves without our being able to prevent them, but Zephaniah is convinced that they will not do so without our consent. At present, he is probably the only one among us who can relay that consent, but he has stated that he will not attempt to do so unless it is unanimous."

"Unanimous aboard Minerva," a voice put in, which Denise tentatively attributed to the cosmologist Victor, "or unanimous between us and Mission Command in Fairbanks?"

"Ideally the latter," the captain replied, with equanimity, "but in the unlikely event of difference of opinion between Minerva's crew and our supposed home base, it would necessarily be up to us to decide that matter . . . bearing in mind that circumstances at Fairbanks have changed drastically since the mission plan was originally formulated there, and that circumstances aboard Minerva have also changed dramatically, in view of Zephaniah's communication. Whatever we do, obviously, we shall be doing on behalf of the entire human race, or what remains of it, and I do not anticipate that any serious difference of opinion could arise anywhere as to where those best interests lie."

The reaction to that statement was almost silent, but Denise had no difficulty judging that several members of the audience had the imaginative capacity to wonder whether such differences of opinion might arise on Earth, even if there were none aboard Minerva. The captain was being deliberately disingenuous.

"I didn't hear every detail of your discussion," Paula put in, "but it seemed to me that you didn't give a great deal of attention to the question of the effect that taking on extra mass would have on our potential range."

"That's for me to work out," said a man that Denise recognized as the technician Birstan. "Until I have precise figures I can't do it accurately, but Zephaniah has been talking thus far in terms of hundreds of kilograms of baryonic matter rather than hundreds of tonnes. You all have some idea of how the matter annihilation drive works and you can all look up the safety margins that the mission specification included, even assuming that the scoops were unable to make any contribution. If that's a reasonable estimate, the diminution of our possible range, even preserving the assumption of the inactivity of the scoops, would only be ten per cent or so, and if Zephaniah can give us the information promised regarding the likelihood of finding planets similar to those in our system orbiting the target star, we shouldn't run out of fuel, any more than we should run out of food, water or respirable air within a mission span of fifty, or even a hundred years. That, of course, is contingent on Mellita's recycling systems continuing working with the same efficiency that they've demonstrated over the last three years, and had previously demonstrated on the Olympus missions, but I see no reason to doubt them. If the presence of our alien hitchhiker causes problems, it won't be its vulgar mass that's to blame. I can't answer for the electronics until I know a lot more about the organism or organisms."

"The observations that Victor and I have made thus far, while we've allegedly been in the heart of the pack, are no help," Savina put in. "A miscellany of anomalies, with no detectable logic as yet . . . but there's definitely something weird going on."

"Definitely," added Alessandro. "Cronos confirms that, but its crew estimate that it will take some time fully to collate and analyze the data their sensors have collected."

"They don't have a Coincidence theorist aboard capable of making sense of it," Helen put in. "That's up to you and me."

"Uncommonly generous of her to bracket herself with someone else," muttered Mireille, who was standing next to Denise now that it was actually possible to stand. "Must be in a good mood."

"If what we're trying to get away from qualifies as an atmosphere of sorts," Denise said, equally quietly, "isn't it your field?"

"I'm a physical chemist, not a Coincidence theorist . . . but maybe I'll take a look."

Elsewhere in the small crowd, Paula ventured, loudly: "Are we just taking our own unanimity for granted, or are we going to take a vote, now that we can raise our hands without going into a spin?"

"We ought to do that, for form's sake," the captain said. "Is there any objection to our continuing to follow our present heading, for the time being?"

No hand or voice was raised.

116

"Entered in the log," the captain stated—again, presumably for form's sake. "The revised data rosters will be posted. Volunteers for Helen's next experiment, please register your names with her, so that she can select the first."

"On what basis?" Mireille asked, this time speaking loudly.

"We can draw lots if you like," Savina put in. Nobody laughed, although Denise was sure that at least two people, in addition to her, understood that it was a joke, of sorts.

"On the basis that you're first in line, my dear," said Helen, "if you care to put your name forward."

Denise saw Mireille look directly at Zeph, who was standing quietly, slightly apart from the rest of the group, observing—while being observed intently himself by at least three other crew members, including Gabrielle. Zeph's face was impassive, but instead of meeting Mireille's gaze, he looked away, first at Helen, and then—perhaps seeking reassurance—at her. Denise shook her head, almost imperceptibly, and hoped that even Zeph, bad as he had always been at picking up non-verbal cues, would be able to interpret the gesture as advice to be patient and not to challenge Mireille in public.

Mireille seemed to be on the point of making a more elaborate comment, but all she actually said, in the end, was, "I'm in, then. I'll go first."

Again she looked at Zeph; again, whether or not he was following Denise's gestured advice, he did not react—but Denise judged that it wasn't because he had nothing to say about the matter.

"Is there anything else that anyone would like to put to the assembly, while we're gathered in the flesh?" the captain asked, in a tone of voice that seemed to Denise to imply that quibbling suggestions would definitely not be welcome, for the moment. None were made loudly, although there was a certain amount of murmuring within the loosely knit miniature crowd.

"In that case," the captain said, "the meeting is adjourned. Thank you all for your attention." It was more a parody of formality than a serous ritual, even though everyone in attendance was now ponderable, perhaps slightly more so than was customary on Earth—but the rate of acceleration seemed to Demise to have stabilized now, with only the slightest tilt relative to the vertical axis incorporated into the ship's design. That was slightly disconcerting, but Denise had every confidence that she could adapt.

As the crowd began to dissipate, Denise made her way to where Zeph was standing. "You didn't need my input into your discussion, then?" she said, keeping her tone scrupulously level.

"I didn't think so," he said, warily. "If there was something else you wanted to contribute, you just had an opportunity. Thanks for helping me to sort it all out beforehand, though—that was an enormous help."

"Still ringing the changes, I see," she commented. "Luke Saverne sends his regards, by the way."

"Who?"

"A young boy who talked to you on Marine Parade—it must have been on the day I came to meet you while you were staying with Mum. He would have been eight or thereabouts at the time."

"The kid. Yes, I remember. He made it through the catastrophe, then?"

"He's in Yorkshire—got a spare ticket. He's sent you a message, but it's probably way down on your priority list."

"I haven't had a chance to look, yet, but it's a very long list."

"The ones at the top will be from Walter Halleck and the Sling techs—but there'll doubtless be some from Marie; the one at the top of mine is a mammoth. She's probably written a book and wants our feedback, to use as publicity. Are you going to talk to Mireille?"

"Yes, of course."

"In secret?"

Zeph blushed. "Yes," he said, awkwardly. "Does it matter?"

"If you mean, have I any objection or comment to make, absolutely not. Be good to her, will you . . . she's had a hard time. I can't look over my shoulder without being obvious, but I suspect that a queue is already forming, waiting for me to step away. Do me a favor and blow them all off in Mireille's favor."

She estimated that there was enough of the old Zeph still left for him to wonder how that could possibly qualify as a favor to her, without his daring to ask. He didn't ask, and didn't take the risk of saying anything at all.

"And write to Luke Saverne when you have a moment," she added. "It'll change his life, and make up for freezing him out on Marine Parade."

"I didn't," Zeph protested. "I talked to him nicely. I answered his questions."

"I can imagine," Denise said. "As I remember, you gave me a hug of sorts, and even I nearly caught a chill."

"As I remember," Zeph said, mutinously, "I was radiating new warmth . . . but any breath of cold you imagined didn't stop you coming round to my new flat at the first possible opportunity and ranting about my having let you down seven years before. We patched up any lack of sympathy, though, didn't we?"

"We did," Denise agreed. "Is Mireille directly behind me in the embryonic queue?"

"No—it's not her style."

"Then barge through the rest and whisk her away. I know it's not your style, but just for once in your life, do as you're told."

Zeph refrained from responding, as he could have done without being utterly dishonest, that he usually did as he was told, meekly, now that he had overcome his youthful bloody-mindedness. Denise took it for granted that he would do so this time, and she looked round for the captain—but he was nowhere to be seen.

As Zeph moved off, hunching his shoulders as he tried to evade would-be questioners in order to make a bee-line for Mireille, Gabrielle stepped in front of Denise.

"Feels good to have weight again, doesn't it?" she said.

"Yes," agreed Denise. "And it's good to be able to ease into it gradually, when I imagine that Minerva could have accelerated from zero to some godawful velocity in no time at all."

"Not policy, when there's no gravity well to climb. Don't be offended that the captain didn't call you, and that he slipped away just now. He's still got long-distance diplomatic games to play with Earth, and he probably thinks he's being kind keeping you and Helen apart for a while—but she'll be pestering you again in no time, even if she has consented to let Mireille and someone else have the first crack at her new variant of Russian roulette."

"Someone else?" Denise queried.

"It took two to bring back a message last time. My guess is that Helen will want to duplicate the format, soon if not for the first experiment in the series, although the captain will want her to take things one step at a time and one person at a time. It appears that Mireille will get to go first, unless she gives Zephaniah a power of veto, and she'll probably want to go alone. Even as far as that, though, there's scope for discussion. Beyond the test run . . . well, your guess is as good as mine, probably better. What do you think?"

"Are you asking me whether I'm going to volunteer to be guinea pig number two . . . or number one, if Zeph can talk Mireille out of it?"

"No, but it's an intriguing possibility. Are you going to volunteer?"

"Are you?" Denise countered. "Isn't getting inside other minds your specialty?"

"I have my own methods for that. I'd rather observe the effects of the machine from outside, at least for a while. Helen appears to have been persuaded or told that she can't simply make her own choice and command compliance, but that won't stop her making suggestions, and you might well be at the top of her list if Mireille changes her mind."

"I can handle Helen," Denise said, confidently, and went on teasingly: "It still seems to me that she ought to have you in her sights as the person most apt to follow in Zeph's footsteps, as the crew's professional empathizer?"

"I don't think she sees that as a qualification," the psychologist replied, with perfect equanimity, "but I might be wrong. If she does want to try her machine on me, I'll just have to ask her to be patient. I've always been a great believer in the virtue of patience."

"You don't mind waiting a little longer to begin psychoanalyzing me, then?"

"Oh, I've already started on that . . . but I don't mind taking my time. Some cases require more studied attention than others." She refrained scrupulously from mentioning that the captain had also given her instructions to make a careful examination and assessment of Zeph's psychological condition, although Denise assumed that he must have done.

"I'm not transparent, then?" she said, instead.

"It's unbecoming to gloat, especially about a presumed opacity. You're a utopian now, and it's a long way to the stars—too far to hold on to inconvenient hang-ups."

Denise did not protest that she was devoid of hang-ups, or deny that the ones she had were inconvenient. *If only . . .* , she thought. Aloud, she said: "If you'll excuse me, I have a long letter to read from my confessor. I doubt that it will grant me absolution for my sins, but at least it will be a welcome hint of home."

"That's good," said Gabrielle. "Even with no absolution, it's a treasure of sorts. Be glad that you have a confessor, even one with whom you can only communicate on-screen. Is she a close friend?"

"She's a minister in the Church of England—she doesn't have *close friends*."

"Please don't take offense—I wasn't implying anything more than what I actually said. However close she was or wasn't, it's good that she's talking the trouble to keep in touch. I fear that I lost contact with almost all of my former friends while I was away on Olympus Four, and when I returned to Earth . . . things had changed. I was retained in the program to help with the preliminaries of Five, and then urgently reassigned to what was then a top secret project—so secret that I wasn't even allowed to know its name. Forming and maintaining friendships in a situation like that is difficult. My parents are still alive and, like you, I have a brother, but I didn't manage to reconnect with them the way Zephaniah seems to have done with you, probably because I wasn't able to make as much effort. So I'm speaking from my own experience rather than purely from a professional standpoint in suggesting to you that any connections you can retain with people on Earth might be a very valuable asset in time to come . . . as valuable in their own way as making good connections on Minerva."

Denise had no difficulty recognizing the hint that, thus far, she wasn't doing very well in making good connections aboard Minerva, but she put her reflexive suspicions aside for the moment and decided to accept that the psychologist was simply being friendly.

"I am glad that Marie is keeping in touch," she said, "and I'll try not to hold the religion against her too much." Privately, she thought that she was also glad that Emily Saverne had taken the trouble to write to her, and estimated that her letter really was a valuable treasure.

She bade Gabrielle an *au revoir* then, which she tried hard to empty of all reflexive hostility, and made her way back up to the cabins. Climbing the ladder reminded her that there was a downside to having an up, but she cursed her perverse ingratitude and instructed herself to delight in her ponderability.

She sealed her pod in order to read the communication in question, and put up the opacity screen, just in case anyone who wanted to use one of the opposite capsules might find her transparent proximity embarrassing.

VIII

As its size implied, Marie's message was not a letter in the ordinary sense, but its precise nature, which she discovered when she obeyed an invitation to put her VR hood on, was a surprise. She found herself in a virtual replication of Kensington Gardens, facing the Watts statue, at the point she had used as a convenient meeting point with various people on a dozen occasions when emerging from her workplace at Imperial College.

Marie had used a library tape of the gardens as a template, but she had spliced in an avatar of herself.

"Hello, Denise," she said. "I don't know what it's like out there in deep space, but I thought you might like to have the illusion of surroundings that are both pleasant and nostalgically familiar. This avatar is equipped with a certain basic versatility—not much more than the average answering machine, but enough to allow you to interrupt the discourse and ask questions to which the program can make polite innocuous replies and slot in sections of text moved from elsewhere, making this more like a conversation and less like a sermon.

"I hope you don't mind, but in the first instance, we'll head directly for the Peter Pan statue and then make our way in a leisurely fashion to the Serpentine bridge to Hyde Park. I have nothing against Physical Energy, but equestrian statues aren't really my thing, and I hardly used to give it a glance in the days when my father used to bring me here for walks when I was a child, whereas Peter Pan was a favorite of his, second in his affection only to the Epstein bas-relief in Hyde Park. It would have been first if it had represented what he called the *real* Peter Pan, but it's the Peter from the play, not the earlier story that he used to read to me, in which Peter is a part-bird Betwixt-and-Between who plays the pipes at Queen Mab's dances, and finds when he eventually flies home that his mother has given birth to another child while he was away, who has usurped her love.

"On the two occasions when I walked through the gardens with you, we barely paused at Peter Pan, but we did cross the bridge into the park and look at Epstein's Rima, so I'm hoping this tape will bring back memories, even though they probably won't seem as pleasant to you as they do to me. Perhaps the Peter Pan statue will strike a chord, because I remember something your mother said when we visited her with you on the day when I bullied you into introducing me to Zeph, about him having been away with the fairies. The account you'd given me of him made him sound something like a Betwixt-and-Between himself, but that was just a gloss I'd put on what you told me; when I got to know him, to the extent that I did, I found that he hadn't been afraid to grow up at all. Now you're both away with the fairies . . . except that the little you were able to say about the entities you call the Bells doesn't make them sound like the creatures carved in the Elfin Oak.

"Forgive my rambling; I know that this Virtual Environment can't have the same resonances of childhood for you that it does for me, but it's within walking distance of Imperial and I know that you came to the real Kensington Gardens a lot during your lunch breaks, for a breath of fresh air, when there was such a thing. Like you, I'm now breathing recycled air, chemically reconditioned, and the prospect of stepping outside is now a lifetime and more away. I know, too, that you won't be able to approve of the gloss I'm putting on your message in commenting on it to the world, but I do believe, sincerely, that through Zeph you really have made contact with God—or the Cosmic Mind as pseudo-atheists like Walter Halleck insist on calling it. I have no objection to referring to God as 'it' rather than Him—I think that the objection that Walter and other pseudo-atheists have to the religious interpretation is more to the personalization than to the fundamental idea."

"Are you on first-name terms with Walter Halleck now, then?" Denise put in, thinking that she ought to try the avatar's supposed ability to interrupt its speech in order to answer questions, like a simple answering-machine AI.

"Yes, I am," Marie replied. "We don't see one another in the flesh, obviously, but I've taken advantage ruthlessly of the introduction you and Zeph kindly provided at Zeph's flat on the night when the Crash didn't go bang, in order to mine him for information relevant to my thesis. Naturally, he didn't approve of me at first, but his resentment at the way he and his Sling have been treated by the government made him grateful for any sympathetic interest, and he's been very forthcoming about the results of his experiments now that the security blanket has been partially removed and he can talk about his old findings. The fact that I'm a young-ish woman obviously helps, of course, as it always does with men of his generation nostalgic for the long-gone days when they could maintain the illusion that women might fancy them, and it's perfectly safe for me to be a trifle shameless while he's in Snowdonia and I'm in the Highlands."

"Hussy," said Denise testing the limits of the avatar's conversational programming—but the program didn't react to the jesting insult, and seemed to be about to return mechanically to the script of the message. They had paused in front of the Peter Pan statue, and Denise looked at it, more intently than she had ever looked at it when it was physically present. Again, she wanted to test the flexibility of the AI integrated into the message, so she said: "Mum took Zeph and me to a pantomime of *Peter Pan* once. I was seven or eight, I think. It was the first time that I realized, fully, that Zeph didn't think like other people."

"Really?" prompted Marie's avatar, moved by the AI.

"Yes. There's a point in the script where Tinkerbell, played by a spotlight, is said to have drunk some poisoned milk left for Peter by Captain Hook, and Peter addresses the audience, telling them she she'll die if they don't clap their hands to signify that the

125

believe in fairies, The entire audience played along and clapped—except Zeph. When Mum told him to clap he just said that he didn't believe in fairies, or milk-drinking spotlights. Anyone else would have clapped simply because everyone else was clapping—but not Zeph. He took it in good part, though, when Mum told him time and time again that he was away with the fairies. After the sixth or seventh time, he even stopped contradicting her."

"That's interesting," Marie's avatar said, with mechanical politeness. "Shall I continue now?"

"Please do," said Denise.

"I've thought a great deal about the nature of Creation, as you can imagine," Marie said, earnestly, "and I think that a lot of the problems that have arisen with the idea historically arise from the crude personalization of the Creator. The Christian religion took a great step forward by substituting Jesus for Jehovah, thus embracing a much kinder morality, but the further humanization of the deity was a mixed blessing, conceptually speaking. Traditional atheism isn't without its faults, though, as I remember trying to explain to you more than once. What you and Zeph have found, it seems to me, supports my cause.

"You'll remember, of course, that of the three fundamental models of Creation, I had objections to both creation *ex nihilo*, as implied by *Genesis* and some versions of the Big Bang theory, and creation viewed as a matter of imposing order on a pre-existent chaos. Atypically, for a theologian, I always favored the model proposed by the first great opponent of divinity theory, Epicurus, as popularized by Lucretius in *De rerum natura*, which imagines creation as the interruption of a pre-existent monotony by a tiny spontaneous modification—*clinamen*, in his terminology—which triggers chains of cause-and-effect that gradually expand and some of which are magnified and complicated by what some physicists like to call the Butterfly Effect.

"In that version of Creation, whether imagined as singular or continual, Creation isn't controlled and managed tyrannically by the Creator, as it is explicitly in the order-out-of-chaos model and implicitly in the *ex nihilo* model. It's more congruent with

Leibnizian theodicy, which attempts to reconcile the idea of God's axiomatic benevolence with the existence of evil by suggesting that the process of Creation and the nature of its raw materials impose certain limitations on what is achievable, even by 'omnipotence.'"

We didn't waste much time on the personal, did we? Denise thought, as they moved away from Peter Pan. She had expected Marie's avatar to respond to the pause and her own anecdote by reverting to waxing lyrical about childhood, but it hadn't. Instead Marie, had cut to the academic meat of her argument and she was now in full flow. Denise smiled wryly at the thought that in Marie's judgment, the statue in the Gardens was the "wrong" Peter Pan.

"Lucretius thought that the introduction of clinamen into the model of Creation could explain the existence of complexity without the need for an active Creator," the avatar continued, "by attributing the evolution of complexity to the accidental amplification over time of a kind of random swerve or nudge, but that isn't very satisfactory, given the observable complexity of the world that we see around us, let alone the hypothetical universe revealed by modern scientific exploration and explanation. As theologians like William Derham and William Paley argued, it's difficult to imagine that such awesome results—awesome not simply in terms of their mathematical and organic complexity, but also their esthetic qualities—could have arisen simply by a statistical accumulation of events occasioned by the natural selection of initial random mutations. Twentieth-century scientists rose to the challenge heroically, and proved themselves not only capable of that imagination but of defending it with the utmost ingenuity, but their arguments always begged the question, assuming the result before organizing the evidence, much as theologians did after having adopted contrary axioms.

"In my view, the apparent impasse generated by the prefatory selection of those fundamental axioms disappears once the idea of the Creator is depersonalized. Many theologians have thought of that as giving the game away, surrendering to atheism, but

127

that's rather simplistic. Although ancient history contains too many misconceptions to have much relevance to modern theology, it's worth remembering that the Epicurean universe, although disposing of gods as ancient religion imagined them, isn't a dispassionate universe in which esthetic and moral judgments become implicitly meaningless. The kind of vulgar thinking that presumes that God has to be imagined anthropocentrically as a person in order to be reckoned 'good' or 'benevolent' is too crude to contend with the conundrums of theodicy and the varieties of religious experience, just as the image of the soul as a ghost temporarily possessing the bodily machine can't stand up to rigorous philosophical analysis. Such problems have to be seen from a different angle if they're to become soluble."

In the Virtual Environment supplied by the library tape, through which Denise seemed to be moving in company with an image of Marie MacLaughlin, the two strollers, having accelerated slightly after passing the Peter Pan statue, had now reached the bridge over the Serpentine, the exit from Kensington Gardens to Hyde Park. The viewpoint slowed down again, and paused on the bridge, as real walkers in the actual London parkland often did, and as Denise had often done herself while strolling idly at lunchtime or after work, alone or in company.

Bridges, she thought, *inevitably have a symbolic significance, marking transitions, to which strollers are sensitive, unconsciously if not consciously.*

Marie's avatar leaned on the parapet and looked down at the water, while Denise looked back momentarily, in the direction of the Serpentine Gallery and the distant Albert Memorial, both of which had survived the Great Flood that had destroyed much of London during at the peak years of the Crash, although both had required routine refurbishment to counter the ravages of time.

"In spite of my best efforts as a pupil and Walter's as a teacher," Marie continued, "I simply can't get a mental handle on the mathematics of Coincidence Theory. He says that it's because when my brain entered the final phase of its physical organization in my teens, it sculpted neural pathways that were subsequently hard-wired—his phrase—and which literally blocked out certain ways of thinking and imagining, whereas at least a few of the kids who learn the fundamentals of the theory in school today will develop different neural pathways as their brains mature, which will enable them to build and deploy different conceptual models. Only a handful will become geniuses like him or craftsmen like Zeph—his terminology again—but all of them, he thinks, will find it easier to conceive of time in a more sophisticated fashion than imagining it as a kind of string with one end at the point of Creation, thus permitting such absurd questions as what happened 'before' the Big Bang, or where God was before he created the universe in order to have somewhere to be.

"As I understand it in my limited fashion, though, Coincidence Theory develops from the observation that elementary particles of matter that are separated in space-time after once having been intimately associated, retain an echo of that association in spite of their separation. They remain connected in some extra dimension, and that association affects their behavior: Coincidence with a capital C. Because of that connection, seemingly trivial in itself, the new structures into which the separated elementary particles are integrated acquire a connection of sorts, and because the nature and activity those structures can affect the behavior of the elementary particles they contain, they can also have slight but tangible effects on the new structures into which their twin particles are adapted. The vast majority of those effects are negligible and imperceptible, but in that regard too there can be a Butterfly Effect of sorts: the effects can sometimes be amplified and augmented by chains of causality that they instigate.

"In effect, Walter says, those connections can be imagined as a near-infinite series of bridges inherent in the structure of the universe, which link points in space-time that are sometimes very distant, effectively binding the universe into an integral whole rather than the mere scatter of independent lumps of mass that it appears to be to our senses. The points defined by those separated particle pairs are continually drawing further apart in space because of the apparent expansion of the universe . . ."

"What do you mean, *apparent* expansion?" Denise interrupted. "I thought the expansion was a fact, just as the length of duration separating the present moment from the moment of the Big Bang is a fact."

"From our viewpoint, that's true," Marie answered, "but the mathematics of Coincidence theory embody other hypothetical viewpoints, from which separations in space-time are only apparent. Thus, when Zeph was in Walter's Sling, it appeared to him that he was looking through a lens into the far future—a whole series of lenses into a whole series of far futures, in fact—but from the viewpoint of the machine itself, there was no separation and the different points in time seemed simultaneous, although the apparent simultaneity generated in Zeph's brain was fragile, difficult to establish, very difficult to maintain, and even more difficult to repeat, because of turbulences or twists in the fabric of space-time itself. Walter thinks that it's only possible when the connected structures harboring the ends of the bridges are possessed of mentality as well as materiality . . . that they have souls as well as bodies, in my vocabulary."

"Hang on," said Denise. "You're going too fast and too far. Zeph always talked about the Sling opening a kind of lens that allowed him to see through time—souls didn't come into it."

"Yes they did," retorted the subroutine engaged by that question, with unusual bluntness. "It wasn't Zeph's physical eyes that were looking through time while he was in the Sling, although his brain translated the stimulations administered by the machine *as if* they were being transmitted by the optic nerve. What he was 'seeing' was visualized by what common parlance calls his mind's eye—the component of the imagination that remembers and formulates imagery in pseudovisual terms."

"Fair enough," Demise conceded. "So he was seeing directly with the optical receptors in his brain, bypassing his eyes—but it was still *seeing*, in neurological terms. He was seeing objects that actually existed in the futures he was looking into . . . wasn't he?"

"In the sense that they were authentic phenomena, yes," Marie conceded, "he was seeing what an observer located at the distant point in space-time would have seen with sensory equipment similar to his . . . but that hypothetical observer, which Zeph called a ghost rather than a soul, had to be constructed mentally, and in order for it to be constructed from the Coincidental particles—those paired with the ones making up his own brain—those particles had to be integrated into structures possessed not simply of a sufficiently similar materiality but of a sufficiently similar mentality: a mentality capable of seeing in the full sense of the word, not merely recording a pattern of light but interpreting that pattern as an image of objects, and attributing identity to those objects."

Not wishing to seem stupid, even to a subroutine of a VR tape that was relaying a slightly confused comment from Marie, which had presumably been added to the core of her letter as a kind of footnote, Denise took up that thread of thought. "You mean that the mind's eye isn't a camera," she said. "What you call 'attributing identity' isn't simply a matter of pattern recognition, after the fashion of facial recognition software—in crude terms, it involves emotional reactions as well as purely mathematical ones. Go on."

The instruction was vague, but the letter took it as an invitation to revert to its script at the point where it had been interrupted.

"You can probably see, given the nature of that crude model, why it's easier to form connections across what we perceive as the temporal component of space-time than the spatial one—in simple terms, why it was easier for Walter to construct his bridge-crossing apparatus than it was for Helen Arkheimer to construct hers, and why Zeph found Walter's neural stimulation machine much easier to operate with the aid of his neural contacts than the one that allowed him to make slight contact with the Bells. Even when the Coincidental contact had been made between his brain and the Bells' informer, he couldn't bring its contents to consciousness—but your brain, once it was connected in series with his, was able to do that. Although material in terms of its actual wiring, the secondary bridge between his brain and yours must have been extremely delicate, Walter says, presumably requiring pre-existing Coincidental associations of some kind forged both before and after your respective births."

"But those births were nearly three years apart," Denise objected. "We're not twins."

That remark hadn't been phrased as a question, but Marie's virtual self seemed to react to the keyword anyway. "Twins do seem to be more prone to forming connections that we can now consider as Coincidental," she said, "which often seem telempathic even to casual observers, especially if the twins are identical rather than fraternal, but ordinary siblings have a greater probability of forming weaker Coincidental links than unrelated individuals, and also a greater probability of being consciously aware of them, even though we had no vocabulary, until recently, capable of allowing us to get a conceptual grip on that awareness. The machines that Walter is presently trying to construct will hopefully be able to make the awareness in question much sharper and more coherent, but the experiments, although promising, have a long way to go."

Denise felt that the missive was being sidetracked into a maze, and that the confusion was largely her fault.

"Why did you refer to *the Bells' informer?*" she asked. "Why not just say *the Bells?*"

"Because we need to avoid being too simplistic," Marie replied. "The ghost mentality constructed at the distant point in space-time, which enables Zephaniah, or another space-time 'traveler' to 'see' remotely, is a collaborative endeavor. The bridge is connecting two mentalities as well as two materialities; what Zephaniah's brain is doing, when stimulated in the right way by the machine, isn't simply *looking*, it's making contact with another mind—but minds can't communicate with one another *directly*; they have to do it via comprehensible constructs, analogous to VR avatars like the one you're looking at."

The words appeared to be spoken by the image of Marie that Denise could see walking through Hyde Park toward the Epstein bas-relief, but Denise knew that it was all fake—not just the backcloth, but the fact that "Marie" appeared to be speaking.

What she had just said had been spliced in from a different tape, and its ultimate author, even if Marie had edited it slightly, was Walter Halleck. It was enough to make her head spin, even though her brain was no longer weightless. The clumsy fashion in which Marie was trying to make a point that she obviously didn't really understand wasn't helping.

"I can see what you're getting at," she lied, knowing that if she tried to sort it out in her head at present she would only get confused, and knowing that she would always have the option of reading the letter again, and of negotiating a variant path through its labyrinth. Wanting to cut to the chase, she said: "What does it have to do with God?"

"It has everything to do with God," Marie assured her, this time reverting to her own unadulterated identity, "just as God has to do with everything."

Pulpit glibness, Denise thought, but kept her mouth firmly shut.

"The point is," Marie continued, "that communication between minds—even the kinds of everyday communication that human minds have evolved over the millennia with the aid of speech—requires a measure of empathy and a measure of Coincidence. The measure varies considerably between human beings, but it has to exist for communication to be possible at all. Where communication is more difficult, as it inevitably is between minds separated in time or space, Coincidence becomes more important—and direct communication between minds, via telempathy, relies almost entirely on Coincidence effects. The intermediary mental constructs permitting that communication have to be contrived—or, as I prefer to put it, *created*."

"But created by people, not by any outside agency," Denise interjected.

"From one viewpoint," Marie conceded, "the creators are indeed the two minds that enter into communication, but that's a secondary process. The medium of communication—or the arena in which the communication takes place, if you prefer that terminology—is what you might call the Cosmic Mind, which I prefer, more accurately, to call God. Without the mental integrity of the universe, what Zeph does, with the aid of Coincidence machinery, would be impossible. The medium in which telempathic communication is possible isn't simply a void in which events happen, as the space through which electromagnetic radiations emanate was once imagined wrongly to be. Supposedly 'empty' space is complex and active, evidently capable of containing life-like phenomena quite different from organic life, and its nature determines, in some measure, what kinds of communication can take place . . . and that applies to telempathic communication just as it does to vulgar space travel. God is ever-present, in our minds and hearts, in our souls. We couldn't exist if he weren't, and the fact of our conscious existence is itself proof not merely of the reality of the soul but its immortality."

Denise could now see exactly where the argument was going, and she took a moment to scan the park, taking particular note of the elm trees that had been planted to replace the lindens and maples that had briefly replaced the original elms killed by Dutch Elm Disease in the twentieth century. Her attention skimmed over the Jelly Baby Family and other absurdities, zeroing in on the Hudson memorial toward which the excursion was directed.

"In order for Zeph to be able to communicate with anyone," Marie continued, relentlessly, "but especially, and vitally, in order for him to achieve a measure of empathy with alien minds, God has to exist. More than that; God has to be good, benevolent and loving. That's a necessary condition of the reality of empathy. Calling God the Cosmic Mind is simply a strategy of depersonalization, which is, in the theology I favor, unnecessary, and which doesn't change the nature of the mentality in question: its necessary integrity, its necessary goodness, its necessary benevolence and its necessary love. Whether you like it or not, Denise, that is what Walter and Zeph—and you—have already proved, and what future experiments will undoubtedly elaborate."

The strolling avatars had reached the Epstein block containing the bas-relief of Rima. Needing time to think, Denise reacted almost reflexively by introducing another interruption.

134

"Have you actually read *Green Mansions*, Marie?"

The real Marie would probably have seen the interruption for the hollow contrivance that it was, but the avatar wasn't programmed to employ that much empathic understanding; it was simply programmed to offer stored answers to questions. "Yes, I have," it replied.

"And what do you think of Rima?" Denise asked, referring to the stylized image of the enigmatic heroine of the novel, and taking it for granted that Marie would have added a footnote to her letter, in view of its planned itinerary.

"Rima is like Peter Pan and Zeph," the avatar replied dutifully. "She's a Betwixt-and-Between, distanced from vulgar humanity by virtue of her empathy with other kinds of beings, an innocent with a direct connection to God—or Nature, if you want to be stubborn in preferring that term—more intimate and more intense than the vague connection sensed by the hapless hero and his peers. She has numerous analogues in the history of religious mysticism, although Hudson, as a nineteenth-century naturalist, doesn't employ the same vocabulary as Saint Teresa of Avila. You ought to read *The Way of Perfection*, by the way; it's an invaluable guide to the contemplative life, which you've now adopted, by necessity."

Denise strangled a blasphemy. Having got the drift of the argument in spite of the tangling she had introduced into it, she felt sure that if she continued the fake walk, it would only become more insistent and more annoying.

"I'm going to pause you for a while, Marie," she said. "I need time to think about what you've just said, but I promise that I'll come back to you when I've done that, and I'll walk with you as far as you want to take me. It's a lot to take in all at once."

"That's all right," said Marie's avatar, with the dutiful politeness of a priest or a computer program. "There's no hurry. I'll see you soon, then."

IX

Denise took off the VR hood, and immediately saw that her screen was flashing a request for a response to a message from the captain. She knew that it couldn't be urgent, or he would have used his privilege to break into Marie's message, but she answered immediately.

"I'm here," she said, "ready to receive orders; go ahead."

The captain's face appeared on the screen. "Thank you, Denise," he said. "It's an apology, not an order. I'm sorry that I excluded you from Zeph's debriefing, but I feared that the discussion would become too complicated if you were there as well, and I needed to handle Helen very carefully."

"I understand," said Denise. "Three's a triad, four's a crowd."

"I see you've been talking to Gabrielle. I'm sorry about that too, but I had to ask her to compile a report on you. Rules and regulations . . . and I need to handle Fairbanks carefully too. It's my job to keep everybody on the same side, with no bones of contention."

"You do realize, don't you," Denise said, "that the assessment she makes will certify me as utterly unfit for shipboard society?"

"No it won't," the captain sad. "It will certify you as fully fit, exactly as required by your *de facto* presence here. Any advice she might think it appropriate to give you as to how to adapt yourself more comfortably to shipboard society will be off the official record, even if it's on tape. Gabrielle knows very well how the game is played—she helped to design it, after all, or at least to modify its design in consequence of her own experience. She passed Zephaniah psychologically fit for Olympus Five, in spite of certain . . . reservations arising from a poor performance on the computer tests."

"Did she? She didn't mention that."

"Of course she didn't—rules of confidentiality. But after five years' service on Olympus Four she was the certified expert with the relevant experience. She was party to the examination of most of the crew of Olympus Five, including those members now on Minerva. You can trust her judgments and her advice."

"I'll bear that in mind. What did you think of Zeph's report?"

"As clear and succinct as could presumably be contrived. Thank you for running though it with him . . . I'm not sure that he would have been able to organize it all so rapidly without your help."

"Do you and Helen have any ideas regarding the danger that the intimacy of the Bells might pose to the ship?"

"Of course—but it's all speculation at the moment. Zeph is . . . looking into the matter. He'll use Helen's machine again, if necessary, but he agreed to tread carefully once I'd acceded to his request to move Minerva out of the ring system. He knows that he's by no means the only person at risk, even though he's the first target in the firing range, so to speak, and he's prepared to tread carefully. He and Helen have negotiated a compromise."

"Negotiated a compromise with you, you mean," said Denise.

"If you like, but I was able to keep my mediation to a minimum, and our discussion was perfectly civilized, as you doubtless saw."

"For a while," Denise observed, pensively, "I thought my insistence on being with him when he woke up had backfired— that my own presence in such close proximity might be counterproductive. It sometimes was, in the old days. He's changed, though. The sojourn on Olympus Five made a different person of him—that must be down to you as well as Mireille—and I think he's now changed again as a result of his contact with the Bells. Do you believe that he's still in contact with them, potentially able to receive more information without going back into the machine?"

"It's an intriguing possibility—intriguing enough to enable Helen to consent to wait and see how things develop, at least in this regard. She wants to put someone else in the machine while we're still in close proximity to the Saturnian intelligences, though, and we had to give her that. She might want you, but you're free to refuse, or at least to wait a while, and that might be wise."

"I know. We have to try to figure out, between us, exactly why that proximity is dangerous if, as Zeph insists, the Bells only wish us well and want our relationship with them to be harmonious."

"It's a hot topic of debate, as you can imagine," the captain told her, "on Earth as well as aboard. Zephaniah's old friend Walter Halleck was cast out into the wilderness for a while, vilified by the suriphobes, but he's recovered his status now that his expertise is being bombarded with new questions, and he's leading the search for potential Coincidence psychics, as recent popular jargon calls them."

"I know," said Denise. "He's apparently in constant communication with Marie, who is busy translating the little she can grasp of Coincidence theory into religious terms, with a slight dose of Peter Pan thrown in for good measure. I had to stop reading her megamissive, because it's simply too indigestible in its relentlessness."

"I've had messages from her too," the captain told her. "Because we were introduced back on Earth, she thinks I'm fair game. She's been refining her seduction strategy on me . . . and I do mean seduction strategy, although her primary aim is to convert me, and she only wants to indulge in virtual flirtation as a means to that end. Fortunately, it isn't my duty to respond in kind."

"It wouldn't have to be a matter of duty," Denise suggested, mischievously. "She's an attractive woman—and she almost swooned the first time she saw you in the flesh. Lust and ambition are a powerful combination, and if she's also prepared to flirt with Walter, who must be as close to being the ugliest man in the surviving remnant of the human race as you are to being the handsomest . . ." She left the sentence unfinished.

138

"You're being very unfair to Walter," the captain replied, in a similar bantering tone. "Didn't you once propose spending the last night of the world in his arms, if the Greenland disaster tipped the balance of the world's doom?"

"I *knew* that flat was bugged," Denise said, with a sigh. "It was a stupid joke. If the world really had ended that night . . . well, I don't know what I'd have done, but it wouldn't have included sexual intercourse with Walter Halleck. You can't have been far away; surely you'd have come to rescue us—for Zeph's sake obviously, not for mine or Marie's."

"Probably," the captain said, and then condescended to modify it to: "Certainly. But I wouldn't have been able to console you until I'd got you all to safety, any more than I was able to do when the alarm bell actually rang."

"You didn't even hold my hand on the plane," Denise remembered. "You held Mireille's, even though she was already holding Zeph's with the other."

"So I did," the captain confirmed. "But you could have completed the ring yourself—all you had to do was reach out. You didn't. Your disdain was evident, although I endured it stoically."

Is that true? Denise wondered, never having thought about it before. Although she remembered feeling a distinct erotic thrill the first time Chris Kemmering had smiled at her, she also remembered that while they were on the plane she had been profoundly indifferent. The situation had been extremely tense, of course, but it would not have been the first time in her life than an initial erotic attraction had vanished rapidly as soon as there seemed to be a possibility of acting on the impulse.

She left the train of thought unfinished, and didn't bother to protest that her failure to reach out it hadn't been disdainful, although she was sure that it hadn't. "And then you saved my life," she said, instead, "although that, of course, was purely a matter of duty."

"Pure and simple," the captain confirmed, serenely. "Sorry, but I have to cut you off now. The latest response from Fairbanks has made its sluggish way across the solar system. We'll continue another time . . . soon."

With that, the screen went blank—but only for a moment. When Denise accepted the next incoming call, Helen Arkheimer's face appeared instead.

"There are matters I need to discuss with you urgently, Denise," the mathematician said. "Is now convenient?" She was calling from the cabin that accommodated her machine.

"No," said Denise, with reflexive perversity. "There's something else I need to do first. I'll call you when I'm ready." She switched off the connection without waiting for agreement.

She exited her own pod and the cabin without even glancing at the one that was opaque and occupied, and headed for the hatch to the common area. Victor, Birstan, Paula and Melitta were there, engaged in animated conversation. It didn't require much mathematical acumen to work out that Gabrielle was probably in her own cabin, in her own pod, and that the other three pods therein ought to be unoccupied, for the moment. Although four pairs of eyes invited her to join the conversation in the common area, with a certain eagerness, Denise raised a hand apologetically and backtracked. Gabrielle's cabin door was open, so Denise only had to intrude her head and say: "May I speak with you?"

"Of course," said Gabrielle, "I'll hop out." She was in the upper pod of the pair.

"I'd rather come in, if that's okay with you," Denise said.

"Certainly," the psychologist said, "but there really isn't any rush to complete the belated regulation evaluation."

"And it's a formality anyway, as you're under orders to pass me fit for duty," Denise said, as she climbed up, and then moved to what seemed to be a suitable position in the pod, assuming a half-lotus position, although it seemed strangely awkward now that she had weight, and she bumped her head in spite of trying to make herself slightly smaller than she was.

Gabrielle allowed the shadow of a frown to pass over her brow. "The captain shouldn't have told you that," she said, after having activated the privacy seal, "especially as it's not strictly true—but the fact remains that there's no urgency, and I'd rather like to make further observations before interrogating you. You'll also have to complete the standard questionnaire at some point for AI analysis."

"I know that you're in no hurry," Denise said, "but I am . . . if only because talking to you in complete confidentiality is the easiest way to avoid Helen for a little longer, given that I didn't want to stay in my own cabin while Zeph and Mireille are catching up and enjoying themselves . . . which I know is stupid, because I'm supposed to be a utopian now and it's something I'm going to have to get used to. The simple fact is that I'm not psychologically adapted to spend the next thirty years on Minerva, and I'm all too well aware of it. In terms of my contribution to the mission, which will only allow me to perform the most elementary monitoring duties until I've gone through the training program, it probably won't matter if I crack up—but if my cracking up were to make things awkward for everybody else, that would be embarrassing. I need to work out how to avoid that. Do you understand what I mean?"

"I do," the psychologist replied, "but I think you might be exaggerating somewhat. I can understand why you want to avoid Helen for the moment—you're not alone in that, alas—but we're all going to have to learn to live with her eventually. As for cracking up and spoiling things for the rest of us, I'm sure that you're underestimating yourself . . . and you mustn't do that. You're here because you're necessary. Zephaniah needs you here."

"And you know that because you psychoanalyzed him when you faked the certificate allowing him to join Olympus Five?"

Gabrielle sighed. "The captain shouldn't have told you that either. I can't discuss with you what I learned about Zephaniah when I assessed his suitability for the Olympus mission, but I can point out that the certification wasn't mistaken. After a few initial difficulties he adapted very well to the mission requirements. He carried out his own roles conscientiously and successfully, and he integrated very well with the rest of the crew."

"Even though Mireille and Savina had to flip a coin to decide who was going to volunteer to screw him?"

"That's an exaggeration too, and a grossly misleading one, but it's not something you and I ought to talk about. I'm sorry that you feel so profoundly uncomfortable at present, but it's mainly due to the pace at which things seem to be moving. The AIs didn't do you any favors by excising three years from your life for physical rest and recuperation while not leaving you any time to adapt mentally to all the changes to which you'd been rudely subjected. It's entirely understandable that you're panicking slightly, but things will calm down now, and you'll calm down too. You'll get through your initial doubts, and you'll integrate with the crew. I'm sure of that."

"Great bedside manner—but bullshit. You don't know me."

"Don't I? I haven't had a chance to interact much with you, it's true, but you must know that as soon as you were press-ganged into the crew, all the records of your life that exist on Earth were collected, collated and scrutinized. There's a lot of missing detail that only you can fill in, if you're willing, but you know how much data is routinely collected on Earth about every person who lives there. Usually, nobody bothers to put it all together in order to build a profile, but in circumstances like yours—especially given the unique features of those circumstances—no effort is spared. I won't be so arrogant as to say that I know you better than you know yourself, but nor will I concede that I don't know you at all."

Denise was momentarily startled by that. "*Merde*," she murmured. After a pause, she added; "At least there are no sex tapes . . . are there?"

"None to compare with Captain Kemmering's in the matter of viewing figures . . . but they wouldn't have been very interesting anyway . . . would they?"

"Low blow," Denise muttered. "But there can't be much data about me as a kid either. It's only when I started working at Imperial that every wall I passed by had ears and eyes, and then only in the corridors of the college—or was the Physical Energy statue in Kensington Gardens bugged too?"

"In fact, it was," said Gabrielle, "and probably still is, as are Peter Pan and Rima, under a thin layer of volcanic ash. It was a strange world that people lived in back there, but it's not entirely surprising that paranoia was rife during the Crash, when the end of the world was so obviously nigh. Please don't worry—I really haven't discovered anything in the torrent of futile information that I gathered that reflects badly on you. I'm sorry that I was obliged to look, because it must embarrass you terribly . . . but getting past that embarrassment is part and parcel of becoming a Minervan. By the time we get to Uranus we'll all know one another intimately, and we'll all feel at ease with it. Experience tells us that."

"Very limited experience," Denise suggested, "or Olympus wouldn't have been such an important experimental crucible. And the manned Olympus missions didn't have Helen Arkheimer aboard . . . or me."

"True—but think how satisfying it will be, for you, for Helen and the system, when we all end up loving one another dearly."

"You mean *if*."

"Do I? Are you really so convinced that you won't be able to love us all, given time and dutiful effort?"

"Yes."

"Because you think you're incapable of loving anyone? Not even your brother or Chris Kemmering?"

Denise contrived a laugh. "The two are hardly comparable," she commented, evasively.

"Why not? They're both decent, honest, intelligent men with a strong sense of duty. They like one another, to the extent of electing without hesitation to serve on a starship together. There's not an ounce of difference between them, except for trivia of no real consequence. And I could use exactly the same adjectives with reference to you, and the fact that a certain self-doubt would incite you to challenge at least two of them doesn't affect the fact that they're all applicable. May I ask you a personal question?"

"Obviously," Denise said. "It's your job, after all—and mine to answer it."

"Yes it is," the psychologist agreed. "Why did you distance yourself from your brother when you were in your teens, given that you could have had a much closer relationship, if you'd made the effort?"

"He didn't make the effort either," Denise parried.

"I know—but I know why he didn't, whereas I'm still slightly puzzled by your neglect. Are you willing to tell me?"

"You're assuming that I know."

"Yes, I am. I'm assuming that even if you weren't aware of it at the time, you know now. It is, as you say, my professional duty to ask, but I really am curious, and if I'm to learn to love you—which is also my duty—it might help."

"Bullshit," said Denise. "And soft soap."

Gabrielle sighed. "Would you rather discuss it with your confessor?" she asked mildly.

Denise nearly qualified that as another low blow, but she knew that it wasn't. "No," she said. "If I have to tell someone, I suppose that you're the one best qualified to listen, and to absolve me of my sins."

"I can't do that," Gabrielle countered. "All I can do is suggest that you absolve yourself. So start with Zephaniah. Why haven't you absolved yourself for real and imaginary sins committed against him in your teens?"

"I can't do that, any more than you can," Denise retorted, "But you're right . . . I can tell you why I drew apart from him when we were in our teens, when I ought to have drawn closer, as he clearly needed to me to do, because he couldn't do it himself. I felt that I ought to give him space, because he was afraid of me. He was afraid of everything in those days, of course, but me especially . . . and I didn't want to hurt him by putting pressure on him."

"I see. And why did you think that he was afraid of you?"

"Because in the period immediately before that I had teased and bullied him relentlessly, like the nasty little girl I was. By the time I was old enough to take notice of the world my father was dead—a belated victim of the Crash—and my mother was looking after us on her own. Because Zeph was . . . difficult . . . she kept very close watch on us, always afraid that in one of his meltdowns he might hurt me. Zeph was aware of that, and it made him very careful of me. He lost control occasionally, but the only person who was ever in any danger of being hurt was him, and I soon learned that I could say or do anything to him without any fear of retaliation . . . so I did. It stopped when he went to secondary school, but when I joined him there, he thought he had a duty to look after me, to protect me . . . and I felt the same about him, because he was obviously having a bad time, even though there was absolutely nothing I could do to protect him, any more than there was anything practical he could do to protect me. Our relationship became a source of perennial amusement to the other kids, and we let their mockery drive us apart . . . and we continued deliberately ignoring one another while he was training to manipulate surrogates with the aid of his implants and I was still studying. When he went to work at the Institute with Halleck I was doing postgraduate work nearby at Imperial, and it would have been easy to meet up and make repairs . . . but I didn't. He was still intimidated by me and I simply didn't make the effort. We only saw one another when we visited Mum, when we were as wary as we had always been while she was watching us. But it still hurt when I read in the news that he'd been hired by the ISA and spirited off to Alaska without even bothering to say goodbye, even though it was entirely my fault. Does that answer your question?"

"Yes—thank you."

"But the damage was repaired when he contacted me from Olympus," Denise felt obliged to add, "and when we met up in London again, everything was different . . . much better."

"Indeed. Do you think that your experience growing up with Zeph affected your attitude to and relationships with other males of the species?"

"Of course it did. How could I help comparing and contrasting, throughout my teens and well into my twenties? How could I help teasing and bulling young men, once I had discovered how easy it was to do, especially while I gradually turned from being a gawky kid into a tolerably attractive post-puberal nymphette?"

"And is that why you think that you'll never be able to adapt to shipboard society?"

"Mostly. I don't get along well with people. To tell the truth, I don't like people very much."

"Because of the way they used to treat Zephaniah?"

"Not just that. And before you point out, smugly, that people on Minerva don't treat him that way any more, I am well aware of that. He's changed . . . but I haven't."

"So you still feel a desire to protect him, and a sense of frustration because you can't?"

"Very clever. Yes I do, and that's why I'm here—a bad reason, I guess."

"Not at all. Do you think he feels the same about you?"

"Probably."

"And do you think that his experiences in childhood affected his attitude to and relationships with other females of the species."

"In spades—but he's changed. Olympus and Mireille have liberated him from my evil example . . . so at least I don't have to feel guilty about having crippled him irredeemably . . . except that . . ."

"Go on," the psychologist prompted.

Denise pondered the thought that had occurred to her before venturing to express it. Eventually, she said: "Except that I worry that he might be even more vulnerable now than he was before. But that's probably just the nasty little girl still lurking inside me, who wants to recover the monopoly on teasing and bullying him that she once had. Perverse nostalgia, I guess."

"Perhaps—but you're right, I think, in judging that he might be more vulnerable now than he has ever been before. He felt comfortable working at the Institute once the Sling began to produce results, and he learned to feel comfortable aboard Olympus

Five. In designing the present mission Helen tried to do everything she could to establish circumstances on Minerva in which he might feel comfortable again . . . but the mission's tribulations might have changed all that."

"You mean that I have. If I'd only had the sense to keep my big mouth shut until I'd had time to think . . ."

For the first time, the psychologist's expression showed surprise. "That's one thing for which you really mustn't blame yourself, Denise. You shouldn't blame yourself for the other things, either, in my professional opinion, but that . . . definitely not. And he remembered anyway . . . except that he won't call it remembering."

"He might not have remembered if I hadn't prompted him—and if my rambling hadn't been on record, he might not have believed what he's presently certain that the Bells put into his brain . . . and still might not."

"You're not thinking about annotated star maps?"

"Of course not. I'm talking about danger."

"You have a theory about what that danger might be?"

"Yes—don't you?"

"Doesn't everyone? Listening to your friend the chaplain explain that he's in communication with a benevolent and loving God hasn't reassured you?"

"Of course not."

"Because you can't believe it?"

"On the contrary—her theology appears to have depersonalized God to the point that there's only a hair's breadth separating her thesis from Walter Halleck's. What scares me isn't the possibility that she's wrong but the possibility that she might be right . . . but in seeing things entirely from her own viewpoint she's ignoring the actual logical implications of her thesis . . . even though the Bible clearly asserts that it's a fearful thing to fall into the hands of the living God."

"Doesn't that passage only apply to those who choose to act in defiance of God's will, and thus invite divine wrath?" Gabrielle objected.

"Probably—but it isn't vengeful wrath that I'm afraid of, in spite of what happened to the Earth three years ago. I'm afraid of something worse than that . . . and so, I suspect, are the Bells."

"Would you care to tell me what?"

"Not until I've talked to Zeph about it . . . and Helen . . . and the captain . . . and Mireille . . . although I suspect strongly that Mireille, at least, is already thinking along the same lines. You can be patient, I'm sure . . . and if not, you have no reservations about eavesdropping."

"True," said Gabrielle. "Have I mentioned that I also like puzzles and guessing games?"

"It's not a game, alas—and I really do have to talk to Zeph about it, if only so that he can tell me that I'm being silly and not to worry my pretty little head about it . . . which would annoy the hell out of me, but I'll refrain from hitting him if he does. After all, we're in utopia now . . . or do I mean prison?"

"It's really not a good idea to think of Minerva as a prison," Gabrielle told her, with a hint of reproach.

"It might be a cozy convent to you," Denise added, "but to me . . . well, I've yet to make any vows, and I can't help feeling that I'm here under false pretences. Helen is insistent that Zeph and I are psychically linked by Coincidence, but if we were, would the story I've just told you have worked out the way it did? Wouldn't we have had the close relationship whose absence from our biographies puzzled you?"

"That's an interesting question," Gabrielle countered. "What do you think?"

Denise laughed. "I don't know what to think. Would I be sitting here with my legs tucked up if I did? But Zeph told me long ago about the hypothesis that human consciousness, as it develops, builds barriers against inconvenient inputs from the unconscious—Marie thinks that her brain can't accommodate an understanding of Coincidence math because the potential neural pathways were blocked before her brain reached its full development. Perhaps Zeph's brain and mine automatically put up barriers precisely to block out the effects of our own Coincidence linkage, which required conscious effort and the intervention of the Bells to be broken down."

"That's an interesting idea too," Gabrielle supplied.

"Which might have some intriguing corollaries, in terms of evolutionary theory," Denise mused. "I'll have to give that further consideration . . . and so will you if you're to complete your psychoanalysis and make your report . . . not just on the possibility of my adapting to life on board, but the possibilities of life on board adapting to any other barriers that might be broken down, between us and, more significantly, between us and the Bells."

Thus far, all Gabrielle's reactions had been purely professional—but the frown induced by that suggestion seemed considerably less artificial. "You might be right," she conceded. "And if you are . . . you really must keep me up to date with your further thinking . . ."

"Because some cases require more elaborate study than others?"

Reverting to bland professionalism, the psychologist replied, almost automatically: "That's true."

Denise believed her.

X

When Denise returned to her own cabin she found that Mireille's pod was closed and still blacked out—but Zeph was not in it. Nor was he in his own pod; instead, he was lying down on his side in hers, evidently waiting for her.

"Helen's looking for you," he said. "She seemed a trifle miffed that you weren't here and hadn't called her. I told her that I'd like to speak to you first, if she wouldn't mind. Clearly she did, but I insisted, and I climbed up here in order to make the point more firmly, symbolically occupying the high ground. The right to give orders has become a trifle confused of late, as I'm sure you've observed."

Denise climbed up into the pod, but she shoved Zeph's head out of the way and resumed a half-lotus position with her back to the screen, tacitly commanding him to do likewise. He obeyed, meekly.

"Helen worked out, mathematically, that you must be talking confidentially to Gabrielle," Zeph observed. "She seemed a trifle miffed about that too, perhaps assuming that you must be talking about her. I assumed, by contrast, that you were talking about me . . . at length, apparently."

"Obviously, you came up in the course of the conversation," Denise confirmed, "but she wouldn't tell me what you said about me when she was interrogating you in Alaska before passing you fit to fly on Olympus, so I couldn't tell exactly what slanders I needed to defend myself against."

"I can assure you that I didn't say anything about you that was uncomplimentary."

"I guessed that, in spite of the fact that you could have vented a lot of resentment and petty spite, in justification of the fact that you hadn't even bothered to say goodbye when you left England—but I made up for it by saying plenty of uncomplimentary things to her . . . oh, don't look like that; not about you, obviously—I mean uncomplimentary things about myself."

The hint of distress that Zeph's expression had taken on deepened rather than seeming relieved by that clarification. "You shouldn't do that, Nise," he said. "You need to be kinder to yourself. You always did, but now more than ever."

"She seems to agree with you, but that's her job . . . and the more urgent need is probably for me to be kinder to everybody else. Kindness isn't a habit I developed while you were away—and you know what a bitch I was before."

"No, I don't."

Denise sighed. "Only because you were in denial," she said. "You can tell I've been talking to a shrink, can't you? But we can talk about our twisted sibling relationship another time. For the moment, I need to talk to you about the Bells."

Zeph seemed slightly surprised. "Not about Mireille?" he queried.

"No—why would I want to talk to you about Mireille?"

"You practically ordered me to go to bed with her. I thought . . ."

"That I'd want a report? No . . . and if I did, I'd ask her."

Zeph seemed slightly shocked by that. "I'd really rather you didn't," he said. "It's . . . well, I suppose I can hardly call it private any longer, as those stupid tapes made aboard Olympus got leaked all over the web, and they're still in circulation back home. Everybody knows now . . . even Mum knew, it seems."

"But they *don't* know, do they?" Denise objected, thinking that if Zeph wanted to talk about it she had better humor him. "All they know is that you and she complied with the moral code that was in force on Olympus. They don't know anything significant. And if I read the hints rightly, even you and Mireille were remarkably unforthcoming in discussing your feelings with one another. And *that's* what I *practically ordered* you to do a little while ago, not . . . whatever else you did."

"Oh. I misunderstood. Sorry."

"But you did talk, as well as . . . ?"

"Oh, yes. Mostly about the Bells, but we did talk."

"Good—unless, of course, it's considered subversive of utopian disciple to talk about feelings, in case it implies a possessiveness unbecoming true spacers . . . but even if it is, you won't get any disapproval from me."

"Don't be silly, Nise. You haven't had a chance yet to see how things work, but you'll have plenty of time to figure it out. The captain will guide you . . . or Gabrielle, if you don't feel comfortable talking about it with a man."

"I suppose I'll have to get used to that, if my duty requires me to screw all of the ones aboard . . . possibly excepting you."

Zeph blushed deeply. "Again, that's ridiculous. The most basic freedom is the freedom of refusal. You don't have to do anything you don't want to do—but it's a long way to Uranus and you might get a little . . . lonely."

"Very delicately put. How sure are you that we'll actually make it to Uranus?"

"The ship will certainly make it, and will go a long way beyond, carrying all its passengers," Zeph told her, putting on a show of utter confidence.

"Even if the presence of its extra passengers is inherently dangerous—to you in particular?"

"We probably won't even know that they're there. It's in their interest as well as ours for us all to make the journey safely, and I have confidence in their ability to figure out how to reduce the danger that they pose . . . with my help."

"But it isn't entirely safe, is it, for us and perhaps even for them? You *know* that . . . but have they been able to explain why?"

"Not yet. I don't believe they're even trying, for the moment. I think they're trying to keep their distance, psychically speaking, for fear of accidental damage, in one direction or the other. They think the possible rewards of the outward voyage are worth the risk, though, for us as well as them. I'm confident that they'll try to communicate more effectively again, once they've weighed up the results and implications of the contact we made with the aid of the machine . . . but that might take a while; they operate on a slower timescale than we do, and I got the impression that they found us . . . surprising."

"Do the possible rewards that you and they have in mind include a closer relationship between humans, the Bells and the Uranian ring intelligences? A broader meeting of minds?"

"Yes, of course . . . a closer harmony."

"Like three choirs of angels singing beneath the throne of God, desirous of learning a new tune and singing together in harmony to glorify the Lord?"

"If the analogy helps you to imagine it . . . Marie MacLaughlin would probably approve."

"She does. But you and I are Nietzscheans, aren't we? When we look into the abyss, we fear monsters and we fear becoming monsters . . . not to mention worrying about how the abyss might react when it looks into us."

"They're not monsters, Nise," Zeph assured her. "I dare say that there might be monsters out there somewhere, and maybe that's an element of the danger that worries them, but the Bells aren't monsters themselves, and nor are the Uranians with whom they want to strike up a closer harmony. Keep it in mind that their great goal is harmony. It's not easy for a whole orchestra of different musicians to coordinate the efforts of its members to produce a symphony of genius, but it's possible, and that's their objective. There's no hostility in them, no aggression. And before you ask, I've considered the wolf-in-sheep's-clothing hypothesis and dismissed it. There are no possible bones of contention between the ring intelligences and the kinds of life that might evolve on planetary surfaces closer to the sun . . . but we *can* do one another small favors, like good Samaritans."

"I believe you, albeit not as fervently as Marie does . . . but I suspect that Marie hasn't really thought it through—not in the direction that my thinking is tending, at any rate. It's not her fault; she's just equipped with a different set of spontaneously generated blinkers. Have you read all the messages that she's sent you?"

"Not all of them. I haven't had time. Have you read all of yours?"

"No. Has the fraction you've read told you the model of Creation she prefers?"

"She told me that back on Earth—monotony disturbed rather than chaos ordered, the initial disruption being a random twitch on the part of one of the components of uniformity, setting off a chain reaction that leads to multiple vibrations and aggregations, eventually building entities that begin to interact, provoking ever greater complexity: a flick of a insectile wing eventually provoking a mighty storm, by chance to begin with, but deliberately as soon as some of the complex entities develop consciousness."

"That's the one. Did she explain why she prefers it to its rivals?"

"Yes. I quite like it for purely esthetic reasons, but she thinks that it offers a solution of sorts to the problem of theodicy: the vindication of divine providence in spite of the existence of evil. But she disapproves of Milton—far too much emphasis on Satan, she thinks, almost to the point of glorification. We went through all that back on Earth—but since your brief report on the existence of the Bells, she's convinced that we've proven not merely the existence of a Cosmic Mind, and 'angels' of a sort, but the fundamental goodness of Creation. She's waiting for further evidence of the immortality of the soul, but she's changed her definition of it sufficiently to make the persistence of Coincidence effects a kind of proof. She also thinks that the ability of machines like Walter's to produce phantoms of a sort is evidence for posthumous immortality, although that seems ridiculous to me. It's certainly not what I'd call immortality, but if she's happy with it, good luck to her. I just wish she wouldn't attribute the notion to me, as she comes uncomfortably close to doing in her commentaries on what she calls the gospel according to Zephaniah."

"By *angels of a sort*, you mean the Bells?"

"No, *she* means the Bells. They're not angels, and it's almost as misleading, as a borrowed label, as Bells. They're organized entities capable of reproduction, with a material component but a much larger component consisting of dark energies of a kind whose existence we had barely suspected before we encountered them. Their physical chemistry is extremely weird, but not without analogy: the Jovian cloud-whales are just as bizarre, in their own way, and we'll probably be able to obtain a much better understanding of their nature and evolution when we understand the nature and evolution of the Saturnian species . . . and the Uranian species, once we're able to observe them at closer range as well. There might well be more strange forms of pseudo-life further out in the system, and further in as well . . . even in the Sun. Our thinking thus far has been far too anthropocentric; life akin to ours probably only accounts for a tiny fraction of lifelike phenomena in the solar system, let alone the universe as a whole. We'll probably be very limited in our ability to interact with other forms of pseudo-life physically, but we can surely interact productively with those that have developed minds, telempathically, if we can master the trick and the artistry of it."

"Interaction that is inherently dangerous," Denise put in.

"Apparently . . . but not so dangerous as to make them unwilling to try."

"Dangerous even for them, as well as for primitive species like ours, in which natural selection hasn't favored the refinement of senses based on Coincidence effects, except perhaps in a few exceptional individuals: seers and religious mystics . . . and occasional identical twins."

"So it seems," Zeph conceded, "although, with regard to seers and religious mystics, charlatans probably outnumber a few authentic examples."

"As with mental reincarnations," Denise added, only partly in earnest. "A few of the people who become convinced that they have lived before might be experiencing genuine transtemporal Coincidence effects rather than simply being deluded or dishonest."

"As the man who has communed with the Dancing Rats and the third-generation Ants, I can hardly deny the possibility of transtemporal communication between humans, especially ancestors and descendants," Zeph agreed.

"But if even a few of those phenomena have an actual neurochemical basis," Denise continued, "the question arises as to why natural selection hasn't favored the refinement of the latent senses in question."

"It surely will, in time," Zeph countered. "We know that it will refine senses of that general kind in all of the future sentient species that come after us in Earth's biosphere, just as it has evidently refined them in the Saturnian ring intelligences. Humans are just too early in the evolutionary process, too primitive for individuals gifted with elementary telempathy to obtain any reproductive advantage from it. History suggests, in fact, that the opposite is true—that people gifted with such embryonic abilities are at a reproductive disadvantage, because they're seen as different and not readily selected as mates."

"Or self-deselected," said Denise, "like Teresa of Avila—one of a whole series of mystics who have embraced and propagandized celibacy as an instrument of cultivating their gift: an essential feature of the Way of Perfection, in her philosophy."

"That too," Zeph conceded. "The human version of original sin, if you want to call it that, seems to be oddly opposed to the cultivation of Coincidence sensory perception, helping to curse the entire human race with a kind of Coincidence blindness. The Dancing Rats had sexual reproduction, as did the Inverts and the plant intelligences . . . but they surely didn't have similar emotional associations . . ." He paused to weigh the implications of that hypothesis.

"Perhaps they were more utopian," Denise suggested. "Better equipped by nature for harmonious social relationships . . . even better equipped than spacers like the captain . . . but not you and Mireille, apparently."

"Very amusing," said Zeph, dryly. "But if the point you're making is serious, then perhaps human . . . animal urges . . . did have an effect, at least in prehistory, opposing the human brain's evolution of Coincidence sensitivities. And perhaps Dancing Rat and future Invert brains *will* differ in that regard . . . just as sexuality in contemporary rats and contemporary ants doesn't have all the complex emotional lumber that human sexuality carries with it. Perhaps the factors that led to the negative selection of sensibilities of that sort are dirty monkey prerogatives. Are you going to suggest to me that an argument of that sort explains my juvenile hang-ups, and that now that I seem to have found my Eve—or my Jezebel—I've wrecked my chances of further advancement on the Way of Perfection?"

"No, I'm not; and in any case, there are more serious issues at stake than original sin even in religious minds, in spite of the preoccupation of the Judeo-Christian tradition with the mythology of *Genesis.*"

"What issues?"

"Bliss, in the term recognized by that tradition—or nirvana: the Buddhist concept of a state of being devoid of suffering, desire or a sense of self . . . the supposed end-point of the cycle of death and rebirth."

"I'm familiar with the notion—but I don't see its relevance."

"Doesn't it seem to you to be closely akin to the kind of monotonous state of being that precedes Creation in Marie's model? Her Christian thought, at least in its mystical variants, accommodates the idea of eternal bliss, or Heaven . . . a state of being that represents the ultimate happiness or joy, which Dante, Milton and countless others have always had difficulty representing in imagistic terms, even with the aid of such notions as choirs of angels incessantly in harmony?"

"Perhaps," Zeph conceded. "What you're implying, then, is that my glimpses of the nature of the Bells and their society, and the sense I get of the fundamental goodness and benevolence of the Comic Mind to which they're Coincidentally linked are akin to mystical glimpse of a paradisal afterlife . . . except that it's not so much post-Creation as pre-Creation . . . which would be the same thing in the philosophy of Eternal Cyclicity?"

"That's right."

"So what?"

"So it seems to me that we might be looking at the danger posed to us by closer contact with the Bells from the wrong angle. When we think of dangers we automatically think of monsters: the threat of pain and harm; the essential features of divine wrath and Hell . . . but what if the danger that you and the Bells sense in your—our—further contact with them isn't divine wrath or Hell at all, but divine grace or Heaven . . . the reversion of our minds to a state of bliss, or nirvana . . . of pre-Creative monotony. Our existence—and, I presume, theirs—is essentially antithetical to that, a product, ultimately, of the disruption of monotony that permits, occasionally, the construction of a different sort of harmony—but a fragile, evanescent sort, perpetually in danger of decaying back into oblivion. Perhaps your prevalent sensation that the Bells, like the future generations of life on Earth, are good, benevolent and kind—and the similar impression gained by religious mystics who think that they've had visions of the divine—actually relates to the inherent tendency of everything created to revert to a more primitive state of monotonous un-creation . . . a reversion to which evolved mentality is necessarily opposed."

"I don't know," said Zeph, dubiously. "It seems suspiciously paradoxical to me."

"As seemingly paradoxical as the existence and evolution of life in a fundamentally entropic universe," Denise suggested. "But it's worth consideration, isn't it? Put crudely, isn't it possible that what the Bells might be afraid of, in enabling you to obtain more intimate contact with them and thus with the Cosmic Mind, is killing you with kindness? Cold, slow-moving, highly evolved creatures like them can cope with the contact permitted by Coincidence sensibility, and exploit it in the process of generating their own complex, quasi-orchestral harmony—but they might suspect that hot, fast-moving, primitive creatures like us might not be able to cope. And human history, it seems to me, is on their side. History suggests to me, quite strongly, that in terms of the crude kinds of harmony that humans can sometimes achieve, the Devil has all the best tunes . . . that our brains, as they develop, build barriers against potential Coincidence effects because natural selection in humans favors the satanic aspects of our behavior: material envy, sexual jealousy and angry violence . . . even to the point of self-destruction."

"But it wasn't us who destroyed the world, Denise; it was a natural disaster, a fracturing of the Earth's crust, like those precipitating previous extinction events. Our great triumph as a species was insulating ourselves—a few of us, at least—from the fatal effects of the latest global catastrophe."

"We were already in the process of devastating our environment before nature administered the *coup-de-grace*. But that's a secondary issue; the point I'm trying to make is that your supposed perception of the fundamental harmony and benevolence of Creation might not be what you think. Marie's primitive religious belief wants the universe and the fate of virtuous human souls, ultimately, to be Heavenly, eternally blissful, and essentially monotonous—but the possibility that the deployment of Coincidence sensibility might provide a short cut to that state of being seems to me to be a dire threat, not a seductive promise. Evidently, those species that have developed more powerful Coincidence sensibilities must have developed ways to avoid their inherent dangers and to exploit them constructively . . . but just because the Bells and the seventh generation intelligences on future Earth can do that, it doesn't mean that we can. We're not equipped, Zeph—not naturally equipped for Coincidental contact with other species more advanced than ours, and with the collective mentality of the universe as a whole."

"Clearly," Zeph retorted, "that's not true. You and I have already done it, and we can't be unique. Other people have done it in the past and far more will learn to do it in future, with the aid of Coincidence technology."

"But will they survive the consequences of the contact? Will *you*, Zeph?"

"Not only have I survived all my alien contacts thus far, Nise," Zeph told her, "but I'm a much better person for it—better than I was ten days ago, let alone ten years. And those species that will exist and thrive in the future, at least some of which are closely related to us biologically, will surely be better than us: more rational, and happier, more harmonious and more loving. It's the way life eventually goes, Nise. It's evidently a difficult and precarious path to tread, but it's the progressive one. You're an evolutionary biologist, essentially backward-looking, but the fact that the natural selection of the human brain has opposed the development of Coincidence sensibilities in the past is only a reflection of past circumstances; things change, and you know full well that genes disadvantageous in some conditions can and do become advantageous in others. The tendency of conscious effort has never been capitulation with the dictates of our genes but the determination to control the circumstances that produced those dictates . . . and that must be true on a universal scale. All evolution of thought leads to greater control and greater freedom from the tyranny of natural selection. It isn't easy, and it certainly isn't free of hazards, but it is the way to go. Perhaps you're right that I'm not well equipped, physically or psychologically, for close contact with the Bells and their perception of further fragments and aspects of the collective mentality of the universe . . . but it's a risk I need to take."

"But as my brother's keeper—which I've always tried to be, albeit very incompetently—perhaps it's a risk that I ought to dissuade you from taking."

"You can't. I know that you mean well, Nise, but I have to disagree . . . even though I have to confess that, insofar as I'm my sister's keeper, I'd rather you didn't follow my example, at least for the time being. Perhaps that makes me a hypocrite, but given that I can hardly deny that the dangers mentioned by the Bells are real, I'd rather you didn't have to face them until you and they can be better prepared. And if it does turn out that I become a victim of contagious bliss, blighted by nirvanic catatonia, the captain will need your help to keep Minerva going as a viable microsociety."

"That's not what I volunteered for, Zeph . . . and you know full well that I'm not equipped for any such role. I've already had my revelation—or shared yours—and perhaps that ought to be enough. I don't want to go to Heaven, before or after I die, any more than I want to end up in Hell. And I truly hope that everything I've just suggested to you is the product of my own unaided imagination, because I'd far rather it was that than a subtle angelic whisper. But either way, you're really not leaving me any choice. If you insist on going forward, you're certainly not going to leave me behind."

"You need to think carefully about that," murmured Zeph. "You do realize, of course, that this conversation can't be kept secret? Others might already be listening in, but even if they aren't, they'll play back the recording . . . and eventually, it will even reach poor Marie. You realize that there's abundant scope for dissent therein, don't you? There are already people on Earth who think I'm the Antichrist, in spite of all Marie's propaganda . . . and that you're already cast in some quarters as another of the Devil's minions. The thesis you've just offered is bound to seem satanic to minds that way inclined."

"The thought had occurred to me," Denise confessed. "The Scarlet Woman of the Apocalypse isn't a role I'll be able to carry off convincingly, though; my credentials as a Babylonian whore are sadly lacking, I fear, even though I lost my virginity before you became an Olympian—but I still think that the wise thing for us to do might be to tell Helen and her machine to go to Hell."

Without even a dutiful pause, Zeph said: "We really can't do that, Nise. I'm committed, completely . . . and in spite of your virtuous hesitations and room for negotiation as to precisely what role you ought to play, so are you."

"I was afraid that you were going to say that," said Denise. "Helen, of course, will tell *me* to go to Hell, probably not politely. The captain will frown and eventually wash his hands of the responsibility in spite of his posturing. Mireille . . . well, I really have no idea what Mireille will say to you, although I'm pretty sure that she's already glimpsed a similar possibility to the one I've just sketched. But I have to insist on the proviso; if, like the stubborn fool you've always been, you won't take my advice, then I'll go with you. If you're going to die of a surfeit of divine joy—which, I agree, is probably the not the worst way to go—then I'm going with you. You owe me that, don't you think?"

"I'm rather inclined to the view that what I actually owe you is to forbid you to do it . . . if I could."

"But you can't. You might think that the days when I could bully or manipulate you into doing what I wanted ended when I was eleven, but they didn't. I've let you off on a few things, and forgiven you for a couple of others, but on this occasion, I'm putting my foot down. The hell with utopian mores—this is between you, me and Coincidence."

"And Harmony," Zeph said. "Don't forget Harmony."

XI

By virtue of an irony of fate, Denise's principal problem, over the Earthdays that followed, was monotony. Because she had not gone through the intensive training program that had been compulsory for the others before joining a spaceship crew, she was unable to carry out many of the obligatory duties routinely attributed to crew members. In truth, few of those duties were strictly necessary; the ship's AIs could operate automatically with the entire crew in hibernation, as the AIs aboard Cronos had demonstrated, but human hands and minds could not be left out of the equation indefinitely, and had a considerable contribution to make to some aspects of the functioning of the ship's systems. Many of those contributions were specific to particular crew members—Birstan, Mellita and the captain had the most demanding physical duties, and Zeph's possession of artificial neural connections made him uniquely valuable too—but the others were not short of demanding work. Information collated by the ship's sensors, whether by direct observation or transmission from Earth, required organization and analysis for which human brains needed to operate in association with AIs, and the organization of the psychological wellbeing of the crew was mostly labor to which the AI contribution was minimal.

Denise found, inevitably, that the only constructive duties to which she could be assigned in the first instance were those involving the routine reception, collation and analysis of information transmitted from Earth. Most of her time when not "on watch" had to be spent in VR, going through a simulation of the training programs that she would have undertaken on Earth had she been recruited to the program in the normal way. Nobody accused her in the meantime of not pulling her weight, but she couldn't help imagining that most of her colleagues must have thought it.

She would have liked to take advantage of her free time by talking to Zeph, but he was too much in demand, and when he managed to escape from interrogation by Helen, the captain or Gabrielle, his first priority was renegotiating his restored relationship with Mireille. Denise couldn't help but feel rudely excluded from his company, and resentful that her own opinions weren't being given the weight to which she thought they were entitled, by Helen, Alessandro, Victor, and even by the captain.

In the meantime, the countdown progressed to the next phase in the program, planned with what seemed to her to be a minimum of involvement on her part. She reacted to the situation in much the same way that she would have reacted on Earth; since study was essential in order to catch up with the training she had missed, she devoted herself to it with a concentration bordering on the obsessive, reacting to her apparent sidelining by isolating herself to an even greater degree from her colleagues, including Zeph. Gabrielle and Mellita made continual efforts to involve her in various collective endeavors, but she maintained a polite wariness, especially with Gabrielle, who had the primary responsibility for guiding her integration into the crew.

"I'm not doing very well in the matter of integration, am I?" she said, sarcastically, when the psychologist visited her during one of her turns on watch in the control room during which the information flow from Fairbanks was desultory.

"Do you mean that you're dissatisfied with your own progress?" Gabrielle asked her, answering the question with a question, as she had an ingrained habit of doing.

"Of course," Denise countered, more as a ploy than a confession. "Do you think I'm being stubborn in my perversity, refusing to do what's expected of me simply because it's expected of me?"

"I don't think so," the psychologist replied, "and I don't think you should beat yourself up because you're having difficulties.

Do you feel that some of your fellow crew members are hostile or disapproving?"

"Hostile, only two—disapproving, all of them, although none of them is likely to say so, especially you."

"Which two?" Gabrielle asked, ignoring the provocation.

"Helen, obviously, ever since I came out against her experimental program. She'd tried very hard to get me on her side, and she blames me for not falling prey to her seductive technique. And Zeph, since I tried to bully him into giving up on Helen's experimental program, and then tried to insist that he couldn't do the next run without my tagging along."

"Only those two?" Gabrielle prompted. "No other perceived hostilities?"

"From Mireille, you mean? No—not at all. She can't say so, of course, to Zeph or anyone else, but she approves of what I tried to do, and she's grateful to me for facilitating her further relationship with Zeph instead of making him feel embarrassed by it. She and I are getting along very well, albeit at arm's length."

"What about the captain?"

"What about him? It's his duty not to be hostile—quite the opposite, in fact . . . but if you mean have I slept with him yet, no."

"Why not?" Gabrielle enquired, with a hint of amusement in her tone.

"Because I haven't wanted to. My internal technology is doing a first-rate job of protecting me from hormonal surges, so I haven't felt any inconvenient erotic impulses, and the idea of doing it as a matter of duty doesn't appeal at all."

"Why would erotic impulses be inconvenient?" the psychologist asked.

"I have a lot of studying to do in order to catch up with basic training, and other demands on my time—reading and replying to correspondence, filling in your psychological questionnaires, etc. etc. You're familiar with my personal history—haven't I always found physical needs inconvenient, insofar as I've experienced any?"

"The recorded data is hardly sufficient to permit me to form a sound judgment. Only you know how and why your relationships on Earth began, and why they ended."

"That's easy," Denise told her. "They began because the men in question wanted to sleep with me, and I sometimes let them, when it seemed that it wouldn't be too burdensome—and if it became too burdensome, I stopped . . . although as often as not, they were the ones who stopped, when the experience didn't live up to their hopes and expectations. We usually parted on reasonably good terms, though. Imperial College before the Crash went Bang wasn't as utopian as Olympus, but it was staffed by scientists, who wouldn't have been prone to amorous turmoil even if end-of the-world anxieties hadn't favored a wider social context of casual amorality, and who felt obliged to conceal it if they felt themselves sickening. But don't worry; I have no intention of remaining strictly and stubbornly celibate all the way to Uranus. When ennui eventually gets hold of me, I'm bound to respond to—or even initiate—an erotic proposition. Then you'll be able to tick off that item in my client profile."

"That will be a great relief," said Gabrielle, introducing a careful dose of sarcasm into her tone, "to the captain as well as to you and me."

"You're taking it for granted that it will be the captain?"

"Aren't you? As you're fond of pointing out, it's his duty—which does make it yours, in a way."

"You're probably right . . . but given my tendency to perversity, I might pick someone else, just to demonstrate my independence."

"I suppose so. Of course, you might change your mind as a result of the further results of Helen's experiments."

"Might I? What results are you anticipating?"

Gabrielle laughed. "I'm not anticipating anything—I'll wait and see. But that's easy for me. It's not so easy for you. You know, of course, the specific timetable that has been agreed?"

"Obviously, as I'm included in it. Helen is putting Mireille into the machine, flying solo, in seven hours' time. Unless something drastic happens to force a change of plan, Zeph and I will follow, in tandem, twenty-four hours later. But you must already know that, so why ask for confirmation?"

"What do you think will happen to Mireille in the machine?" Gabrielle asked, instead of answering the question—although it was easy enough to deduce that she had wanted to measure and evaluate Denise's attitude to the timetable.

"Nothing, I hope," said Denise. "It seems to me that the best outcome, for her, would be that no communication is established. That doesn't seem unlikely. Mireille probably isn't equipped for it, and the Bells probably have no interest in trying to institute such a communication with a novice at present. They might react to our attempt to open communication, but I hope that they'll prefer to wait—assuming that they can—until Zeph and I are back online and make their own move then."

"Move?" Gabrielle queried.

"Certainly. Having analyzed and assessed what they obtained from Zeph last time, surely they'll have made a plan to obtain more. Just as the Dancing Rats were always glad to be contacted by Zeph, while retaining a profound indifference to his substitutes, I think the Bells will be far more eager to establish communication with him than with Mireille."

"You're assuming that they'll approach the contact with a view to obtaining information rather than communicating it?"

"Of course—but it's a two-way mirror; in trying to form a better idea of Zeph and human nature, they'll make themselves more . . . I don't know how to put it: not visible, obviously. Tangible? Accessible? I don't know. Their brain-analogues, of course, are accustomed to contacts of that sort, with other entities of their own kind, and although the process is clearly not unproblematic, they know how to go about it. Zeph has experience of contacts with beings of his own kind—by which I mean Earthly minds— and even with the Jovian cloud-whales, but he really didn't do very well during the earlier attempts to make contact that were initiated by the Bells. Whether he and they are better prepared this time remains to be seen."

"And where do you fit in?"

"Exactly as I did last time: as a semi-conscious eavesdropper on Zeph's unconscious mind, whose presence probably won't be irrelevant even if his consciousness contrives to eavesdrop itself, or even to open the door to deliberate communication. I might be even more relevant if I can remain fully conscious this time, rather than babbling semi-incoherently in a somniloquistic trance."

"And do you think that if Zeph is in danger—of whatever sort—you might be able to save him?"

"I certainly hope to be able to help him save himself . . . or to drown with him . . . but preferably the former."

"Are you sure?"

"That I prefer the former? Absolutely certain? Heroism trumps suicide in the motivational stakes, don't you think?"

"Certainly. But the situation is more complicated than a simple pair of alternatives. Sacrifice and suicide aren't the same thing."

"I suppose not—but I'm not thinking of what I'm doing as sacrifice, any more than I'm thinking of it as suicide. I want to be with Zeph because it's where I belong, and because I think that he has a better chance of coming through unharmed if I'm there. He knows I'm right, although he feels obliged to oppose my participation because he thinks he ought to protect me from any danger that might materialize. But the objective is to live and learn, not to die or have our brains scrambled. Or are you the kind of psychologist who always assumes that people mean the opposite of what they say and that everyone has an unconscious death wish?"

"I'm not familiar with any psychologists of that sort, and I'm certainly not one of them myself."

Slightly surprised that the psychologist had actually answered a question straightforwardly rather than by retaliating with a counter-move, Denise was quick to seize an apparent advantage by saying: "Eros and Thanatos are dead and buried in contemporary psychology, then? We've progressed so far beyond the pleasure principle that the death wish is now a matter of intellectual paleontology?"

"Do you disagree that that would constitute progress?" Gabrielle countered, reverting to type.

"Personally, no—but I knew some people back on Earth who would probably have argued that no one would ever volunteer for a space program if they didn't have an unconscious death wish."

"But you said yourself that heroism trumps suicide in the motivational stakes."

"And you said that sacrifice and suicide aren't the same thing. I'd wager that Marie MacLaughlin has met plenty of people who would credit all martyrs with a death wish, although she wouldn't agree with them herself."

"Have you exchanged further communications with her?"

"Yes—a new sally came through a couple of hours ago, but I haven't opened it yet. It's rather long, although by no means as massive as her interactive stroll through the parklands of virtual London—probably a conscientious rebuttal of my underhanded attack on the notion of Heaven and a strident denial that mystical bliss can be equated with pre-Creative monotony . . . but she'll forgive me for my blasphemy; it's her job. Have you tested the feeling among the crew with regard to that thesis?"

"I haven't taken a census, but the impression I get is the expectable one: that they think it's an interesting thesis, but that they're reserving judgment."

"Very diplomatic . . . and expectable, as you say. What a polite crowd you are."

"We," said Gabrielle, mildly.

"Pardon?"

"You said *you*, although you meant *we*. We are a polite crowd, as you say. You're not alone in wanting to preserve a little elbow room in our midst. We all do . . . that's part and parcel of being a successful polite crowd."

"That sounds suspiciously like counting successes before they're hatched."

"I don't think so," the psychologist said, brightly. "The mission has had a couple of hitches, but on the whole, I think we've coped with them well, as a team."

"But we're still in difficulties. Whether tomorrow's experiment is a success or not, Helen's series has a way to go, and she'll want to keep plugging on until it produces the results she wants. If it doesn't, she's bound to get fractious."

"Of course. But we'll all plug on, as you put it. That's the mission, which we're handling very well, just as the people on Earth are handling their mission very well, in spite of difficulties far graver than ours. Helen will carry on too, keeping any disappointments she might suffer under control. There might be disagreements as to the precise design of her program and its pace, as it develops further, but that kind of debate is healthy. Everything so far suggests that further successes are possible, albeit difficult of practical achievement. Walter Halleck and his new associates will follow a parallel program on Earth. The Age of Coincidence has arrived there, and there's no turning the clock back. After a momentary hesitation, the Cabal now seem to be fully behind him."

"He certainly seems to think so," Denise agreed. "His recent letters to Zeph seem to be mostly triumphant crowing. Like Helen, he believes that his machines are capable of creating super-humans who will be able to draw enlightenment from a universal fount of knowledge. According to his most recent slogan, the human species has to evolve or die—but he's a mathematician, not an evolutionary biologist, so he finds it easy to ignore the fact that the general rule, thus far without exception in our family tree, has always been evolve *and* die . . ."

"To make way for more competent species," Gabrielle suggested.

"Perhaps . . . but just because we all think we're on the Way to Perfection, it doesn't mean that any of us will ever get there; all we can be sure of is that the vast majority will fall by the wayside and perish. The gospel according to Physics says that in the long run, entropy and monotony are bound to win. In the meantime, even the most beautiful harmony will eventually decay, and far more false notes will be struck than true ones."

"But all that can't detract from the esthetic splendor and beauty of the symphony, while it lasts," Gabrielle insisted. "Entropy can destroy everything, ultimately and many attempts at creation will fail—but the heat death of the universe can't prevent all the things that have been created in the interim from having existed, and all the failed endeavors don't detract from the glories of Creation."

"Nicely argued," Denise conceded, in a lukewarm tone, "but I fear that you're as unlikely to convert me to optimism as Marie is to convert me to theism."

"Perhaps you shouldn't count your failures before they're hatched, Denise," the psychologist suggested, with consummate politeness. "Who can tell what the future might bring?"

Denise suspected that her interlocutor knew perfectly well that she was quoting her mother, and that she had contrived the coincidence deliberately. She didn't bother to object that she would regard her non-conversion to optimism as a success rather than a failure, because it was all too obvious that the argument could simply be flipped.

Another batch of zipped communications came through, and Denise returned her attention to her screen in order to save them, unzip them and sort them before redirecting them internally to different destinations. None was an order or an urgent communiqué requiring consultation with the captain, but he materialized at her elbow anyway, as Gabrielle slipped away with polite discretion.

"All quiet on the Earthward front, Captain," she said. "Weather bloody, but humankind tucked up safely, for now. Everything on board going like clockwork, including Gabrielle's motivational pep talks."

"Good to know," said the captain. "I hope you don't feel that Gabrielle is harassing you. She seems to be taking the compilation of her official report on you very seriously, even though its conclusion is foregone."

"She's being professional and conscientious," Denise said, feeling slightly guilty about her own mutedly expressed hostility. "Surely you'd expect nothing less?"

"Indeed."

"And she isn't harassing me; our conversations are proving to be very educational. I didn't know that the idea of the death wish had fulfilled itself by dying in the realm of theoretical psychology—did you?"

"It isn't something I'd ever thought about," said the captain.

"No? Well, as a military man and a spacer, you wouldn't, lest you begin suspecting that you might have a death wish yourself."

"Do I detect a hint of aggression in that remark, Denise?"

"Of course not—I was just thinking aloud."

"Oh, don't be embarrassed about it. Gabrielle would probably think that it's a healthy sign. But then, she feels obliged to interpret almost everything as a healthy sign."

"Obliged as a professional psychologist, or merely as a compulsive optimist?"

"Both. Should I assume that you regret the death of the death wish in psychological theory? That you feel a certain compassion for it?"

"Oh, absolutely," said Denise, playing along with the joke. "As I was just explaining to Gabrielle, as an evolutionary biologist I'm well aware that billions of ignominious deaths are a necessary consequence of the progressive evolution of life on Earth, including the eventual death of our entire species. How will the Dancing Rats ever be able to dance, if they don't have our graves to dance on? Of course we have a death wish, individually and collectively—and so we should. If psychologists have given up looking for it, in spite of the evident fact that we all succeed in dying, it hardly does credit to their science."

"Perhaps they've just abandoned the terminology while retaining and refining the fundamental idea," the captain suggested. "As a mere military man and spacer, I wouldn't know."

"False modesty doesn't suit you, Captain. Good leadership requires a certain swashbuckling arrogance, don't you think?"

"No, thank God. Most of all, it requires tact . . . which can sometimes be mistaken for false modesty, especially by observers who are addicted to false modesty themselves."

"Is that an accusation?"

"Merely a general observation. I have too much respect for you to think that your modesty is false merely because it's a trifle exaggerated. Your brother might have set you a bad example in that regard, although it's a very slight failing, if it is one."

"Zeph has always been very slight in his failings—and very good at setting bad examples."

"Isn't that a trifle unkind?"

"No, but it wouldn't matter if it were. I'm his sister, so I have a license for it. I'm careful in using it nowadays, though, as befits a good shipmate."

"I'm glad. He needs all the moral support he can get at the moment."

"Are you accusing me of letting him down?"

"Again, no, merely making an innocuous observation."

"Well, I'm sure that Mireille is doing her best to provide him with moral support, as he is for her. They're warming up for her attempt to contact the Bells by ringing a few changes of their own. There are some kinds of morale-boosting for which a sister is inadequate . . . or at least inappropriate. Fortunately, we have a full team ready to step in to keep his spirits up."

"And yours, Denise. You have a full team on hand too, if there's anything you need."

""I know—but the others are all respectful of your *droit de seigneur*, so there's been no rush to volunteer. Fortunately, my morale doesn't need boosting, so there's no need for you to worry about it . . . and no need for you to supervise me while I'm on watch, if that's what you're doing. It's not as if doing sentry duty on the com stream is a complicated job. The poor folk at Fairbanks who have to decide which abuse to censor and which to forward to us for a laugh must have a much harder job, although I'd quite like to see a little lunatic raving occasionally, to break the monotony."

"I think you might be overestimating the ingenuity and persistence of the Earthbound opponents of Minerva's mission. They'll be waiting as avidly as anyone else for your next report, and hoarding their wrath until it's incited. I suspect that Walter Halleck's hate mail has dwindled away too. Not that we care what crazy Earthers think, do we?"

"There's the arrogance I was looking for, *mon capitaine*. No, the only opinion that counts is that of the Master of our Mini-Universe, and we all have faith in him—except Helen, alas."

"She's coming round, gradually," the captain assured her, "now that we've achieved a fundamental philosophical harmony."

"Yes, but is the sex any better?" Denise bit her lip as soon as she had fired off the quip, but the captain only laughed.

"I hope so," he said, "but hers isn't the only mediocre report I've had recently, so I must be losing my touch. Either I'm getting old or familiarity is beginning to breed contempt, with so many people aboard who've served with me before. Or perhaps your disdain is contagious."

"I don't think so. Half the female crew members seem to pity my abstinence, and the other half seem to resent it, as if it were an implied criticism. Even Helen doesn't approve, but that might just be a reflection of her general disapproval of me, the human species and everything that isn't mathematics."

"She'll forgive you instantly if you and Zeph give her some data to get her mathematical teeth into in her encephalograph traces when she hooks you up to her machine again. She's half-forgiven you simply because you're willing to try . . . and she's not immune to the anxiety that the machine might do some damage, or permit some damage to be done. Unfortunately, three years of working under stress while you were asleep seem to have left me with little to offer her in the way of morale-boosting, and it seems that Alessandro has flattered only to deceive in that regard. We all have hints of perversity about us, but some are more difficult to cater to than others . . . and no, that isn't an accusation, just a general observation. What Helen needs—and what you and Zeph need too, is a morale-boosting contact with the Bells . . .

especially with the ones stuck to the outside of the ship, if they're already there. I'd be grateful to you if you could clarify that . . . and if you could be a little more apt in your labeling in future. I've forgiven you Bells, because it was a spur-of-the-moment thing, but this time, you've had time to prepare."

"I have a sneaking suspicion that you could go on," said Denise, "and on . . ."

"Of course—but I mustn't. I don't want to seem to be feeding suggestions to you. I'm not afraid of the conspiracy theorists who might accuse us of rigging the game, but I do want to beware of the possibility of undue influence. You need to go into the session with a clean mind."

"I think you mean an open mind. That I might be able to do. Clean, no, even though I'm notoriously virginal aboard Minerva."

"Poor choice of words—I apologize. I did mean open."

"No, it's my fault—I deliberately misconstrued what you meant by clean . . . my sense of humor getting in the way again. At Imperial that sort of childishness passed for witty banter, a sort of verbal slumming. I need to remember that Zeph and I are the only Brits aboard, and that no one outside the municipal boundaries of Oxbridge—which, with typical geographical perversity, somehow annexed Kensington and Bloomsbury—ever understood academic wit even in Merry England. Not appropriate for our present location, although I manage to suppress the ridiculous giggle every time someone says Uranus. Thank God we're not going via Rhea."

"A rhea is a bird," the captain pointed out, pretending mystification.

"And an ass is a donkey. Let's change the subject."

"Fine, as long as we don't go back to the death wish. Birstan and Victor would like to deploy the scoops while we're still moving relatively slowly in matter-rich space, but I'm hesitant to license it because we don't know what effect it might have on the Ring's pseudo-life forms. If you and Zeph could possibly get a hint of an answer to that dilemma, it would be helpful, especially to Victor. Captain Fulsom is being very cautious aboard Cronos, but even if he decides to give in to temptation, Victor will want his own particle collection and so will Savina. Without prejudice to your open mind, obviously."

"Obviously. Anything else on the wish list . . . apart from the fabled annotated star-map, of course."

"No, let's try to keep it simple to begin with . . . and let's see what they want to tell us, if anything. I'm trying hard not to be too optimistic, but it's difficult."

"I'm trying hard not to be too pessimistic, but it's equally difficult. You and I are not exactly two peas in a psychological pod, Captain."

"That's good. Complementarity is Harmony without monotony. And everything might change in six hours time. Mireille might surprise us all."

Denise, the diehard pessimist, didn't know whether she ought to hope that he might be right or dread the possibility . . . but mostly, she just hoped reflexively that he turned out to be wrong and that Mireille would survive the machine without any tangible effect, in case the alternative spoiled any surprises that she and Zeph might be able to pull out of the magician's hat, if they managed to avoid having their minds blown.

XII

When Denise returned to her cabin she found Mireille there, sitting in her open pod, not looking at the screen or wearing a hood, but not lost in meditation either.

"Zeph isn't with you?" Denise couldn't help observing.

"No," was the flat response—sufficiently flat to trigger a suspicion in Denise's mind that seemed oddly horrible.

"You don't mean that he's cuddling somebody else?"

"No—but if he were, it would be perfectly all right. We're not on Earth, Denise; different rules apply. On Olympus, he probably wouldn't have . . . cuddled anyone else if I hadn't told him to, but he's adapted now. If Savina asked him, he'd oblige . . . as he should."

"Savina?" Denise queried.

"Or anyone else—but she seems to have the possibility on her mind. You know why. Can we talk about something else? Did any news come through while you were on watch?"

"Nothing significant—although I must admit that I was somewhat distracted. Gabrielle decided that I needed a final session on her metaphorical couch and the captain wanted to feed me a few subtle hints before tomorrow."

"They shouldn't do that," Mireille opined. "It's unsporting. But they both had a go at me when I was last on watch; I think they're working in tandem."

"I can understand why the captain might want to prime you, while strenuously denying that he wants to compromise your open mind, but surely Gabrielle has no need to compile a report on you?"

"She has us all under observation—it's her job, until things settle down . . . and some cases require more sustained attention than others, as I'm sure she's told you. I was drafted belatedly too, remember . . . for reasons that she probably finds psychologically fascinating. In her eyes, I must be almost as interesting as you are . . . no offense intended."

Denise laughed. "None taken. I'm surprised that you've been left on your own, though, with only a few hours to go before Helen puts you in her machine."

"I haven't," Mireille said, dryly. "They knew you were coming off watch, and they knew you'd come back here. Effectively, they've left me alone *with you*. Don't ask me why, because your guess is as good as mine—probably better."

Surprised by that judgment, Denise began speculating aloud. "I'd hardly be the number one choice as a potential morale-booster," she observed. "Do you think they might be expecting me to talk you into ducking out?"

"I don't think so," said Mireille. "I can't see any reason why anyone would want me to do that, and I certainly wouldn't have the courage to make an utter fool of myself by backtracking now."

"But you do have reservations? I got the impression when I formulated my thesis about the threat of exposure to divine joy that you'd already thought something similar, and you saw what happened to Zeph on his first trip in Helen's hallucination machine. You know how dangerous it might be."

"Of course—why do you think I volunteered to go first, ahead of Zeph?"

Denise frowned. "But going first isn't going to protect Zeph," she objected. "Even if the machine killed you . . ."

"Don't be ridiculous, Denise. I don't have a death wish, and fond as I am of Zeph, I wouldn't sacrifice my life in response to some pointless quixotic impulse that, as you say, probably wouldn't save his. I've told you before that I'm in this purely for selfish pleasure, but you seem to be insistent on trying to impose some stupid traditional mythology on your speculative account of my psychology."

While speaking, Mireille reached out with her left hand, tacitly asking for help in climbing out of the pod. Automatically, although she could not see the necessity and was surprised by the gesture, Denise gripped the hand and provided the requested support, while saying: "Then I don't follow—why did you volunteer to go first, ahead of him . . . of us."

"Because I want my share of the glory that you and he are hogging. It should have been me the first time, not you. I should have been the one linked to his mind, not you." Although she was now out of the pod and on her feet, Mireille had not let go of Denise's hand, and Denise looked down at the clasped digits for a moment while she thought about what the other had said. Mireille saw the glance, but let a few more seconds go by before detaching her own hand.

"I don't believe you," Denise said, in a slightly belated response to Mireille's claim.

"No?" the Frenchwoman said, casually. "Well, that's your prerogative. Has it occurred to you that the reason we've been left alone isn't so that you can talk to me but so that I can talk to you?"

"No, it hadn't. You're the one who's about to take the immediate risk; I still have twenty-some hours in hand . . . assuming that nothing happens to you that might occasion a delay."

"I'll try to make sure that it doesn't," Mireille said, "but it would be far too tedious if nothing happened. Personally, I'm hoping for a hint of the innate joy of creation, aren't you? In moderation, obviously . . . nothing to excess, as Epicurus prescribed . . . and Socrates, and practically everyone else. But you do have a tendency to pathological self-denial, don't you?" As she made the last remark she reached out with her right hand and touched Denise lightly on the cheek with her fingertips, in what might have been intended as a quasi-maternal or sisterly gesture made to assure her that no offense was intended.

"Do I?" Denise parried, feeling slightly uncomfortable. "It doesn't seem that way to me."

"Obviously not—the first symptom of self-denial is to deny itself. I'm sure that Gabrielle would have told you that, if she wasn't so perennially evasive. I'm also sure she'd tell you that you can have sex with your brother if you want to, because old Earth taboos have no force on Minerva and no one would bat an eyelid—but she's probably waiting for you to confess the desire." Her right hand was dangling by her side again, but the Frenchwoman was still reaching out with her gaze, probing, as if trying to read Denise's mind—but there was no hostility in her expression, merely concern.

"I don't have any such desire," said Denise, keeping her voice scrupulously level, as befitted a crewperson, and suppressing her discomfort.

"No? Well, if you did have a tendency to pathological self-denial, you would think that, wouldn't you, just as you'd probably extrapolate it into a refusal to have sex with anyone at all? But don't mind me—I'm only a chemist, not a psychologist. I'm probably talking nonsense. And Helen's only a mathematician. However well she understands the math of Coincidence theory, she's all at sea when it comes to the psychological implications . . . as we all are, including Gabrielle . . . and Zephaniah, who likes Dancing Rats but still hasn't made much progress understanding his fellow humans. Do you think Walter Halleck is having any better luck on Earth?"

That, at least, was a question to which Denise felt that she could make an innocuous reply. "I doubt it," she said. "I've met him, and he's almost as devoid of empathy as Zeph used to be." She emphasized the final phrase slightly, for rhetorical effect.

"I agree," said Mireille, "I've read his file. But it does mention that he dotes on his daughter. The word *idolizes* is used—just as it was in Marie MacLaughlin's assessment of your attitude to your brother."

"As I told Zeph at the time, that's just her habitual vocabulary," Denise said. "I wouldn't read too much into the word's use with regard to Walter either, no matter who put the note you're citing into whatever file you've consulted. I get the impression from Gabrielle that modern psychology has abandoned all its primitive Freudian nonsense."

"I dare say you're right. I thought the matter worth mentioning, though, if only to make it clear that I wouldn't have any objection, any more than the rest of the crew, if . . . well, it's a dead issue, since you say so. I'm sorry."

"No apology is necessary," Denise said, scrupulously. "This is Minerva; there are no taboo subjects, and by the time we get back from the stars several decades from now, absolutely everything will have been laid on the table and dissected. We'll probably be in our nineties by then and hopefully much wiser, albeit just as vigorous, if the promises of modern medicine can be taken seriously and ennui hasn't provoked us to mass suicide."

"Always provided that contact with the Cosmic Mind and some of the weirder entities of Creation hasn't proved disastrous, one way or another," the Frenchwoman added, in a casual fashion that surely had to be contrived.

"Of course," Denise agreed. "In twenty-four hours, though, we all ought to be in a better position to estimate the likelihood of that. And you can be sure that I won't begrudge you your share of the glory, if that's really what you want."

"What else could I want?"

"An interesting question—but you'll forgive me if I don't rack my brains over it for the time being. I have others on my mind. I really do wish you the best of luck, though, in the pursuit of all your desires." Denise suppressed an impulse to offer a hand to be shaken, suspecting that the other might respond with an accolade.

Mireille only laughed. "That's almost worthy of a Frenchwoman," she said. "We're wasted on these Americans, aren't we? I wish you the best of luck too, Denise, in the pursuit of all your desires. Let's compare notes in twenty-four hours, shall we, and raise a glass—metaphorical, alas—to mutual understanding?"

"Let's," said Denise, and made as if to climb into her pod, intending to put on her VR hood and continue her current training program—but Zeph came in, looked at Mireille and then at her, and said, apologetically: "Sorry to interrupt, Nise, but I need to speak to Mireille."

"That's okay," Denise said. "I'll seal my pod and give you some privacy—or leave, if you'd prefer.

Zeph blushed. "No," he said, "That's not necessary." Even so, he climbed into Mireille's pod, and the Frenchwoman followed him there, immediately blacking out the surface. Evidently, she felt that privacy was desirable, if not strictly necessary.

Denise changed her mind about the VR pod, and left the cabin.

Birstan, Victor, Mellita and Savina were in the common area, sitting cross-legged on the floor in a circle below one of the screens but not paying any attention to it. They were all holding hands, but Birstan and Savina broke apart as they shifted in order to make room for Denise to join the group. She sat down in the vacant place, employing her customary half-lotus rather than the sartorius position that the others were affecting. She had not been aboard long enough to know how conventional that kind of circular formation was, but she kept her hands to herself for the time being, and no one seemed to take offense.

"How's Mireille?" Victor asked. "She seemed a trifle nervous earlier—tetchy, one might almost say."

"So would you be," observed Savina, "if you'd had the guts to take first watch in Arkheimer's machine."

"Which you should have done," Mellita put in, "as a good cosmologist, instead of leaving it to a meteorologist to volunteer."

"Actually," said Denise, "Mireille seems to be fine. Zeph is keeping her company now. She was just regretting that we wouldn't be able to have a drink together when we both get back from the shores of infinity."

"That could be arranged," said Mellita. "It's against regulations, but regulations really are made to be broken occasionally. Few things are easier to synthesize than liquor. The captain has turned a blind eye before, on Olympus Five."

"I remember," said Birstan. "I had a headache for days. I'd lost the knack of holding my drink . . . but Mireille took it in her stride. If I remember correctly, though, Zephaniah didn't indulge."

"He didn't mind indulging back on Earth," Denise recalled, "but according to the captain, I shouldn't be aboard at all, given the alcohol problem of which I was allegedly on the verge, according to my file—so I think I can assume that it won't upset me too much."

She had the satisfaction of seeing one or two of the others react with evident surprise, but perhaps not quite for the reason she had anticipated. "The captain actually said that to you?" Savina said, reaching out insistently with her left hand to take Denise's right. "Not like him at all. He really is losing his touch, and not just in the sack."

"It was a long time ago," Denise said, apologetically, "back on Earth—and it wasn't a reproach. Technically, he wasn't the captain at the time."

"That's even worse," Victor pointed out. "Back on Earth, he shouldn't have been talking about the starship at all. If one of us had let a word slip, we'd have been canned."

"He had to talk about it," Denise said, regretting that she had brought the matter up. "He wanted to make sure that my decision to come to Fairbanks instead of heading for Snowdonia was as fully informed as possible, and Zeph and I had already guessed what it was that he was being recruited for. The captain didn't tell me anything that I didn't need to know, and Helen would have told me a great deal more if the disaster hadn't unfolded before she could brief me herself. She didn't care whether or not I drank—in moderation, I hasten to add—she just wanted me aboard because of my presumed Coincidental association with Zeph. She wanted Mireille for the same reason . . . similar, anyway . . . but you all knew that, didn't you?"

"Not officially," Birstan observed. "You weren't the only one who missed out on a thorough pre-launch briefing, by any means, and Helen was . . . absorbed during the brief interval between take-off and the AIs putting us all to sleep. We're playing catch-up too, and I'm far from certain that we're fully caught up yet. The captain is doing his best, but . . . we get the impression that Helen isn't exactly helping."

"Nice understatement," Savina observed, still holding on to Denise's hand. "Poor Chris had to be awake with her while we were all asleep—it's no wonder he's not quite his old self."

"Mireille says that she was much better during that interval," Mellita said. "It's only since things became complicated again that she's become hardly bearable. Many people . . . like her find considerable numbers of people difficult, while a company of three would have been less stressful."

"Three's a triad, four's a mob, as Gabrielle would say," murmured Savina. "Let's hope she acclimatizes."

"She will," Victor predicted, "once she's put her machine through its paces and cemented the proof of its efficacy . . . assuming that the trials do have that result."

"I wouldn't be sorry if they don't," Savina said. "Sorry, Denise."

While the xenobiologist added the final phrase, her hand gripped a little harder, but Denise resisted an impulse to pull away—in fact, it occurred to her that perhaps she ought to close the circle by reaching out to grab Birstan's hand . . . which suddenly reminded her of the incident aboard the plane carrying her from the heart of England to Alaska, and she reminded herself privately that she hadn't been disdainful then, and wasn't being disdainful now. Aloud, she said "No apology necessary" to Savina, and added: "I've wished more than once that the dream was just a dream, a spontaneous delusion of my unconscious . . . but I have to trust Zeph's endorsement. I wouldn't blame you if you didn't feel the same."

"The universe would be a less interesting place if it did turn out to be a delusion," Victor said, "but perhaps that wouldn't be a bad thing."

"Galileo has a lot to answer for," Mellita observed, with contrived lightness. "If he hadn't invented that bloody telescope, we might still be snug in our feather beds, perfectly satisfied with Aristotle's lovely crystal spheres."

Nobody bothered to correct her assertion that Galileo had invented the telescope, or her blithe suggestion that the heliocentric theory would never have caught on without it. Instead, Birstan said, pensively: "But even in a hypothetical Aristotelian universe, Dante was able to travel in his dream to the sphere of Saturn, where he found the paradise of the contemplatives, and discussed the terrible decadence of the church with Peter Damian. It was a pleasant vision. His companion, Beatrice, became even lovelier there, and more radiant."

"Just like Denise," Savina put in, again squeezing Denise's hand to assure her that the joke did not contain any hostility.

"And like us," Birstan continued, "Dante went on in his paradisal dream to the sphere of the fixed stars—but not via Uranus, which couldn't exist in his cosmology. Beyond that sphere, he went on to the Primum Mobile, the abode of the angels, and then to the Empyrean, where he was able to confront God, and had a sudden flash of understanding in which everything became clear to him—but which he couldn't express—and his soul became aligned with Divine Love. Not a fate that Denise can envy him, apparently, even though she's about to accompany her brother on a similar dream excursion."

"I doubt that mine can make me as lovely as Dante's Beatrice," Denise said, with a sidewise glance at Savina, "who was, if I remember correctly, much younger than me, at least as Dante remembered having seen her. And I certainly hope that I don't meet the same fate, fusing with the Cosmic Rose while her companion returned to Earth alone to tell his story."

"But that's not why you don't envy her and Dante, if the reportage can be trusted," Birstan said, refusing to accept the evasion.

"The . . . reportage is correct," Denise conceded. "I'm fine with Zeph visiting the sphere of the fixed stars, but I'd rather he didn't go to Heaven, or its secular equivalent, and I certainly don't want to go there myself. I'm an authentic heretic. Aren't you?"

"I'm an engineer," Birstan said. "Obviously, I don't hold with ludicrous images of angels pollinating cosmic roses, and sets of three circles that are both different and the same. So yes, I certainly hope that your Divine Comedy has a better punchline than Dante's."

"Our," Mellita put in.

"Pardon?" said Birstan.

"You said *your* when you meant *our*," Mellita said. "We're all aboard the same dream-ship. Zephaniah might be piloting it and Denise keeping the log, but we're all passing through the rings. And correct me if I'm wrong, but didn't Dante simply title his work the *Commedia*. The *divina* was added later by a commentator."

"I believe you're correct," said Birstan. "My apologies, Denise: I hope *our* Comedy has a better punchline. And apologies to you too, Mellita. We are, indeed, all in the same play, even if some of us are only spear-carriers. Let's not forget our duty to pedantry."

"Amen," said Victor. "The trouble is that, even though Galileo did invent a telescope—or, at least, was the first to apply one to the study of the Heavens—thus transforming our understating of the universe and paving the way to real space travel, we're all still haunted by bloody Dante. Even we—the five of us, supposedly among the finest of scientific minds—still see the world in terms of his symbolism, broadly if not in detail. His model of the physical universe is wrong, but even that's still magnificent, in its way . . . and his symbolic account of the failings of the human soul remains all too plausible. As geniuses go, Dante beats Galileo, Newton, Einstein and Walter Halleck hands down in terms of colorful imagination and narrative verve. With all due respect to Zephaniah and you, Denise . . . and Mireille too . . . I think your chances of finding a better punchline for Birstan are rather slim."

"I agree entirely," said Denise, "but if Marie MacLaughlin's favorite model of Creation is sound, and my quasi-satanic reinterpretation has anything to recommend it, my . . . I mean *our* . . . un-Divine Comedy can't have a punchline at all; its esthetic appeal isn't contained in any tidy conclusion, or any simplistic vision of the Empyrean. Dante's universe was determined by predestination; everything in it is orientated toward its assumed end—but what we now know about evolution suggests that earthly life isn't like that at all, and nor is the role of the human species within the much vaster pattern of existence. And if I do get a chance to see equivalents of the Cosmic Rose and the triple circle of the Cosmic Mind, I'll try to formulate my own sermon, in spite of the risk of ending up in Pandemonium."

"Bravo," said Savina, with yet another pressure of the fingers to defuse any hint of sarcasm. "I wish I could say things like that."

"Whatever happens tomorrow, Sav," Mellita observed, mildly, "you might still get your chance—and if traveling to Uranus inside the body of an angel enables us all to develop our latent Coincidence sensibilities, we might all get a chance to give the Cosmic Mind a little good advice before it loves us to death and the patient AIs bring Minerva home from the stars as a coffin ship. Do you think the dome people will give us a nice funeral?"

"Probably," said Victor. "Then they'll take her out again, leaving Saturn behind on the far side of the sun, and five members of her crew will gather just like us to hold hands defiantly and discuss whether or not they ought to spit in the eye of the Cosmic Mind . . . metaphorically speaking, obviously."

Defiantly? Denise thought. *Are we being defiant? I don't think so—but what are we doing, then?*

Perhaps, she thought, the other four were simply reproducing a pattern that had become conventional on Olympus Five, three of them having been members of that crew—but it was difficult for her to imagine Zeph sitting as she was doing, in the tailor's position, stitching commentaries on Dante or anything similarly fanciful. On the other hand, the limitations of her imagination wasn't a sound argument, and she had been assured that Zeph had adapted and had been integrated into the crew of Olympus. The fact that he had not had sex with Savina didn't necessarily mean that he hadn't held her hand, and felt the pressure of her fingers informing him that her undiplomatic remarks were not intended to be hurtful.

"Mellita is right," she said, aloud. "We are all in this together, because, in the ultimate analysis, we're all just tiny fragments of the Cosmic Mind. We're looking at the situation from our own minuscule viewpoint, as a matter of our endeavor in trying to make contact with that mysterious mind, but we ought not to forget that the perspective could be inverted, and we could envisage what's happening as the consciousness of the Cosmic Mind endeavoring, in its own incompetent fashion, to make contact with us with us, via pseudoangelic messengers."

"*Incompetent?*" echoed Birstan. "You imagine the Cosmic Mind as incompetent?" His tone was not incredulous, merely a trifle provocative.

"Definitely," said Denise. "That's self-evident . . . and perfectly understandable, if we accept the Epicurean model of Creation rather than the alternatives."

"I see what you mean," Mellita was quick to say, enthusiastic to add her support, having felt that her own opinion was being endorsed. "Traditional religion sees its God as pre-existent to Creation, already fully formed and meaningful. Denise's thesis sees the Cosmic Mind as a product of Creation—*the* product of Creation—presently at an early stage of development, a mere fourteen billion years or so after the Big Bang. The future dominant species of Earth's nöosphere will be more in tune with it, which will certainly be an achievement on their part, but it will have moved on by then to a greater maturity. The better connections obtained by the rat-descended sentient species and the ant-descended sentient species will really be an achievement on the part of the great collective of individual minds, seen as a slowly evolving and still juvenile whole."

"So there you are, Denise," said Savina, smiling. "If the baby Cosmic Mind makes contact with you again, don't expect an adult conversation—and look out for tantrums."

Birstan was following a different train of thought. "Perhaps Dante was genuinely inspired in likening the angels of the *primum mobile* to pollinators of a Cosmic Rose," he said, "which is to say, to the bees of a hive making emotional honey with the intellectual pollen they collect, increasing the sweetness of the universe. Not that I'm saying that the analogy of Bells producing Harmony is no good . . . just that there are other possibilities, which needn't be disdained."

"Did Dante's symbolic bees have symbolic stings?" asked Victor.

"In other words," Savina suggested, ignoring Victor's flippant question, "it won't be a matter of Mireille trying to make contact with the ring intelligences when Helen hooks her up to the brain-boosting machine, it'll be a matter of opening her mind to the contact that the ring intelligences, operating as primitive agents of the immature Cosmic Mind, are trying to make with her?"

"That seems to be a distinction without a difference," Birstan riposted.

"Not quite," said Denise, "but very nearly."

"Because the evolving mind of the Universe, forged out of Coincidence effects, has been striving to make such contacts since the beginning of time?" Birstan queried.

"Not *striving*," supplied Savina. "That's teleological thinking. It's surely an innate tendency, not a conscious effort. The universe is still young, the Cosmic Mind still infantile—but we're a tiny educational step on the way to its maturity . . . *we* meaning the entire human race, the five of us, and the blessed prophet Zephaniah—no insult intended. On a smaller scale, the ring intelligences have been making groping attempts to Coincide with us ever since we took off, and they still are, at the present moment, albeit tentatively."

"The fledgling Cosmic Mind must have been initiating such provocations accidentally—*attempts* isn't any less teleological than striving, Savina—since the dawn of human consciousness," Victor mused, "but Coincidence events are only partly distance-independent. Humans have never been as close to any of the more active agents of universal thought before . . . and probably never will be again. Even without the aid of Helen's machine, we'd be more vulnerable now than any human beings have ever been in the past. And whether Dante's bee-like angels had stings or not, we've been warned that there are dangers in the rings as well as sympathetic intelligences. No entity capable of putting ideas in our heads is hostile to us—but that doesn't mean that we can't get stung. Perhaps Dante didn't imagine the blossoming of a Comic Rose because roses were seen in his day as the most beautiful of flowers, but because roses have thorns . . ."

"It's not necessarily the case that humans won't have other opportunities in future," Mellita said. "Minerva and Cronos have long lifetimes ahead of them, even if their crews have to rotate watches. And the Cabal and Walter Halleck now seem to be seeing eye-to-eye about the future of Coincidence technology, so Minerva might not be the last starship, if Fairbanks still has the technological capacity to build another, and Helen's and Halleck's machines might be the precursors of generations of better ones . . ."

"If the gloss we're all putting on our present situation isn't purely a matter of human imagination," Birstan suggested, "perhaps we can enhance the effect . . . if we close this circle." He offered Denise his free hand as he spoke.

Denise didn't take it. "No," she said. "The circle is good, but I don't believe it should be closed. I've been here before, but the accusation of disdain because I didn't close it then was unjust . . . in fact, it was anything but. I don't doubt for a moment that the gloss we're putting on the situation is purely a product of our five imaginations, filtered through our various packages of knowledge and our various personalities; but that doesn't mean that we don't qualify as a whole of sorts, or that the whole in question isn't also an aspect of larger collectives, a molecular aggregate within a ghostly body. We're undoubtedly taking some inspiration from our surroundings, and from one another . . . but that's in the nature of inspiration, and the nature of our kind of Comedy . . ."

Noises up above interrupted her, testifying that Zeph and Mireille had emerged from the cabin where they had been in conference. Although their footfalls were very light, Denise had no difficulty deducing that, while Mireille was heading directly for the cabin that containing Helen Arkheimer's machine, Zeph was coming to the hatchway to the lower deck.

He did not come down the ladder; he merely put his head into the gap and studied the group of five momentarily, gesturing a salute before turning away to follow Mireille. Silent and casual as it was, the gesture broke the mood of the colloquium.

"They're going a little early," observed Savina.

"The machine takes a long time to tune in to the patient's brain waves," Denise said, "so they'd already be running late if it weren't for the fact that Helen has carried out preliminary electroencephalographic investigations of Mireille's brain while we five were all asleep. She also has the data collected during her first experiment to take into account now, but that shouldn't cause much delay. Mireille will have to be a little patient, but not as patient as Zeph had to be while Walter Halleck was tuning him in for Slingshots."

"But Zephaniah's only going to observe, isn't he?" Savina said. "He's not going to be hooked up with her."

"No," Denise confirmed. "That privilege is reserved for me. He'll stay in the operating room to watch, and the captain will doubtless come down from the control room to join him, but there's isn't enough space there for a larger audience. We'll have to watch from here, or from our pods. Not that there'll be a lot to see . . . or hear, unless Mireille suffers a sudden attack of somniloquism. If a contact is established, it will probably put her to sleep, or into a trance state."

"The suggestion that she stay alert, pay attention and talk will have been firmly planted," Birstan observed. "Whether it will be effective is a different matter—but I'm sure that Mireille will do her best."

"I don't think we should retire to our pods," Savina said. "In fact, we might do better to summon Alessandro, Paula and Gabrielle from theirs in order to join us. I don't say that a shrink and an information-collator are necessary, but they'd both have a contribution to make to the gestalt."

"Alessandro has taken over from the captain on watch," said Victor, "and Gabrielle is monitoring the operation from her own station. She'd probably argue that five is already a crowd."

"Not relevant, in the circumstances," Mellita judged, while Birstan reached up to the screen control panel with his free hand and activated its functions. He displayed Helen's operating room, where she was already busy adjusting her apparatus. Mireille was supine, the upper part of her head fitted into something that resembled a complicated VR hood. Helen was wearing a similar headset, which was tuned in to the monitors attached to Mireille's head, in order to display electronic data collected from Mireille's brain on a virtual screen inside the visor.

A few moments later, Paula appeared in the hatchway. Unlike Zeph, she descended the ladder. As expected, Alessandro and Gabrielle had not responded to the invitations sent to them, or bothered to send apologies.

"I didn't know there was a meeting," Paula said, a trifle reproachfully.

"Neither did we," said Birstan, offering her his free hand. After a moment of puzzlement, she took it, and sat down. She looked at Denise, but the latter refused her hand.

"You can operate the screen for us," Denise said. "You're far more expert than I am."

Paul shrugged. "What are we talking about?" she asked.

"The nature of the Cosmic Mind and the inability of Western eschatological thinking to escape the imagery of Dante," said Savina, succinctly. "Don't worry—you'll fit right in. You've probably read the damn thing in the original Italian, as well as the Apocalypse in Hebrew."

"I've only read Dante in translation," Paula said, "and the *Book of Revelation* too . . . although I incline to the opinion that the latter was originally composed in Greek. Why invoke the Apocalypse? Are we expecting a Day of Judgment?"

"We are," said Savina, "although, like Denise, we don't know whether to hope for a Rapture or dread it . . . and we can't remember whether Dante's soul-rose had thorns, or whether his bee-angels had stings. Perhaps you can tell us?"

"I can tell you that you appear to be talking nonsense," said Paula, "or, at the very least, mixing your metaphors and mythologies recklessly, as usual."

"Cross-pollination, in search of a hybrid vigor of ideas," Mellita supplied. "Two minds are better than one, it's said . . . although, if Gabrielle were here she'd probably tell us that five constitute an orgy, and that six has never been reckoned a magic number."

"You're all mad," Paula observed, with a sigh. "If I'd been on Olympus Five, the discussion you're carrying over might have been a lot more orderly . . . assuming that anyone would have bothered to pay any heed to my advice."

"They might have been even more confused," Mellita suggested. "As librarians go, you're not exactly the traditional bespectacled pedant with a bun, always calling for quiet. Thus far, my mind's eye sees you more as a Wagnerian Valkyrie collecting the souls of the intellectual warriors of the past from the battlefield of Ragnarok."

"I'll take that as a compliment," said Paula, "given that the Earth has just gone through the mother of all disasters, and picking up the pieces of its intellectual heritage has become urgent and vital work, enough to occupy a legion of librarians for years. But I can see that Mireille is being snugly hooked up to the machine as we speak, and I'm sure that Denise would rather see herself as a volva than a Valkyrie."

"I have no idea what a volva is," Demise confessed, stressing the first vowel lest it might be confused with a u.

"It's from the same mythology," Paula explained. "A volva is an Old Norse wise woman or seeress. It's a more sedentary profession than valkyrie; Strabo alleges that their duties were said to involve cutting the throat of prisoners of war over cauldrons in order to extract prophecies from the blood-flow, but he's a notorious fantasist, so I shouldn't take any notice of that slander, if I were you."

"I agree," said Birstan. "If you need an imagistic vocabulary to draw on next time you have a vision to interpret, Denise, stick to the Latinate classics. Dante's *Paradiso* will hopefully be apt, but the *Inferno* might be best avoided, for much the same reasons as *Götterdämmerung* and the Apocalypse. Keep thinking honey, not vinegar."

"I doubt that I'll have a choice," Denise said, trying to suppress an incipient intoxication in her mind that was certainly not due to alcohol, and probably not to nectar. "Zeph is the seer, not me; I'm just his amanuensis."

"That's not entirely obvious," commented Victor. "His account and yours agree, apparently, but your narration came first chronologically. He had the big reputation, because of his previous successes with Halleck's prophecy machine, but that doesn't prove that he should have the priority in the new joint declaration."

"Yes, it does," Denise said firmly, still fighting the mysterious intoxication. "I know my place. Not because I'm only his little sister, but because that's the way it was and is. He's the one with the wide open mind, the principal conduit of the Cosmic Mind's substitute for divine joy. Mireille understood that—that's why she's being tuned into the machine now. She doesn't know whether it can contrive a direct link for her, but she thinks that she'll recognize the phenomenon if it can."

"If she thinks that Zephaniah giving her an orgasm or two has provided her with a unique link to the exaltation of the Cosmic Mind, she's a silly girl," opined Paula. "No such effect was noted by the other women with whom he had intercourse aboard Olympus Five, both of whom apparently disagreed with Mireille, rating Birstan and the captain as much better lovers. One has to make allowance for individual tastes, but even so . . ."

"Who told you that?" Birstan objected, sharply. "I wasn't aware that any such rating was going on, let alone that it's become a matter of public record. That's directly contrary to the conventions in force aboard Olympus, and to common sense. Our sexual encounters weren't and aren't competitive."

"Absolutely not," Savina agreed. "I certainly didn't rate my . . . interactions for any kind of league table. Did you, Mel?"

"No," said Mellita. "Your data is imaginary, Paula, and your judgment of Mireille absurd. I've known her for years, and I can testify with certainty that she's not silly. If her connection with Zephaniah has allowed her to perceive something via a sixth sense, I'm ready to accept it as real."

"Remark withdrawn, then," Paula conceded. "I'm the outsider here; I shouldn't try to set myself against the Olympian clique. I see you've let Denise in, though, presumably in Zephaniah's honor."

"We just summoned you to join us, literally," Birstan pointed out. "There's no clique. The Valkyrie comparison was intended as a compliment. If Denise is right and the circle is enabling us to pick up some kind of resonance from alien minds in the proximity, let's all try to cooperate, shall we? You say you've been here before, Denise—what happened?"

"I was on a plane with Zeph, Mireille and the captain. It looked for a moment as if we might not pull through. We all joined hands, except that the captain and I left a gap in the circle. I wasn't aware of blacking out, but we all went into an altered state of consciousness, and seemed to lose some time. It didn't feel as if I were dreaming—just thinking . . . but now I'm pretty sure that it was some kind of Coincidence effect. Helen certainly seemed to think so, when I told her about it . . . just before she crashed the car we were in and the feed to my oxygen mask was ruptured . . . but I think the crash really was a coincidence-with-a-small-c."

Paula fiddled with the screen controls and brought up a set of electroencephalograph traces. "Mireille's," she said. "Looks perfectly normal . . . no, wait, some activity is registering."

"That's because Zeph is speaking to her," Denise said. "Turn up the audio and we'll be able to hear what he's saying."

"He's reciting something," said Birstan. "A poem—*Kubla Khan*, I think. although it sounds peculiar."

"That's not very long," observed Victor. "Unless, of course, he can take over where Coleridge stopped and finish it. I don't suppose he knows anything longer, or more rhythmic, Denise?"

"Not as far as I know," Denise said, "but it's not *Kubla Khan*, its *Cobbler Ken*, which is why it sounds peculiar. It's Zeph's own variation on the theme: 'In Sutton Hoo did Cobbler Ken a shapely pleasure dame decree . . .' I haven't heard it for more than a decade—he was only a kid when he made it up. Don't ask him to explain it . . . he used to have a whole prepared routine for deflecting the question and saving his embarrassment, which only added to the nonsense. It's not a good sign that he's reciting it, though; it was prescribed as a device to help him keep calm when stress threatened to become too much for him. He must be desperately concerned for Mireille."

"You must know something equally rhythmic and far longer, Paula," Mellita suggested. "We can feed your voice through, if it would help—and if Helen will permit it."

"I'm not sure that it would," Denise said. "It's a personal thing . . . but Gabrielle might be a better judge than me."

"It might be better to stick with Zeph's own voice and for him simply to repeat his repertoire," the librarian opined. "It's his choice, though. Look at the alpha on the EEG trace. She's going into a trance. If he's doing it for her benefit, it's working . . . I assume."

"That depends," Mellita suggested. "If she simply falls asleep, without dreaming . . ."

"Oh, she's already dreaming," Paula said. "Look at the traces that the screen's capturing from Helen's hood—and the eye movement that's clearly visible in the visual image behind her lowered eyelids. The question is, will she remember anything when she wakes up? There's no trace of somniloquism thus far . . ."

The librarian spoke too soon. Abruptly, Mireille's eyes opened, and she sat up—or tried to sit up, even though she was strapped to the couch and had little scope for movement. Then she screamed—and Denise felt the scream ripping through her head like a sharp blade, causing her to faint.

*

XIII

Denise rocked backwards, but because of her position she fell slowly, and she felt the blood that had retreated momentarily from her brain flowing back again as the back of her head made contact with the floor with the mildest of bumps. If she lost consciousness, it was only for a second or two, but the interruption of thought was sufficiently disruptive to make her confused as to where she was and what she was doing. It was with some surprise that she felt Savina's fingers clench, as if seeking support from her hand—support that Denise was in no position to lend, in purely mechanical terms.

Sorry, Denise thought, automatically, and let go of Savina's hand, which permitted the detachment. Then she shook her head, trying to clear it of the confusion.

For a moment or two, the confusion resisted—but then it gave way and Denise got a grip on her train of thought again. She became aware that someone was leaning over her, looking down at her with evident concern. She recognized Paula, who had evidently sprung to her feet rather than falling. A medley of voices told her that other people were nearby, and as she blinked, she saw from the corners of her flickering eyes that other people were also on their feet. Savina was still supine, and Birstan too, but the others seemed to have resisted the shock successfully, if they had felt it at all.

Still mysteriously intoxicated, Denise heard herself giggle.

"That's no rose," her lips murmured. "That's a thistle . . ."

Victor, who was bending over Savina, said: "She's okay. She isn't hurt."

"Nor is Birstan," Mellita was quick to supply. "Did we all feel that brain shock?"

"I certainly did," said Victor. "Where the hell did it come from? Mireille?"

Denise, like everyone else, looked at the screen. Even from the awkward angle—she had not yet managed to sit up, although she was propped up on her left elbow—she could see that Mireille, having screamed, had fallen back on the couch, and she could hear Helen Arkheimer saying to the captain and Zeph: "It's all right! It's all right! She's fine! Don't panic!"

In fact, they had not panicked. Neither of them had made a move.

No casualties, then, Denise thought. *But what was it? And where did it come from, if not from Hell?*

She became aware that everyone was looking at her. She was the expert; she was supposed to know . . .

She made an effort to sit up and straighten her back, bracing herself to stand and face the inquisition—but it was Birstan, also sitting up again, who answered the unvoiced question.

He laughed. "Idiots!" he said. "It was us! It was autosuggestion! We hypnotized ourselves with all that rambling talk about stings and thorns."

"And did we hypnotize Mireille too?" asked Victor. "She was the one who screamed."

"That was just the trigger," Paula countered, as if in support of Birstan. "It startled us, and made us imagine the pain."

"That pain," said Mellita, "was *not* imaginary. You felt it too, didn't you, Denise?"

"Yes," Denise confirmed. "The pain was real."

"As real as the phantom pain in an amputated limb," Paula objected.

"But . . ." Mellita began, perhaps about to argue that although an amputated limb might be ghostly, the neural impulse traveling from the stump to the pain receptors in the brain was real enough.

She was, however, interrupted by Savina, who had also sat up straight, and who was lifting her free hand in order to point at

198

the screen. She did not speak with any particular vehemence, but what she said commanded attention nevertheless.

"Look, Denise," she said. Denise realized that the xenobiologist was pointing at the time display in the corner of the screen. It was at least thirty minutes ahead of the time that her memory told her it ought to have been showing.

"That time loss didn't happen when I fainted," Denise said. "That really was momentary. Was it afterwards, while I was still dazed?"

"No," Savina said confidently. "We'd already lost the time before the scream, without even noticing. That's why we felt disorientated . . . and no, Birstan, it wasn't autosuggestion because we'd been talking about drinking."

"But why would a Coincidence effect make us lose the perception of time?" Victor asked. "That doesn't make any sense."

"It wasn't a direct effect," Denise said. "It's probably an aspect of the defense mechanism that our brains have developed in order to insulate them from Coincidence effects. There was an attempt at contact—which really was an *attempt*—to which our brains reacted . . . reflexively, I suppose we'd have to call it. But it was probably a side-effect—the primary target of the attempted communication was surely Mireille . . ."

"Who seems to be merely asleep," Victor observed. "Helen is monitoring her brain via the virtual displays on her visor. Nobody up above is panicking. Whatever happened, it hasn't done her any more harm than it has done us . . . which is, unless my eyes are deceiving me, hardly any . . . almost none."

No one contradicted him, but Denise read uncertainty in more than one gaze as she stood up straight and scanned the people surrounding her attentively. *But how did we lose the time?* she asked herself. *It wasn't just me; it was all of us. It's not as if we went into a coma—we just* jumped. *Time itself jumped, at least within the ship . . . or within the entity that is riding on the hull.*

"We don't know that for sure," Paula said. "We won't know how Mireille is until she wakes up."

"Are we quite sure that it hasn't done *us* any harm?" Mellita asked. "I don't believe that I lost consciousness, even for a second, but some time has definitely gone missing, and as Savina says, I was weirdly disorientated for a least a few minutes *before* the scream and the stab of pain. We can only have perceived a fraction of whatever happened to us while time was . . . compressed. The pain was momentary but we don't have the slightest idea what other effects there might have been . . ."

"If I dreamed in mysterious interstices in the flow of my conscious thought," said Birstan, "the memory of the dream has been erased. Has anyone fared any better?" He was looking at Denise, although the question had been addressed generally.

"Not me," said Denise. "But Mireille might have done . . . and Helen's fancy brain-scanners will have recorded all the associated electrical activity. Neither we nor the AIs have yet been able to make any sense of the traces we have in store . . . but as the sample size grows, patterns might become clear. And tomorrow, when I'm hooked up in parallel with Zeph, there's a good chance that we'll be able to repeat the party trick."

"A *good* chance?" Victor repeated, tacitly challenging her casual implication that the likelihood might be a good thing.

"A high probability," Denise corrected herself.

"A greater danger," Savina suggested.

"Perhaps," said Denise. "But if Mireille really is uninjured, I'm already committed. We all are."

"Mireille's waking up," Paula observed. "That's quick—you were out for a long time after your epoch-making speech, and the AIs kept Zeph in a light coma for days, with the captain's approval."

"Helen must be satisfied with the EEG recordings," said Victor. "Hush—Zephaniah's about to question her."

They could see on the screen that Zephaniah had, indeed, stepped forward as soon as Helen and the captain had removed the hood from Mireille's head and laid it gently on the pillow of the pod. Helen was already removing the supplementary electrodes.

"How do you feel?" Zephaniah asked.

"Fine," said Mireillle. "Better than fine, in fact. I felt a little dazed while the electrodes were being positioned, and it continued for a while once everything was in position and the hood was lowered, but that's surely perfectly normal. Before the machine was switched on I felt quite calm . . . perhaps a little too tranquil. I tried to stay awake, but it wasn't working—I could feel myself drifting into a narcoleptic trance almost immediately. In all honesty, Zeph, I don't think the garbled *Kubla Khan* was helping. Nonsense verse, imperfect scansion, limited rhymes. I lost track of time . . . of everything. I didn't see anything inside the hood, and once your voice had faded away, I didn't hear anything either. I was just . . . well, lost in space . . . everywhere and nowhere . . . but if that's what the Cosmic Mind feels like, continuous Creation must be a very tedious business . . . unless, I suppose, it was taking a nap, or resting on the Sabbath. Damn! I was sure *something* would happen."

"It did," said Zephaniah. "You tried to sit up, and you screamed."

"No I didn't." Mireille seemed quite positive.

"Yes you did," Zephaniah told her. "We can play it back to you, if you like."

"Go on."

Zephaniah half-turned, and the captain operated the control panel beneath the cabin's screen.

The repetition of the scream did not produce the slightest pain in Denise's head, even with the aid of memory. It was just a scream, seemingly with more surprise in it than fear or horror.

"That's not me," Mireille said, without hesitation. "I don't scream like that. I'm French."

"It was made by your vocal cords," Zephaniah told her, "but it's possible that your voice was just a resonance of a sound originating elsewhere. Did you hear the scream?"

"No."

"Your eardrums and auditory nerves registered it," Helen reported. "Your physical reaction was exactly what would have been expectable if the scream were your own."

"I didn't hear it," Mireille insisted.

"Everybody else did," the captain put in. "Some people down below are reported to have fainted, and all of us—the three of us here, the six down below and presumably Gabrielle in her pod and Alessandro in the control room—felt a stab of pain."

"I didn't feel any pain," Mireille said. "Nothing at all."

Zephaniah could be seen nodding his head, although the significance of the gesture was profoundly unclear. "They pulled out," he said. "As soon as they felt an effect they pulled out. What we experienced was a kind of ripple effect, but they were careful not to hurt Mireille. They really are learning, and doing their best to protect us."

"But the clock jumped," the captain objected. "I didn't lose consciousness, but time actually skipped. If they can do that . . ."

"I don't think it was deliberate," Zeph said "Again, it was a side-effect. It doesn't appear to have done any harm . . . and I think it's happened before, even without the involvement of the Bells . . . you were there, captain."

"But that was just a temporary lapse in attention," the captain objected. "Time didn't actually stop, or skip. That's surely impossible."

"In terms of conscious apprehension, it's clearly not," Helen put in. "The instruments didn't record anything—it was something that happened in our brains . . . if it had only happened to one of us, it wouldn't seem so strange; it's the simultaneity that's amazing . . . but it might not be as rare as might be imagined, if it's usually only a matter of seconds, and often passes unnoticed. It's hardly unimaginable, given what we know about the relativity of space and time, and the fact that Minerva has already traveled fast enough *en route* to Saturn to have suffered a slight relativistic distortion relative to Earth. We'll experience more pronounced effects between here and the stars, won't we, Victor, as we get closer to light speed relative to the sun?"

"Evidently," Victor replied, from the common space, "but that's a known effect, calculable with the aid of elementary math. This . . ."

"Merely serves to remind us that the ring intelligences are odder than we imagined, and that their experience of the world is fundamentally different from ours," Helen said, with her customary conviction. "But our minds are back in ordinary clock time now, and no one—Mireille included—seems to be suffering any residual effect."

"I feel fine," Mireille interjected. "I didn't feel a thing. I didn't even hear myself scream."

"In its way," Helen said, now poring over the machine's instrument panel, although she was still wearing her hood, in which multiple displays of information must have been simultaneously available, "that non-reaction is as significant as the fact that the rest of us did feel it—sharply enough, apparently, to cause four people to lose consciousness momentarily."

Four? thought Denise. *Alessandro or Gabrielle fainted too, then.* She did not bother to wonder which, for the moment.

Alessandro's voice came over the communication link almost immediately. "It wasn't just us, Captain. Captain Fulsom is reporting an incident aboard *Cronos*. No casualties—everyone has recovered completely . . . but they felt the shock of pain . . . all fourteen of them, I think."

"I didn't feel anything," Mireille repeated.

"That's not what the electroencephalographs say, my dear," Helen put in. "Your pain receptors show a spike . . . it's only your consciousness that ignored it. But it wasn't just your pain receptors that reacted—there was also a spike of activity in the nearby parts of the brain that were once labeled pleasure centers, or addiction centers . . . and that took far longer to fade away Do you feel any euphoria?"

"No," Mireille replied, automatically, as she sat up and swung her legs off the couch—but almost immediately, she retracted the denial. "Perhaps a little . . . yes, perhaps more than a little. As I said, I feel fine . . . better than fine. But that's only natural, isn't it, having come through . . . not that I ever expected *not* to come through. It's not relief I'm feeling; it's just . . . lightness. It's nothing like . . ." She broke off without completing the comparison.

"Nothing like the feelings you have when you're in bed with Zephaniah, the captain or me," Helen completed, with her usual tactlessness.

Mireille didn't offer any confirmation or contradiction. All she said was: "I didn't scream. I don't." Her expression betrayed the fact that she was aware that it was a lie, but couldn't understand how she had managed to scream without being aware of it.

"Neither does Zephaniah," Helen noted, although it was not obvious to whom the remark was addressed, or why she had made the observation.

"Ease up, Helen," the captain ordered. "But you're right: the absence of any memory is as significant, in its way, as an actual memory would have been. That's the datum whose significance warrants enquiry. We ought to recognize, however, that it's not so very unusual. People suffering from shock often blot out any sensation of pain and the memory of the perception that triggered the shock. I've seen wounded soldiers react in much the same way as Mireille, remaining quite calm and even reporting a feeling of lightness . . . for a while. Has her production of endorphins showed a similar spike?"

Helen had to check a recording device that did not have a virtual display in her helmet, but she answered the question affirmatively without delay.

"But I haven't been wounded," Mireille said.

"Not physically," the captain told her, "but your body has that capability of reaction, as most human bodies do. It's not particularly extraordinary."

"It's damnably inconvenient," Helen retorted. Almost immediately, however, she added: "But there *was* a contact. The ring intelligences definitely reacted to the operation of the machine. There's no doubt about that."

"Yes, there is," said Zeph. "There was a reaction, but there's nothing to prove that it came wholly, or even partly, from the ring intelligences. We have no idea how many pseudo-living entities there are in the vast plane of the rings. Whatever reacted to the activation of the machine might be no more intelligent than a Jovian cloud-whale, and perhaps quite different. That could be where the danger lies in trying to amplify our response to Coincidence effects while we're in this region. Mentality isn't just the prerogative of creatures participating in our kind of sentience. The ring intelligences with which I've made contact previously participate in the general benevolence of life and pseudo-life, but they might not be alone out there . . . in fact, I know they're not."

"It didn't do me any harm," Mireille insisted. "Helen's right— the failure to register a memory is inconvenient, but there *was* a contact, and it didn't do me any harm. You say that some of the people on the lower deck were knocked unconscious. Have any of them reported any injuries?"

"No, they haven't," the captain told her, "but the fact that they reacted at all is a trifle worrying. They *have* reported hearing the scream and feeling pain . . . and Cronos is already a million miles away, albeit still in close proximity to the ring. Being inside the machine might actually have insulated you from the effects of the reaction to its activation."

"But there's absolutely no reason not to go ahead with to-morrow's trial," Helen was quick to put in. "There's every reason to think that Zephaniah and Denise, operating in tandem, will do at least as well as before, and perhaps much better. This was only a tentative test, remember. Tomorrow's run is the main experiment."

"True," said the captain, "But . . ."

"There are no buts, Captain," Helen insisted. "We could have wished for something better from today's run—I certainly did—but the fact remains that it was a limited success, which offers us every encouragement for tomorrow. Don't you agree, Zephaniah?"

Zephaniah hardly paused before replying: "Yes, I agree—but I shall have to consult Denise. She reacted more strongly than most of those down below, and it might be unwise for her to take part."

Denise immediately stabbed the screen's control panel with an insistent finger.

"I'm fine, Zeph," she said, "and more enthusiastic now to go ahead with the experiment than I was before, in spite of the risk. We need to know the answers to all our questions, and you and I are the ones best qualified to seek them out. It ought to be us and it ought to be soon. Humankind will never forgive us if we hesitate now."

She was aware as she said it how absurdly pompous that last remark was—but she was still suffering from a mild intoxication, even though not a drop of alcohol had passed her lips. Like Mireille, she felt fine—better than fine—and she was suffering from a sudden fit of atypical optimism that contrasted strongly with her mood of only a few hours before. Was that part of the after-effect that they were all denying having experienced?

"Captain?" said Helen Arkheimer pretending to ask for permission dutifully now that she knew that the answer was a *fait accompli*.

"I'll consult with Alessandro," he said, for form's sake, "but I see no reason at present to change the program. Tomorrow's experiment will go ahead on schedule unless something comes up in the interim to dictate otherwise."

Seeing that Mireille was free from the last attachments from the machine and that Zeph was putting a protective arm around her to draw her out of the cabin, Denise hastened up the ladder in order to meet them. She and they went into their own cabin, but no one had time to close the door before Helen Arkheimer slipped through it directly behind them.

"Denise," the mathematician said, "did you get anything? During the contact, said you see or hear anything?"

"That's not the way it works, Helen," said Zeph. "The question is, Nise, do you know anything now that you didn't know before?"

"Not so far as I know," she said, "but if you play the tape of the conversation we were having before the screen, you might be able to pick up some suggestive hints. It was entirely a product of our collective imagination, but we were working together, prompting one another. We might have picked up something without being consciously aware of it. We were definitely a little high, but that could have been the effect of our own adrenalin." A thought struck her, and she continued without a pause: "The fourth person who fainted was Gabrielle, right?"

Zeph looked at Helen, who nodded.

"Who was alone in her capsule?"

"Yes," said Helen

"Was she watching on the screen, as we were?"

"No," said Helen. "She was wearing her VR hood, using a telepresence link to my monitor—but she couldn't have seen anything I didn't, and she doesn't have my expertise in reading the brain monitors. You had the key indicators on your own screen, so she couldn't see very much more than you could."

"I'm going to check on her," Denise said. "Look after Mireille, Zeph."

Only a few strides separated the two cabin doors. Denise knocked, but entered immediately, before Gabrielle had had a chance to say: "Come in."

"I'm all right," Gabrielle said, instead. She was sitting up in her open pod, having removed the headset through which she had been monitoring Helen's machine. "I passed out for a moment, but only for a second or two. I've already reported to Alessandro, who's on duty in the control room, that I'm fine."

"Good," said Denise. "Did you hear the scream?"

"Yes."

"Was it yours?"

Gabrielle frowned. "It was Mireille's," she said.

"It was her voice," Denise agreed, "but she denies that it was her scream. It wasn't mine, and neither Savina nor Mellita laid claim to it. Was it yours?"

"I told you, no. I don't scream."

"Mireille said the same—which is an odd denial to issue, don't you think? But no matter; you felt the pain too?"

"I felt something, reminiscent of a dagger plunging into my brain without bothering to cleave through the skull. You?"

"The same. But it wasn't a dagger, was it?"

Gabrielle thought about that, with the scrupulous seriousness of a conscientious scientist. "It felt more like a sharp instrument than a fang, a sting or a thorn," she said, eventually, "but no, it wasn't the illusion of a knife or scalpel wielded by the hand of an assassin or a surgeon. I didn't get the sense that it was an *implement*; perhaps it was something more akin to a flash of lightning . . . but the memory is already hazy, getting lost even as I try to bring it into focus."

"Did you lose a slice of time?"

Gabrielle glanced at the time display on her screen. "It's later than I thought," she admitted, "but I'm not aware of any breach in the continuity of my memory. If I lost time, it didn't leave an appreciable gap."

"What were you thinking about before Mireille was hooked up to the machine?"

"I can't remember—why do you ask?"

"Try to remember. I ask because you had that hood on and couldn't have overheard what the six of us down below were talking about. If some of the same ideas occurred to you, it might be significant."

"Oh. Well, I remember Zephaniah reciting a poem, which was garbled but recognizable as Coleridge, which made me think of opium. The poem that Zephaniah was parodying was supposed to have been composed in an opium dream, as I remembered it, and I wondered, naturally, whether it was a symptom of something odd happening in Zephaniah's brain. Then I thought about poppies—fields of poppies—and I tried to remember whether opium poppies are red or white . . . and I wondered whether cross-pollination might produce pink poppies, which I couldn't remember ever having seen, and I wondered whether ring pseudo-life includes plant-like organisms that absorb and exploit solar light, even way out here, and whether, if so, they have pollinators, or whether they rely on the tides . . ."

"Tides?" Denise queried.

"Yes. I'm not a cosmologist, obviously, but I remember reading somewhere about there being tides in the atmosphere of Saturn, just as there are in the atmosphere of Jupiter, but far more complicated, and that there are bizarre tides in the rings too, caused by gravitational interactions between Saturn and Titan, and also Rhea, which the Cronos Mission was supposed to investigate. I'm not a xenobiologist, either, but I wondered whether the unusual tidal effects around Saturn were as important to the evolution of pseudo-life in the locale as the interaction of lunar and solar tides are said to have been to the evolution of life on Earth—about which you'd obviously know far more than me. That's all I can remember . . . my mind was just drifting really, outside my specialism. It often does, I fear . . . but that's not unusual for people like us. It's useful, for spacers . . . a crew needs a cross-pollination of interests and ideas, as well as a broad spread of literal seed, if it's to thrive, socially and intellectually. Ask the captain . . . or Zephaniah . . . or any of the others. Sorry—I don't think any of that is likely to answer the question you asked. Or does it?"

"Perhaps. I'll be sure to let you know if I notice anything that seems significant—but I agree with you that something was happening in Zeph's brain that prompted him to recite *Cobbler Ken* . . . almost a reversion to his childhood mentality. As to the rest, check the tape of the conversation down below and make up your own mind. You'll find it interesting anyway . . . and at least it might help convince you that I'm making belated progress integrating with the crew."

"I'll do that," Gabrielle promised. "Perhaps I should have answered the call when I was invited to join in, but I was monitoring Helen monitoring Mireille . . . did I mention that I liked puzzles?"

"Yes," said Denise. "I'll get back to Zeph now, if you don't mind. He and I need to compare more notes before tomorrow."

"Of course," said Gabrielle. "Thanks for dropping by."

Denise returned to her own cabin, which still seemed a trifle crowded, although it only contained its usual residents; Helen was still there, with Zeph and Mireille, all three of them standing in the aisle between the pods.

"Gabrielle's fine," she reported. "Everybody is fine, it seems—suspiciously so, it seems to me. We're all a little intoxicated, and have been for some time. We all felt the spike of pain and reacted to it, but that wasn't the only event occurring in our brains. There was a slight and slow inebriation beforehand, which we didn't even notice—but your sensors registered the neural effects in Mireille's brain, Helen, and mapped them too. Did your machine pick up similar effects in my brain, and Zeph's, during the first tandem experiment?"

Helen hesitated. "It depends what you mean by *similar*," she hedged, pulling a face: a grimace that Denise classified as that of a mathematician confronted by an ugly equation.

"What I mean," said Denise, impatiently, "is: did the impulse that triggered both the pain receptors in Mireille's brain and the pleasure centers have any parallel in the patterns of stimulation in my brain and Zeph's during the first contact? My consciousness has blotted out any memory of pain or pleasure, but your monitors were mapping neural activity in our brains, so you must know whether the same centers were activated in a similar way."

"It isn't that simple," Helen said. "Even pain isn't as easy to define, neurologically, as you might think, although subjective descriptions only identify a few different types, and there are a limited number of neural pathways connecting to various termini within the cerebral cortex. Pleasure is much more complicated, objectively as well as subjectively, and theoreticians are still divided as to whether the relationship between pleasure and pain places them as opposed points of a kind of continuum of affect, or whether there's a definite category distinction. The neurological evidence is ambiguous, deeply confused by the fact that as neural pathways develop in maturing brains, different trajectories are carved out."

"But they aren't really *carved out*, are they?" Zeph put in, even though he had used the same analogy himself.

"Not literally," Helen replied, "but sculpted nevertheless, in a sense. As brains develop, neural pathways die selectively. In humans, unusually if not uniquely, that selective dying continues

210

for more than twenty years after birth, affected in complex ways by experience of the environment. The role played by consciousness in that kind of neuronal sculpture is peripheral, but vital."

"And it affects the development of reactions to pain and pleasure," Denise supplied.

The mathematician still seemed unhappy, as if being forced to think about matters that had little exactitude about them actually caused her a kind of discomfort.

"There isn't sufficient stereotypy in human brains to permit the kind of analysis your earlier question asked me to carry out," she said. "I can't give you a good estimate of the degree of similarity between the reactions of your brain and Mireille's with regard to neuronal stimulations perceived as pleasure, because such perceptions are too idiosyncratic."

"What Helen is saying," Mireille contributed, "put crudely, is that although most people feel pain in response to the same environmental stimuli, and experience it in much the same way, pleasurable responses to environmental stimuli are much more various, and the subjective experience of pleasurable sensations also appears to be more variable . . . sorry, that isn't quite as simple as I was trying to make it."

"The most important point," Zeph interjected, "is surely that the role of learning is markedly different in the two cases. Although a few people can learn to suppress or modify pain consciously, it's rare; by contrast, it much easier for people to learn different kinds of enjoyment—everyday parlance routinely speaks about acquired tastes. As I remember, when so-called pleasure centers were first identified in the brains of rats, they were identified as clusters of neurons that, if stimulated, resulted in compulsive repetition of the stimulating actions . . . but it soon turned out that the situation was variable even in rats, and when human experiments were undertaken, the results showed a much greater variability."

"Complicated, as I said," Helen observed. "The neurology of pain can be treated mathematically without too much difficulty, but the neurology of pleasure, or joy, or whatever you care to call it, is more difficult to generalize, even with the aid of Coincidence theory."

"It works in mysterious ways," Denise suggested, sardonically.

"Yes, it does," Helen acquiesced. "But the problems aren't insuperable. If my data can be cross-correlated with Walter Halleck's, we might be able to accumulate a sufficient sample size to begin extracting some statistical generalities."

"Good," said Denise. "Let me know how that works out. For now, I want to talk to Victor, after I've given Zeph a hug."

"I really am perfectly fine," Zeph assured her, although he accepted the hug with what was, for him, a perfectly good grace. For good measure, Denise also hugged Mireille, who seemed startled, but not offended.

Victor was still down below in the common area, involved in an intense discussion with Savina.

"Forgive me for interrupting, Victor," Denise said, "but have you, by any chance, cast an expert eye over all the data that Cronos and previous probes have accumulated relating to tidal effects in Saturn's atmosphere and the rings?"

"Not really," said Victor, seemingly slightly annoyed by the interruption—but he repented immediately and went on: "Although Saturn and Titan are the only major players, eighty-some other moons and millions of moonlets inside and outside the rings make exact calculations impossible even for the smartest AIs."

"I've tried to make some preliminary observation of tidal effects in the internal oceans of a couple of ice-worlds, in order to compare them with the data Olympus collected," Savina put in, "but the probe data is cursory and the Cronos crew has hardly begun to collate it, let alone supplement it. Mireille must have looked at tidal effects within Saturn's atmosphere, but she must have been waiting for further data as well. I don't think either of us has generated any conclusions, but you should ask her about it."

"As well as gravitational tides," Denise said, stubbornly addressing Victor, "aren't there also so-called electromagnetic tides, the effects of which interact with them?"

"It's sloppy terminology," Victor said, sternly, "but if you mean that gravitational tidal effects are subject to modification by cyclical electromagnetic effects, that's true—it's very obvious in the vicinity of Jupiter, but might be less pronounced hereabouts."

"And such tidal effects could potentially be used to map the distribution of dark matter in proximity to Saturn—specifically in the rings?"

"Theoretically, yes," Victor admitted, with a sigh, "but the math is so horrendously complicated that I doubt that even Helen Arkheimer would be able to do the calculations with the aid of a battery of AIs . . . not to mention the fact that the data are strangely inconstant—nobody knows why."

"I can guess," Savina supplied, unable to resist the opportunity to show off. "Pseudolife studies are in their infancy, but if the rings of Saturn are replete with entities exhibiting life-like behavior, much of it in their dark matter aspect, it would play havoc with the kind of measurements that we can make of electromagnetic and tidal cycles, as well as other things. As a matter of fact, I was thinking about the possible effects of Titanic tides on the evolution of pseudoliving entities in the rings during our discussion a little while ago, when my mind wandered briefly. I was holding your hand at the time, Denise, and I thought that I really must compare speculative notes with you."

"We really must," Denise agreed, "once I've refreshed my mind regarding recent theory relating to the role of tides in the evolution of life on Earth."

"You ought to liaise with Gabrielle as well," Victor suggested. "She's done work on possible psychological consequences of tidal and electromagnetic effects on the human brain—it's all very vague and speculative, but worth a consultation."

"Yes," said Savina. "We talked about that on Olympus Five, although neither you nor Gabrielle was on board. Zephaniah will remember—or, if he doesn't, Alessandro certainly will." She could not resist the temptation to add, curiously: "Has this got something to do with what happened a little while ago?"

"Peripherally, yes," said Denise. "I feel as if I'm trying to put together a giant jigsaw puzzle from which most of the pieces are missing . . . but there's a big picture in there somewhere, and it might be very useful, at least for my own satisfaction, if I could get an idea of it before tomorrow."

"That's a rather sharp deadline," Victor observed. "People spend lifetimes trying to work out tiny corners of the great cosmological enigma without getting much past square one."

Denise looked around the room, which was now empty apart from the three of them. She made no comment, but Savina evidently made a judgment as to what she might by thinking. "Mellita and Birstan are . . . in conference," she said. "Paula went to look for the captain—but they won't be long. Paula's very . . . efficient."

Denise looked at her with slight surprise, and then looked at Victor. "I see," she said. "I'd better leave you to your . . . discussion, then"

Neither of them blushed.

Denise went back up the ladder to her own cabin, where Zeph and Mireille were still in conversation with Helen.

"Back so soon?" said Helen, in a tone more suggestive of sarcasm than surprise.

"Victor's busy with Savina," Denise retorted, watching Helen's eyes for a reaction, although she could not detect any.

Helen turned back to Zeph. "Would you come over to the machine cabin, please?" she said. "I need to take some measurements. It won't take long."

"Of course," said Zeph, and followed her.

After a brief pause, Denise looked at Mireille. "Don't look like that," the latter said. "They really have gone to take measurements—it wasn't a euphemism. And don't look at *me* like that, either."

"I'm not," Denise assured her. "I'm just surprised that the hand-holding circle down below seems to have become the prelude to an orgy. I can assure you that I don't have the slightest urge to join in."

"And if you had," Mireille supplied, "you certainly wouldn't be looking at me. Perhaps I ought to feel offended."

"My brain evidently doesn't process induced euphoric feelings in that way," Denise said. "It's too late for experience to carve out new neural pathways now, though. I'm past thirty."

"So are we all," Mireille pointed out. "But it wasn't too late for Zeph's brain to forge new connections when he first went to work for Walter Halleck . . . and my guess is that it still wasn't when he signed on for Olympus, perhaps because several years of having his brain stimulated by Halleck had maintained its flexibility, or perhaps because he was simply a slow developer. Either way, he was still able to sculpt novel neural pathways when . . . but you know all about that now. Was Victor any help to your earnest cogitation?"

"Not really . . . his mind seemed to be on other things. In fact, Savina was more helpful than he was."

"I think you'll find that that's generally true. Savina's tactless, but very obliging, and she speculates freely . . . much more so than Victor."

"She suggested that I talk you . . . about tidal effects in Saturn's atmosphere, that is."

Mireille laughed. "Did she? Well, she probably meant exactly that. Sometimes, I wonder how things might have developed on Olympus if she hadn't won that stupid coin-toss . . . or lost, depending on your point of view. I'd like to believe that what Zeph experienced with me was at least special, if not unique . . . but maybe it wasn't. And maybe—horrible thought that it is—he'd have obtained even more pleasure with Savina. Stupid, aren't I? And heretical to the ideals of Olympus. That's partly why I volunteered to go into Helen's machine . . . but you'd already worked that out, along with everyone else. I really wish that I'd got more out of it than an unconscious scream. I'll try not to be terribly jealous of you tomorrow, but if you can deliver another soliloquy, I won't be able to help it. And you will, won't you? You're tuning up for it as we speak . . . and saving yourself."

"There's no reason for you to be jealous," Denise said, reflexively.

"Says the most famous woman on Earth, the voice of the Oracle, who believes that she's on the verge of an understanding that no one else has. Sure, I get to screw Zeph occasionally, and you probably won't, at least for a while, but one thing you don't understand, as yet, is how little that matters. Did you really want to talk to me about tidal effects in gas giant atmospheres? I've hardly started on the Saturnian data, but I found some interesting correlations between Ganymede's orbit and the life-cycle of the Jovian cloud-whales, which might be applicable by analogy to the influence of Titan on the Saturnian ring life forms."

"I'm sorry," said Denise.

"For what?"

"I'm sorry that you didn't get to deliver a speech—a commentary on a connection with the Bells."

"It's hardly your fault. One way or another, your brain is wired for it, and mine doesn't appear to be. All I can do, it seems, is scream. But I didn't scream when it mattered . . . when I made my minuscule contribution to the formation of Zeph's neural pathways. That was pure pleasure, and I don't scream with pleasure."

"It wasn't minuscule," Denise told her, ignoring the sarcasm. "I spent fifteen years of childhood making my contribution to the experiences that molded his neural pathways, and hardly made a dent, so far as I can tell—but when he came back from Olympus Five he was no longer the same person. I think he'd experienced what French terminology calls the *coup de foudre*—the thunderbolt."

"That metaphor is used by different people in different ways," Mireile informed her, scrupulously. "Some employ it as a euphemism for orgasm, others as an equivalent what the English cliché calls *love at first sight*—but that kind of love is an invention of troubadours, refined by Romantic poets and adopted by novelists as a convenient justification for the marriages with which they formulated the ritualistic denouements of their plots. The poets, in particular, tend to revel in the ambiguity as well as the indirection, but the romantic mythology of love has no place aboard a starship, and it's not what Zeph experienced on Olympus Five any more than it was when he met the Dancing Rats in Halleck's Sling . . . oh, *merde*, I'm rambling like a drunken idiot. Anyway, I've told you before that you don't understand . . . yet. It doesn't matter—Zeph understands, at least a little, the particular pleasure that we experienced together, and why it's deceptive simply to file it under the designation of love . . . and Zeph is the one to whom the ring intelligences are connected by some kind of twisted telempathic thread. And I strongly suspect that the person he needs to take his dictation is you, and only you. If it were me . . . well, it might turn out to be entirely the wrong kind of *coup de foudre*. I'd probably scream. I'm willing to bet that you won't."

Denise didn't have time to reply to that evidently intoxicated speech. Zeph opened the cabin door. "Helen needs you in the machine cabin, Denise," he said. "She's recalibrating the machine and needs some baseline measurements of your present resting brain activity. The readings will probably be much the same as the last set of measurements she made—mine weren't very different—but it's a necessary precaution, after what happened just now. Sorry."

Resting? Denise thought. *If she thinks my brain is resting, she's sadly mistaken. I can't even put a slight brake on it.* Aloud, she said: "That's all right. I'll leave you two lovebirds alone, then." She looked at Mireille as she said it, but the Frenchwoman didn't react to the provocation of the term—and even Zeph failed to blush.

XIV

Denise stood beside the captain and Mireille while Zeph was being strapped in and hooked up. The wallscreen was blank, for the moment, and Denise resisted the temptation to ask the captain to put up a view of the chamber below, in order to see whether a group had assembled there, and whether they were holding hands.

"Who's on watch?" she asked the captain, instead.

"Paula," he replied. "But don't worry—she'll be following every second of the experiment with rapt attention."

"She won't be able to do that if the clocks jump forward again," Denise said, "and it won't be the same if she has no one to hold her hand."

"You've done this before," the captain reminded her, in his most soothing voice. "When this run is over, you'll be a veteran. Just remember, if you feel the urge to make a speech, that every human being in the system will be listening in—even those on Earth, who will have to hear your words on the bounce, which will stretch the time delay to two hours."

"I'll try to bear it in mind," Denise said, "but it might not be easy. Anyway, this time Zeph might be able to speak for himself, and humankind won't have to receive his message secondhand, as well as *on the bounce*, as you put it so eloquently."

"I'm a soldier, remember. I can't recite poetry, like Zeph. How did he memorize all that, and why?"

"I can still hear you, Captain," Zeph interjected, pushing away the adapted VR hood, which Helen Arkheimer was just about to fit over his head. "I memorized the Coleridge poem when I was at school, on the advice of a psychologist who was trying to help me cope with my . . . condition, and I cultivated the habit of reciting it, in full, when I needed to calm down, like a sort of epic mantra. Such was my perversity as a child, though, that I soon began varying it, making a parody of it . . . and then I made up an absurd backstory for the first couple of lines of the parody, which I could trot out when people mocked me if they caught me reciting. Cobbler Ken became an English folk hero, the inventor of the souled boot, which occasioned a great leap forward in arse-kicking contests, and the stiletto heel, which brought about a crucial elevation of the female bum. If I had to spin it out I made Cobbler Ken the Jewish cobbler in the old joke who made a repair when the Pope's shoe was punctured during a walkabout, and put a sign in his window saying *Cobblers to the Pope*, prompting his Christian rival to put one up saying *Knackers to the Chief Rabbi* . . ."

He stopped, evidently having observed signs of frank incomprehension on the part of the captain, Helen and Mireille. "You have to be English to appreciate it fully," he added, and looked at Denise in quest of support.

"That's right," she said, scrupulously keeping a straight face, "although there are plenty of people even in England who have no idea where Sutton Hoo is, and the joke only works properly if the Chief Rabbi has a horse."

Nobody else laughed, which made her wonder whether the double act had really been as funny as it had sometimes seemed when she was ten years old. She met Zeph's eyes before Helen finally lowered the hood, and she added: "Wasted on foreigners, I fear. I haven't heard that load of codswallop since I was thirteen— it brings back memories. Thanks."

Nobody asked her what codswallop was, presumably content to draw an inference from context and reluctant to admit that the Cobbler references were beyond their ken.

"Sometimes," Zeph said from within the hood, "I still recite it when I feel stressed. I was worried earlier . . . for Mireille . . . although I was only pretending to be doing it for her benefit."

"I knew that," said Mireille. She and the captain were the only bystanders inside the cabin, but the door was open and Denise, still unhooded, was able to see that Gabrielle, Victor and Savina were immediately outside—which meant, she calculated, that Alessandro, Birstan and Mellita must be watching on screens.

"Feel free to do it again if it helps you," Helen said to Zeph, "but your EEG trace looks good to me . . . very calm, in fact."

"Walter used to play music at one time during the tedious preliminaries," Zeph said, "but it was for his own benefit, not mine. Mozart, Chopin, Bach . . . chamber music, I think it's called. I don't think he really liked it very much, but he had an image to maintain. He switched it off when he got down to serious business, though. The Dancing Rats had markedly different tastes, to judge by their jigs, but I couldn't hear anything in the Sling once it was activated . . . except for Walter's prompts during the final run."

"I can play music, if you like," Helen offered. "You name it, the library will have it. Or poetry on audio, if you prefer."

"The *Paradiso* might be interesting," Zeph said, "but I'm told that it loses something in translation, and I probably need to avoid influencing my impressions unduly. Let's opt for rapt silence, shall we? Unless Denise has other ideas."

"I've got more ideas than I know what to do with," Denise told him, "but they don't need a soundtrack."

"You might not need a soundtrack," observed Mireille, "but back on Earth they're not going to broadcast dead air if you don't have anything to feed them. They probably have Beethoven's setting to Schiller's *Ode to Joy* on standby . . . unless nationalism prevails in England and they play the Saturn movement from *The Planets*."

"Inappropriate, if so," Helen opined, without specifying why. She stood away from Zeph's capsule and said: "Your turn, Denise." Her voice was scrupulously level, but her expression was a taut frown of concentration.

Denise took her position obediently in the lower capsule, and lay still while the mathematician made all the necessary connections, very methodically. "How are the EEGs?" she asked, for the sake of saying something.

"Fine," Helen replied, tersely and noncommittally.

From the corner of her eye, Denise saw the captain take Mireille's hand, but she wasn't sure whether it was for her benefit or his. Then the hood was fitted and she was consigned to darkness.

"At this moment," Denise said, "which is to say, when the signal reaches her in about two hours' time, Marie MacLaughlin will be saying a prayer for us both—and for herself, of course, because she'll think that she's with us in spirit."

"Did you ever get all the way to the end of that interminable virtual stroll through Kensington Gardens and Hyde Park?" Zeph asked.

"Eventually," said Denise, "but I must confess that I kept asking her avatar questions, in order to break up the flow. The walk was a closed loop, going all the way back to Physical Energy via Peter Pan. She did throw in a prayer then, but it seemed to me that it was a trifle incongruous, in front of a pompous equestrian statue with that title. Did you write to Luke Saverne, by the way?"

"Yes, I did," Zeph said. "Briefly—I didn't have a lot to say—but I told him I remembered him and wished him well."

"Good," said Denise. "That will mean a lot to him. Mum would have approved."

"I'm beaming all my readings immediately, along with the audio and visuals, so that Walter Halleck can monitor them in Wales," Helen put in. "The Cabal might not approve, because they still think of him and the Shangri-La team as mavericks, highly likely to go off-message, but they're still stuck in the twentieth century. This is the future."

"Given that it has to be relayed, the information will only reach Wales and China if and when the members of the Cabal want it to," the captain observed. "My feeling is that they'll consider it politic to let it through, though. They seem to count Halleck as a key asset to the whole human race now."

"He'll love that," said Zeph. "He might finally be able to shrug that almighty chip off his shoulder if he thinks that the world is finally giving him his due. His daughter and his grandsons will be very proud of him, and justifiably so."

"Not as justifiably proud as mine will be of me," said Helen Arkheimer, a trifle acerbically.

"I didn't know you'd ever had a child," Denise said.

"I haven't," said Helen, curtly, "but before I left Earth I donated one of my ovaries to Fairbanks. The Cabal won't waste the genes contained in all those ova. I've probably got a dozen offspring in embryo by now, with more to come—and without the bother of having to give birth to them. I expect the Cabal have used Halleck's sperm at least once."

"If he has any viable ones left," Zeph suggested, dryly, presumably as an alternative to challenging the mathematician's hyperbolic boast. "He's in his late sixties, remember."

"Oh, they've probably had some on ice for twenty years," said Helen casually. "They're the Cabal; they make provision. They tend to be a little pedestrian in their thinking, though. They probably haven't even thought of fertilizing one of my eggs with your sperm, in a spirit of open-ended experimentation."

"Do they have any of my sperm?" Zeph asked.

"They're the Cabal," Helen repeated. "You went through basic training at Fairbanks. Of course they have your sperm—probably enough to father a thousand children. If and when Halleck and the Chinese team begin to identify potential telempaths, they'll hardly be able to wait to start inseminating the nubile females. When we get back to Earth in fifty or sixty years' time, we'll both be able to meet our genetic offspring, but whether any of them will be ours in the narrower collective sense is a different matter. We can only hope . . ."

I still have my ovaries inside me, Denise thought, *with all their cells unplundered. I won't have any children waiting for me on Earth, if I ever . . .*

She did not finish the subvocalized thought, because it was at that moment that time braked. At least, that was her first

222

thought, although she realized almost immediately that there was something fundamentally wrong with the conceptualization. Time had not slowed down within the world, or even within the neural pathways of her brain; it was continuing there, she assumed, as normal. What had changed, suddenly, was her subjective perception of the passage of time . . . and she knew full well, even though she could not remember the detail of it, that something similar had happened to her more than once before. Less than an Earthday had passed since she and her fellow crew-members had "lost" half an hour or so, when time had been somehow compressed, or her perception of it had skipped forward, but that had not been the first occasion on which she had "lost" consciousness of time, in company with others. This time, though, she was aware of the compression, or the skip. It was as if she had taken a strange kind of existential sidestep into a temporal no-mind's-land.

She tried to say something, but there was no tangible response to her attempted mental command from her mouth or her vocal cords. Her consciousness seemed to have lost contact with matter as well as with time. It was not, however, a standard out-of-body hallucination of the kind anesthetized people sometimes reported. She had a sense of being located inside her skull . . . but she could not feel her head, or the hood in which it was contained. If Helen was still speaking, the sound was not reaching her consciousness, even though, she assumed, her eardrum must still be reacting, in the objective time with which she had somehow lost her connection.

But the machine hasn't even been switched on yet, she thought. Then she added: *But it will be. Coincidence effects are partly time-independent; they can provide the illusion of time travel . . . in fact, the reality of time travel, or at least transtemporal sensation, the formation of ghosts. This time, when the switch is thrown, I'm not going to lose consciousness. If I dream, it will be lucidly. And if I speak, it will be lucidly. I can do this; this time, tricky Coincidence hasn't cut me off completely. That's progress—presumably the Bells' progress rather than mine, but it all counts. If I can only get a grip,*

I can stay in control. I managed to speak before, albeit in an altered state of consciousness. This time, I can do better.

When she contrived to "speak," however, she knew that she was not making any sound. She had not yet "got a grip."

Zeph? she subvocalized. *Are you there, Zeph?*

But Zeph wasn't "there"—not yet, even though they were still Coincidentally connected. What *was* "there"—except that there wasn't actually a *there* in which to be, any more than there appeared, for the moment, to be a *then*—was something else entirely.

She was blind and she was deaf. She had a vague impression of sound waves *out there*, but they were distorted; although they were presumably reaching her eardrums normally, the neural signals were being distorted when they reached her brain. She had a vague impression of electromagnetic radiation within the range of visual perception, but if any such stimulus reached her retinas through open eyes, the images were scrambled thereafter. And yet, she was aware of *something* that was neither sight nor sound, but a curious kind of touch . . . a touch that was difficult to categorize, in qualitative terms, but was strangely pleasurable: euphoric and well-meaning.

Her brain, she knew, was being pressured by mysterious means, but it didn't hurt—far from it. Even the Bells, if she had intuited their first machine-aided communication correctly, had observed that Zeph's brain was taking a "battering," although it hadn't caused him any pain or, it seemed, left any permanent scars. What she was receiving, unconsciously, seemed more akin to a soothing massage.

This is it, she thought. *This is what seers and mystics mistake for divine joy, for divine benevolence and bounty. This is the illusion of the grace of God, the mercy of the Lord and the exaltation of the Holy Spirit . . . except that it's not supernatural. It's something perfectly natural, even inevitable, a fugitive aspect of the fact of conscious existence . . . and it's fragile, evanescent, and delicate. If I'm to maintain concentration upon it . . . if it's possible for me to maintain that focus . . . I have to keep my balance . . . I have to avoid falling . . .*

224

I have to avoid vertigo. But it is *possible. Others have done it and others will. And I'm good at it, at least in collaboration with Zeph, my better half. I haven't had to fast, or pray, or mortify my flesh, or recite mantras. All I've had to do is be me. I have the equipment; all I have to do is* be.

But she knew, too, that it wasn't that simple—that there was nothing simple about mental *being*. Being, in fact, was difficult, especially for minds like hers. People thought that existence was easy, that it required no effort, but they didn't understand; they didn't know what they were doing, let alone what they might do with a certain amount of effort, and a little assistance. They didn't even understand what it was to be . . . really *to be*. Potentially, they were all creators. In actuality, they *were* creators because they couldn't be otherwise . . . but in what a paltry fashion! People routinely created more people, they created works of art, they created ideas, and most of all they created themselves, but how terribly incompetently, how terribly meanly! They sculpted themselves, carving out neural pathways in their developing brains while they hadn't become too set in their ways, while they hadn't become existentially paralyzed. While they were still young they were always making and amending neural pathways, shaping and blocking and polishing, albeit unconsciously . . . but how ham-fisted they were, and how crude their chisels were! Not that it was entirely their fault; as creators, they could only work with the raw materials they had, and human brain-tissue was very limited in its malleability . . . and as for the unconscious scalpels of human thought . . . but the potential *was* there, if only it could be mastered, and understood!

And even those individuals who succeeded in *being*, to a useful degree, in the fuller sense of the word, still had a further step to take in order to be capable of true feeling. Most human brains, in fact, automatically built both conscious and unconscious defenses against feeling, for good physiological and psychological reasons, with varying degrees of success . . . and those who let those barriers down, even a little, exposed themselves to risk, even to peril. But it had to be done, selectively, if any useful communication were to be established, even between human beings, let alone between humans and entities like the Bells.

It had to be done *now*, while there was a new opportunity to be grasped, even though "the world" had already ended, in more ways than one. There were risks, but there were also rewards. One had to speculate to accumulate . . . and the door to speculation was now wide open, thanks to Helen's machine and the efforts of the Bells.

This is the beginning, Denise thought, and she repeated to herself again: *I can do this* . . . and she was convinced that she could. A novel connection had been made between conscious apprehension and the exotic input into the normally unconscious part of her mind, and it wasn't slipping. She was dreaming lucidly, and the dream was real. She had *a grip*. Now, it was a matter of using the grip, of manipulating the input, of controlling the bliss and holding off the entropic dissolution.

This is Creation, she "said" to herself, carefully. It doesn't start with *let there be light*, or even *let there be life* or *let there be love* . . . which surely would have been a better starting point for the Biblical God. and wouldn't have been so blinding, in spite of what proverbial wisdom says about love. Nor does it start with *I think therefore I am*. Enlightenment requires much more than seeing, and much more than believing, and thinking is insufficient proof of being . . . real *being*. In the beginning is, indeed, *the word*, which is neither a bird not a worm even though it has metaphorical wings and is perfectly capable of sickening roses . . . but the word is incomprehensible in the beginning, because meaning hasn't yet been attached to it, and it's replete with ambiguities because in the beginning, it lacks vowels. It's not enough to *hear* the word, even when you've improvised vowels, you have to find the *meaning*, and that's hard, so hard that *hard* doesn't even begin to describe it . . . so hard that it would need an entirely new dictionary to compile the merest description of its hardness.

Stay calm, Denise, she instructed herself. *You're getting high and developing logorrhea. You can't help that, of course, but you have to avoid getting carried away. You have to get back to time and place* and true meaning, and you have to hold on to them. No matter how high you're taken, or how slippery concepts become as you try to build auditory associations for them, you have to keep control. Now . . .

In the beginning there is . . . nothing? Chaos?

No, and no.

Not nothing, and not chaos. Monotony? Yes, and no. Metronomic monotony, tick and tock. Repetition . . . ambiguity. In the beginning there is *potential*, potential for something to happen . . . so much potential that something *has* to happen, eventually. Even in the very beginning there was a waiting, an expectation of something happening, and there still is, in every new beginning.

What was, and is, and always will be waiting to happen? A disaster?

Oh, yes, always a disaster . . . but not *only* a disaster. Disasters are impatient, they don't wait long . . . but within potential there is also something patient, something undisastrous, something that might exist, and which is far worthier of existence than mere disaster, something that can make existence worthwhile. It has no name—obviously, since nothing has a name yet, even a lousy tetragrammaton, and finding the right one will be no easy matter, because everything that springs to mind will be imperfect. Harmony? Love? Grace? None of the above . . . they're too down-to-earth, inapt for space travel, inapt for Saturn's rings, inapt for the elusive mathematics of Coincidence, incapable of capturing the beautiful ambiguity of Coincidence, the fundamental perversity of existence, the slipperiness of meaning.

I'm really in contact with the Cosmic Mind, Denise thought. *My latent telepathy has been activated—not by Helen's switch, which hasn't even been thrown yet, but by the echo of that stimulus, rippling through time, and the effort of the Bells. And that's just as well, because when the stimulus eventually hits full on, my mind isn't going to be able to control my brain's reaction. Hopefully, I won't have an epileptic fit, as Zeph did, and I won't even scream, like Mireille; perhaps I won't even feel the virtual scalpel slicing through my being . . . but chaos is waiting and the center won't be able to hold for long. I only have a limited amount of time—perhaps only seconds or minutes, objectively—but time is elastic now, and the brakes are on. Now is elastic. Maybe I can't think coherently, or clearly, but thinking is still possible for the moment, drunkenly . . . and this time, I can feel my memory grasping it. But I have to focus, to fixate, to organize, to begin to feel . . .*

Where's Zeph?

Nowhere.

Denise realized—and was exuberantly delighted to find herself capable of realization—that not only was she more fully Coincidental with Zeph, and peripherally Coincidental with the Bells, but that she was also faintly Coincidental with . . . well, almost everything, to varying degrees . . . degrees that varied along a spectrum so vast as to be almost infinite. But she knew that she needed to concentrate; she needed to focus on the particular Coincidence that she had with her brother, because that was her conduit to feeling the presence of the Bells. She needed to focus on Zeph: not what she thought about him, but what she *felt* about him.

That wasn't so very difficult, once she turned her full and sympathetic attention to him . . . which, she admitted, wasn't something at which she had ever been particularly competent—quite the reverse, in fact—but things were different now. Zeph was different, she was different, and she was, at last, free to feel about him what she ought to have felt, and had to feel *now*.

She loved Zeph, She always had, although she had always been shy about saying so, just as he had, but that love was naked now, devoid of protective clothing, and because she loved Zeph she couldn't help having warm feelings not just for him but for everything with which he and she were Coincidental: the Bells, and the future Earth, and the past and future Universe . . . not because she was able to look into that abyss, but because, for the moment, the ultimate abyss was capable of looking into her. For the moment, her love for Zeph was true, because it was magnified, and complicated, and held far more than their two selves in its embrace.

228

And there *was* a moment. She was no longer outside time—the true time that, from a mathematical viewpoint, had neither direction or duration. She never had been, objectively speaking, but now she was no longer subjectively detached from the tidal *flow* of time. The tides afflicting it were complex, incalculable, only vaguely predictable, but that wasn't entirely a bad thing. And for the moment, her grip seemed solid and secure . . . and meaningful.

Zeph! she yelled, silently, *I'm here, I'm here!*

And the yell echoed, not merely in Zeph's mind but elsewhere and elsewhen, albeit faintly. But it was only in Zeph's consciousness, she knew, that the echo was not merely a yell, and was, in fact, not a yell at all, because it became a *word.*

In the end, as in the beginning, she reminded herself, is the incomprehensible word . . . the enigma . . . but I'm a creator too; there's a sense in which I already know the word, and the meaning . . . but spelling it out is reducing it, simplifying it, trying to move consciousness along the continuum, away from the scream of pain toward the thrill of pleasure, trying to render *being* more bearable. I've been thinking of telepathy as something distinct from the five familiar senses, which are all sophistications and refinement of touch, but it isn't really so very different; it too is a kind of touch, but it's more complicated, more sophisticated. Mind has at least as many dimensions as space-time, and perhaps even more. Even ordinary touch—seeing, hearing and holding hands as well as direct stimulation of erogenous zones—can be loving, and can embrace a component of Coincidence, but telempathic touch is much more so, and perhaps necessarily so.

I'm in contact with the Cosmic Mind . . . with its innate tendencies . . . its innate *conflicting* tendencies, its yin and its yang. Marie is right, in a way; substituting the notion of the Cosmic Mind for that of God is really a terminological shift, albeit a significant one . . . and she's right, too, about the problem of theodicy, even when secularized, being thorny and difficult of solution . . . but not impossible, for philosophy and for science. The point of that science, though, is not to dwell too much on the Cosmic Mind but also to think in parallel about the Cosmic Brain, the Cosmic Bell: to think more materialistically, even though the materialistic contribution to thinking is so very minimal, in appearance. Think about the Universal brain, Denise, the Almighty Bell, rather than the Cosmic Rose, and what happens in the Almighty Bell when the clappers strike; at the very least, that's surely a slightly better analogy than blinding transcendental light.

Creation . . . Evolution, if you prefer, as you're bound to do, as a biologist . . . is a matter of sculpting new neural pathways to channel and facilitate thought, or deflecting and fusing established ones, whether in baryonic matter or dark matter . . . but it isn't easy, because there isn't an omnipotent and omniscient sculptor outside the Cosmic Brain, armed with chisels and scalpels, gravers and polishers, expertise and a plan, any more than there is outside the human brain . . . and it's inherently dangerous, because it isn't possible to know in advance exactly where the new pathways will lead or what effect the reconnection of existing pathways might have, and the first rule of experimental biology is that you can never do just *one thing*. There are always unintended side effects, even when there's existing knowledge on the basis of which to build and plan. But the internal sculpting, and the polishing, the work of art and the work of creation, aren't something you can *not do*, even when your brain seems set and sclerotized, even when you're completely unconscious of it . . . as you normally are, because selective unconsciousness is an essential part of *being* . . . and, more importantly, of *learning* to be, and learning to feel.

Why do separated pairs of elementary particles remain linked? Why are there pairs of particles in the first place? Why does the universe contain the elements of Coincidence? If it didn't, of course, it wouldn't exist. Nothing would exist. But that's not an answer. Why *does* anything exist? Why isn't there nothing? Why are even the things that look like nothing—the voids of interstellar space—not actually nothing but vast reservoirs of potential, infinities of ambiguity? Existence exists because the pairs of particles aren't really pairs rather than unities at all, any more than they're really particles rather than waves; because it's a better analogy to say that they're *resonant* rather than *connected*.

Everything is ambiguous, even monotony: tick and tock, ebb and flow, being and nothingness, the fundamental tidal rhythm of everything . . . which seems so simple, so tedious . . . but it isn't, because everything isn't unitary but multiple, because the basic gravitational equation, the squaring of the existential circle, is only as simple as *pi*, which isn't very simple at all, since it recurs infinitely, and not repetitively, and the interactions become very complicated very quickly . . . so horrendously complicated that even a genius as mighty as Helen Arkheimer, supported by a legion of AIs, couldn't complete the computation within the lifetime of the universe.

And that's why Creation exists, how it begins and how it continues, and how its complication is augmented, evolving, not only generating structure, and chemistry, but also esthetics and virtue, so that Creations continually produce new secondary creators, many of them unlimited by crude gray matter, clumsy human hands and inept humanoid thoughts and feelings . . . angelic bees, pollinators of the great Cosmic Thistle . . . but not, as Dante imagined, simply to keep the same cycle of reproduction revolving endlessly, forever unchanged, forever monotonous. *Smart* bees, capable of artificial selection, molding the subsequent generations of the Thistle along with themselves, not just to maximize the production of nectar with which to make honey, but also to transform the thistle esthetically . . . in order that it might one day become a rose, and better than a rose.

Don't get carried away, Denise. Stay high, go higher, but don't get carried away . . .

Smart bees, smart angels . . . bees that communicate by dancing, because they have no physiological apparatus for making sound, and all their words are gestures. Nor is that their only limitation. They're anchored to their particular hives . . . but they're aware of others. As pollinators of the Cosmic Thistle, they need, or perhaps merely want, to enhance that potential communication, just as all active entities have a tendency to self-enhancement, to grow, to multiply, to surf the tides of time, to improve, to *create* . . . to *be*.

Why?

Because. Be cause. Because it's hard to be and hard to cause, but impossible to be without being a cause. Mere wordplay—except that there's nothing mere about wordplay. The word is the beginning and wordplay is everything else. Play is what begins and continues the work of making the word comprehensible. Play can brake time or break it . . . or wring or ring it, compress it or impress it. Play isn't just what *is*; it also embraces what *isn't*, or isn't yet; it embraces ambiguity and potential.

Play is make-believe, but as manufactures go, there's something essentially corrupt about that particular one; the product of belief is wrong, ersatz, paralyzing; it leads in the end to the ultimate madness, the sin of faith, of belief for belief's sake, belief devoid of rationality. The point of the game isn't to believe, but to see *beyond belief*. Play is more important than that, more creative than make-believe. Play is about authentic possibility, and possibilities really are endless.

Where are you, Zeph? Denise thought, deliberately. *I'm getting lost in a mindfield here. I need to get a handhold inside* your *mind. For the love of Heaven, Helen, switch on that bloody machine!*

Somewhere, or somewhen, perhaps in answer to her plea or perhaps not, it seemed to her that time, which had remained in semi-suspension for far too long, even though it was no time at all, ticked over at last, or perhaps tocked in automatic reaction, like an echo. At any rate, it seemed to Denise that Helen actually did switch on the bloody machine, defiantly.

Why defiantly? Denise couldn't tell; selective unconsciousness was blotting that out. But that was good.

At any rate, the switch was thrown. There was a shift in the dream, a transition.

But so far as Denise could tell—which, she had to admit to herself, might not be very far—nothing actually *happened*. As far as she could tell, nobody screamed. As far as she could tell, nobody had a quasi-epileptic fit. But that was good, because that wasn't the tale she had to tell.

It's no cause for disappointment, Denise thought, at first. *There ought to be something, but not that . . . something else.* Almost immediately, though, she amended the idea: *No*, she thought, *there ought not to be something, because the absence is more significant than the presence, in this instance. The impact on my brain has been suppressed, damped down and, at least crudely, shaped. I've made progress, and not simply by blocking out part of the attempted communication. I've adapted, I've coped. Old as I am, I'm trying to forge a new nexus of neural pathways. I'm building on past experience. I'm changing. And even though I'm doing that psychosomatic resculpting blindly and unconsciously, I'm conscious of the fact that something is happening. I haven't excluded myself entirely, and my thought processes are dancing a frantic jig. I'm letting myself in on the business of being . . . and I'm enjoying it. Being is fun, once you get used to it, or even if you don't. It's an acquired taste, but Being is good and good is Being.*

She paused in her thought process, but time didn't stop again. That was beyond her ability. In fact, everything was beyond her ability; she wasn't *able* to do anything except bear witness . . . but that, she could definitely do! She was conscious; she was *there* . . . wherever or whatever *there* might be.

There ought to be Zeph now, she thought, *and Chris, and Mireille, and the others, although they're mere ghosts, just shadows. At the very least, there ought to be more Denise—not to mention the Bells, which ought to be ringing carillons, and angelic bees of some sort, which ought to be pollinating Cosmic Thistles of some sort, amending their evolution. It's slow work—but the Cosmic Thistles have been growing, like unstoppable weeds, ever since the Big Bang, and perhaps thistles, like nettles, have to be grasped if they're to do no harm.*

If only I had clever hands . . .

Dante, Denise guessed, hadn't understood his own dream . . . but nobody ever does. When he saw the warning notice bidding all those who entered to abandon hope, he mistook it for the entrance to the Inferno—which it was, obviously, but not just that. It was the entrance to the Comedy, which could only be entered by those who abandoned any hope of a plot, any hope of a denouement, any hope of a punchline . . .

But I'm not abandoning anything, Denise asserted. *Not hope, not joy. I can do this. But where the hell is Zeph? I need Zeph.*

"I'm here," Zeph said, then—but only to her, behind the protection of a virtual privacy screen. *"I'm here, if there's any here to be in, and I'm dreaming, but it's all confused . . . can you hear me, Nise?"*

"I can hear you," Denise replied. And, much to her surprise, she *could* hear him—literally *hear* him—as well as *being* him. And she could also speak. She could speak aloud—and not, in her case, behind a screen. She could be heard. She knew that Zeph couldn't make himself heard, in spite of the intensity of his feeling . . . of *their* feeling . . . but she could. She was as high as a kite, but she was lucid. She hadn't been carried away. And Zeph was there, actually *there*; and as long as she had a grip, Zeph wouldn't get carried away either. He couldn't speak, in such a way as to be heard by anyone else, but he could make himself understood to Denise, and she could speak—not somniloquistically, this time, but consciously.

What can you see, Zeph? she asked, even though she knew it was a silly question.

Nothing, he replied. *You know that. But I can feel. I can feel the vibrations, the Bells, the carillons, the tocsins, the knells, the concert. It was easier back in the Sling. It was easier making sense of the dances and the semaphores, and even melding with the sentient Earth, with which I had a kinship as well as a Coincidence. The Bells are different: diffuse, turbulent, confused. They're taking a battering, but they're used to it . . . and importing the side effects of that battering into my poor gray brain isn't easy. It doesn't hurt . . . in fact, it's strangely pleasant, but that doesn't mean that it isn't a threat. Can you feel it, Nise?*

234

"Yes," Denise replied, "but it's muted, more like stroking than battering. And as you say, it's strangely pleasurable . . . but confusing, disturbing, worrying . . . "

You're right . . . it's too complicated, too convoluted, too paradoxical; it's musical, not cacophonous, but it could drive a man mad, or deaf . . . mercifully, you're here, keeping me anchored, keeping me sane, siphoning off the excess emotion, preventing me from meltdown. I'm acrophobic . . . but while you're here, I won't fall . . . You mustn't let go, Nise; you mustn't let go.

I won't. Denise promised, hoping that it was a promise that she could keep. *Just hold on, Zeph. Just* be. *Leave the talking to me. I can do it. I have to do it.*

That was true, she thought, and necessary. She had to speak, not just to Zeph, but for the record. It wouldn't be easy, she knew. Zeph was confused, and afraid, in spite of the tide of joy that was buffeting him like a turbulent wind and she was confused herself, having real difficulty maintaining her equilibrium . . . and all she had to work with were words: fragile, evanescent, stumbling words. She was a ghost, an avatar, a soul, a virtual person with only a tenuous anchor in materiality, but she was *here*, and she was conscious. She was a scholar, for fuck's sake, a *philosophe*, an evolutionary biologist, a pedant. If she couldn't keep the words more or less straight, more or less coherent, who could? So she could talk to Zeph, and *for* Zeph, and also for the record. Zeph could hear . . . and perhaps, just perhaps, *everybody* could hear . . . the whole bloody human race . . . who, just for once, would actually be listening.

So prick up your fucking ears, she thought—but she knew that she couldn't and mustn't say that out loud, because she was a utopian now, and there were principles and protocols to be observed. She had to keep the words under control. No obscenities, no matter how readily they leapt to her poor, paltry vulgar thoughts by way of emphatic punctuation marks. She had to keep a clean mind, so far as she could.

I don't understand it, Nise, Zeph said. *I can feel it . . . the benevolence . . . the joy . . . the music . . . the dance . . . but I can't understand it. I can't turn it into words. Can you feel it, Nise? Can you feel the joy?*

"I can feel the Bells, Zeph," Denise replied, trying hard to choose her words carefully but not sure that she was succeeding completely, "and what lies beyond them . . . but as for joy . . . certainly, but maybe not exactly in the way you mean. As for understanding . . . I have the feeling that I'm beginning to . . . I can certainly *feel* the Bells, though; they aren't making any sound, but I can feel the vibrations of their carillon . . . and so much more. If they felt any louder, or went on too long, I think I'd go deaf, like poor Quasimodo swinging on the bells of Notre Dame, but I think I have it under control, for now, damped down in the campanile of my skull to a tolerable level. I can sense the harmony of the chimes without their intensity cutting through me like a dagger. And I think that I can sense something of the meaning.

"You were right the first time, Zeph: they'd like to go with us to Uranus, and then to the Oort Could, and then to the stars. It's a selfish desire, but it also resonates with a broader purpose. It will be a good thing—not just for them, or for any other intelligences with which they might be enabled to have intimate intercourse, but for the whole brain . . . I mean, the whole universe, the cosmos . . . so I'm giving them permission, even though it's not really my decision. It will fit in harmoniously with the greater pattern, in time and in space. It's not so much a purpose, because a purpose implies a definable end, and that's not what the Bells or the Universe want. They don't want predestination, a fixed denouement, because that's not the kind of story theirs is. It's an exploration, an infinite series of beginnings, an infinite series of words, none of which will ever be THE END.

"And we really do need to help them, Zeph—not because we might get something in return, and not because we couldn't actually prevent them from coming with us if we wanted to, except by refusing to go, but because it's the right thing to do. We can't give them fully informed consent, but we can give them consent based on the information we have, and the dream that we have, the dream that we represent, and are . . . the human dream.

236

So that's what I've done, Zeph, It's a *fait accompli*, although it will take decades to unfold. If anyone disapproves, I'll have to talk them round . . . anyone aboard Minerva, that is. On Earth, opinion is bound to be stubbornly divided, but the people on Earth no longer represent the human race. We do. That sounds arrogant, I know, but it's simply a fact. We're *here*, wherever here is . . . and now, now that there's a *now* again. We're ringing the changes . . . you, me, and the other ten crew members. We're all in this together, forever and ever, with no *amen*."

You won't get any argument from me, Zeph said. *Keep talking . . . the opportunity might not last for long, and it might not be easily repeatable. The automatic reaction of your brain might block off further communication at any moment—like poor Quasimodo, as you say. I'm holding on, as best I can, and I'm sure that I can, as long as you can hold on to me. Don't worry about the joy; I can feel that for both of us; I can feel the harmony. Just concentrate on talking, on finding words. I can't do that, but you can, having always been a blabbermouth, even when you had nothing to say. Together, we can be a whole. Keep talking.*

Denise kept talking, hastening as much as the seemingly turgid pace of her thought and the precariousness of her equilibrium would permit.

"There are thousands of species of ring life-forms," Denise said, "and that's just Saturn's rings. The Bells aren't the only sentient species, but there aren't many in Saturn's orbit. On a universal scale...well, the arithmetic soon becomes horrendous, uncountable even, though they can't all be perceived, or all felt, however faintly, from here.

"Organic life like ours is only a tiny fraction of life in the universe, and there are many chemical species even of that, all evolving slowly, in many directions, but mostly toward their own planetary or nebular consciousness, to their own mental totipotency, because it's the most fecund way to go, the way that will permit them to make the fullest and the most esthetic contribution to the universal story . . . which definitely isn't a tale told by a idiot, even if it begins with naivety and will take a long time for its intelligence to become clear to its meaner component minds. Wherever there is the capacity for physical reproduction, self-reproducing systems develop, and wherever they develop, they evolve. Wherever there is metronomic monotony, there is also clinamen, the potential of variability, of evolution, of natural selection and eventual directional self-selection. And although self-selection doesn't always lead to intelligence, and probably leads in the opposite direction as often as not, sometimes—which is all it takes—it produces a story possessed of originality, style, wit and sequels . . .

"The process takes a very long time, and there are countless glitches along every conceivable path, but the universe is big enough, and sufficiently divided, for the possibilities to seem endless, and perhaps they really are. At least, we can hope so. Perhaps that's why the universe is expanding, because if it didn't keep growing it wouldn't be able to contain itself. Infinite as the possibilities are, though, some certainties remain: death and taxes, as the old saying has it. There's no evolution without death, and there's no change without entropy. The Bells and their kin live for thousands of Earthyears, but they're born and they die, like us and everything else. Like all other active creators they begin to die before being born, and they begin to age before being young, let alone reaching maturity. That's the nature of being, but in the meantime . . .

"We humans exist at a very early stage of the evolutionary story, even on Earth, let alone in the solar system or the universe, but we're already dying, already under the threat of decay without having reached the full potential of our development. We're only just beginning to develop a notion of our own identity, our vulnerability and our mortality, but we're also only just beginning to develop a true sense of our real achievement and the potential that we had, which hasn't gone to waste, in spite of appearances, because nothing really goes to waste. Even excreta are useful in fecundation, but the human race hasn't only produced shit; it's produced intelligence, art, protective domes and Minerva. And we're here. Helen Arkheimer might think that's entirely due to her genius and bloody-mindedness, but it's actually the result of hundreds of thousands of years of collective progress . . . progress amid strife, admittedly, but there really isn't any other kind . . .

"The Bells are much older, as a species, than we are, having been here before life on Earth first emerged from the sea on to the land, but they're also younger, in terms of their own potential development. They work on a slower timescale, but also a more malleable timescale. Because their sensorium is primarily based on Coincidence effects, they have a peculiar relationship with both space and time, a complex existentialism. Their capacity for movement is limited, but their tenuous multidimensional bodies overlap and intertwine, which is imprisoning in one sense but liberating in another, loveless in one way, but brimming over with love in another. Human minds can hardly begin to cope with the kind of complexity that is their everyday experience, and there's nothing surprising in the fact that they've evolved a mentality that's the metaphorical equivalent of a cross between a tortoise and a porcupine, but that they still retain the innate potential of mentality itself, however fugitively. You and I are proof of that, Zeph . . .

"The Bells are limited in both time and space, because that's a fundamental condition of life, and of being in a more elaborate sense of the term, but the conditions of their existence—their environment—permit more flexibility in that regard than could ever be permissible for planet-bound entities living within the kind of temperature range that we need to sustain our metabolism. They're much bigger than that and only comfortable in a temperature range much closer to absolute zero, but that circumstance permits matter to exist in states far more exotic than our pedestrian range of solid, liquid and gas, and permits complex interactions between baryonic matter and dark matter, and between electromagnetic energy—light in its broadest meaning—and various dark energies. The capacities latent in that kind of existence, and that kind of being, are exploitable; they allow Bellkin minds to tie seeming knots in time, and they find that impossible to avoid when they make attempts to communicate telempathically with mentalities of our kind. That makes their intimate presence very disconcerting and very disruptive for limited linear minds like ours, which have difficulty negotiating temporal glitches, even though they have some capacity to induce them, but the possibility of negotiation exists . . .

"There's competition between the species in the rings, and violence, including wars, but you're absolutely right about their fundamental benevolence, Zeph; their natural inclination is to avoid harming other mentalities if possible, even others as different from them as we are, and their own mentality elevates that inclination to the rank of a principle, a desire and a duty. The entities with which you and I, Zeph, are temporarily linked are doing their utmost to protect us from the harmful effects of their presence. They have various kinds of love, and they also experience hatred, although most of them disapprove of themselves and others for the latter. Their reproductive processes include interactions analogous to sex, but mostly more complicated than the crude bipolar distinction that causes so many complications for us in spite of its apparent simplicity. Perhaps perversely, perhaps even paradoxically, the complexity of their physical options of reproduction make those negotiations seem less problematic to them, and less conflict-ridden, but they're by no means immune to . . . emotional turmoil. Seen from one angle, they're as different from us as it's possible for us, or for them, to imagine . . . but it's not so very difficult to find basic analogies . . . similarities . . . harmonies . . . coincidences . . .

"We can be friends, Zeph. We will be. We are. Mutual adaptation might be a stern challenge, but it's not insuperable. It wasn't easy to get this far and it certainly won't be easy to go any further, but the possibility is there, if we can summon up the will, and are willing to accept the risks.

"Nothing is guaranteed, Zeph. Everything, everywhere, is constantly changing, constantly ebbing and flowing . . . and the tides around Saturn are so complicated that paltry arithmetic can't begin to cope with their calculation.

"Like all tides everywhere, those local tides don't just affect the atmosphere of Saturn or the oceans inside the ice worlds. While we're here they affect our fluid brains and the liquids inside our neurons. And the gravitational effects interact with the tidal effects in the electromagnetic environment. We're all victims of those tidal effects . . . the Bells and their kin as well as us. Such control as we have over ourselves and our environment, such creativity as we can exercise, is never completely free—but nevertheless, we and they *can* swim against those tides, we and they *can* survive and thrive in spite of being perennial victims of entropic changing circumstance. And if those tides didn't exist, if they hadn't always existed, we wouldn't be here at all; no one would. The everpresence and the limitless arithmetical complication of those tides is the backcloth against which all creativity happens . . .

"Am I getting this right, Zeph? I know that I'm only your amanuensis, that the thinking I'm doing is really more your thinking than mine, but I'm doing my best to take the dictation. Am I getting it right? I'm afraid that I might be making mistakes."

Don't be ridiculous, Nise. We're a pair . . . a strange couple, perhaps, as far from being twins as two children of the same womb can be, but Coincidental, in the best sense of that perverse and ambiguous word. You're providing the voice, but you're not just reading from a script. So I can't tell you whether or not you're making mistakes, and I certainly can't correct you. But we needed each other in order to pull this off. Apart, we'd only be disconnected halves of a pair . . . although that doesn't mean that we can't be parts of other pairs as well. Our relationship doesn't have to be exclusive . . . in fact, it can't be. The whole point of our being here . . . of our being, and of our being here . . . is to help to forge something wider, something bigger, something more powerful, to help to bring light into the shadows to help beings capable of being at least to be, and perhaps to be better . . . to be better . . . to be . . .

"Okay," said Denise, trying to stop her virtual head spinning drunkenly. "I get it, Zeph . . . or I'm beginning to . . . but I fear that I'll have to call it a day, for now. We're getting vertigo and feeling sick. Things are beginning to whirl and dissolve . . . I'm sorry, but I'm losing my grip, and my mind, and it doesn't seem, any longer, to be a slow process . . .

Feeling is weakening, Zeph told her, *like a candle guttering in slow motion . . .*

"I know," Denise told him. "Hold on. Hold tight."

Where Alf the secret reiver ran through caverns measureless to man, down to a sinless see . . .

"Damn! Throw the switch again, Helen, for God's sake. We're at the end of our tether, and if you don't throw the switch now, I fear that one or both of us might go deaf . . . or worse."

There was no perceptible delay. Shadow Helen threw the switch immediately, and Denise fainted—again. She could feel the blood flowing away from her brain as her carotid arteries contracted defensively, in an incipient panic attack.

But she didn't lose control. She pulled herself together. She didn't scream and she didn't have a fit; if she lost herself at all, it was only momentarily, for an unperceived second or two. Time didn't jump, or flip; it maintained its subjective coherency in spite of a certain elasticity. She felt a turbulent tide rocking her brain and confusing her mind, but she knew that she still *was*, and would continue to *be* . . . not exactly as she had been before, but that didn't matter, because nobody ever really was, from one day to the next, or one moment to the next. The important thing was to be able to make the jump without stumbling, and to land safely, still running, if that were humanly possible . . .

XV

The residue of the intoxication, with all its attendant confusion, didn't last long. Helen Arkheimer hadn't finished detaching all the electrodes from Denise's scalp when the blood flow returned to normal, and full, apparently stable identity with it. It seemed to happen very rapidly. When Denise opened her eyes the VR hood had been removed and the mathematician was leaning over her, and speaking in an urgent whisper.

"You're fine," she said. "Whatever happens, *you have to tell them that I was right.*"

Denise had no idea what the other woman was talking about, or why she was emphasizing her words so emphatically. "Is Zeph all right?" she asked, urgently.

He was misquoting deliberately, she thought. *I've heard him do that many a time before, even as a kid, and it's perfectly normal, perfectly Zeph. Maybe at first it was just to annoy the shrink, but that doesn't affect the fact that he was being creative, refusing to get stuck, refusing to be imprisoned by the printed words, deliberately venturing into the deep romantic chasm that slants down a red hill athwart a sudden cover . . . good, good, keep on running . . .*

"He's fine," Helen assured her, hastily—too hastily, Denise thought. "No fits, no pain, much as I expected. All the indicators pass him fit."

The fucking indicators don't know, Denise thought, relaxing her self-censorship and permitting herself the meaningless expletive. *They can only go on appearances and precedent. They have no fucking idea . . .*"

"Oh, shut up, Helen," interjected another voice—the captain's—cutting off Denise's own silent objection. "Look after Zephaniah, to the extent that you can, while I finish unfastening Denise. *Are* you all right, Denise? *Really* all right?"

Am I? Denise wondered. *A damson with a dulcimer . . . devoid of a plum . . .*

"So far as I can tell," she confirmed, in a perfectly steady voice, so far as she could tell. "I feel fine . . . slightly euphoric, in fact . . . evidently buoyed up by endorphins, now that my blood flow is normal again and my brain is floating quietly in its own disciplined tidal fluids. I did speak, didn't I? Aloud, I mean?"

"Oh, you spoke," said the captain, with evident relief in his voice. "And how. I thought you were never going to stop."

"And I made sense?"

"You were . . . reasonably coherent," the captain confirmed, more than a trifle carefully. "As to how much sense you made and what it all meant . . . that will doubtless be under discussion for some time, here and elsewhere, and the debriefing is going to take a long time, but for what it's worth, you convinced me." He finished releasing the last of the gentle straps securing Denise to the cushion of the capsule. "Stay still for the time being," he instructed her, in a commanding manner, before turning his attention back to Helen. "But the fact remains, Helen," he said, in a tone of voice that was almost level, "that you disobeyed a direct order. That's a court martial offense."

"Good luck with that," retorted Helen, defiantly. "Hold your court martial, if you like, and convict me of high treason. Relabel the lab cabin the brig and lock me in for life . . . but that won't affect the fact that I was right and you were wrong. I did what it was necessary to do, and everybody knows it, now, whatever they were screaming before."

"Screaming?" Denise queried, raising her head from the pillow, in spite of the fact that it was still a trifle fuzzy and the fact that she had been ordered to remain still. "Who was screaming? Not me, I hope?"

Not me but Zeph, she thought, although she contradicted herself immediately. *No, he didn't scream. He should have done, but he didn't. He'd taught himself how to keep a lid on his melt-downs. In Sutton Hoo did Cobbler Ken a shapely pleasure doom decree . . . but bottling the screams up only works momentarily, building up pressure . . .*

"No," said the captain, "not you. But we were all watching your EEG trace, to the extent that we could. We all saw the evidence of your brain going crazy, and we all had one eye on the clock. When the numbers skipped forward for more than an hour, we all knew that something was seriously awry, although nobody collapsed or twitched. Nobody was actually screaming, I suppose, but there was certainly shouting as soon as the clock was ticking again—a sharp difference of opinion and a certain amount of hysteria. Paula started it, I think. She shouted: 'Abort the test! Abort!' but she was only echoing my thought, although she voiced it before I did and repeated it in an undisciplined way. You didn't hear her?"

And mid this tumult herded from afar . . .

"No," said Denise. "I didn't hear anything . . . not from the shadows. I was aware of your presence . . . all of you . . . but only that. The only voice I heard was Zeph's, and I knew that he wasn't speaking audibly, in a way that could be heard by ears. I screened out all the rest, except for the Bells . . . I had to . . . Something's amiss. What did I miss?"

The captain continued his narrative: "Mireille shouted: 'Don't!' Then everybody else joined in, on one side or the other. I ordered Helen to abort the experiment, not to throw the switch . . . but she threw it anyway. I feared that it might kill you, or Zephaniah . . . but it didn't . . . which doesn't affect the fact that Helen disobeyed a direct order, in spite of having formally ac-cepted and acknowledged the fact that she's under my command. She might be crowing for the moment, but she had no reason to believe that activating the machine wouldn't damage both of you . . . especially after what happened last time, when Zephaniah nearly died . . ."

"No, he didn't," said Helen, flatly. "He had a brief epileptic episode, which calmed down almost immediately. His life was not in danger."

Yes it was, you silly bitch . . . it's just that your dumb AI indicators and your hidebound mathematical mind couldn't see it . . .

"You don't know that!" snapped the captain. "He'd spent the previous three years in a coma, damn it. He's my crewman, my responsibility. So is Denise. You didn't have the slightest idea what was happening to her when her brain went haywire, let alone when the clock skipped. Throwing that switch was just a crazy gamble—and this is a starship, not a casino. We do not gamble with people's lives."

"Oh, don't be ridiculous, you stupid man!" Helen retorted. "This whole expedition is a monumental gamble with all our lives, and to pretend otherwise is intellectual treason. The experiment had to go ahead, and it did . . . and no one can possibly deny, after what Denise said, that it was a success."

Denise sat up in the pod, only slightly unsteadily, free of the last of the electrodes and all constraint and still feeling positively euphoric, albeit as drunk as a skunk. She bumped her head, not for the first time, but it didn't hurt. "It was me, Captain," she said. "I'm sorry."

"What was you?" Chris Kemmering demanded.

"It was me who told Helen to throw the switch. I needed her to throw the switch . . . or throw the dice, if you prefer. I know you couldn't hear me at that point, because I didn't have voice control yet, but I still gave the order. I don't think Helen had any alternative but to respond. We're all inside the Bells' mindfield. I'm not saying that she didn't have free will, but what she did was necessary. I knew that, and I gave the order. *It's all my fault.*"

"Whether you were making sense before or not," the captain opined, the anxiety in his voice intensifying. "You're not now."

"With all due respect, Captain," Mireille put in, "but I think she is. I didn't know before . . . or don't remember having known . . . but I know now, now that my head is beginning to clear.

246

What Denise said might have sounded odd, but it does make sense . . . and if any of us doesn't understand, the fault is in us, not in Helen or Denise."

Denise saw Chris Kemmering raise his eyes toward an imaginary Heaven, evidently thinking that Denise was not the only one making no sense, that the nonsense was contagious, and that it was great pity that a sane man like him should end his career saddled with an entire crew as crazy as a sackful of monkey-nuts.

"It doesn't matter," Denise put in, swiftly. "It's done. I'm fine—but you have to save Zeph, if you can."

Could I revive within me, her sympathy and song, to such a deep delight 'twould win me. No, no . . . that's right, just an accurate quote. It mustn't *be right . . . and all should cry, Beware! Beware!*

"He's breathing normally," Helen reported, stubbornly. "His EEG traces are . . . anomalous, but he's no longer fitting. He isn't conscious, but all his other organs are functioning normally. His heart is beating, his lungs are pumping. There's no cause for concern, let alone panic."

And close your eyes with holy dread, for he on honey-dew hath fed, and drunk the milk of Paradise . . . no, no, it's stuck, it's stuck . . . fight it, Zeph change it, improvise . . .

"He should have woken up, though," the captain muttered. "Shouldn't he, Denise? You were coupled . . ."

And how.

"He was higher than me, but I was holding on," she said aloud, her voice sounding oddly dull, and defeated. "I swear that I didn't let go until the switch was thrown. He was still thinking then, still communicating, still creating, still improvising. He was very confused, but that goes with the territory . . . unless the AIs have put him into another bloody coma?"

That thought added a note of hope to her voice, but it was quashed almost immediately.

"They haven't," said Helen. "You blacked out briefly too, I think . . . he's just taking a little longer to come round. There's no cause for concern."

I didn't black out, Denise swore, cursing herself for not having that excuse, and cursing herself again for reflexively looking for an excuse, instead of taking the blame that was her due.

"*Stop saying that*, you stupid woman," the captain repeated. "There's *every* cause for concern. Paula, what's your reading of the EEG traces?"

"Unreadable, Captain," Paula reported from the operation room, regretfully. "The AIs are confused; there's no precedent to draw on . . . but in all fairness, the fact that there's such an active set of traces is surely a good sign in itself. His mind is working. He's just dreaming."

"No," Mireille put in. "Even from the limited readout on the screen, I can see and I can feel that something's wrong. He's not dreaming . . . not *just* dreaming, at any rate. Something else is happening inside his dream. Something bad, something disastrous."

Denise wanted to say *Let me see*, but she knew that it would be pointless. The EEG traces would be meaningless to her; she had no command of that arcane language—and in any case, she *knew*. Like Mireille, she could feel Zeph dying, like a candle guttering in slow motion. Instead, she repeated, dully: "It wasn't Helen's fault, Captain. She might have thrown the switch, but it wasn't her decision."

"She disobeyed a direct order," the captain repeated, but with less conviction than before.

"She had to, Captain," Denise insisted, beginning to babble and realizing why Zeph had accused her of being a blabbermouth. But at least she wasn't simply reciting poetry, even with variations; at least she was making it up from scratch, however ineptly. "I don't mean to be insubordinate, but Mireille and Helen are right. The contact had already been made before the machine was even switched on, and it had to be completed. Once the knot in time is tied, it has to be pulled tight. The disaster was waiting, it couldn't be avoided. You're the captain, and you're responsible for your crew; you want to protect us . . . but we can't be protected by refusing to engage with the Bells. Their mere presence is hazardous, and will continue to be hazardous, but they're learning, as we are, and we're helping them to learn. We'll never be able to talk to them even as coherently as Zeph was able to talk to the Dancing Rats by means of sign language, but we *can* co-exist, and serve one another's purposes . . . and we need to do that."

"Can they give us a list of nearby stars with worlds bearing our kind of life?" demanded the captain, skeptically.

That was good, Denise thought; it was always good to have something practical to focus the attention, in order to recoil from turmoil and death.

"A list might take me a while to compile," Denise said, astonished by the evenness of her tone, "but I know the location of every Earthlike planet in the galaxy now, and I can mark up any star map you care to display on a screen. There are half a dozen within fifteen light years."

"How Earthlike?" Mireille asked, dubiously—but not skeptically.

She believes me, Denise thought. *She knows that I can do it, and she's recoiling too, putting up a makeshift barrier between thought and feeling, turning away from the guttering candle . . .*

"Capable of sustaining organic life, with oxygenated atmospheres," she said. "The Bells can't promise us humanoids, rats or sentient insectiles, but they can guarantee life and mentality, even at the distance from which they're viewing . . . or, rather, feeling. Trust me; I can do it." She could tell by the expression on Chris Kemmering's handsome face that he wasn't convinced, although he wanted to be. She went on: "If we can reach Uranus successfully, and introduce the Bells to their neighbors, Birstan and Victor, with a little input from me, will be able to plot a course from there that will take Minerva to another Earthlike planet within decades, to the abode of a sentient species that is physically and mentally equipped to talk to us, at least with the aid of some kind of semaphore or whistling . . . and a species that we have every reason to expect to be benevolently inclined. Whether we can all get there in one piece, I don't know, and by the time we arrive we probably won't be the same people that we are now . . . but I know that I can help program Minerva's AIs to get the ship and its passengers there. After that, if all goes well . . . in fact, even if things go badly . . . you or Birstan will be able to bring Minerva home, unaided if necessary, after completing the mission. I can't make the calculation off the top of my head, but I'm pretty sure that we can do it well within the space of what passes nowadays for a normal lifetime . . . barring disasters."

Babble babble, tail and dribble . . .

"Barring disasters?" repeated the captain, reflexively.

"That's right. Our traveling companions might be dangerous . . . but they might also help us to avert more and worse dangers than they constitute in themselves. The void between the stars isn't as empty as it seems, and no matter how far away from the nearest useful star we are, we'll always be inside the sentient universe, able to sense its presence, within a mindfield that can't be absolutely safe for feeble creatures like us. There are no guarantees . . . the odds will even be against us . . . but we really don't have any alternative. We're the human race. For the time being, at least, no matter what the Cabalists of Fairbanks might think, humankind's entire future is in our hands and minds."

Our clumsy hands and our stupid, incompetent minds . . .

Captain Kemmering hesitated, but Paula's voice came over the communication link. "I'm sorry, Captain," she said. "This is my fault. I panicked when I realized that time had gone awry again. I gave you the wrong advice. If anyone should be held accountable . . ."

It isn't you . . .

"It's not your fault, Paula," the captain said, dutifully. "It was an understandable reaction—understandable to me, at any rate, because mine was exactly the same. The blame, if there's any blame to apportion, is entirely mine and I'll take it, as duty demands. Now, pay attention; we have nearly four hours in hand before the initial reaction from Earth reaches us. That's when the serious debate will start . . ."

Too late, Denise thought. *Far, far too late. The person from Porlock is battering on the door . . .*

"Wait!" said Paula. "I spoke too soon. Helen, are you getting this?"

"Of course I am," the mathematician snapped. "Don't panic!"

"What's wrong?" the captain demanded, as Denise leapt out of the pod, losing her balance as she did so and stumbling.

The captain caught her and held her upright. "Don't panic," he echoed, albeit in a fashion extremely unlikely to nip any incipient panic in the bud.

Everybody panicked.

Denise turned her head so that she could see the wallscreen, which was displaying an image of Zeph, with a set of EEG traces and other indicators stacked at the bottom of the screen.

"*Fuck*," said Denise forgetting the fact that she was undoubtedly still talking to the world, or would be in two hours' time.

"*Merde*," said Mireillle, like an echo. "*Do* something."

Denise knew that Mireille had to know, even as she said it, however, that there was nothing that a mere mortal like Helen Arkheimer could do. Whatever could be done, the medical AIs were already doing. Zeph was as fully hooked up as anyone could be to the most expert medical assistance in the solar system—but he was flat-lining. His heart had stopped, and the hectic activity that his brain had been manifesting a few moments before was fading away, with alarming rapidity. He wasn't fitting, and he wasn't screaming, but he was definitely and manifestly dying, his life ebbing like a guttering candle, no longer in slow motion.

He had been too high, and he was falling.

It wasn't the Bells' fault, Denise knew. They had done everything possible to sustain him and let him down gently, but they were only unhuman, only mortal, older than humankind by far, but also younger, more naïve. They meant well, but they were maladroit. They had been overconfident, and Zeph had paid the price for that overconfidence, as well as his own and Helen Arkheimer's.

She noted, however, while being slightly surprised by her own lack of hysteria in the wake of her brief panic, that the expression on Zeph's face was utterly blissful, a perfect expression of joy. He wasn't glad about dying, she knew, but he was surely glad about having lived, and about having lived the life he had, even though he was dying before reaching the age of forty. His had been an uncommonly eventful life, a full life—fuller than any human life had ever been before—and he was glad to have lived it, and glad to have risked it. He hadn't been blaming anyone as the light of his life had been snuffed out; he had maintained his benevolence to everyone . . . even her. He hadn't even been forgiving anyone, because in his view there was nothing to forgive.

Lucky sod, Denise thought, and then cursed herself for thinking it.

And in any case, she told herself, just because the clock was stubbornly clicking on for her and Minerva, it didn't necessarily mean that subjective time hadn't stopped in the nick of time for Zeph, in order to hold eternity within his final hour.

Denise heard an angry sob, but it wasn't one of hers; it was Mireille's. Even so, the captain tightened his grip on her arms, evidently afraid that she might collapse. Victor had to leap through the open doorway in order to catch Mireille, although Denise suspected that she would have been able to catch herself before she actually fell over.

"Take Mireille back to her pod, Victor," the captain ordered, his commanding manner instantly coming back in full force. "Savina, go with them. See that she's fully hooked up to the medical monitors, and don't leave her alone. Gabrielle, do the same for Denise. Don't argue, Denise; I want you under total observation and supervision until I'm convinced that all danger has passed. Helen and I will take care of things here, with Birstan's help. The rest of you, stay at your posts and await orders."

Before he had finished speaking, the captain had started handing Denise over to Gabrielle, who had pushed past Victor and Mireille. Denise was not in need of support in order to stand up and walk; indeed, she still felt perversely euphoric and quite calm, although her consciousness knew full well that her immediate physiological response to the disaster was utterly inappropriate, and that her present lack of feeling was utterly absurd.

I'm in shock, she thought, surprised at being able to think it, and cursing the pedantry that she had been trying so hard to maintain while babbling. Meekly, she allowed Gabrielle to steer her across the space between the cabins and maneuver her into the lower pod on the left-hand side: Zeph's pod. She lay still, almost corpse-like, while Gabrielle hooked her up to the AI monitors, even though she knew perfectly well that the precaution was unnecessary.

Best lie still, she thought, *until the grief kicks in. It probably will, when the shock wears off. And how. It isn't as if I've only lost a brother; I've just lost the other half of my being, more literally than any other human being has ever done. And it's partly my fault. But I really didn't let go until the machine was switched off. I didn't let go while he was still channeling the Bells. And they didn't let go either. If it had been humanly or unhumanly possible to sustain him, I and they would have done it. They needed him, probably more than I did . . . and they loved him, perhaps more than I could. There was nothing anyone could have done. It was just a disaster waiting to happen, which got sick of waiting. He very nearly pulled through . . . but he was too high, and no one could have hung on to him, no matter what we did. But still, it was my fault. If I could turn back time . . .*

She had to suppress an urge to laugh, then, although she knew that it was the stupidest joke that had ever sprung unbidden to her mind, if it even qualified as a joke at all.

Gabrielle had finished connecting a drip to the venous connection in her arm. Denise could actually feel the interface—but she knew that the AIs weren't feeding through anything but monitoring nanobots. Their mechanical subconscious had already judged, correctly, that no sedation was necessary, and no metabolic supplementation.

"Comfortable?" Gabrielle asked. She was crouched in the space between the pods, back-to-back with Savina. Victor had already gone, presumably to help the captain and Birstan to carry Zeph's cadaver to wherever it had to be carried.

"Perfectly," Denise confirmed, automatically.

The psychologist had a good beside manner, but Denise had no difficulty reading in her expression that the answer disconcerted her somewhat. It wasn't that she didn't want Denise to be comfortable, just that she was alarmed by what seemed to her to be an unnatural lack of reaction to the fact that Denise had just watched her brother die.

You don't know the half of it, Denise thought. *You only watched. I felt* him die. *That was the real shock, the paralyzing shock.*

"Don't worry," Denise said. "Not about me, anyhow. I can't tell you that everything will be all right, because it isn't and it won't be . . . but worrying won't help. Just follow the captain's orders."

Gabrielle took her by the hand. Reflexively, Denise tried to pull away, but Gabrielle, equally reflexively, only gripped harder. "Don't be selfish, Denise," the psychologist said. "I need it even if you don't. Just for a moment, please."

That made all the difference; Denise immediately clasped the other woman's hand, not merely politely but affectionately.

"How's Mireille?" Denise asked.

"The indicator readings are okay," Savina supplied, speaking from behind Gabrielle. "Physically, she's fine. Mentally . . . that will take time to ascertain. Try to relax, Mir. I'm not going anywhere. Cry if you want to; it's all right."

"Never mind me, you idiot," said Mireille's voice. "Look after Denise, for Heaven's sake."

"It's all right," Denise called to her. "I think I'm in shock, temporarily insulated from my own feelings. I can still sense the Bells . . . distantly, but they're there. If they had eyes, they'd be watching, but all they have is an exotic kind of feeling. That's all I have too, for the time being, muted at present . . . and I have a suspicion that it's not going to go away any time soon."

Victor returned, coming close enough to stick his head through the open doorway. From the corner of her eye, Denise was able to see the head in question shake, significantly. Zeph was still dead, then. She hadn't doubted it for an instant, but the confirmation was still a slight stab in the gut. The stab didn't hurt; she felt it, but it didn't hurt.

I was right, she thought. *I'm insulated—but not by any physical anesthetic. It's psychosomatic, purely mental. Not like me at all . . . but then, I'm not the same me that I used to be, even an hour ago. Old neural pathways have been dammed and redirected, without any tangible effort at all. The changes have been rung. Perhaps for the best . . . although I might not be the best judge of that, being inside the campanile looking out. Just because I didn't much like my old self, it doesn't mean that I'll like my new one any better.*

"Don't worry about me, either," Mireille called to her. "If I'm being torn apart by grief, I can't feel it, for now. The shock might be about to wear off, but for the moment, I'm as steady as a true Frenchwoman ought to be. Think of me as Jeanne d'Arc."

More like Jeanne Dark, Denise thought. *Who are you trying to fool?*

"I might start blubbing any second myself," Denise replied, insincerely, "but I know I mustn't scream. I'm a spacer now, albeit a bad one. There are principles and protocols, and responsibilities too. Gabrielle," she went on, withdrawing her hand from the psychologist's, gently but insistently, "can you bring up a star map on the screen for me, including every G-type sun within twenty light years of Sol, with a baseline in the plane of the galactic spiral, adjustable north and south thereof. Then, if you don't mind, detach the keyboard for me and help me to sit up."

"You don't have to . . . " Gabrielle began.

"I do have to," Denise corrected her, "and I have to do it right away. The whole bloody Earth will be on tenterhooks . . . and anyway, it will keep my fingers busy. You'll have to surrender my hand for a while, I'm afraid, but you can hold Savina's spare one . . . she's much better at hand-holding than I am, anyway."

"I don't think . . ." Gabrielle began.

Denise interrupted her, swiftly. "Yes, you do," she said. "You're a psychologist; you can't help it. Think, and think hard. Keep thinking . . . and keeping feeling at bay. You won't be conscious of doing it, but if you don't keep a lid on it, you'll be broadcasting that feeling, initially to the rest of the crew and a handful of Bells, but eventually, however faintly, to the entire ring system, the entire solar system, and the entire universe. Better not to, if you can damp it down, for the moment. You too, Savina, and especially you, Mireille. We'll probably have to let it out eventually, but it doesn't have to be mere babble. If we work in chorus, while we still have the residues of our unnatural calm, we might be able to put the Cosmic Mind itself in dignified mourning, as it ought to be. Not a sparrow falls, remember. The disharmony needs to be registered, and regretted. I don't have to weep yet, but I'm very much afraid that I might not be able to help it as soon as my fingers stop dancing, and embroidering Coleridge won't help me. When I do weep, I want it to be honest, and I want the whole bloody universe to know it . . . to feel it. The pattern of universal evolution just lost something unique, something precious. We need to understand that, so far as we can, in order to feel it properly, in order to make that tiny mark on the infinity of emotion, that tiny blot of disaster on the infinity of joy. Think, damn it . . . and when the time is right, feel . . . don't hold back. Do as I say, not as I do. For the moment, I'm in command, even though I'm babbling like a lunatic . . ."

While she was speaking, her fingers did their work, with uncanny discipline and precision. Evidently, her mind was sufficiently compartmentalized for her motor nerves to do exactly what they had to do. She typed, accurately and efficiently. Gabrielle and Savina watched her. Mireille couldn't see her, because the others were in the way, but she knew what was happening . . . and they all obeyed her order, even though they had to know that she was not in her right mind.

It turned out that she was right, after all, about the blubbing. As soon as her fingers finally stopped pecking at the keyboard that Gabrielle had detached from the wall and placed in her hands—as soon as the star map had been flagged and annotated to an acceptable level of seeming adequacy—she started weeping, and once she had started, the weeping rapidly became uncontrollable.

She had seen Zeph weep like that, during his childhood melt-downs, and she knew that there was nothing to be done about it but to let it go, let it wear itself out. So she let it go. Throwing her own advice to Gabrielle out of the metaphorical window of her soul, she stopped thinking, and just let herself feel, no longer even caring whether what she was feeling was being communicated dimly to the crew of Minerva, or to the Bells, or to anyone or anything at all, content to let it wash over her and through her, like an irresistible but complex tide.

Part of her was dead, she thought, but most of her wasn't; she would live; time had her securely in its metronomic grip, within its insistent perceived monotony, and time was all that she needed, for the time being, in order to return completely to her trivial, normal self, to be that self, in insofar as being was now possible, and insofar as her self was still recognizable.

In a way, it might have been easier if it wasn't; then she might not have felt so guilty.

In the meantime, Gabrielle took hold of her right hand again, more firmly and more affectionately than before, and, even though it must have required a certain amount of contortion on both sides, Savina took hold of her left hand, completing a closed loop of sorts in which Mireille was the fourth component.

This time, Denise knew, it was the right thing to do. This time, the chain ought not to be left open. This time, tactile continuity was required, emotionally and esthetically.

After all, they were all in it together—if not for life, at least for a long, long time.

When the flood of tears abated, she made her voice scrupulously calm and sensate, and said: "How long will the autopsy take?"

"A long time," Gabrielle told her. "Don't think about that."

"How can I help it?" Denise retorted. "Who's doing it?"

"Mellita and Helen, primarily," Gabrielle told her, only a trifle reluctantly. "They're supplying the hands, at any rate, with Victor standing by to assist and record. The AIs are playing their part, but the whole operation is being beamed to Earth. It will take four hours for suggestions and queries to come back, but there won't be any shortage. The captain is monitoring at close range at present, but he'll have to leave them to it very soon to go back up top, in order cope with the feedback from your speech, with help from Paula and Alessandro. That feedback will run and run, in spite of the long time gap. My professional opinion might not be worth much any more, but for what it's worth, Denise, it really might be best not to think about the autopsy, if you can. You were right about the star map, though; it might be best to keep your fingers busy, even if it means letting go if my hand."

"No," Savina put in, her voice sounding more than a trifle fractious. "Don't let go. With all due respect, Gaby, to hell with your professional opinion. God, I wish I hadn't won that stupid coin-toss on Olympus."

"You didn't win," said Mireille. "You lost—and you had plenty of time to take your turn, if you'd wanted to."

"No I didn't . . . once you'd marked the territory . . ."

"Considering that you're holding hands with both his lover and his sister," Mireille retorted, "I really don't think that's an appropriate remark."

"No?" Savina seemed unrepentant. "Gabrielle wouldn't want us bottling things up, would you, Gaby?"

"I thought my professional opinion had just been consigned to hell," the psychiatrist retorted, amicably. "But for what it's worth, given that all four of us seem to be in a slightly strange emotional state, and that two of us are supposed to be lending moral support to Denise and Mireille, I really think we might find more profitable directions in which to turn the conversation. I think you'll agree, Savina, that when it comes to entitlements to express regret and remorse, you really aren't at the head of the queue."

"I was just setting an example," Savina retorted, "but if you can think of a more appropriate topic of conversation than Zephaniah, in the circumstances, by all means introduce it."

Good luck with that, Denise thought. *Meandering with mazy motion . . . oh, shut up, Coleridge . . . and lay off the laudanum . . .*

"If I understand correctly what Denise said while the machine was active," Gabrielle said, "and given what we all observed beforehand, the machine doesn't have to be activated in order for us to be feeling the presence of the ring intelligences, and that certainly isn't going to stop now that she's issued an invitation to them to stick with us . . . assuming that they can. I'm not consciously aware of any profound effects myself, but it seems to me that Denise, and perhaps Mireille, might be. Obviously, the captain will want to debrief you both personally, in full, but too many things are happening just now that require his attention, and the annotated star map you've just forwarded, Denise, will add a further complication, so he probably wouldn't object to your talking to us first, especially as I've been ordered to look after you. Does that meet with your approval, Savina?"

"Absolutely," said Savina. "Sorry I spoke. Give us more inside dope, Denise, if you can . . . and if it's not too painful."

"It isn't," Denise assured them, although she wasn't at all sure why it wasn't. "First of all, I don't believe that any of you are in any immediate danger. The danger that existed while we were still in the vicinity of the C-ring arose primarily from the multiplicity of . . . quasi-life forms with which the ship was in physical contact. We're already far enough away for that contact to be drastically reduced, as is Cronos. As for the passengers we're carrying, they'll be able to exercise deliberate restraint, and focus, and even supply a measure of shielding. I can't give you any absolute guarantees, but I can assure you that we're far safer now than we would have been if they hadn't been able to warn us to move away from the dangerous position to which our mission plans inadvertently brought us, and safer than we would have been if I hadn't acceded to their request to accompany us, physically and mentally. Zeph has paid a heavy price for that, alas, but in slight compensation, I believe that we really are in a healthy situation now, fully equipped for a successful mission to the stars, detours included."

"Thanks for the reassurance," Savina said, "but it would be a good deal more reassuring if Zephaniah were still around to provide a second opinion . . . *ouch!*"

Denise deduced that the hand with which Savina was holding Mireille's hand had just been squeezed, hard—but neither of them broke the circle.

"It was my fault that he died," Denise said, bluntly. "I should have realized that it wasn't safe to let go. I wasn't able to hold on, and I should have pulled him away much sooner. I let him down, just as I'd done half a hundred times before, ever since we were children."

"I don't believe that Zephaniah would agree with that judgment, Denise," said Gabrielle, softly.

"I'm sure that he wouldn't," Mireille put in.

"So am I," Denise agreed. "For all his troubles, he always leaned over backwards to be kind to me. He would never blame me for anything, even things that were clearly my fault. I didn't return the favor. Blaming him—silently, at least—became something of an ingrained habit . . . but that's beside the point. The point is that I knew that he was only able to report back verbally on what he was sensing while he was in contact with the Bells because Helen's machine had linked him with me as well, enabling me to hear him. I knew that I had to hold on to him, to provide him with an anchorage, and I didn't. I let go . . . too soon."

"When you say that you didn't," Gabrielle suggested, "don't you mean that you couldn't?"

"Same thing; either way, the failure was mine. The only reason I'm here, nearly a billion kilometers from home, and the only motive I had for being here, was to hold on to Zeph, and I failed him. Whether he would blame me or not, you can, and you should—especially you, Mireille."

"I don't believe you," said Mireille, flatly. "I think that if there was anything humanly possible for you to do, you'd have done it. Blaming yourself isn't reasonable, and it isn't healthy. And even if your only reason for being here was to keep Zeph company, it doesn't mean that you no longer have one. We need you now, because you're our best surviving link to the Bells. You still have an obligation to Zeph, and to us. You're entitled to grief, as I am, but you're not entitled to wallow in self-blame. So, weep again if you need to, but don't forget that you still have duties to fulfill, to the captain, to me, to Helen, and even to Savina. Why do you think we're all holding hands, still pretending to be a team as hard as we can? Because we're going to have to be a team for real, aren't we, for the rest of our lives? You're not the only one who was only here, two billion klicks from the nearest bottle of Bourgogne, purely and simply to keep Zeph company . . . but we can't any more, so we'll have to make do with one another, won't we? And we'll have to hold on, whether we like it or not, because if we don't, we'll all end up flatlining."

"If I understood what Denise was saying correctly," Savina retorted, "we might end up that way anyway, sooner rather than later."

"I understood that too," Gabrielle put in, "but there are only two choices: either we carry on with the plan that Zephaniah and Denise have mapped out for us, or we quit and head back to Earth . . . and that isn't really a choice, is it? We might have free will, but some decisions are still impossible. Our itinerary is Uranus, the Oort and Target, and then home—and unless and until we reach Target, turning Earthwards is simply not an option, because we can't return home empty-handed."

No one objected to that, although it seemed to Denise that Savina might, if she had been so inclined, have argued that they wouldn't be returning home empty-handed even if they set a course for Earth right away. But Savina had to know, as well as everyone else did, that if they were to do that, the Bells and the Universe would never forgive the human race, and the residuum of the human race would never forgive them.

"And it *was* my fault," Denise whispered, rebelliously. "He always needed someone to look after him, and he didn't always make the best choices. He was lucky, on Olympus Five, to have Chris and Mireille . . . and lucky to have got away from Walter Halleck for a while. But coming back to Earth, to me and Helen Arkheimer . . . his luck ran out there."

"Stop it, Denise," said Mireille, trying to sound mild. "And don't repeat that to Chris—he puts on a sterling act, but he's not as tough as he wants to be, and if you're blaming yourself, try to imagine how he feels right now, watching actual scalpels cut slices out of Zeph's brain. He really didn't have any alternative but to do what he did, any more than Helen had. Tell him that, if he asks for reassurance, or even if his military discipline won't let him. We all have a responsibility to one another, which is why we're here, now, not letting go, even though we're only holding hands. So let's all hold on, shall we? At the risk of degenerating into horrid cliché, it's what Zeph would have wanted. Believe me, I know."

Denise did believe her, and also believed that she knew. "I'm sorry," she said, to no one in particular. "I'm not quite myself at the moment."

"That's understandable," Gabrielle assured her, although Denise judged that she was speaking more for the record than for her. "As you said earlier, you're in shock . . . the psychic beating you took from the Bells has left you with a certain existential concussion. It might be a good idea if you were to get some sleep."

"It might be a good idea," Denise agreed, "but I'm not sure it would be possible . . . and I certainly don't want the kindly AIs stepping in to save me from myself again. If it's a choice between existential concussion and coma, I'll take the concussion. Anyway, it wasn't a beating. Zeph took a battering of sorts, obviously, but not me. I thought of it at the time as being more akin to massage, but . . ." She stopped, having temporarily run out of babble.

"But what?" Savina prompted.

"I don't know. It wasn't *like* anything."

"Not sex, then?" Savina queried. "Not divine joy?"

"Sex is your idea of divine joy?" Denise countered, skeptically.

"No," said Savina. "But isn't it supposed to be, at its best? Mireille?"

"Is *that* why you've had a sudden fit of belated jealousy?" Mireille countered. "No, as Denise took a certain amount of trouble to tell us while she was delivering her sermon, what mystics and religious fanatics sometime mistake for divine joy has nothing to do with sex."

"She wouldn't know," Savina snapped back—but didn't add any of the supplementary remarks that had probably sprung to her mind. Denise refrained from squeezing her fingers aggressively.

"It wasn't like sex," she said, instead. "So far as I can tell, at any rate—but Savina's right; my own meager experience might not be anything to go by. It wasn't any kind of metaphorical rape or other penetration. It was just a kind of touch, intimate but not hurtful. It wasn't hostile. At worst, it was clumsy . . . inexpert. Hopefully, it will improve . . . I'd rather that, I think, than go on trying to build barriers in my mind in an attempt to lock it out, assuming that my conscious mind has the authority to do that. In time . . ."

"You mean that you're going to go back into Helen's machine again?" Savina said, skeptically. "Don't you think that would be taking dutiful risk a bit far?"

"Perhaps," said Denise, "but it will have to be done, eventually . . . and not just by me. As the captain might put it, we might not all be in the same existential boat, but we're all part of the same flotilla. Once you've caught a glimpse of infinity, you can't simply look away."

"I haven't caught any such glimpse," Savina parried, "and even if I had . . ."

"You're a xenobiologist, Savina," Gabrielle reminded her, mildly. "It isn't a purely theoretical science any more, and you're on its cutting edge. You've been to Jupiter to study cloud whales; you came here in order to study the ring quasi-fauna . . . and now we're heading for the stars, with alien passengers. Your field has suddenly become a lot more complicated than you ever imagined possible . . . but you're here, with a unique opportunity of study, and a unique opportunity to provide much-needed enlightenment. If not you, who? If not here and now, where and when? Are you really going to leave any accessible stone unturned?"

Savina sighed. "Bloody psychologists," she murmured.

"There's no desperate hurry," Denise pointed out. "It's a long way to Uranus, let alone the stars. By now, Birstan should have calculated the basic trajectories that will allow us to reach . . . Target, and he'll be able to give us an approximate timetable."

The door opened, as if on cue, but it wasn't Birstan who appeared in the gap; it was the captain.

He only had a slight frown of puzzlement on his face as he surveyed the group.

"I came to obtain a progress report," he said, "and to relieve Gabrielle. How are you feeling, Denise?"

"As well as can be expected," Denise replied.

"Mireille?"

"A trifle restless, to tell the truth," said Mireille. "May I have permission to go up to the ops room and help monitor the incoming traffic from Earth?"

"You're still hooked up to the medical apparatus," the captain pointed out.

"Needlessly."

"All right," said the captain. "By all means unhook yourself and stretch your legs, if you feel the urge. You're relieved, Savina. Is there any cause for concern regarding Denise, Gabrielle?"

"None, medically speaking," the psychologist reported. "And to all appearances, Denise is more-or-less *compos mentis* . . . gibbering a little, but surprisingly well disciplined, emotionally speaking, which proves that she's an exceptionally well-balanced individual."

Denise suppressed the denial that was on the tip of her tongue. Instead, she said: "How's the autopsy coming along?"

The captain winced slightly. "I'd rather not attempt a verbal description," he said. "You're a biologist, but I'm a trifle squeamish, in spite of supposedly being a highly trained killer. I'm sorry, but there are things you and I need to discuss. You'll have to compile a formal report, obviously, as soon as you feel up to it, and we'll have go through the debriefing procedure by the book when we have time . . . a *lot* of time . . . but as I say, there are things I need to ascertain immediately. Is Gabrielle right in saying that there's no need for concern?"

While he was speaking, the circle of hands broke up. Gabrielle

264

went out immediately, but Savina lingered until Mireille had detached herself from the medical monitors; then they left together, leaving Denise alone with the captain. She detached her own monitors, but she didn't climb out of the capsule.

"Yes," she said, in answer to the captain's question, "she's right, with regard to my wellbeing. I'm not going to die just yet. But that's not the only cause for concern, is it?"

She left it at that, waiting meekly for the captain to initiate the list of potential causes for concern.

He didn't. Instead, he said: "I'm truly sorry, Denise, about Zephaniah. I think I did what I could but . . . well, it's the first time I've lost a crewman, and there's no way to escape the feeling that it's my fault."

"It isn't," Denise told him, "and it's your responsibility . . . your duty . . . to isolate yourself from that feeling and to keep control. The task ahead of you is an order of magnitude more complicated now than it was before . . . but I'll give you what advice I can. This is only the beginning. You really need to be a captain now, and the best captain you can possibly be; but we're a team; we'll all pull together."

His expression suggested that he wanted to express gratitude, but all he could actually contrive to say was: "Even Helen?"

"Even Helen," Denise said. "She's never been able to love anyone before, but things are different now. She'll need help—we all will—but we can do it. Trust me, I *know*."

XVI

Chris Kemmering made himself as comfortable as he could in the gap between the opposed pods, but he made no move to grasp Denise's hand or contrive any other gesture of familiarity.

"I *am* sorry," he said. "One way or another, I messed up."

"No you didn't," she told him. "And I'm not prepared to let you share my guilt, no matter how much you want to, for reasons that I've just explained. I should be apologizing to you—I let you down as well as Zeph."

The captain had too much self-control to rush to contradict her and start an argument over which of them had a better entitlement to their instinctive guilt feelings.

"I suspect that the AIs might have put you into a precautionary coma if I hadn't fiddled with the programming," he said. "I'm not sure that I was right about that, either."

"I am," she said. "I don't want to be unconscious. Even if hearing the Bells ringing faintly is still confusing me slightly, I want to stay awake. And I'm making more sense than some people seem to think. Some people on Earth might take it for granted that everything I said was mere crazy ranting, but you know better, don't you?"

"Yes," he said. "I can't claim to understand it all, but I believe every word. I wish I'd asked Paula to send a copy of *Kubla Khan* to my palm-pad, though, or to transmit an audiotape."

"It wouldn't have done any good. Zeph was trying to recite *Cobbler Ken* mentally, although you couldn't hear him, and to play with the words the way he used to do. It wasn't working.

He was beyond the reach of petty trickery like that. But I should have held on."

"Even at the risk of being dragged down with him? Are you sure it was you who let go, and not him?"

Denise hadn't thought of that, but she dismissed it as irrelevant.

"As I told you before," she said reflexively, "he used to misquote the poem deliberately," she repeated, "playing with the sounds and ideas. I think it was precisely for that reason that it worked far better than any repetitive *Om mani padme hum* when he was a kid. That certainly couldn't have saved him, then or just now, but it kept him going, kept his mind actively searching for oddity. As to what might save us, or at least keep us going until we get to where we need to go . . . we'll all have to think about that carefully and constructively . . . and eccentrically."

"Helen asked me to apologize to you too," the captain said, tacitly shelving her train of thought for the time being. "She'll come to do it herself eventually, but she's going to be tied up for a long time. The investigation of Zeph's . . . being . . . is going to require a great deal of effort and ingenuity . . . urgently."

"It's very kind of her, I'm sure," Denise said, "but I'm not letting her steal any of my blame either."

"That wasn't really why she was apologizing," the captain opined. "She was apologizing for having made an incorrect calculation. She *hates* having made incorrect calculations. She'll never forgive herself. But she really did love Zephaniah, even though she wouldn't have thought of it in those terms. She probably thinks that she's too rational to grieve, but she isn't. It's perhaps as well that she has something with the requisite intensity to occupy her hands and mind."

"She hardly had three conversations with Zeph," Denise pointed out, "and they were entirely devoted to pressuring him into going along with her plans. The two of them never had a single instant of genuine human rapport . . . which isn't at all surprising, but isn't an excuse."

"Perhaps they didn't," the captain agreed, "but I know Helen a little better than she knows herself, and she isn't the pure calculating machine she'd like to be and pretends to be. I couldn't touch her heart, and nor could Mireille, but it's not untouchable, and the fact that she couldn't attain any kind of human rapport with Zeph in the course of a handful of conversations doesn't mean that she didn't appreciate his value and isn't feeling the horrible void that his absence is going to leave in her soul. If her hands weren't busy, she'd be weeping. Let's cut her a little slack, shall we?"

"It's our duty, after all," Denise agreed, without too much sarcasm.

Chris Kemmering didn't bother to agree with her, although she knew that he did. Denise could tell that there was something else on his mind, something that he was not saying.

"I'm going to get out of this stupid capsule now," she told him. "I need to stretch my legs even more than Mireille does. And I certainly don't need sleep, induced or natural. I still haven't got over waking up a few Earthdays ago to be told that I'd been away with the fairies for three years . . . three years of the prime of my life—and don't tell me that they don't count. I might have been in suspended animation, but I was still aging, physically. It was three years out of my lifespan—three good years. And poor Zeph was asleep too. He couldn't afford to lose them . . . no matter how tedious they were for you. I know the value of alertness now. But you must be in need of sleep yourself—it's been a stressful time for you too, and you can't have had much recently.

"I have my duty to keep my brain active and my upper lip stiff," the captain reminded her, with the ghost of a smile, and without making any move to reduce the embarrassment of his presence so that she could make a dignified exit from the pod. "And Fairbanks, obviously. The data deluge will begin any minute, and will doubtless be relentless for at least forty days and forty nights."

"Will they want me court-martialed, do you think, for exceeding my authority in giving the Bells permission to hitch a ride to Uranus?" Denise asked, figuring that if he still had more to say and wanted her to stay where she was for the moment in order to hear it, she might as well oblige him. "Do you?"

"No, of course not. I won't say that you'll be universally hailed back on *terra firma* as the greatest heroine the world has ever seen, but you're certainly light years ahead of the next best. My bet is that the trolls who've been screaming that you were deluded or corrupt will mostly feel obliged to fall silent, for diplomacy's sake if not because they've been converted by your expanded sermon. If your friend Marie weren't a Protestant, she'd probably start a campaign for your canonization."

"My canonization? You mean Zeph's."

"Actually, no. Dying used to be a good career move for martyrs, beatification-wise, but this is the twenty-second century; survivors get all the press, and the star map that will shortly be hailed by all the believers as the new model of the conceptual universe has your fingerprints all over it."

"But it'll take decades for anyone to ascertain whether even one of my indications is correct," Denise pointed out. "And the skeptics will simply refuse to believe any information that we might eventually be able to send back from the star that Gabrielle seems to have dubbed Target. Surely the skeptics will continue to claim that it's a Cabal plot calculated to keep the herd in line by supplying them with a distraction and an illusory hope."

"Perhaps, but the story is too good, and the mystery packed into it is far deeper than anything that the Cabal would have packed into it for propaganda purposes . . . or anything that the skeptics are likely to believe that you cooked up yourself. The cranks who credit you with being an evil genius will be hard pressed to believe that you're that much of a genius . . . or that evil, in fact. Perhaps it wasn't such a mistake for your parents to name you Denise, after all—it's not easy to think of a less likely name for an evil genius."

"I'm glad it no longer meets with your disapproval," Denise said. "But the fact remains that it will be a long time before we can provide further evidence to justify the star map, and belief in it is bound to be hard to sustain."

269

"I disagree; the long wait will maintain the suspense and stimulate the discussion," the captain opined, "which is always good for the reputation of prophets; and belief in the reality of Coincidence math and its practical applications will surely progress by leaps and bounds now that Walter Halleck and the Shangri-La gang have been given free rein. They'll do their bit to boost your reputation. Hopefully, you'll avoid sainthood, but you'll have to get used to being the next best thing to a demigoddess that humankind presently possesses. Don't let it go to your head, though; on Minerva you're still just a crew member, and I'm still the captain." His tone of voice was light and bantering now, as befitted a thoroughly professional lie.

"A crew member who has ninety per cent of basic training still to undergo," Denise observed, a wryly. "Not exactly an asset, in that regard, and perhaps quite superfluous to the mission now that you have the star map on file." She didn't mean it, but felt obliged to put on a show of false modesty in case she was suspected of letting things go to her head.

The captain laughed, dutifully. "I think the star map has earned you enough moral credit to get you all the way to Target, and back. The name wasn't my idea, by the way, or Gabrielle's. We had to find something to substitute for its official catalogue number, but I wasn't quick enough off the mark, and neither was Helen, for once. Victor got in first. He's a trifle prosaic in his thinking, as you've doubtless observed."

"I haven't actually had time," Denise reminded him. "I was even slower off the mark, obviously—I could just have pre-empted Victor and simply stuck a label on the map. I was in too much of a hurry even to think about it. It would have been polite, I suppose, to call it Zephaniah's Star . . . or Corcoran's Star. Denise's Star was obviously out of the question . . . but Dad couldn't have had any idea, when he stuck me with the name, what a burden it would eventually turn out to be."

"Why were you in such a hurry?" the captain asked.

"I'm not entirely sure," Demise admitted, "but I did feel a sense of urgency. Perhaps I was afraid that I might lose the information the Bells had imported into my mind . . . that it might slip through the cracks of memory, like a dream . . . but I don't think it will. The connection seems firm now . . . and permanent, although I suppose that I have no reliable means of judging that."

The captain seemed to be making an effort to digest that assertion and calculate its implications.

"You can still feel their presence now?" he queried, although it had to be a rhetorical question. "Even though they're no longer . . . talking to you?"

"They can't talk to me without Zeph—he was the one who had the psychic telephone line. On the other hand, I think I've always been able to feel their faint presence; I suspect that everyone can, however feebly, even over interplanetary distances . . . but I'm only now learning to recognize that presence for what it is . . . cosmic background radiation, psychically speaking. Now that I have recognized it, I hope to refine my discrimination considerably, and get to know its components much better, but it won't be easy."

"And it won't be without danger?"

"Obviously not. I don't feel imperiled at present—but neither did Zeph, until the moment when he fell. All his life, the abyss was there, and the unconscious part of his mind was aware of it, but it's only in the last few days that the realization made its way through the labyrinth to consciousness, and only today that the vertigo caused him to fall."

"To fall where?" the captain queried, curiously.

"Into the metaphorical caverns measureless to man . . . the deep romantic chasm."

"That's Coleridge again?"

"Word for word. Not the only viable metaphor, by any means, but the first one that came to Zeph's mind. Mum's fault, and that of the shrink who prescribed it . . . but they meant well. They were only trying to help."

The captain was pensive, a train of thought having been triggered. "Do you think . . . ?" he began.

"That Coleridge's opium dream might have permitted him to obtain a momentary and fragile contact with some fragment of the Cosmic Mind?" Denise interrupted. "Probably. He'd undoubtedly have thought of it, in poetic language, as his Muse, if he'd bothered to attach a label at all—and whatever vague stimulus might have arrived from outside, the words were his, and hence the genius. But that's an unnecessary digression. The point is that, for the moment at least, I'm not only in . . . resonance with our passengers but conscious of it. It might be a disaster waiting to happen, whether I lie down in Helen's machine again or not . . . so there might, in fact, be a certain urgency in the situation."

"Well then," said the captain, still striving to keep his tone light, "we'll just have to look after you as best we can, as befits the care due to humankind's greatest asset."

"Just an ordinary crew-member," Denise reminded him. "Look, I really do need to get up, if only to stand upright on my feet for a while—and to resume my duties, obviously. I don't need baby-sitting any longer, so if you don't mind...."

"Of course you don't need baby-sitting," the captain agreed, a trifle uncertainly, "but you might find it convenient to confine yourself to quarters for a little while longer, lest you get mobbed. You do have to write your report while the experience is still fresh in your mind, and . . . to be honest, I need to bring you up to date with a few more things. Then, if you don't mind, I'd like to exercise my captainly authority to keep the other interrogators at bay for a while longer, or at least to let the other vultures in one at a time. The military mind, you see—excessively devoted to order."

"I don't know," Denise replied. "The condolences might become a trifle tiresome offered in series, repetitively; it might be better to get them out of the way all at once . . . although you seem to be assuming that yours can be taken for granted."

"I suppose I am," the captain agreed. "It's not an easy subject to address, for me. I'm only a military man up to a point, remember. Zephaniah was . . . more to me than just a crew member . . ."

"I know," said Denise. "But you really don't have to tiptoe around the subject. Zeph's dead . . . and if I understand the . . . principles correctly, his body will have to be recycled, like all the other organic matter aboard. We'll all end up eating his substance, along with our own reprocessed shit, and there's no point in being squeamish about it."

The captain seemed genuinely shocked by that remark, but he pulled himself together with due discipline. "That's inaccurate," he said. "There are several steps between feeding raw materials to the thermosynthetic converters and turning the resultant crops into food, and in this particular instance there are . . . complications."

"What sort of complications?"

The captain hesitated, manifestly embarrassed. "Your reaction thus far is . . . a trifle unexpected," he said, after a pause.

"You've seen me weep, if you were keeping one eye on me while the other was tracking the autopsy," she said. "I've moved on now. I don't need Gabrielle to explain the common phases of grief to me, and I figure that it's probably best to go through them at a gallop. And I don't need to eat Zeph's substance in order to integrate him into me. His soul is still with me, and always will be."

"His soul?"

"If you'll forgive the religious metaphor. His mentality . . . something of it, at least. Once fused, it can never be entirely separated again. It's not a kind of immortality that Zeph would have wanted, or that Marie MacLaughlin would endorse, but it's something. What sort of complications?"

"I think you might need more time . . ."

"I don't. What sort of complications?"

The captain was manifestly still hesitating. Denise could read the signs of his internal conflict, but she knew that his sense of duty would prevail.

It did; even so, he tried to be diplomatic. He had had abundant practice in that regard.

"I know you haven't read the mission plan," he said. "Nobody has—not the fine print, at least—but you know its outline, and its provisions . . ."

"Oh, cut to the chase, Chris," she said. "There's a vacancy aboard, and a readily available way to fill it. So what are you going to do? Draw lots to see who gets permission to get pregnant, and by whom? Or are you blushing scarlet because you want to make a proposition to me?"

"Are you sure that you're not still in shock?" the captain parried.

"Absolutely not. I won't say I've never been saner, but I've certainly never *felt* saner. So spit it out. What's the procedure going to be? If you call for volunteers, the situation could become far too interesting for comfort."

"That's not the proposition that has been put to me," the captain said, colorlessly.

"By whom?" said Denise, but immediately added: "No, let me guess—by Helen. She wants to carry through the suggestion that she made while she was hooking us up for the crucial contact. She wants to do a little selective breeding of her own and have Zeph's baby posthumously?"

"Not exactly," said the captain. "She's more ambitious than that. She reckons that with the stem cells she can harvest from Zeph's body while his tissues aren't completely dead, she can clone him. She takes the view that his . . . talent must have been largely genetically determined. At Fairbanks, she says, they only have his sperm. We have the whole genome . . . including, if you're willing to make a donation, a precise copy of the mitochondrial DNA contributed by his mother's ovum, mounted in a viable host cell."

"Why didn't I think of that?" was Denise's carefully controlled response. "And me an evolutionary biologist. So you're offering me a replacement brother, younger than me this time instead of older. Are you expecting me to play mother?"

"Popular wisdom has it that it takes a village to raise a child," the captain said, having recovered all of his own composure in confrontation with Denise's apparent equanimity. "The proposal is that we all share the parenting . . . although you would have a privileged position within the team."

"And a veto over the plan?"

"Effectively, yes, although you don't have any legal power of attorney over the substance of Zeph's body, including his DNA. He signed a contract."

"Of course he did. I never got around to it, myself . . . but that's a moot point. Mireille is on board with this, is she?"

"I don't know; I haven't had a chance to ask her, or anyone who wasn't present down below when Helen voiced the plan, scalpel in hand. No objection has been raised as yet, but there's no point taking any kind of vote until I get clearance from you. We'll need unanimity, I think—effectively, everyone has a veto, but I had to consult you first . . . and I wanted to do it before Helen had the chance to put it to you directly. I thought that, for once, the bull shouldn't be released into the China shop until I'd had a chance to see how the porcelain is stacked."

"Nicely put. But everyone will be able to see the logic of Helen's argument won't they? She is, after all, a mathematician of genius . . . and the arithmetic of the present instance isn't particularly challenging. We've just lost our Coincidence magician, but we have a chance of producing another, from scratch, if we act quickly. The powers-that-be on Earth, will approve too, I presume. Helen is probably right to assume that she has, or will have, children back on Earth, if her arrogant assumptions about the value placed on her ova by the Cabal are justified."

"They are," the captain confirmed. "She's a product of the Cabal's clandestine eugenic program; as am I. I've checked; she does indeed have two children at Fairbanks, one of them conceived some time before she was assigned to Minerva. Not clones, of course, and carried by surrogate mothers, but half hers genetically . . . and there are bound to be more in future."

"Will any of them be yours?" Denise asked.

"I can't be absolutely certain, but I'm confident enough simply to say no—and I have no knowledge of what use the Cabal might have made of my sperm, or might plan to make of it in future, having no say in the matter. I signed a contract too. I suspect my genes are a long way down their list of priorities, now that they're having to be . . . more economical in their choices. On the other hand, the sperms can stay on ice for as long as necessary . . . and circumstances do change."

"You're a certified hero, and an exceptionally handsome man. Volunteers ought to be queuing up to bear your children."

"The Cabal doesn't call for volunteers, and for the moment, they're rationing pregnancies as well as food and air. They're a long way from the New Eden at present . . . and probably almost as far from any Revolution in prospect. They've learned enough from history not to let it repeat, as tragedy or farce. Are you going to veto Helen's plan?"

"Of course not. How could I put you in the position of having to decide whether or not to overrule me with your hidden iron fist? We're spacers, remember—true utopians, always striving for unanimity. I haven't signed the famous contract or gone through basic training, but I'm no less committed for that. How could it be otherwise?"

"You're a surprising woman, Denise Corcoran," the captain said, and added: "I knew I liked you the first time I saw you, but I wasn't sure why. It wasn't just the ash-blonde hair, the pretty face, and the fact that you're nearer to my height than the women who made it through the selection procedures for long-haul space travel Maybe it was Coincidence; either way, I'm glad that my intuition didn't let me down."

Denise still had enough innate self-deprecation in her new self to remind herself that "ash-blonde" was a polite term for a shade that connoisseurs of beauty might simply dismiss as "dull," and that her slightly-above-average height would be regarded as a deficiency rather than an asset by many men, even those as tall as the captain.

"Helen would definitely tell you that it was Coincidence," she remarked.

"Of course—but I'd like to conserve the idea, even if it's an illusion, that my expert judgment counted for something. She's doubtless mustering her arguments as we speak in anticipation of a long quest of persuasion, but she won't be sorry to find that they're unnecessary."

"Of course not—she knows her limitations as a diplomat, and even though peace has been officially declared, she wouldn't trust you to carry out a delicate mission on her behalf as far as she could throw Minerva on the surface of Saturn. It's only a matter of hours since you were calling one another stupid and looking as if you were about to strangle one another . . . not to mention the threat of court martial."

"I did go over the top," The captain admitted. "Conduct unbecoming an officer. I'll give myself an official reprimand in the log . . . but she did disobey a direct order and I'm by no means convinced that I was wrong to issue it. If she had obeyed it, Zeph would still be alive."

"Perhaps, but he'd never have forgiven you. Sooner rather than later, he'd have forced the issue, I don't say that he had a death wish, but he was absolutely determined to take the risk. Don't blame yourself. I don't."

"Does that mean that you don't blame me, or that you don't blame yourself?"

"The former, of course. Naturally, I blame myself. I always do. That's why I can advise you so sincerely not to do it—no good ever comes of it. Can I go up to the control room now? I'd like to be on hand when the data deluge reaches its full intensity. I'll help with the unzipping of the files and the preliminary sorting, if I may. As the likely target of the lion's share of the verbal lapidation, I'm surely entitled."

"I'm not convinced about that, either," said the captain, "but I suppose you'd better go, if you want to. I'll join you shortly; I need to check in on the autopsy first, and get a progress report from Birstan. I want to be up-to-date when the questions start flying like arrows, and it's my responsibility to frame the replies. It's not that I don't have confidence in Alessandro, but . . ."

"But it's your duty as captain," Denise finished for him, when he showed no inclination to do it himself.

"Precisely," he said, apparently glad of the support. "And thank you."

"For what?" she said, although she knew.

"For everything," he replied, only a trifle over-generously, in Denise's not-so-humble opinion.

XVII

As Denise had anticipated, the control room was crowded. It only contained three workstations equipped with chairs, which were occupied by Alessandro, Paula and Gabrielle. Mireille and Savina were standing behind them, each trying to keep an eye on two screens simultaneously. Four hours had now elapsed since the transmission of the first experimental data, including the beginning of Denise's commentary. Not everyone, it seemed, had wanted to wait for the end. Expectation had bred impatience, and the first trickle of reaction was already coming through.

In spite of the fact that something was actually happening, Savina came away from her station behind Paula's chair as soon as Denise appeared, claiming her attention without hesitation. "You were in conference with the captain for a long time." she observed. "You must have been making quite a report."

""It's all on the record," Denise countered. "You could have listened in if you wanted to hear it."

"We already had plenty of fuel for discussion," Savina told her. "One step at a time, as the captain would say. If I said anything to offend you, I apologize. I know you didn't dig your fingernails into the back of my hand the way Mireille did, but I got the impression that you might have sympathized with her."

"There's nothing to forgive," Denise assured her. "Have your richly fueled discussions reached any conclusions?"

"Not really—hardly surprising, as we were all coming at it from different angles, and it's all so vague. Personally, I have to accept what Gabrielle said, with her irritating habit of putting her finger squarely in the pulse. I'm a xenobiologist, and my subject matter is in the middle of taking the greatest leap forward in its history. I hadn't quite realized the significance, at first, of the fact that you connected . . . telempathically with the aliens some time before Helen switched her machine on . . . that you had a link already established, left over from your previous . . . encounter. I hadn't realized, either, the implications of the fact that the aliens could distort our perception of time regardless of the machine. That could happen again, I assume, at any time?"

"Apparently," said Denise.

"And you are still linked to them . . . permanently linked, in fact?"

"Probably," Denise agreed, waiting to see where the line of questioning was going.

"But even without that link, the aliens would be able to make the clocks jump forward—to snatch time from our consciousness while it continued to elapse for the machines? They could have done that without being telempathically linked to any of us."

"I think so."

"So it could happen again, at any moment?"

"I suppose so."

"At your command . . . or your request?"

That, Denise thought, must be what was on Savina's mind. She almost wished that she could simply say yes and lay claim to a superpower that she certainly did not possess, but honesty prevailed. "I doubt that," she said. "In any case, at present, I have no way of issuing any such request, and certainly don't expect ever to acquire any entitlement of command. Why would I request it, even if I could?"

"I don't know," Savina replied, with a hesitation suggestive of the possibility that an idea or two might have occurred to her, "but you are trying to establish a better communication with the aliens, aren't you? If you succeed . . . eventually, you will be in a position to make requests of them, just as they were able to make a request of us via Zeph?"

"It's a possibility," said Denise warily.

"And did the permission you apparently gave them to ride with us to Uranus include permission to play tricks like that with our minds?"

"Ah," said Denise. "No, it didn't . . . but since you raise the question, the invitation I attempted to issue to them was a trifle vague, and I don't know how liberally they might have construed it. I wasn't exactly in a position to draw up a formal contract and have a lawyer look it over. For what it's worth, though, I'm convinced that our passengers will tread very carefully indeed. I don't believe that they'll want to play tricks with our minds again, as you put it, until they're quite sure of not doing any harm. They know that we're trying to establish better communications—I think they'll be content to let us try, for the time being, only attempting to help us out if they think they can. They live slowly, and they know the value of patience."

"And what about messing with the ship?"

"That's hardly in their interests," Denise pointed out, "as they're relying on it to transport them to Uranus, and Minerva only has one backup, at present. They've surely learned from the accident that triggered the AIs' precautionary reaction, and I'm certain that they'll be very discreet indeed until they know more."

"I'm not so sure about that," Savina retorted. "Nor is Alessandro."

"Why?" Denise asked. "What's happened?"

Alessandro swiveled round in his chair. "The scoops are active," he said.

Denise remembered that Chris Kemmering had remarked, at one point, that it might be as well to activate the scoops, in order to draw in dust, which ought to include ice particles as well as various potentially useful minerals, while Minerva was still in relatively matter-rich space. The ship was a long way from Saturn's atmosphere now, but the rings had a tenuous atmosphere of a sort, which must extend for a long way in space, perhaps as far as the orbit of Rhea.

"So what?" she said cautiously.

"So there's no record of the captain or any crew member having issued an order or flipped a switch, or of the ship's AIs responding to any kind of automatic trigger. I can't be sure that it isn't an internal glitch, but I suspect that the operation was motivated externally."

"You mean the that Bells riding with us might be responsible?"

"I don't know," Alessandro replied, with exaggerated caution. "What do you think?"

I don't know, was Denise's automatic reaction, but she stifled the impulse simply to say it, because the fact that she didn't know might carry extra significance. Would she know, if the Bells had done it? *Should* she know?

"Why would the Bells want to activate Minerva's scoops?" she asked.

"You tell us," said Savina. "You're the expert."

"No, I'm not," Denise countered. "I've only established a fugitive telempathic contact with one or more of their minds. Their physiology is your department. To me they're just tenuous ghosts."

"And you think I'm in a better position to make assessments of their physical nature?" Savina's sarcasm had a hint of resentment about it, but she was striving to make her tone amicable, as a good utopian should. "Alessandro's more qualified to do that than I am, and he's mystified. So is Victor. You're the one who seems to have landed us with the hitchhikers; isn't it up to you to figure out what their dietary requirements might be, and what they might do to supply them?"

"Not really," said Denise. "But I assume that I'm right in thinking that there might be valuable information to be gained from whatever the scoops pick up, no matter why they've been activated, and that there isn't any significant risk in their activation? We have a lot yet to learn about the rings and the ring intelligences . . . and every little helps."

"That's true," Alessandro conceded readily enough. "I'm certainly not complaining about the activation, and Victor's already looking forward to analyzing what the scoops pick up—but if it was the aliens who deployed the scoops, without asking us, it might be slightly worrying, don't you think?"

"No," said Denise decisively. "If they've done it—and there still seems to be an if about it—I'm certain that they'll have done it for good reasons, and that they would have consulted us if there had been any way to do so. We have to trust them, don't we? We're all on the same side; what's in their best interests is in ours, and *vice versa.*"

But even so, she couldn't help adding, mentally, *it's hardly comforting to think that our passengers mighty be taking it into whatever they have instead of heads simply to make use of Minerva's facilities. The incident might be trivial in itself, but it helps to remind us how vulnerable we are, and that the Bells could exterminate us with ease, if they wanted to. They need Minerva to take them to Uranus, but they won't necessarily need us to fly her, once they've figured her out . . .*

She put an immediate damper on that train of thought.

"I'll try to voice your concern, Savina, if I can figure out a way to do it," she said calmly.

Savina seemed to have more questions in mind, but she was interrupted by Mireille.

"Excuse me, Savina," the chemist said, "but I need to talk to Denise."

"Go ahead," said Savina, after a moment's hesitation. "Don't mind me."

"In private," Mireille added.

"Oh!" said the exobiologist, putting a wealth of suggestion into the monosyllable "In that case . . ."

Mireille met the unvoiced implication was a basilisk stare, but made no verbal reaction. "Please, Denise," she said, indicating the hatchway.

Denise looked at the three screens, which were all registering and sorting incoming information, but it was all encoded for the moment, and Denise knew that it would take some time before the receiver AIs were ready to put any but the tiniest fraction in clear.

"It's okay," Paula told her. "Anything for your specific information will be fed straight through to your account; you can access it just as easily from your capsule as from here, and you can tap into the captain's feed at the flick of a switch—you won't miss anything."

"Of course," said Denise, dividing the remark between Paula and Mireille, and she followed Mireille meekly back down to the cabin she had recently vacated, which was now empty, the captain having had several other priorities to juggle.

Mireille pointed at her open pod. "Don't mind Savina," she said. "She can't help it. To be clear, though, I don't want to have sex. If I wanted sex, I'd exploit the captain, as usual, when he has a few minutes to spare, but I doubt if I'll be feeling like it for quite a while. I do want to talk, though, in private . . . genuinely in private, and talk to you, specifically. I know that the captain has probably demanded that you make a formal report as soon as possible, and then make yourself available for extensive debriefing, but he obviously gave you permission to come up to the control room, so he's leaving you some latitude, for the moment."

"It's perfectly all right," Denise assured her. "After you."

Mireille climbed into the capsule first, and sealed it as soon as Denise had assumed her customary half-lotus, with her head slightly bowed. The privacy lock was activated; if the captain and the AIs could be trusted, no recording was being made.

"Do you might if we lie down?" Mireille said. "Not facing one another, though. I'd rather you had your back to me. I need to talk . . . to you . . . but I don't need you staring me in the face."

"All right," said Denise. "Whatever you need." She lay down on her side. Mireille assumed a similar position; she put her right hand on Denise's shoulder, but the contact wasn't intimate, it could as easily have been construed as a light push rather than a gesture of affection.

"I'm sorry," Mireille said. "There are rules . . . principles . . . that I ought to observe, but I've broken them before, and . . . I need to break them again. I need to talk about Zeph. Gabrielle would doubtless think that I ought to spill it to her, but . . . I wanted to talk to you instead. Is that all right?"

"Perfectly," Denise assured her, repetitively.

"Because I think you might understand," the Frenchwoman added.

Denise thought it superfluous to agree, or to promise that she would try, and remained silent.

"Not that I understand myself," Mireille went on. "So perhaps you'll even be able to help me explain, although that isn't necessary, any more than giving me absolution for my sins."

"Sins?" Denise queried.

"You're not the only one who let him down—who let go when she ought to have held on . . . I was way ahead of you there."

No you weren't, Denise thought. *I was doing it, relentlessly, long before you ever met him*—but she didn't want to start a competition. "There was nothing you could have done," she assured her interlocutor, instead.

"Not when he was in the machine—long before. I abandoned him. I told myself that it was the best thing to do, and the necessary thing to do, under the Olympus mission rules, to which I'd made an oath of allegiance, but I knew that I was lying. I shouldn't have accepted my release from rehab while Zeph's debriefing still had weeks to run. I was nostalgic for Paris, but that was a trivial matter; in the circumstances I should have stayed with Zeph, even if Mission Control would have frowned. He needed me. He wouldn't admit it—he actually told me to go, promising to keep in touch . . . but he didn't even do that, having been infected by Chris Kemmering's one-step-at-a-time philosophy. I let it happen.

"You can't imagine how glad I was when Helen contacted me, and ordered me to go to England as soon as she'd introduced herself. I couldn't even be bothered to ask why. Then a diplomatic car picked me up at Heathrow and drove me straight to the flat in Kensington . . . Zeph's flat. I thought that I was being thrown into bed with him, or at least being given permission to take up where we'd been forced by protocol to leave off . . . but I was just left kicking my heels for hours while he was in secret conference with Helen. We hardly had a chance to say hello before we were being bundled into a copter and flown to the middle of nowhere, without a word of explanation except some military jackass repeating 'It's a Code Triple Red.' The captain turned up once we were on the plane . . . which was a great relief, because we knew that he knew, and was sympathetic . . . but all he did was dump you on us and disappear in search of an update.

"The only information I got was what you let slip, because . . . well, you were there . . . I was . . . confused. But at least the decision had seemed easy to make when all I knew was that it was a chance to join Zeph on another space mission. Luck, I thought, was on my side . . . it wouldn't have taken much to make me believe in destiny . . . except that Zeph . . . well, it's very difficult to know what he's thinking, especially when there are rules and protocols to be followed. We had been together for seven years, screwing for five, at sparse intervals as regular as the sense of decency that prevailed aboard Olympus permitted, and when we thought that we had genuine privacy, but even so . . . I was never confident that I could deduce what he was thinking and feeling, and I think he had the same problem, even though I wasn't as guarded as him. I should have been more open. I should have . . . made a better connection. I let him down."

"It wasn't your fault," Denise said

"It wasn't his," Mireillle countered. "We used to lie like this, you know, back-to-front . . . well not exactly like this, in closer contact . . . but the point is that we were together, relaxed. Given that it isn't very comfortable to sit up straight, even for people who aren't as tall as you, it's a very convenient position . . . but with him, it wasn't just a matter of convenience. The others . . . . well, they'd all been taught that it isn't polite just to cut and run, but with the others, it was just a matter of being polite. Not Zeph; his interest didn't disappear with the . . . climax. He enjoyed the sex, obviously, but he also enjoyed, perhaps almost as much, simply being with me. That, I think, looking back, was what made all the difference; that, for me was what truly constituted love. But I couldn't tell him that . . . not just because of the stupid rules, but . . . I don't know why. I always intended to . . . and I knew I should when I saw him stepping into that tricked out capsule of Helen's the first time . . . but I didn't, even then. I didn't tell him what I felt. And now it's too late. So I'm telling you instead, because I feel a crazy need to get it off my chest. It's not the same, obviously and it's not adequate, but it's something. I'm sorry."

She didn't have anything for which to apologize, but Denise didn't think there was any point in telling her that.

"A little while ago," she said, instead, "Marie MacLaughlin took me for a virtual walk through Kensington Gardens. She meant well, and I appreciated it, even at the cost of listening to her sermonizing, but I had a mischievous impulse to keep interrupting her and making her digress. I told her that I'd once been to a performance of *Peter Pan* when Zeph and I were kids. It was a special treat. When the members of the audience were asked to clap their hands to bring Tinkerbell back to life, he wouldn't do it. Mum was horribly embarrassed, because she hated him not behaving like other people, making a display of the fact that he was different, ill-adapted to social conventions, and she thought that he was just being bloody-minded, as she put it, but I knew that he wasn't, that it was something deeper than that, just as Cobbler Ken wasn't just a way of taking the piss out of the psychologist who was trying to adjust his alternative sanity for him.

"I read later that when the play was first performed, the author had no idea whether anyone in the audience would be prepared to clap, on behalf of a spotlight, and he gave instructions to the orchestra that they were to put down their instruments and provide the necessary applause. In fact, everybody clapped, as they always do . . . except for Zeph. But Barrie didn't know that. He had no confidence in his ability to create the effect for which he was striving. Zeph is the same; he doesn't have an atom of confidence in the effect that he might have on others, even when he's trying hard to have an effect, so, mostly, he hesitates to try. He doesn't initiate. He's too patient by half . . . more than half. I'm not in the least surprised that he didn't know how to talk to you, even after he'd learned to love you. And he does love you, and not just in a dutiful way, as required by the contract he's signed. For him, as for you, the principles are irrelevant; it's a matter of pure pleasure. It's just that, for him . . . pleasure is too difficult to manage."

"You're speaking in the present tense," Mireille observed.

"Yes," Denise agreed. "The hell with linear time. Do you know what Helen intends to do?"

"Yes. Paula was multitasking, tracking the autopsy. She heard every word and passed it on to Alessandro, who passed it on to Savina, who . . . but you know how these things work. Are you going to let her do it . . . Helen, I mean?"

"I can hardly stop her. And why would I? There really is a chance that Zeph's exceptional Coincidence sensibility is genetic. Minerva might need someone with that ability, even if it will require thirty-some years to develop it to the same extent. Helen will be hoping that she and the Bells can bring it out faster than that. But the child won't be Zeph. He will be my biological brother, but he won't be Zeph. I'll doubtless love him but he still won't be Zeph, will he?"

"No," said Mireille. "Quite apart from the fact that I'll be sixty when he's twenty, we couldn't possibly have the same relationship. There might be an element of Coincidence in relationships, which we experience subconsciously without ever being aware of it, but that doesn't mean that it's all there is. And even if it did, making a genetic clone of Zeph couldn't reproduce the Coincidences of the atoms making up his body, even if Helen feeds him on a diet of his own reprocessed flesh. I wouldn't put it past her, but I don't believe that it could work. And talking about him in the present tense can't make any difference to the fact that you and I saw him die in that capsule, and the fact that the ghouls who are trying to capture the psychosomatic changes made to his brain, with the aid of scalpels and a microscope, can't possibly succeed."

"I know," said Denise. "I'm not in denial. You only saw him die; I felt it. I wasn't certain at the time exactly what I was feeling, but I definitely felt it. I'm still feeling it. The captain thinks my reaction is strange, and he's probably right, but I can't help that. I can still feel him—not as if he were still alive, enjoying some kind of afterlife . . . which will doubtless disappoint Marie . . . but nevertheless, I can still feel him, in the present tense. And it really is tense, if you'll forgive the wordplay. I expect it will wear off eventually, but I can still feel him, and although he's silent for the moment, I suspect that I'll be able to hear him sometimes, if only mangling *Kubla Khan* as only he can. Perhaps it's an illusion . . . but given that we'll be living inside a gaggle of invisible alien hitchhikers for the next forty or fifty years, who can bend time, it would be trifle overpedantic to insist on the old boundaries between illusion and reality, don't you think?"

Denise realized as she finished the speech that she had needed to talk about that too, specifically to Mireille, the one person of whose sympathetic understanding she could be absolutely sure. She hadn't been conscious of the need before, but it had been there, and she had caught up with it now. She doubted that it would be the last realization with which she would only catch up belatedly.

"Perhaps it won't fade away," Mireille said. "Perhaps the ghost can cling on to a kind of existence, in the extraordinary circumstances . . . but I don't envy you. It isn't just the flesh that I'm going to miss, but without the flesh . . . the pleasure couldn't be the same. And I don't mean that in just a vulgar way. I don't mean simple sexual intercourse, I mean the way that, when we were lying like this, he would put his arms around me, in order to be close."

As she spoke, Mireille put her arms around Denise's shoulders, and mimed holding her close. She was, of course, actually holding her closely . . . but Denise knew that it had to be very different. She didn't try to pull away, though. She didn't need Gabrielle to tell her that it was a time for building and bonding,

"He never does that to me," she said. "He can touch me, and sometimes wants to hug me, but he always finds it difficult, even after all these years. As a child, he was practically phobic about it. It distressed Mum more than me. To tell the truth, as a child, I

288

didn't really care. It didn't bother me. I guess I had a reluctance of my own. I didn't have to grit my teeth in order to kiss somebody, but . . . well, as you've observed more than once yourself, I had a certain difficulty with it. When he came back to Earth after seven years on Olympus, I forced him to hug me, and he did it with a good enough grace, but I was making a point, not seeking . . . closeness. I'm not really cut out to be a spacer."

"No one is," said Mireille. "We all have to pretend. Some of us are better than others, but that's a mixed blessing; some of us forget how to set the act aside and be ourselves, and even when we remember, it takes special circumstances to bring it out. But being on Olympus or Minerva isn't much different, for me, from being in Paris. Rules, principles, barriers, performances . . . they're not just artifacts of space travel; they're universal facets of human life. It's just that we're more conscious of them here. But if Zeph had to die here, I'm glad I was here with him, no matter how much progress I hadn't yet made in getting closer to him, and no matter how much it hurts, for various reasons."

"Me too," said Denise. "And he's glad that we're here . . . not just on Minerva, but here, now. He didn't want to die; he'd far rather be with us in the flesh, but if he could really talk to me . . . to us . . . in anything but gnomic whispers, he'd want to remind us that the direction and duration of time aren't absolute, that there are hypothetical viewpoints from which they're meaningless. I'm no mathematical or Coincidental *übermensch* . . . unlike Helen, I don't have a neuronal configuration that will allow me to understand advanced math, let alone like it, and unlike the Bells, I can't pause the perception of duration, but I can still talk about Zeph in the present tense, and if anyone tries to correct me, I can simply tell them to go to hell, and leave me to my madness."

"Alternative sanity," Mireille corrected her.

Denise didn't tell her to go to hell. Instead, she said: "We can do this—you and I, and the captain, and all the others. There'll be risks, but the Bells will protect us as best they can. And if you and I don't make it back from Target, we can be glad that we tried, and glad that we lived in such a great adventure. What else would we have done with our lives that could have been better, or happier, even if the Crash hadn't gone bang? We're lucky . . . very lucky . . . to have had the opportunity to be heroes. The least we can do is try to live up to the role."

"Just like Jeanne d'Arc," said Mireille—although Denise couldn't help translating it as "Jeanne Dark."

"You and I have touched the truth," Denise said. "I suppose, strictly speaking, we only condescended to let it touch us, but it still counts. We probably can't save the human race from extinction, and we certainly can't save ourselves from pain and distress, but we've already achieved much of what we could, and we're fortunate that we have more yet to attempt—that it isn't over, and won't be over for a long, long time. You and I and don't want to write THE END to the story, because that isn't the kind of story that it is. We've imported some meaning into the beginning, which is a feat in itself, and we ought to be glad that we can go on, without having to feel or reveal a denouement."

"It is a pause, though," Mireille said, "even if we still have reports to write and briefings to undergo, even before we set forth on the epic journey to Uranus and beyond. It's a pause, and I'm glad of it, because I needed to pause, to take stock."

Denise turned over to face her interlocutor and look her in the eye. "Do you mind?" she said.

"Of course not," said Mireille, "Although . . . what I said earlier . . . still applies."

"Me too," said Denise, "but I think, now, that at least I can look at you, and I ought to. We're going to be together for a long time, and this probably won't be the last time that we feel a need to talk to one another . . . about Zeph. Can we agree that we have nothing for which to apologize, nothing for which we need to forgive one another, or ourselves?"

"That might not be easy," said Mireile, "But I'm certainly willing to try."

"It'll be a beginning," Denise said. "And that, after all, is all that Creation is: an infinite series of beginnings."

Pompous idiot, she thought, and even though she wasn't under undue stress, for the moment, even though she was now looking Zeph's heartsick lover in the face, she recited, privately: *If I have freedom in my love, and in my soul am free, Angels alone that soar above, enjoy such liberty.* Zeph, she knew, would have changed the words and made nonsense of it, in the interests of rebellious absurdity, but she figured that there would be all the time in the world for that, and in the meantime, having contrived a pause of sort even without stopping the clock, it would be best to hang on to such meanings as she had, and try to retain a little of the ordinary person that her father, in his innocent fashion, had always wanted her to be, even while she set forth steadfastly in the convoluted recesses of her mind to be a hero.

A PARTIAL LIST OF SNUGGLY BOOKS

MAY ARMAND BLANC *The Last Rendezvous*
G. ALBERT AURIER *Elsewhere and Other Stories*
CHARLES BARBARA *My Lunatic Asylum*
S. HENRY BERTHOUD *Misanthropic Tales*
LÉON BLOY *The Desperate Man*
LÉON BLOY *The Tarantulas' Parlor and Other Unkind Tales*
ÉLÉMIR BOURGES *The Twilight of the Gods*
CYRIEL BUYSSE *The Aunts*
JAMES CHAMPAGNE *Harlem Smoke*
FÉLICIEN CHAMPSAUR *The Latin Orgy*
BRENDAN CONNELL *Unofficial History of Pi Wei*
BRENDAN CONNELL *The Metapheromenoi*
RAFAELA CONTRERAS *The Turquoise Ring and Other Stories*
ADOLFO COUVE *When I Think of My Missing Head*
QUENTIN S. CRISP *Aiaigasa*
LUCIE DELARUE-MARDRUS *Amanit*
LUCIE DELARUE-MARDRUS *The Last Siren and Other Stories*
LADY DILKE *The Outcast Spirit and Other Stories*
CATHERINE DOUSTEYSSIER-KHOZE
    The Beauty of the Death Cap
ÉDOUARD DUJARDIN *Hauntings*
BERIT ELLINGSEN *Now We Can See the Moon*
ERCKMANN-CHATRIAN *A Malediction*
ALPHONSE ESQUIROS *The Enchanted Castle*
ENRIQUE GÓMEZ CARRILLO *Sentimental Stories*
DELPHI FABRICE *Flowers of Ether*
DELPHI FABRICE *The Red Spider*
BENJAMIN GASTINEAU *The Reign of Satan*
EDMOND AND JULES DE GONCOURT *Manette Salomon*
REMY DE GOURMONT *From a Faraway Land*
REMY DE GOURMONT *Morose Vignettes*
GUIDO GOZZANO *Alcina and Other Stories*
GUSTAVE GUICHES *The Modesty of Sodom*
EDWARD HERON-ALLEN *The Complete Shorter Fiction*
EDWARD HERON-ALLEN *Three Ghost-Written Novels*
RHYS HUGHES *Cloud Farming in Wales*
J.-K. HUYSMANS *The Crowds of Lourdes*
J.-K. HUYSMANS *Knapsacks*
COLIN INSOLE *Valerie and Other Stories*
JUSTIN ISIS *Pleasant Tales II*

www.ingramcontent.com/pod-product-compliance
Lightning Source LLC
Chambersburg PA
CBHW020359110726
47899CB00006B/1785